She walked over to his corpse to retri— moment to mutter a two-word prayer for him. No time for anything more. Whatever cruel god had sent Sandan through those doors did so as a gift to me.

And as I took Whisper in hand, I knew it'd just be rude to waste it.

Over the crate I was hiding behind. Dagger flipping in my hand. Feet moving as I swept up behind the closest thug. Arm around his waist, pull him close, bring the dagger up.

Like I said, I'm no good in a fight.

But killing?

Yeah, I know a thing or two about that.

The thug started to say something as I grabbed him, but whatever it was came leaking out of him on a crimson torrent as I drew Whisper's edge across his neck. He started squirming as the life bled out of his throat, his blood spattering my arm.

Messy death. But I needed it messy.

His companion whirled around, didn't even get a chance to comprehend what was happening before I shoved his bleeding friend at him. They went down in a heap, one of them screaming, the other trying his damnedest to scream.

And I was already running.

Up on top of a crate, then another, and another until I was up high. I felt the wind split, wood shudder as a dagger sank into the wood where I had just been.

But I couldn't stop. I couldn't turn. I couldn't let Chariel see my face.

I kept running, leapt up to the shelf, darted to the window. I grabbed the frame, swung my legs through. The wind shrieked past my ear. I felt a metal kiss upon my cheek. The narrowest sliver of blood wept down to my jaw.

The last favor any god was going to do for me today . . .

The Pathfinder Tales Library

The Pathfinder Tales Library

Shy Knives

Sam Sykes

A TOM DOHERTY ASSOCIATES BOOK
New York

PATHFINDER TALES: SHY KNIVES

Copyright © 2016 by Paizo Inc.

Maps by Crystal Frasier

A Tor Book
Published by Tom Doherty Associates
175 Fifth Avenue
New York, NY 10010

www.tor-forge.com

Tor® is a registered trademark of Macmillan Publishing Group, LLC.

The Library of Congress Cataloging-in-Publication Data is available upon request.

ISBN 978-0-7653-8435-5 (trade paperback)
ISBN 978-0-7653-8434-8 (e-book)

Our books may be purchased in bulk for promotional, educational, or business use. Please contact your local bookseller or the Macmillan Corporate and Premium Sales Department at 1-800-221-7945, extension 5442, or by e-mail at MacmillanSpecialMarkets@macmillan.com.

First Edition: October 2016

Printed in the United States of America

0 9 8 7 6 5 4 3 2 1

Inner Sea Region

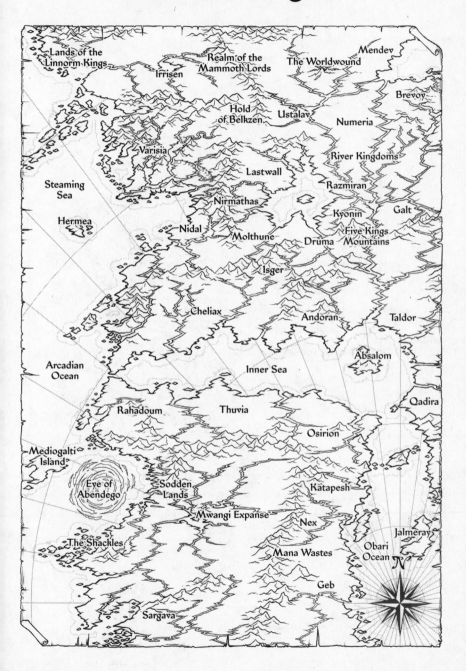

Taldor

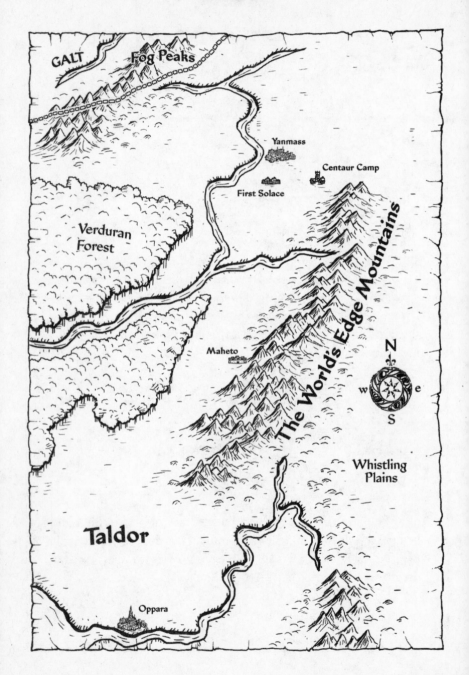

1

Sociality and Shackles

Shaia Ratani."

This wasn't how I wanted to be introduced.

"Approach."

My chains rattled as I shuffled slowly across the floor on bare feet. Despite the multitudes of burning candelabras stretching down the hall on either side of me, the tattered rags I wore failed to ward off a chill. Even if I hadn't been walking the length of a hall so grand and drenched in opulence, I would have felt small.

"That's close enough, thief."

I stopped. The shackles around my wrists seemed heavy enough to pull my eyes to the ground. In the reflection of tile so polished you'd pay to eat off it, I could make out someone looking back at me, black hair hanging in greasy strands before a face covered in grime.

My face.

"Shaia Ratani," a deep, elegant voice said. "You are accused of a thousand crimes against the aristocracy of Taldor, the most heinous of which include larceny, fraud, extortion, assault, assault with a deadly weapon, assault with intent to murder, unsanctioned use of poison, trespassing, public indecency . . ."

I was hard pressed to think of any legends that began like this.

". . . and consorting with deviant powers."

Hell, I couldn't even think of a good tavern story that began like this.

But it was bards who were concerned with how stories began. In my line of work, you learned early on that it's only the ending that matters.

"You may look up, thief."

Bold, commanding words from a bold, commanding voice. You'd think, upon looking up, that they'd belong to a bold, commanding man.

Those were not the first words you'd think upon seeing Lord Herevard Helsen. They *might* have been the thirty-second and thirty-third ones, if you were generous.

Tall and thin as a stalk of corn and with ears to match, the aristocrat who stood upon a raised dais at the end of the hall seemed an ill fit for his fancy clothes. Hell, he seemed a poor fit for his own home.

While his hall was bedecked with tapestries and servants standing at attention and portraits of strong men and women with strong, noble features, Herevard, with his weak chin and shrewd eyes, shifted uncomfortably. Like he could sense his ancestors' disapproval emanating from the portraits and was already imagining what they'd say if they could see him now.

I never knew them, but I imagined they probably wouldn't be pleased to see a filthy Katapeshi girl in shackles dirtying up their halls.

"Understand this, Miss Ratani." Lord Helsen spoke down an overlarge nose at me, as though the dais he stood upon wasn't high enough to separate us. "I have had you brought from my private dungeons at the behest of another. A mission of mercy that relies entirely on your ability to be civil. Do you understand?"

That would have sounded significantly more authoritative if his face weren't beaded with sweat. I chose not to call attention to that, though. I merely nodded and received a nod in exchange.

Lord Helsen glanced to his side.

"She was captured not two months ago. My guards found her robbing my study. She's been serving penance in my dungeons ever since, my lady."

"Penance?" another voice chimed in. A lyrical birdsong to his squawk: soft, feminine, gentle.

I wasn't sure how I hadn't noticed the woman standing beside him before, but the moment she spoke, I couldn't see anything else in the room.

Had Lord Helsen not addressed her as "lady," I might never have guessed her to be a noble. She certainly wasn't what you'd think of when someone mentioned the word, let alone what I'd think of. Her dress was a simple thing of white and blue linens, easy to move in and functional—words that make aristocratic tailors cringe. Her brown hair was clean and washed, but not styled with any particular elegance. She didn't look especially rich.

Pretty, though.

Or at least, she might have been. It was hard to tell, what with the massive spectacles resting upon the bridge of her nose.

"Penance, my lady." Lord Helsen nodded to the woman. "As you know, Yanmass's laws are rather . . . archaic when it comes to crimes against the gentler class." He chuckled. "Why, I'm told that Lady Stelvan, upon finding a vagrant in her wine cellar, appealed to the courts to have him walled up inside and—"

"*Please!*" The woman held up a hand. "Er, that is, Lord Helsen, I do not need to be privy to the details."

"Of . . . of course, Lady Sidara." Lord Helsen made a hasty, apologetic bow. "Regardless, I couldn't let her walk away freely. Time to reflect upon her misdeeds in the dungeons seemed adequate." He glanced back toward me. "I suspect that she will be ideal for your purposes."

"Purposes?"

I hadn't intended to sound quite so alarmed when I spoke. I hadn't intended to speak at all.

Lord Helsen hadn't intended me to either, judging from the annoyed glare he shot me. "Yes, thief. Purposes."

I bowed my head.

"The Lady Sidara has need of someone with particular . . . talents," he continued.

I nodded, head still lowered. Somehow, I figured it was going to be about this.

The three things nobles hate most, in order, are losing money, bad wine, and being reminded they have the same needs as anyone else. No matter how big your house is or who you pay to wipe your ass, eventually everyone needs a treasure stolen, a throat cut, or something set on fire.

They might have used words like "talents," but nobody needed dirty work done more than a noble.

And they didn't come nobler than they did in Taldor.

"She is firmly bound, my lady, and no danger at all." Herevard gestured to me with one white-gloved hand. "You may inspect her at your leisure."

Lady Sidara cast him a nervous look before glancing back at me. I was, at that moment, keenly aware of every inch of grime on my skin, every ounce of weight in my chains, every tear in the raggedy shirt and trousers I wore. Something about this woman, with her drab dress and giant spectacles, made me feel naked. Vulnerable.

Unworthy.

Still, she wasn't the first person to do that to me. Certainly not the worst person, either. I kept my head respectfully low, my body reassuringly still as she approached me.

One dainty hand reached out as if to touch me, but she seemed to think better of it and drew it away. I averted my gaze as she studied me from behind those big round spectacles.

"You're not Taldan," she said. "From the south, maybe?"

Lord Helsen spoke from the dais. "She's Qadiran, my lady."

I stiffened at that. My hands tightened into fists, only relaxing when Lady Sidara spoke again.

"Not Qadiran, Herevard. Her features are a little too fine." She hummed a moment before her face lit up. "Ah! Of course. You're from Katapesh."

Herevard yawned. "Same thing."

Still, I couldn't help but raise an eyebrow. Not a lot of people from Taldor appreciated the difference between us southern nations, let alone a noble.

"You poor dear," she said, eyeing the sorry state of my dress and hygiene. "Listen. I know this might seem . . . unorthodox. It certainly wasn't my first choice. But I have . . . an issue." She glanced around, as though wary of who might be listening. "An issue that Herevard said you might be able to help with."

I cast her a sidelong look but said nothing. As if embarrassed, she turned away and readjusted her spectacles.

"I can't give you the details here," she said. "Nor can I promise it will be easy. But I can promise you'll be adequately rewarded. I'll see you safely exonerated of your crimes and granted a handsome sum besides, in exchange for your assistance." She drew herself up, fixed me with a hard look. "Of this, you have my word, Miss Ratani."

Funny how words, common as they are, seem to mean an awful lot to some people. Nobles and their heritages, wizards and their spells, paladins and their oaths—words mean a lot to the kind of person who woke up one day and heard a higher calling.

I once heard that calling.

Then I put the pillow over my head and went back to sleep.

People like me, we don't put much stock in words. We know how cheap they are. We know how quickly they spin on glib tongues and how swiftly they scatter on the floor. People like me, we needed firmer stuff.

"I know this must sound odd," Lady Sidara said. "Is there . . . is there anything I can get you? To help you make up your mind?"

I took a breath and spoke softly.

"A drink."

Lady Sidara nodded and made a gesture to Herevard. Herevard, in turn, gestured to a nearby servant. The servant ran to a table set up against one of the hall's walls and, in a few moments, came rushing up to me with a goblet upon a tray. I took it, nodded my gratitude, first to him and then to her. I closed my eyes and took a long, slow sip of cold, refreshing liquid.

And immediately spat it out.

"What the hell is *this*?" I snapped at the servant.

"W-water!" he replied, holding up his tray like a shield.

"Well, did I *ask* for water, Cecim, or did I ask for a gods-damned *drink*?"

"S-sorry, Shy!" he cried out, cowering. "Sorry, Mistress!"

"'Shy'? 'Mistress'?"

It wasn't until I looked and saw Lady Sidara, her mouth wide open in puzzlement, that I realized I *might* have just ruined things.

"What did you call her?" The noblewoman glanced from Cecim to me, and the puzzlement turned to irritation. It was a full-blown scowl when she whirled upon Lord Helsen and saw the thin nobleman quaking upon the dais, the sweat on his face having gone from beads to big as moons.

"What did he call her?" she demanded. "What's going on here, Herevard?"

"Uh, well . . . that is . . ." Lord Helsen's tongue seemed two sizes too large for him at that moment, and he fumbled over his words. "You see, Lady Sidara, when . . . when we make mistakes and . . . and things are said . . . and we try to make them right, and . . ."

"Ah, give it up, Herevard," I said. "Whatever excuse you're choking on, it's obvious she's not going to buy it."

Lady Sidara turned to me, shock wrestling with outrage on her features as she watched me unfasten the shackles around my wrists and drop them to the floor.

I looked up at her, blinking. "What?"

"You . . . you're not a prisoner at all!" She pointed a finger at me that would have been accusing had it not been so dainty. "You *lied* to me!"

"If you'll recall, good lady," I replied, holding up my liberated hands in defense, "I didn't say ten words to you. Any lying came specifically from *that* man."

Lord Helsen squirmed under my finger, flailing as though he could pull an excuse from thin air. But instead, all he did was thrust a finger right back at me and let out a rather unlordly screech.

"She was *blackmailing* me!"

"I was not!" I shouted back. "I asked you *specifically* what the information was worth to you! *You're* the one that came up with the number!"

"Oh, don't you turn this on *me*, you lying Qadiran—"

"*Katapeshi!*"

"*ENOUGH!*"

To look at her, you wouldn't have thought such a little lady could come up with such a bellowing voice. But it seemed Lady Sidara, breathing heavily, holding her hands up in a demand for silence, was a woman of more than a few surprises.

"No more lies." She split her scowl between me and Lord Helsen. "And no more blaming. The truth. Now."

The nobleman and I exchanged glances for moment—or rather, *I* exchanged a glance and he gave me a look that suggested he might soil himself. At that, I just rolled my eyes and sighed.

"All right, fine. What I did might, in some countries, be construed as blackmail." I waved absently toward the dais. "I got some information on Herev—" I caught myself; didn't want to rub salt in the wound. "—on Lord Helsen and asked him what it was worth to him to keep it quiet."

"And what *was* it worth?" Lady Sidara asked.

"Two months in a nice bedroom at his manor," I replied. "Waited on hand and foot by Cecim here." I shot a glare at the servant. "Who should damn well *know* by now what I mean when I say I want a drink!"

Cecim squealed and scurried off, still holding his tray up. I sighed and looked back to Lady Sidara.

"Anyway, when he said you had a job that needed doing, we made up this bit about the private dungeon." I gestured to my clothes and grime. "Though had I known it would turn out like this, I wouldn't have bothered painting so much dirt on myself."

Lady Sidara frowned.

"And what information did you have to make . . ." She gestured over me. "*This* seem intelligent?"

"Well, I—"

"You *swore* you wouldn't tell!" Lord Helsen piped up, his face a red-hot contortion of embarrassment.

"Herevard, what good do you think *not* telling her would do?" I looked back to the noblewoman and sighed. "I found out about his mistress. A lovely little halfling woman who visits his chambers every other night." I shot her a wink. "Herry likes his short women."

Lord Helsen's mouth hung open. His eyes looked like they were about to roll out of their sockets. I had no doubt that, if I could have read his thoughts, they'd be mostly my name attached to variations of the word "strangle."

Frankly, I wasn't sure what the big deal was. I always thought they looked cute together.

Lady Sidara, for her part, didn't seem particularly upset, either. She slowly turned a sweet, sad smile on Lord Helsen.

"Oh, Herevard," she said. "We've all known about Numa for years now."

"W-what?" Lord Helsen said. "Everyone? All of Yanmass?"

She nodded gently. He made a soft whimpering sound.

"Even Lady Stelvan?"

"She was the first to know, Herry."

"Well, then." I kicked off my ankle shackles and sent them skidding across the hallway. "I guess we've all learned an important lesson about honesty today." I began wiping the painted-on grime from my skin. "And it seems my time with Herry is at an end. Give me a couple of hours to have a bath and I'm all yours, my lady."

"What?" Lady Sidara looked at me, anger flashing across her features. "You assume I'd still hire you now, after . . . after . . ."

"Oh, what? You were happy to have me when you thought I was a thief, but now that I'm an extortionist, you're too good for me?" I rolled my eyes. "A touch hypocritical, don't you think?"

"It's not that! It's just . . ." She rubbed the back of her neck, helpless. "This . . . this is a delicate operation, one that I am intent on seeing carried through. I need people I can trust."

"Liar."

She looked at me like I had just slapped her. "What?"

"If you needed people you could trust, you would have found a knight or a brave warrior or some lovesick noble. What you *need* is someone who can get the job done, and the fact that you're here tells me that the people you can trust simply can't do that."

She fixed me with a long, methodical stare. And though it made me feel every bit as naked as it had the first time, I held my ground and my smile like a sword and shield.

"And can you get the job done?" she asked.

"Are you still going to pay?"

"I will."

"Then I can." I turned to walk away toward the hall's exit. "But, as I said, let me get a bath first. I'm not going to talk business covered in filth."

"Yes, fine, whatever." Lady Sidara stalked behind me. "Glad to be doing business then, Miss . . ." She paused. "Is your name even Shaia?"

"Of course it is." I glanced over my shoulder, spared her a wink. "But my friends call me Shy."

2

Bathwater Deals

I suppose I should have felt worse than I did.

Shortly after our little arrangement was exposed, Herry fled sobbing to his chambers up above. I was told he spent roughly half an hour weeping over the indignation of his noble peers knowing of his indiscretions. I couldn't quite imagine what he was going through, really; nor was I quite certain what, exactly, I should have done to appear sensitive after shattering a man's self-esteem.

I was *fairly* certain that lounging in a bathtub the size of two oxen wasn't it.

To the uninitiated viewer, this might all seem a tad heartless.

And I swore, by Norgorber's left nut, that I would feel bad about it.

Later.

Guilt was something I had in small supply to begin with—in my line of work, it's not what you'd call a useful commodity—and I certainly wasn't going to squander what time I had left in Herry's household on it. For the moment, every sense I had left to me was reserved for the bath.

I had washed away the grime within minutes of entering it, a two-foot-deep ivory basin set into the floor of a nicely rounded chamber filled by servants who, even now an hour later, still came by to replenish it with jugs of hot water. I leaned back, feeling the chill of the ivory in my arms as I draped them over the rim, feeling the warmth of the water seep into me, the steam shroud me like a blanket and bid me to go ahead and close my eyes and pretend I was a real lady of class.

Ah, Sem. If you could only see me now.

I just might have let myself enjoy that thought.

"May we finally discuss business?"

Were it not for certain people intent on ruining the atmosphere.

I cocked open one eye, glanced to the side of the chamber where Lady Sidara stood a polite distance away—so polite, in fact, that I might have been offended. After all, it wasn't like I was *that* dirty.

"I believe," she said, as forcefully as her educated enunciation would allow, "that I have been exceedingly patient with you, Miss Rat—"

"Shy," I corrected her.

"Very well . . . Shy. I *ought* to have you reported to the authorities for what you put poor Herevard through. The fact that I have not only abstained from that, but also waited as you tended to your vanity, would suggest that my faith in you is already being stretched."

"While I'll be sure to thank Norgorber for your saintly patience," I replied, maneuvering over to the other rim of the basin, "I have two points of advice for you, Lady—"

"Dalaris," she interjected. "My name is Dalaris."

"Dalaris," I said. "The first? Never pretend going to the authorities is an option when you're talking to a woman like me. Whatever you require of me, it's going to go a hell of a lot easier if we both don't pretend that what we're doing is the sort of thing we need to involve lawful types in."

She stiffened at that, the realization doubtless striking her like a slap across her face. Yet she slowly loosened with a long, resigned sigh.

"Agreed," she said. "And the second?"

"The second is that it'd be much easier for us to talk if you'd turn around to face me."

Now, I could only see the back of her head, but I would have paid to have seen the face she was making at that moment. If the way her body went tighter than a bowstring was any indication, it was worth at *least* twenty gold.

"I . . . I will *not!*" she said. "You're indecent."

"I mean, that depends who you ask, but at the moment, I'm merely naked."

"It's immodest!"

"Well!" I said, mock indignation creeping into my voice. "I don't know what you heard about Katapeshi, but I promise you, my lady, I don't have anything you don't."

"It's not that! I assure you, I have nothing but respect for—"

"Relax, dear. I'm teasing you." I leaned forward on the rim, laying my chin on my folded arms. "I'm just saying it seems a little odd that you'd ask me to murder someone if you're too reluctant to look at me."

Lady Sidara—Dalaris, I mean—didn't loosen like she did before. When she turned around, it was so slowly I thought I could hear her joints creaking. But regardless of how hard she held herself, her voice was soft, meek. Almost afraid.

"I don't want you to murder someone," she said, looking at me at last. "I want you to find out who murdered my husband."

And there it was again. That look. That eerie feeling that made me feel even more naked than I was. Like she *knew.* Even from behind her spectacles, her stare felt like a knife on my flesh.

I resisted the urge to turn away—I'd look rather stupid doing that now, after all the lip I had just given her. I forced myself to look at her, into those big round lenses, and speak.

"Go on."

To my unspoken gratitude, she averted her gaze once more and sighed.

"You are obviously not from Taldor," she said. "I would wager you've not spent much time in Yanmass, either?"

I didn't take her for a gambler, much less a good one, but she was dead right about that.

Set in the plains in the northern part of Taldor, where the dying empire's borders had contracted after a number of messy secessions from its former vassals, Yanmass wasn't a city people like me went. Unless they came to serve people like Dalaris, that is.

It had begun as a small trading outpost where caravans were gouged by tax collectors on their way to be gouged by other tax collectors in the capital of Oppara. Eventually, that wealth had attracted the attention of nobles, who found the rolling plains to be an ideal vacation spot. Word spread, and nowadays the people who lived in Yanmass were mostly aristocrats who had no desire— or ability—to hack the political scene in the capital.

"I've spent time in Herry's library," I replied. "I know a little of the city."

"How much is a little?"

"Enough." I paused, choosing my next words carefully. "My trip to Yanmass was a tad . . . spontaneous, if you will."

"And if I won't?"

"Then you'd better learn to." I turned, reclining on the rim of the tub and beckoning a nearby servant to come add more water. "Anyway, I know enough of this place to know it's like any other rich man's city. A den of snakes wearing silks, each one of them speaking gentle words and trying not to be noticed as they unhinge their jaws to swallow the others whole."

"That is . . . a disgusting metaphor, Shy," Dalaris replied. "And frustratingly apt, as it were. Those 'snakes,' as you so eloquently call them, have been feeding on House Sidara for years now. *My* house."

"I gathered that much."

"In truth, it can hardly be called a house anymore. Sidara was a name that helped build Yanmass, the noble protectors who guarded the weary travelers who came this way. Then the other nobles came and picked us apart until we became what we are today."

"And what are we, my lady?"

"Me," she replied simply. "I am the last heir to House Sidara. All that remains of our holdings is my manor and a handful of servants after my mother died of a fever not two years ago."

"My condolences."

I said those words like I meant them because I most certainly did. Everyone needs a hard-edged woman in their lives, especially someone like Dalaris.

"My sole regret is that her last days were not peaceful," the noblewoman continued, sighing. "She was wracked with concern for me before she passed, and went to considerable lengths to ensure that I was looked after."

My ears pricked at that. I glanced at the servant, made a dismissive gesture. I rolled around to face her once again, fixed her with a hard stare. "How considerable?"

"She arranged a marriage," Dalaris replied. "A union to ensure that Sidara's legacy would not be lost and that I would be cared for. After considerable negotiation, she persuaded the heirs of House Amalien to take me in."

"Ah," I said. "And this is where your husband came in."

She nodded. "Gerowan—" she paused, catching herself, "—*Lord* Gerowan Amalien agreed to marry me." She looked down at the floor, her voice growing soft. "Today would have been our wedding day."

She took a moment to simply stare at her feet. A moment I was inclined to give to her; if we were to talk business, I wanted her composed. She did not look back up, instead beginning to pace back and forth as she continued to speak.

"House Amalien deals primarily in ore," she said. "They refine metal dug out of the mountains by the dwarves in Maheto and send it north to Galt. Galt always needs more metal."

Ah, Galt. Short on everything except corpses. Rife with money-making opportunities, if you can stomach all the blood.

"So, what? Your husband was killed in a bad deal?"

"No," Dalaris replied. "He was on a routine journey to a caravan-rest just west of the city to check on a shipment heading north. There, he was killed." She glanced up at me. "By centaurs."

"Centaurs," I replied, flatly.

"You don't sound surprised."

"Well, don't get me wrong, I wasn't exactly *expecting* them. Odd that they should be in Taldor, but if you're asking me to be surprised that centaurs killed a guy, I'm going to have to ask if they were all wearing pretty dresses while doing it."

"They were not, and you *should* be surprised. I certainly was when I heard that the thirty-five guards they keep stationed at that caravan-rest were insufficient to ward off a raiding party." She eyed me, suspicion on her features. "Because the guards were not present."

I quirked a brow. This *was* getting interesting. More interesting than theoretical fashionable centaurs, at least.

"For the past few months, a clan of the horse-people have been harrying the local caravans. It's alarming enough that they're so well organized as to have been successful, but they've also shown an unusual sense of diplomacy, permitting caravans to go unmolested in exchange for a portion of their cargo.

"But on the day Gerowan was killed, they were brazen enough to attack a fortified position. They came thundering across the plains in broad daylight, launching fire arrows at the caravan-rest. The guards mounted up and took pursuit, chasing them off into the hills to the east. Not twenty minutes later, another war party attacked from the south. They came in, grabbed some cargo, and ran out. And when they left, Gerowan was dead."

I took in every word, furrowing my brow. "So you want me to . . ."

"It can't be a coincidence, Shy. Centaurs attacking in such coordinated fashion? Gerowan was nowhere near the cargo they seized. They sought him out. Maybe Gerowan was killed by them, but it wasn't their idea to do so. *Someone* ordered my husband dead."

She came to a stop and fixed me with those hard eyes of hers.

"And I want you to find out who."

I simply looked back at her for a moment.

People not quite as worldly as myself might have called her crazy for seeing a conspiracy here. After all, the Inner Sea isn't exactly a safe place, and there were sure as hell safer places in it than the outskirts of Taldor. Monsters killed people all the time; it wasn't outside the realm of possibility that they could do so in a country that couldn't afford to watch its borders anymore.

And yet . . .

Maybe it was what she said, or maybe it was the way she said it, so full of conviction, but something just didn't make sense.

Centaurs attacking a position they couldn't overrun, provoking the guards and then fleeing? Another party arriving right after only to kill one man and take a few crates?

It sounded like either a conspiracy or one hell of a coincidence.

And in my line of work, you learn to stop believing in coincidences in a damn hurry if you want to stay alive.

"Herevard said you were resourceful," Dalaris continued, at my silence. "And I suppose you must have been to blackmail him. Until I know who was involved in this, I can't tell anyone else. If you have any sense of justice—"

"I do," I interrupted her. "Same sense of justice that anyone else has." I rubbed two fingers together. "How much is this worth to you, my lady?"

She couldn't have *not* been expecting that, yet I could tell by her frown that she was still annoyed by my question. Perhaps she had been hoping I harbored some hidden heart of gold beneath all the grime I'd cleaned off myself.

I couldn't bear to tell her that this wouldn't be the first time I would disappoint her.

"Five hundred," she said.

"Gold?"

"Platinum. A third up front, the rest upon completion to my satisfaction."

A third. Smart girl. Five hundred shiny pieces wasn't enough to retire on—not with my tastes—but it'd be a fool who walked away with only a third when she could have it all. Still, it wasn't the most satisfying number she could come up with. And this sounded like an *awful* lot of work. But then again, my gig with Herry had just met an untimely end.

Also? My bath was getting cold.

That sealed it.

"What the hell," I said, rolling my shoulders. "I'm in."

Her face lit up like a kid on her birthday. She smiled so wide I damn near thought her face was going to split apart.

"Really? You will?"

"Give me a moment to get dressed and we'll be on our way."

I stood up out of the basin. Immediately, that glow on her face turned a deep shade of crimson. She sputtered several things that almost sounded like words, desperately searching for a place she could look that *wasn't* full of naked Katapeshi woman.

I was half-tempted to stand there a little longer, just to see if she'd explode. But it wasn't like I was getting paid by the hour.

I slipped out of the basin, made my way to a nearby mirror, and checked myself out. Might as well make sure everything was in working order; I'd be charging her extra if I came out of this with any scars.

My hair was just the way I liked it: short in the back, long in the front, and black as night. Time in Herry's wine cellar hadn't seemed to diminish me at all: beneath my skin, I could see lean muscles cord and tense, ready to get back to work. Nary a curve on me, but I had always been built short and thin like a dagger. When I was younger, I cursed myself for this.

Had I known what I would eventually grow up to be, I might have appreciated the thematic appropriateness.

Herry hadn't objected to my using his bath one last time, though he *had* made sure to make my eviction clear by having my effects sent down in a trunk that lay nearby. I kicked it open, pulled out my leathers, and dressed in quick succession: black boots and leggings that fit me snugly, a belt and gloves to match, and a short-cropped vest coming down to my ribcage that some in Qadira might have said was far too short and many in Katapesh would have said was far too long.

But no wardrobe was complete without a bit of metal. And I found mine at the bottom of the trunk. The last bit of home I kept with me, a short curved dagger in a black leather sheath. I took him by the handle, pulled him out. He was as sharp and shiny as I had left him.

Whisper.

"Look lively, darling," I said, sheathing him and attaching him to my belt. "We've got a job to do."

I sprang up and walked to Dalaris, who had taken a discreet position facing the door. I tapped her on the shoulder and she nearly jumped out of her skin. The look of relief on her face that I was clothed was short-lived, replaced by a rather peculiar look at the state of my leathers.

"*That's* what you're wearing?" she asked.

"Yeah. Why?"

"I . . . well, it seems a touch immodest." She glanced at my vest. "At least, for a woman named Shy."

"Yeah, well . . ." I rolled my eyes, pushed past her and toward the door. "I should have told you I got my nickname from a guy named Jeb the Ironic."

3

Cold Coffins for Rich Men

Just like you can't really understand a wound without understanding the weapon that caused it, you can't really understand a city like Yanmass without understanding a nation like Taldor.

Of course, the ailing empire's many woes were about as common knowledge as water being wet, which is how I knew all about the disastrous years of failed military expeditions, which led to breakaway colonies gaining independence, which led to an impotent senate bickering atop the ruins of a fast-crumbling infrastructure.

Which led to where the empire was today: a withered old man of a nation pressed between the hulking shoulders of Cheliax, its former thrall turned infernal rival; Andoran, the boorish upstart with its notions of "democracy" and "liberty"; and Qadira, its rather forward neighbor to the south. It was an ongoing bet among the few politically savvy gamblers which nation would swallow up Taldor first.

And if even a Katapeshi girl knew that Taldor was screwed, you could damn well bet that the Taldans themselves knew exactly *how* screwed.

The wheels of Dalaris's carriage rolled over a pothole, jolting me out of a trance. I leaned over to the side of the cabin and flipped open the window, peering out into the streets of Yanmass.

Funny, but to look at the city with its nicely paved streets and tall manors, you'd think the average Taldan could pull gold out of his stool.

Greenery was everywhere, with trees and hedges planted in small plots to give a healthy contrast to the gray cobblestone streets they lined. As the carriage rolled past, I could see great works of art: carved statues of famous Taldan heroes, elegantly flowing fountains, monuments to former glories. But even as beautiful as these were, they seemed trifling against the majesty of Yanmass's manors.

Like the nobility that had settled here, the houses were old and brimming with prestige. Their domed roofs stretched high to the sky. Their stained-glass windows were broad and glistened like rainbows in the sunlight. Their many marching pillars resolutely held up many powerful eaves.

To look at them, you'd think Taldor was doing pretty damn well.

That is, unless you looked closer.

Even with the carriage going as slow as it was, I almost missed the finer details of those houses. The domed roofs included slots where the massive heads of ballista bolts peeked out. Behind the glass windows I could see iron shutters ready to slam down and prevent entry. And there were a few pillars rigged to fall over and bring those noble eaves crashing down on whoever might be trying to get in through the front door.

"The people of Yanmass are well prepared," I noted, mostly to myself.

"Preparedness and paranoia aren't the same thing."

I glanced across to where Dalaris sat, staring out the other window and doubtless seeing the same thing as me. Her brow furrowed above her tremendous spectacles.

"Back when Qadira came surging up across the border, many nobles of Oppara decided that a vacation to Yanmass would be quite ideal," she said. "And as the war dragged on, they figured more permanent establishments would be worthy investments."

"They're expecting an attack from Qadira?"

"Not Qadira. At least, not *only* Qadira. Most of them are paranoid about Cheliax bringing its devils down to seize control. Or Andoren revolutionaries making a mess of things. Or Galt. Or the centaurs. Ask enough nobles and I'm sure you'd find at least *one* who was worried about the possibility of invasion by an army of intelligent monkeys riding on the backs of dragons and firing crossbows that shot fireballs."

I clicked my tongue. "Makes sense."

She whirled, fixed me with the kind of suspicious stare that I usually only got from guards, priests, and ex-lovers.

"I'm going to have to ask you to elaborate on that," she said, "else I'm going to have to rapidly rethink my opinion of your intellect."

"When it comes to watching one's gold, it pays to think of every possible way you could lose it," I replied. "You get a lot of money, makes sense that you'd spend a lot to keep it."

She sniffed. "And you would know, would you?"

"I would." I grinned. "I *am* from Katapesh."

"You keep saying that like you expect me to know what it means."

"It means I know rich people. I know they get their gold by taking it, I know they *keep* their gold by assuming others are coming to take it, and I know what they'd do to prevent that from happening."

"You make it sound like all nobles are villains," Dalaris said. "Scheming little plotters who think of nothing but gold."

"Aren't they?"

"I'm not."

"And how well did you say your house was doing?"

Under most circumstances, I would have felt a little pleased with myself for that line. And when her face screwed up in irritation, I certainly did. But then she had to go and ruin it by looking pointedly away.

The wounded look that crossed her face then would have almost been petulant if it weren't so pained. She swallowed something hard, her lips twisted into a bitter frown, as though I had just flung a knife at her rather than a few insults.

I've never been good with emotions; no one in this line of business gets very far if they consider other peoples' feelings. But damned if that look she tried so hard to keep me from seeing didn't make me want to wrap my arms around her and tell her it was all going to be okay.

If she were my type, I might have.

But I liked them a little taller.

"How much farther?" I asked. "To the temple of Abadar?"

Changing the subject seemed like the next most merciful thing. And she was quick to perk up at it. All business, this girl.

"Not far," she said. "We just passed the Stelvan estate. The temple is at the edge of the noble district, where it meets the commons."

I nodded. That made sense. Worshipers of the merchant god liked being at the center of rich and poor, I'd noticed. They said it was so they could serve all walks of life. I preferred to believe they knew as well as anyone that a poor man's gold weighed as much as a rich man's.

"I admit to being surprised that you'd use Abadar's services," I said. "You don't seem the type to be one of his faithful."

"I'm not," Dalaris replied sharply. "But Gerowan's family observes. As we were never officially wedded, it was their decision to inter his body with Abadar." She looked away. "Frankly, I don't see the point in going. It's disrespectful."

"Respect is for bodies who go pleasantly in the night," I said. "As we're fairly certain that Gerowan didn't get that honor, I'll have to take a look at his body to find out exactly what *did* happen."

"I assure you that we've already seen to that," Dalaris said, the subject clearly putting her on edge.

"You had a good look at the corpse?"

"The *priest* inspected the *body,* yes," Dalaris said, forcefully. "All proper arrangements were made and, at his brother's insistence, a spell was even cast to communicate with his spirit."

"And?"

"And everything suggests that centaurs killed him." She frowned. "Including his spirit. It looks hopeless."

I folded my arms across my chest. "I'm starting to think you don't *want* me poking around your dead husband's corpse."

"I *don't!*" she snapped back. "At least, I don't want him desecrated. If there was anything I thought you could gain from inspecting him further, I would allow it, but—"

"There is."

"Like what?"

"I'm not sure."

"Then how can you know you'll find anything that Gerowan's brother and the others didn't?"

"Because they were looking for closure," I replied simply. "And I'm looking for a murderer."

The carriage rolled to a stop. The door opened. Standing before us was an older gentleman: hard face behind a hard beard, wrinkled body under wrinkled clothes, the kind of gray hair and deep lines that you only got from honest labor. Looking at the man made me hope I'd be dead before I saw any of those things.

"Here," he grunted as he produced a stepping stool and set it down before the door.

Lady Sidara had no servants left besides this man, the others having all left to serve at more expensive houses. And as he snorted and spit on the cobblestones, I was starting to see why he wasn't serving someone else.

"Thank you, Harges," Dalaris said, gesturing to me to exit first. I did, then reached back to take her hand and help her out—Harges didn't seem like he was in a hurry to do so. "We'll be brief. Please see to it that you water the mares."

She gestured to the two horses drawing the carriage—workhorses about as old as Harges was. He nodded at her and she turned to leave. I paused, glancing at him as he mopped his brow.

"The temple probably has water," I offered. "You want to come?"

"Nope."

"Why not?"

"Don't like priests," he said. "Don't like rich men. Don't like priests of rich men."

I decided I liked Harges.

I hurried up a simple stone walkway stretching down a simply cut lawn leading up to a simple stone building with tall doors and high windows. You'd never guess it was a temple if not for the symbol of an intricately wrought bronze key hanging over the doors. The sigil of Abadar.

Admittedly, I was a little surprised. The god of merchants was obviously popular in Katapesh. And though I hadn't spent an *awful* lot of time in my home country—enough to know that I hated it, at least—I had vivid memories of sprawling golden doors and great, expensive tapestries dedicated to Abadar.

I supposed that just because he was a god of merchants didn't necessarily mean he was a god of wealth.

But then, in Katapesh, wealth was a god unto itself.

"Let me do the talking," Dalaris said.

She reached up, knocked three times upon the door. After a few moments of silence, she reached up and knocked three times more. After another, longer few moments, she did so again, three times more. And again, silence.

That was about the time I pulled my dagger free from my belt and slammed its pommel against the door three times. The sound echoed through the building within, and the doors shook on their hinges. Dalaris glared at me as I resheathed my dagger.

"What?" I asked. "I didn't say a thing."

If she were going to chew me out about that, it would have to wait. The doors creaked open. A man's face with the sort of cheeks that suggested too much wine and too little labor peered out. His eyes, cautious and shrewd, widened a little at the sight of Dalaris.

"Lady Sidara," he said. His gaze drifted to me, looked me over and narrowed again. "And company."

"Apologies for the intrusion, Tessan," Dalaris began.

"*Lender* Tessan, if you don't mind," the chubby fellow replied. "I take it you desire to come grieve over Lord Amalien once more?"

"I do, Lender," she said.

"It is typically considered polite," he paused to let that word sink in, "to arrange an appointment before arriving." He waited a moment, as if we might simply turn tail and run out of embarrassment. I folded my arms and glared at him, and he sighed. "But I am under instructions to allow you to see Lord Amalien at your leisure, as per the wishes of his brother, Lord Amalien. The *other* Lord Amalien, that is."

"My thanks, Lender," Dalaris said, bowing.

"You are welcome to enter," he said, turning an eye toward me. "Your Qadiran friend, however—"

"Katapeshi," I interrupted.

Tessan's cheeks pulled his face into an impressive frown. "It's quite rude to—"

"That is," Dalaris said, quick to impose herself between us, "my Katapeshi friend was also a dear friend of Gerowan. I've come to escort her as she pays her respects."

From over her shoulder, I could see the emotions play out on Tessan's chubby face as he went from irritated to suspicious and, finally, to apathetic. Abadar's people didn't seem to mind most transgressions, presuming they were paid adequately for them. And whatever Gerowan's brother, the *other* Lord Amalien, was paying, it must have been enough to excuse this interruption.

He pushed open the doors. His tall and heavyset frame was covered in gold and white robes, a heavy bronze key hanging by a chain around his neck. He stepped aside and gestured in.

"Please, come in."

We did so and he eased the doors closed behind us. The interior of the temple was sparser than I remembered the ones in Katapesh being. Certainly, it was clean: the pews were all of high-quality wood, the candles burned with a nice clean smell and carpets were arranged for the comfort of kneeling worshipers. But there were none of the splendid gold statues or fantastically wrought ivory altars I had seen in Katapesh.

From windows, at least. I was never invited into the temples proper.

This temple had a simple stone altar with Abadar's key carved upon it. The place had a nice, well-lit atmosphere that was still slightly foreboding. And this temple had only a few people—dressed both nicely and shabbily—kneeling in supplication. That didn't surprise me much. Few came to Abadar unless they needed something.

Like us.

"Follow me, if you please." Tessan walked past us, gesturing for us to follow. "Lord Amalien is right through here."

He led us down a nearby hallway that was dotted with doors on either wall. At the third door on the left, he stopped and fished out a key ring from his belt. With no particular hurry, he sorted through them and opened the door into a modest room that was just a little larger than an alcove. It was lit with candelabras at all corners to complement the daylight seeping in from the high window overhead, and dominated by a rectangular wooden table.

All in all, this might have been a pleasant little breakfast nook, had it not been for the dead body.

Dalaris cringed at the sight of him. I blinked. Tessan checked his nails.

Long and slender, his skin just slightly darker than the white funeral shroud he was dressed in, a man lay upon the table. His hands were folded over his belly, eyes closed, black hair and goatee stylishly trimmed. Clean, peaceful, smelling vaguely of flowers.

Gerowan Amalien, late husband.

A pleasure to meet you, at last.

"As per his brother's wishes, we have continued to weave spells each day to preserve the cor—" Tessan caught himself, cleared his throat. "To preserve the body, Lady Sidara. Though Lord Amalien's contract compels me to tell you that we will be concluding this service at the end of the week, that he may be interred in the family crypt."

"A week."

Dalaris spoke the word simply, a grimness in her voice that caught my attention. Not that she sounded callous or anything, but not an hour ago, this woman looked like she was ready to burst into tears. Now she spoke with a solid sorrow, an acknowledgment, a remorse—but nothing else.

"A week, Lady Sidara," Tessan said. "Any further services must be renegotiated."

"That means," I interjected, "that all services you offer are still available."

Tessan regarded me carefully. "It does."

"Would you kindly permit us to speak with the corpse?" I asked.

To my credit, I kept the revulsion out of my voice. I found spells that allowed communication with the other side profoundly creepy. Sure, some said that the dead had a lot to teach us, but that never seemed to make much sense to me.

They were dead, after all. Whatever they did in life, they couldn't have been *that* great at it.

"Apologies," Tessan replied. "I meant that services are available to House Amalien." He inclined his head to Dalaris in what was almost respect. "To which you were never officially joined, my lady."

I didn't give her the chance to do more than frown at that, pushing past her to stand before Tessan. My voice slid low as a knife under a table, and I leaned close to the priest.

"It's I who should apologize, dear lender," I said. "We haven't been entirely truthful with you."

"Shy!" Dalaris exclaimed.

I held up a hand without looking back at her. "You see, sir, I was not lying when I said I was Katapeshi, and I was not lying when I said I was Lord Amalien's friend." I gave him a knowing look. "I am his Katapeshi friend. And he owes me a debt."

It would have been slander to say that Tessan had no manners. He at least *tried* to conceal the sneer of disgust he shot my way.

"What manner of debt?" he asked.

"Money," I replied. "The kind of money that calls a woman all the way to Taldor from across the Inner Sea. The kind of money that would merit me requesting such a service from you."

"I see." As a priest of Abadar, the fellow couldn't help but be impressed. But as a particularly lazy bastard, the fellow couldn't help. "Well, best of luck with that. But it's really not my—"

"Very well, sir," I replied. "I've no mind to press you further. If you'll just give me your full name, I'll be happy to send it to my superiors and let them handle it. I really don't get paid enough." I offered him a smile. "Refresh my memory, it was Tessan what?"

In this line of business, pulling a knife on the right man can get you far. But that's messy work. Pulling a lie is quicker, cleaner—and besides, the annoyed glare he gave me in exchange for my smile was infinitely more satisfying than sticking some fool.

See, I'd met people like Tessan before. No longer a novice to be taken care of, not yet a high priest to order others around, he had likely been sent to Yanmass to prove himself, and likely deeply resented that.

Too old to be adored, too young to be respected, he was doubtless the middle child in a family of thousands: uninterested, unhelpful, and unmotivated by the thought of anything but work.

Or rather, the thought of avoiding it.

And so we locked eyes for a moment, my smile digging into his scowl like it had claws, as I let him work out just how much trouble it would be to deal with debt collectors.

Katapeshi debt collectors.

"Very well . . ." I began.

That did it.

"One moment," he sighed as he trundled to the head of the table.

I shot Dalaris a grin over my shoulder. She shot me a confused look, like she wasn't quite sure what had happened. I couldn't tell if she was impressed with my lying or if she just hadn't seen a lie before.

Either way, I liked her a little more.

My attentions were drawn back to the table as Tessan took Gerowan's face between his hands. He shut his eyes, began to murmur words that hurt my ears.

I probably should have mentioned—to Dalaris, at least—that I didn't care much for magic. It always seemed to me like cheating. That wouldn't offend me quite so much if it were cheating I could do myself, but I never had a knack for it.

I clenched my teeth, steeled myself for what would happen next.

Regrettably, it happened very quickly.

Gerowan didn't move much. His eyes didn't shoot open, he didn't shoot up and dance a jig; really, I didn't even know if there were a spell that could do that. But his mouth opened ever so slightly and I heard the faintest sound of wind whistling.

I leaned forward, whispered.

"Is that you, Gerowan?"

"*. . . yes . . .*"

His voice was a rasping, echoing thing, as though spoken from a great distance away and still far too close.

My skin crawled. And given that I had enough skin on display, I wagered Dalaris probably saw that and was a touch offended. I ignored her and continued. Everything I knew about talking to corpses was that they only ever answered questions, and they were thematically appropriately cryptic.

"Where is the money you owe me, Gerowan?" I phrased it vaguely enough that I hoped his answer would be just as cryptic.

"*. . . I . . . don't . . . know . . .*"

Good. That probably wouldn't draw too much suspicion from Tessan.

"Who killed you, Gerowan?" I asked.

"*. . . cen . . . taurs . . . descended . . . fire . . . fear . . . pain . . .*"

"How did you die?"

"Really," Dalaris whispered, "we went over this once before, there's no need—"

"*How* did you die?" I spoke louder.

"*. . . stabbed . . . in the . . . back . . . tried to . . . flee . . . had to . . . escape . . .*"

"How many centaurs were there?"

"*. . . don't re . . . member . . .*"

"What weapons were they carrying?"

"*. . . axes . . . swords . . . fire . . . fear . . .*"

I bit my lower lip. I almost hated to ask this next part, but . . .

"Gerowan," I said, "what were your last thoughts of?"

"*. . . last thoughts . . . of . . . lady . . . lady . . .*"

"Is this really conducive to your collection?" Tessan's voice jolted me back to my surroundings. His suspicious glare caught my eye. "Did your superiors ask you to traumatize his widow if you couldn't collect his debts?"

I glanced over my shoulder and cringed. Dalaris was looking away, her face buried in one hand. Yet her hand was so mercilessly small that I could still see the despair on her face.

Sorry, kid. I wish I hadn't.

"All right, all right." I waved a hand at Tessan. "Shut it down."

I had no idea how magic worked beyond the fact that it annoyed me, so I had no idea if one *could* just "shut it down." Tessan seemed happy enough to do it, though. He broke contact and the unnatural half-life fled from Gerowan's corpse, leaving him in mostly peaceful repose once more.

"Satisfied?" Tessan asked.

"Not even a little," I replied with a sigh. "But I suppose you've done all you can." I stared at the corpse for a moment. "You can leave now."

"Leave?" Tessan quirked a brow. "Leave you alone with the corpse?"

"Unless you want to stand around as I take a sketch for my superiors in Katapesh." I shrugged. "I'm a bit of a slow artist, though, so it could take a while."

"What on earth do you need a sketch for?"

"Have you never been to Katapesh, sir? Death is the only thing that releases a man from his debts, and then only if you're *damn* sure he's not coming back. My superiors will want evidence."

"I was hired by the Amalien family to safeguard this man's corpse and will *not*—"

"Norgorber's nuts, man, I'm not going to spoon him." I gestured over my shoulder. "Lady Sidara will be watching me like a hawk, if that soothes you any."

Both he and I looked to Dalaris. She seemed to regain her composure enough to afford him a brief nod. He looked at me once more and I didn't blink as I waited for his apathy to triumph over his suspicion.

It did in rather insultingly short order and he left the room, muttering something I might have taken offense to if I weren't already pushing my luck here. I waited, counting the seconds until he had left, then quietly eased the door shut. I glanced at Dalaris.

"Keep a lookout," I said.

"A what?" She blinked.

"A lookout." I walked to the table holding Gerowan's corpse. "Watch the door, listen, tell me if anyone's coming. You know, like when you and your friends were sneaking wine from your mother's cabinet."

"I never *did* that!"

"Really?" I glanced over Gerowan. "Well, there's nothing to it. It's just three steps: keep an ear out, keep quiet . . ."

"And?"

"And . . ." I seized Gerowan's funeral shroud in both hands. "Don't scream at what I'm about to do."

To her credit, she didn't. But when she saw me hike his shroud up over his face, exposing his death-pale body below, I could tell that she wanted to. Hell, by the look on her face, I could tell she wanted to do a lot more than scream. To her credit, she didn't do *that*, either.

"You said!" she settled on protesting. "You *said* you wouldn't desecrate his corpse!"

"I *implied* I wouldn't. I *said* I wouldn't spoon with him, and I'm not." I ran fingers over his body, hooked them under his side. "Besides, I'm not desecrating him. You'd know if I were."

"Then what are you doing besides causing me to once again regret ever laying eyes upon you?"

I grunted, pushed, rolled Gerowan over with great difficulty. I was about to ask Dalaris for help, but thought better of it. I'd never been what you'd call particularly religious, but I was pretty sure that asking a widow to help someone strip her dead husband was some kind of sin I wasn't ready to commit.

"Did he say anything else?" I asked. "The first time you spoke with his body? Anything different than what we just heard?"

"Not a word." Dalaris approached the other side of the table, desiring at least to keep a close eye while I was messing with her husband's carcass. "Was something he said amiss?"

"Not to him," I replied. "He said centaurs came with fire and fear, and he's right. He said they carried axes and swords, and they do. He said he was stabbed in the back . . ."

I looked down to the wound: below his right shoulder blade, a long, jagged cut where a blade had entered, pierced his heart, and exited with a minimum of fuss.

"And he was."

"Then what's the problem?"

"The problem is this." I pointed to the cut. "Look at it."

"I'd rather not."

"Then just listen. It's just one cut, in and out. Clean."

"It's hardly clean," Dalaris replied, blanching. "Look at it. It's all . . . jagged, ugly. Someone stabbed him in a hurry."

"No, someone stabbed him and then made it look like it was in a hurry." I ran a finger just below the wound. "See here? The tearing came from a knife twisting."

"How can you tell?"

I shot her a look that asked her to consider very carefully whether she wanted to know the answer to that question or not. She grimaced and, looking away, decided she did not.

"More than that, though," I said, "this isn't the work of someone in a battle, least of all a centaur. They're efficient soldiers, but they're not clean. If they had brought him down, they would have stabbed him a few more times just to make sure he wasn't going to get back up."

"So, he . . . wasn't killed by centaurs?"

"You sound surprised."

"I expected he had been killed on someone else's orders," Dalaris replied. "Not that he had been killed by someone else entirely." She looked at me carefully. "You're certain?"

"Not yet," I replied. "I can be *more* certain, obviously." I sniffed. "How far away was the caravan-rest he was killed at?"

"It's a few miles out of town."

"Can we get there before sundown?"

"If we hurry."

"Best hope Harges watered the horses, then." I turned to leave. I had made it to the door when I noticed she wasn't following. "What?"

Dalaris blinked at me. She slowly looked to her husband's corpse, lying on his belly, funeral shroud up around his face, ass in the air. Then back at me, expectantly.

I rolled my eyes. "Oh, fine. I'll fix him. But for the record, it was *you* that said we had to hurry."

4

Digging with
Our Hands

Sem once said to me: "Cities are the beating heart of the nation, but caravans are the blood that it pushes through."

Of course, right after that came: "It's easier to cut out an artery than a heart, so that's why we're waiting on this road."

Sem had a saying for everything. Not all of them were true, but both of those were. And they were sayings that thieves and nobles alike lived by.

Yanmass's caravan-rests, as the name implied, were originally oases and clearings where mounts could be watered and inventories tallied. Eventually, bandits came to appreciate the appeal of a caravan that didn't move. So merchants reached out to nobles, who fortified them. And eventually, nobles came to appreciate the same things that the bandits had.

Sem once said to me: "Honest thieves never need to fear death. The devils and demons will always take a noble first."

I really did miss Sem sometimes.

Like right then.

"So, let me get this straight." I pointed to the low-slung wall that stretched all around a dirt patch several hundred feet wide. "The centaurs came over the wall here?"

"So I've been told," a voice said from behind me. "I was off chasing the first raiding party with the rest of them when the others came calling."

"Huh. Did you happen to find out how many?" I asked.

"I'm told somewhere between three and fifty. The only ones that saw them were some feather-spined merchants who likely hid at the first sign of trouble. Good luck getting a real answer out of them."

I glanced around the little dirt patch that had been given the name of First Solace. Like most caravan-rests, it wasn't much more than a wall surrounding four large warehouses and a crude tavern. Still, it didn't need to be much to serve its needs. Several wagons were parked here, with several more merchants busying themselves rubbing down their horses, pitching tents to spend the night, or haggling with tax collectors bearing Yanmass's colors.

No sign of damage on any of the warehouses beyond a few superficial burn marks. None of the chaos and massacre that usually followed a bandit raid. The merchants looked more worried about the tax collectors than the possibility of another attack.

"Well, since this place is still standing, I'm going to guess it wasn't fifty," I said. "And given that they didn't knock anything over, I'm guessing it couldn't have been more than ten."

"Why, madame, are you suggesting that our merchants might not have the most trustworthy memories?"

I shot a grin over my shoulder and received a grin in turn. The guardsman standing behind me was young—the tall, lean kind of young that came from humble beginnings and saw law enforce-ment as a means of dying with a greater legacy than a patch of manure to his name.

So I assumed, at least. I had just met the fellow.

"I'll trust their memories when it comes to debts, nothing else." I shot him a curious look. "What'd you say your name was, sir?"

"Sandan." He hastily removed his helmet, letting black locks tumble as he offered a bow before me. "Sandan Klimes, madame."

"Been a while since anyone doffed their hat for me, Sandan," I replied with a grin.

"Aye, well, been a while since I met anyone worth doffing it for, madame." He cracked that boyish grin at me again. "I don't see many out here that aren't money-grubbing merchants, let alone a nice Katapeshi girl like yourself."

"And here I thought we all looked like Qadirans to Taldans," I said, sounding a tad more impressed than I'd like.

"To most, I suppose. But I can tell. It's the hair. Katapeshi always have such nice hair."

It's a short list of things that a man can do to impress me, and he had just ticked two of them. If I hadn't been on the job, I'd probably have seen if he could get the other three.

But I am nothing if not a professional.

"You've got a talent for details, Sandan," I said. "And your time in humoring my questions is appreciated. Can you tell me what the centaurs took?"

"Not much, madame." He replaced his helmet. "They swept into a nearby warehouse and made off with some crates. Not many, though." He scratched his chin. "They were already gone when we came back from chasing the others."

"And how many were there in the first raiding party?"

"Hard to tell, madame." He turned a baleful glare over the wall, like he was convinced they'd come back at any moment. "We've been having trouble with them for months now. They come running out of the nearby woods, fire on our caravans, then disappear once they've grabbed some loot."

"But they'd never attacked a caravan-rest before?"

"Never," Sandan said. "They move so fast, we couldn't count how many were out there, shooting arrows over the walls and running out of range before we could fire back. We eventually mounted up and chased them, and that's when the rangers moved in."

I paused. "Rangers?"

"That's what some of the other guards are saying. See, the first party came with spears and axes and such, typical sort of tribal warriors. The second party, though, they came with beasts."

"What kind of beasts?"

"Wolves. A whole pack of them, I'm told. I think they were brought in to spook the remaining horses and prevent anyone from fleeing. The other guards said they were being driven by centaurs carrying bows. Wouldn't be the first time they figured out how to do that."

A lot of this sounded strange.

Not the centaurs attacking people; outside of a few eccentric horse-folk who preferred city life, your average centaur was as savage and unruly as your average bugbear, if more reclusive. But the way Sandan described them: hitting and running, fleeing to bait guards into chasing them, then coming in with wolves?

And all just to make off with a few crates and kill one noble?

I supposed it *could* have just been a case of them testing out a new raiding strategy, but that'd be one hell of a coincidence.

I believe I've made my position on coincidences quite clear.

"So, madame," Sandan said, "you really think this'll help you take care of the beastmen?"

I blinked, stared at him blankly for a moment.

Oh, damn it. What the hell kind of lie did I tell him to get him to talk? Think, Shy, think. What did I tell him I was? A grieving widow? No, he'd never buy that. A detective? That's ridiculous. Adventurer?

"Well," I said, "that bounty's not going to collect itself."

He nodded. I held my sigh of relief.

Adventurer. Always a safe bet. Some random person walking around asking questions about centaurs and murders, people get suspicious. But they'll tell any maniac clad in armor and carrying sharp edges anything so long as he calls himself an adventurer.

"Sure I couldn't talk you out of it?" he asked, grinning. "Killing centaurs is dangerous work." He glanced my leathers over. "And, no offense, but you don't look quite built for the job."

"You've got your talents, I've got mine, sir," I replied. "And one of them happens to be collecting money from dead nobles."

At this, his face fell a little. "Ah, yeah. I heard about Lord Amalien. The dead one, that is. Bad luck for him. Better for his brother, I suppose."

I felt a cold shiver through my body, the kind I only get when I'm about to get paid or stabbed.

"Oh?"

"Lord Amalien—er, that is, *Alarin* Amalien, the younger brother—usually comes to First Solace to check the inspections. He was held up that day, though. Gerowan came in his stead."

Sandan, I could kiss you.

Hell, I just might have right then and there, if I didn't know it would make him follow me around like a puppy for the rest of the day. After that elucidating bit of knowledge, I felt as though I'd have to be alone very soon.

"Well . . ." I rubbed the back of my neck and sighed. "His brother's money's not going to go bad. I suppose I could take some time before leaving." I eyed Sandan. "What time's your shift end?"

The boy nearly burst out of his armor, so bright did he light up at that question. I couldn't help but let my grin grow a bit bigger as he fumbled over himself, trying to regain some semblance of composure.

"Er, ah, in about three hours, madame. If you're free, I'd happily buy you a—"

"Don't finish that sentence," I said. "In three hours, I'll tell you what you can buy me."

"S-sure, madame!"

"And enough of this 'madame' business." I winked. "Call me Abetta."

"Abetta." He tasted the name, found it sweet. "I'll see you soon!"

I didn't let my frown show until he had scurried back to whatever post he had to be watching.

I hated to do that to him, really. He was so nice and helpful. Didn't hurt that he was handsome, but you can find a hundred pretty men as surely as you can find a hundred pretty knives and they're all just as likely to hurt you. But that boy had something. His smile, I think. He had an honest smile.

Because he was an honest boy.

Which meant I couldn't have him anywhere near me.

And so long as his mind was occupied with who he thought I was, he wouldn't be paying attention to who I actually was. For the next three hours, he'd be in as much bliss as his imagination allowed. And in the next two, I'd be long gone.

I checked my belt, patted Whisper's hilt to make sure he was there. With a tug on my gloves, I was off across the dirt patch that called itself a caravan-rest.

I had convinced Dalaris and her carriage to linger on the outskirts of the caravan-rest. Whoever was behind Gerowan's death—and I was quickly forming ideas—it wouldn't do for them to know that his widow was looking into it. Until I could get something firmer than conjecture, I wanted to keep our investigation out of anyone's notice.

Fortunately, that wasn't hard to do in First Solace.

Every rogue from Katapesh to Molthune has an opinion on how best to be sneaky. Some recommend black leathers, some recommend coming out only at night, and so forth. But it's always been my personal experience that your average fool is so wrapped up in his own life that he won't even notice you if you simply don't say anything.

And lest I sound too harsh on merchants, they were good for exactly that. Everyone here was far too busy haggling with other merchants, fretting over missing inventory, or screaming at tax collectors to notice a lone woman walking swiftly across the lot to the nearby warehouses.

It wasn't hard to find which ones the centaurs had raided—two of them had nice, pristine bars on the door while the one in the middle had been smashed by a firm kick and was being held together by a chain with a padlock. Nothing I couldn't pick, if I had the time. But somehow, I thought several dozen merchants would notice me getting near their money like that.

I disappeared into a small gap between the warehouses, edged my way through it to the rear. A small alley ran between First Solace's wall and the warehouses—not quite enough space to maneuver guards through, but more than enough for my purposes.

I glanced up and saw a window set in the warehouse's wall, high above. Well out of reach for your common burglar, but I hope by now we can all agree that I was far from common.

I paused, took in the distance between the wall and the window. It'd be close, but I thought I could make it. With another glance to make sure no one was around, I leapt onto the lip of the wall, then turned and leapt to the warehouse. One hand found the sill, the other worming fingers under the window's lowest edge.

No lock that I could feel; they relied on good old reliable rust to keep it shut. And though it took a bit of unfashionable grunting, I managed to push the window open and haul myself up and over the sill.

My feet landed with a wooden *thunk*. I swayed precariously for a moment atop a stack of crates. The warehouse was simple and efficient in design: crates had been stacked around the edges, and a shelf had been built into the wall to bear the heavier burdens, a ladder resting against it nearby. Amid the drab dust and wood, the only color seen was the various merchant sigils painted upon the crates.

I made my way down the shelf to the floor of the warehouse and glanced around.

Ten centaurs and a mess of wolves had made their way in here. They escaped with a few crates. Couldn't have been too many. The problem would be discovering which ones they took and for what reason.

Among the various, shall we say, *nonstandard* humanoids of the Inner Sea, centaurs tended to get a lot more credit than the two-legged kind. With a few of them abandoning their barbaric ways and integrating with civilized nations, armies occasionally found them quite useful as scouts and cavalry. They were powerful, fearless, and proud.

But no one ever called them subtle.

Or clean, for that matter.

Fortunately, no one ever accused Taldans of being in a hurry to tidy up, either. Someone had made a go of cleaning the aftermath of the centaurs' incursion, but they hadn't made it very far. I could see gouges in the floor where hooves had trod and crates had been dragged. And here and there, spatters of dried blood.

I wondered if any of it was Gerowan's.

That was just one more thing I wouldn't be telling Dalaris, along with the possibility that his brother might have been the one to kill him.

I know, it might seem like a leap, but to me it seemed more like a hop. Family is all well and good until concepts like inheritances come up, and then murder starts to sound more efficient than dealing with lawyers and contracts.

But I wasn't being paid for speculation.

My thoughts now were for following that trail of carnage to a nearby wall. There, I found some crates in relative disarray against the neat stacks of the rest of the warehouse, as though someone had reorganized them not quite as thoroughly as they had the others.

I leaned over one. Upon its lid were several painted seals, each depicting a different sigil: a long scepter upon a golden field, a pair of crossed bronze rapiers, a hand clenching an orb . . .

Hey, I knew that one!

I recognized House Helsen's seal almost immediately. I supposed I would have had to, with how often I saw it around Herry's manor while I was a "guest" there.

So, these were all noble seals, then. I supposed it made sense that they would all put their stamps on crates. It was a pretty common practice in Katapesh, too, for merchants to indicate their alliances to would-be looters. A message, spoken plainly: "Screw with one of us, you screw with all of us."

Thieves' guilds tended to do that, too.

Of course, we were doing it *before* it was fashionable.

I couldn't tell by looking at the crate why the centaurs had gone after these ones in particular.

But that's why I brought a knife.

I drew Whisper from his sheath, worked his blade under the lid. It took a bit of doing, but I managed to pry off the nails and crack the lid open a touch. I worked him around the lid's edge, bit by bit, until I could ease it off with the faintest squeak of nails. When the time came to leave, I could just slide it back on, no one the wiser that I had been here.

That might seem a bit unnecessary. After all, all I had to do to not be noticed was be slightly less messy than a centaur raid. And truth be told, I wasn't sure why they would go after crates in the first place.

Wasn't sure, that is, until I opened the lid.

Two dozen longswords. Nine stout battleaxes. Two bundles of javelins. Six sheaves of arrows. All of them made with fine steel and polished to a high, glossy shine.

Yeah, I could see why a centaur might want this.

They might be mighty warriors, occasionally even decent soldiers, but they were still savages, which meant their best black-smithing techniques probably began and ended with hitting metal with a hammer until it looked like it would hurt. Weapons this well made, a centaur would kill for. Mostly so he could do more killing.

And I guess they *had* killed for it. But how did they know to take these crates, specifically?

That thought hung around my neck like a lead weight as I reapplied the lid and banged it shut with Whisper's hilt. I had just gotten halfway through the nails when I noticed it.

A red stripe, so dark as to be nearly black, ran along the outside of the crate, just beneath the lid. I would have thought it to be paint if it hadn't been applied so sloppily. And it had been painted beneath the rim of the crate, as if someone didn't want it to be noticed.

I leaned down and squinted at it, and that's when something made my nostrils quiver. I could barely make it out, at first: a whiff, the ghost of a scent. It wasn't until I had my nose right up against the wood and was inhaling deeply that I could place it.

Hog's blood.

If you promised never to ask me how I knew that, I'd promise never to lie to you. At that moment, I wouldn't have even been able to think of a good one to tell you, because, at that moment, it all made sense.

Hog's blood. At the edge of the crate, applied covertly and faded. You wouldn't notice it right away, maybe not at all if the lighting were bad. No human would be able to smell it.

But a pack of wolves . . .

That's why they were here. Someone was sending them weapons. But for what reason? And how did it involve Gerowan?

"Wrong place, wrong time" was an answer that was quickly losing water. Back in Katapesh, there was no such thing as a wrong place or a wrong time. There was always a time and place for killing someone who knew something they shouldn't.

Like Gerowan might have.

Gerowan. Who was here when his brother, Alarin, should have been.

Dalaris wasn't going to like this.

"You hear something?"

I dearly hoped I would get to tell her.

"I hear you wasting time. Open the lock, you idiot."

Voices. Outside. Men. Two of them, at least.

Keys jingling. Lock turning. Chains rattling.

Any time now, Shy.

I leapt to my feet, hurried to a crate beneath the shelf on the far wall, and ducked behind it. I pressed my back against the crate, slowed my breathing. Whisper was in my hand, close to my chest, ready to be used if I needed him.

Which I dearly hoped I wouldn't.

I don't know if it's obvious by the way I hid like a coward, but I was rather unhandy in a fight.

5

Well-Dressed Blades

Killing, I was fine at. Lying, even better. But like most professionals, I didn't like doing anything I was good at for free. I
wasn't being paid by the body to begin with, let alone the bodies of
a couple of porters hired to lug crates.

Rusty hinges creaked as the doors swung open. Daring to poke
my head up as much as I was able, I saw the two men enter. And
as soon as they stepped out of the afternoon light and into the
shadows of the warehouse, I felt my heart drop.

I would have killed a hundred porters to avoid having to deal
with these men.

Their hair was nicely oiled. Their beards were stylishly
trimmed. Their clothes were finely cut silks that fit each of their
long, lean forms perfectly, and their black-and-red trim was a
perfect match for the rapiers hanging at their hips. One of them
moved to brush stray dust from an otherwise impeccably clean
outfit and I ducked back behind the crate and held Whisper a little
closer to my chest.

You could be forgiven for thinking, at that moment, that I had
a fear of men in fancy clothes.

But only if you had never heard of the Brotherhood of Silence
before.

All of this—the sweat forming at my temples, the way I held
Whisper—might have seemed a bit much for a couple of thugs.
After all, every country had its thieves' guilds—and I knew a

number of them quite well. But to say Taldor had a problem with thieves' guilds was like saying a plague victim had a runny nose.

In poor countries, your average guild is a rut of urchins picking pockets and bashing peoples' heads in dark alleys. In nicer countries, your guilds are into smuggling, heists—all the classics. But only in Taldor did you find a thieves' guild that actually held political office.

Because that's what the Brotherhood was: the whisper in every greedy noble's ear, the knife in every honest king's back, the face in the crowd you couldn't quite pick out, and that made you wonder why your blood ran cold when it looked at you. It'd be a misnomer to call them thieves; really, they were just straightforward politicians.

You might have wondered how I knew all this.

Just like you might have wondered why I was hiding in Herevard's manor.

Just like you might wonder why it was my heart was hammering like it was going to burst out of my chest.

And I would have promised to answer you, if I ever made it out of there alive.

"It reeks in here," one of them said. "I don't think they're ever going to get the smell of horseshit out of the wood."

"I don't think they even tried," the other one replied. "You'd think they'd take a little professional pride in their work."

"That's the problem with the world today. No gods-damned standards."

"Norgorber's truth, that."

Silence fell. All I heard from them was the shuffling of feet as they went about their business. I slowly leaned out as much as I dared.

They had clipboards in hands, going down the line of crates and boxes and inspecting them. They would glance them over, make a note on their parchments, occasionally mark one of them with a piece of white chalk, probably to let a smuggler in Yanmass know what crates to look for. Standard, if low-rank, stuff.

But I wasn't interested in their activities. My eyes were on their clothes. In other countries, thieves occasionally identified themselves by scars, tattoos, what have you. But here in Taldor, they had class. And the classier a Brother, the more people would be pissed if you killed him.

Fortunately—or as fortunate as could be, given the circumstance—these particular associates didn't look too classy. They had nice clothes, nice hair, but their poise was stooped and their hands callused from honest labor. These were thugs that had climbed the ladder through violence—and in the Brotherhood, that ladder didn't go very high at all. The Brotherhood liked muscle just fine, but valued diplomats and thinkers. These two would be missed, but only as long as it took to replace them with another pair of idiots.

I let out a low breath, already running over how I'd kill them. They were on opposite sides of the room, slowly making their way around. Once one of them got close enough, I could get the drop on him: come up behind, clamp a hand down, cut his throat. Minimal fuss. That'd give me maybe ten seconds before his partner noticed, during which time I could put Whisper in his kidneys.

It would have to be a straight kill, though. They both looked like they spent a lot of time beating up people much bigger than I was. Like I said, I was no good in a fight.

I took up Whisper, tightened my grip, and waited for one of them to get close. But just as I was about to spring, the doors swung open again.

And whatever god had been watching over me up to this point promptly turned its eyes away.

A woman walked in; my breath died with every step she took. Her long, pointed ears twitched, and suddenly the sound of sweat sliding down my temple was deafening. She came to a stop, and I had one long moment to appreciate just how much shit I was in.

An elf. Tall and thin, her body a spear wrapped in black silk. Her face was full of iron-hard edges, her mouth a thin scar beneath a long nose. Her hair, the color of fresh snow, was neatly trimmed around her giant ears. And she had those eyes: those big, freaky eyes that all elves have.

Cold as a gods-damned night.

She didn't do a damn thing more than step into the warehouse, hands folded neatly behind her back, and stare at the thugs.

She didn't have to. I cold feel my blood run cold at her presence, like the world had just collectively held its breath. And in the gravelike silence that followed, my worst fears were confirmed.

"Oh, hell," one of the thugs all but whimpered. "Madame Longstride."

Chariel Longstride.

Hell.

Damn.

Shit.

No, no, no, no, *no*.

My heart pounded. My blood froze. Any thoughts I had of fighting my way out of there grew legs and ran right out of my head. Any thoughts I had of leaving there alive followed. And if I'd had any voice left in my throat, I'd have been screaming.

So yeah. Not great, this situation.

"Well?" Chariel spoke in the soft, lilting tone that had been a lullaby for the hundreds she had put in early graves. "What did you find?"

"None of our stash is missing, madame," the other thug, just *slightly* less intimidated, said. "Whatever the beastmen were looking for, we didn't own it."

There was a long stretch of silence. Long enough for me to realize that I had been holding my breath this entire time.

This probably seems a bit dramatic. You might have found it weird that I should be acting that way at the sight of an elf.

You might have found it weirder that two men of that size were terrified of a woman that slight.

But then, you didn't know Chariel Longstride.

Nobody knew Chariel Longstride.

She was a ghost. A ghost that the Brotherhood called upon when they needed someone dragged down to Hell. For the list of people on the Brotherhood's bad side was long, and as of very recently the name "Shaia Ratani" had gotten bumped up somewhere uncomfortably close to the top.

Hence, you'd understand when I clenched everything at the sound of her sighing.

"A raid. Fantastic," she said. "I was called all the way out here to see a centaur raid."

"That's . . . that's good, right?" the first thug asked. "No harm to us, Madame Longstride?"

"My dear," she replied, "does it make sense to use two-hundred-year-old wine to water a potato farm?"

A long pause. "Uh . . . no?"

"I permit people to say exactly one stupid thing around me before I get irritated," Chariel said. "Were I you, I'd hedge my bets and just stay silent." She snorted. "If everything else is in order, I see no reason for us to linger."

Feet shuffled. Floorboards creaked. If I weren't terrified, I'd have started laughing.

Leaving.

She was leaving. Just like that.

I heard them walk toward the door, heard the door swing open. All I had to do was wait for them to be gone and make a break for it. Norgorber's nuts, but I felt a bit stupid for being so worried. All that fear and it was going to be this easy?

"Wait."

Apparently not.

Floorboards creaked. I heard Chariel's light step stride over to the corner of the warehouse where I had just been. I glanced out the side of my eye, saw her lean down beside the crate I had inspected, the crate whose lid I had pried open . . .

. . . and hadn't finished securing.

Chariel slipped a finger under the lid, tilted it up a little, heard the nails squeak.

"Someone has been here."

From somewhere inside her sleeve, a short blade leapt to her hand like an overeager puppy. I dared a little movement and slunk back further against the crate, clutching Whisper tightly. I couldn't see her anymore, but I could feel those big, freaky eyes as they swept across the warehouse.

Just as keenly as I'd felt them the last time I'd seen them.

She drew closer to me, her footfalls going soft as she realized she wasn't alone. I was left with silence. Silence in which I could hear my heart pounding. Silence in which I could hear every creak of wood as the elf slowly searched her way closer toward me. Silence in which, if you strained your ears, you might hear me praying to any god to answer me.

"Hello?"

I blinked.

Usually, gods didn't answer quite so promptly.

"Is someone there?"

Nor with quite so much uncertainty.

I heard footsteps again—Chariel rushing toward the door. The two thugs were taking up positions in case they needed to back her up. I glanced up, saw one of them standing just behind her, the other standing not far from my hiding spot. Their eyes were locked on the doors as the unluckiest man in the world entered.

"No one's supposed to be here," the guardsman said as he walked in. "Haven't you heard there was an attack?"

My heart stopped pounding just long enough to sink into my belly as I recognized the voice. I glanced over the crate and saw him standing there: boyish face peering out from under his helm, boyish hands on his sword.

Sandan gods-damned Klimes.

Ah hell, kid.

"We have." Chariel's body was rigid as a viper, and though I couldn't see her eyes, I knew they'd make a snake's look kind in comparison. "We're simply taking care of some business. Walk away."

"Business needs to be cleared with the captain," Sandan said, eyeing the elf. "We're on high alert."

"Boy," the thug behind her said, "take her advice."

One thing I'd never accuse the Brotherhood of being was dumb. I found myself desperately wishing that Sandan would listen to them, that he'd turn around and pretend he never saw this.

But he was an honest boy. An honest boy who had an honest job, an honest sword, an honest life.

And really, really bad luck.

Sandan seized his sword. "By order of Yanmass and Grand Prince Stavian, I order you to—"

His sword was about halfway out of its sheath when the dagger's hilt reached his jugular. His voice died in his throat and his eyes bulged out like they didn't believe what had just happened.

Chariel had that effect on people.

She walked over to his corpse to retrieve her dagger. I took a moment to mutter a two-word prayer for him. No time for anything more. Whatever cruel god had sent Sandan through those doors did so as a gift to me.

And as I took Whisper in hand, I knew it'd just be rude to waste it.

Over the crate I was hiding behind. Dagger flipping in my hand. Feet moving as I swept up behind the closest thug. Arm around his waist, pull him close, bring the dagger up.

Like I said, I'm no good in a fight.

But killing?

Yeah, I know a thing or two about that.

The thug started to say something as I grabbed him, but whatever it was came leaking out of him on a crimson torrent as I drew Whisper's edge across his neck. He started squirming as the life bled out of his throat, his blood spattering my arm.

Messy death. But I needed it messy.

His companion whirled around, didn't even get a chance to comprehend what was happening before I shoved his bleeding friend at him. They went down in a heap, one of them screaming, the other trying his damnedest to scream.

And I was already running.

Up on top of a crate, then another, and another until I was up high. I felt the wind split, wood shudder as a dagger sank into the wood where I had just been.

But I couldn't stop. I couldn't turn. I couldn't let Chariel see my face.

I kept running, leapt up to the shelf, darted to the window. I grabbed the frame, swung my legs through. The wind shrieked past my ear. I felt a metal kiss upon my cheek. The narrowest sliver of blood wept down to my jaw.

The last favor any god was going to do for me today.

I couldn't stop now. I slipped out the window, darted down the alley, stuck close to the edge of the wall as I ran for the gate.

Keep moving, Shy, I told myself. Just keep moving. Chariel had two corpses to deal with. I was out of there quick. She might have guessed I was a woman, but she wouldn't know who I was.

She couldn't. She didn't see my face. She didn't see my face. She didn't see my face.

I kept repeating that. As I ran through a cluster of merchants, as I ran past a pair of inattentive guards, as I ran out of First Solace, blood still on my hands.

6

Hoofbeats

I mpossible!"

It's not that I *blamed* Dalaris for her disbelief.

"Simply unbelievable!"

This couldn't be easy, after all. It's one thing to suspect a plot around one's murdered husband, another thing entirely to have it confirmed. And to have his own brother implicated in it had to have been upsetting.

"You're surely mistaken!"

So, like I said, I didn't blame her for not believing me.

"That's just . . . just . . ."

But after two hours of her expressions of incredulity, my sympathy, patience, and restraint were all wearing thin.

"You seem to have run out of synonyms, darling," I said. "Should I take that to mean you're ready to listen to me, or shall I fetch you a thesaurus?"

From across the carriage's cabin, Dalaris fixed me with a glower. That, at least, was an improvement from the scowl she had first given me when I told her everything. And though she was still the same shade of incensed red, she at least seemed to be receptive to listening.

"Look, here's what I know." I leaned forward, elbows on my knees. "The centaur raids are connected. There's no way they launched two perfectly timed raids by coincidence. Someone sent them there to get crates of weapons out. Gerowan was killed in the process."

"I don't doubt that," Dalaris said. "But to suspect Alarin, his own brother . . ."

I rolled my eyes. If the idea of one noble murdering another was unthinkable to the heir of Sidara, it was little wonder their house was in decline.

"I know what I saw," I said. "There were sigils on the crates they took: Herevard's sigil, and a long scepter on a gold field."

"That's House Stelvan's sigil," she said. "But they're arms dealers. It's simply unthinkable that they'd set weapons up to be taken."

"Which leaves the last sigil I saw: two crossed rapiers."

Dalaris's face sank. Her head followed, drooping down as she rubbed her temples. "That's . . . that's the sigil of Amalien. Two swords, two siblings."

"Makes sense to me," I replied, leaning back in my seat. "Amalien smuggles someone else's weapons to the centaurs. That's a loss in profit for the other nobles and he secures the gratitude of a bunch of murderous and armed horse-folk."

"That's where it all falls apart," Dalaris shot back. "The nobles of Yanmass are forever waiting for the day Taldor collapses. They hold onto their gold like a dwarf in rigor. For what reason would they *give* arms to centaurs?"

I sniffed. "I guess that's what you're paying me to find out."

Dalaris fell silent at that, dropping back in her seat with such vigor that she seemed to think she could just sink into it. I had seen that face before—on the faces of wives discovering faithless husbands and children discovering that heroes don't win.

Life's rough. Rougher still if you spend time thinking it's not.

She needed time to process this. I was inclined to give it to her. I eased the door open, stepped onto the carriage's railing. She glanced at me with concern, but the day I couldn't handle myself on a moving carriage was the day I found a more boring profession.

I made my way to the front of the carriage, where Harges sat. If he had any objections to me joining him, he didn't voice them.

Rather rude of him. I could have used the distraction.

Because every time I closed my eyes, all I could see was Sandan. Sandan's wide eyes, Sandan's honest smile, Sandan's blood weeping out onto the floorboards as he choked on Chariel's dagger.

Don't get me wrong, I was no fool. I knew people died—good people or bad—and I knew a few who had died because of me. But Sandan was an honest boy. The deaths of honest people have never sat well with me.

And every time I saw his body hit the floor in my mind, I saw Chariel standing over him. And the cut on my cheek started to burn. Had she recognized me? I was dressed differently, wore my hair shorter, but she had those eyes that seemed like they could see right through any lie.

I wanted not to think about it. Any of it: Sandan's death, Chariel . . . But I'd been in this business too damn long to believe trouble went away just because you didn't think about it.

So instead, I stared out over the horses. The plains rolled away beneath us, slowly giving way to rising underbrush and trees. The guards at First Solace had said the centaurs came out of the woods nearby. Seemed to make sense to me—centaurs could traverse the difficult terrain easily; a full mounted guard, perhaps not so much.

It wasn't exactly easy for a horse-drawn carriage, either. But an unanticipated benefit of Sidara's declining fortunes was an upgrade in functionality. In Yanmass, the sturdy carriage with its wagon wheels and its two farm horses would be considered positively unfashionable. But here on the plains, the carriage and the horses handled the terrain without complaint.

"Dalaris says you know these woods," I said, glancing at Harges.

"Mm-hm," he grunted, not bothering to glance back.

"Says you grew up playing in them."

"Mm-hm."

"I'm not crazy for thinking that we'll find the centaurs here, am I?"

"Mm-hm."

Harges didn't say anything else. Harges didn't even look at me. I liked Harges.

At any rate, I assumed either he or Dalaris would voice an objection to my plan if they had one. It seemed to me that, if the centaurs were the only lead I could point to, finding them would lead, one way or another, to Gerowan's murderer.

Harges had heard the plan. He hadn't said anything.

He took the reins in one hand, then reached down into his boot. He pulled out a dented flask, unscrewed it, and took a long sip. He smacked his lips, then handed it over to me.

I *really* liked Harges.

I was well on my way to enjoying his offering—it smelled like whiskey, about as old as he was—when the carriage came to a sudden stop. The horses whinnied, but didn't protest further as Harges drew back on the reins, causing me to spill the liquor over my leathers.

"If I was drinking too much, you could have just grunted," I muttered at him, vainly trying to brush the liquor from my clothes.

Harges didn't reply. He didn't seem to be listening. He hopped off the seat and stalked to the nearby underbrush, eyes on the ground.

Brush and scrub grass rose up densely here, the vanguard to the forest proper, which loomed tall not a mile away. The evening cloaked the sky in pale purple as the crown of the sun slipped over the horizon. But there was more than enough light for me to see absolutely nothing that would have caused such a sudden stop.

"Harges?" The carriage's door opened and Dalaris stepped out. "Why have we stopped?"

I hopped down to join her, keen to know as well, as we walked to him. He knelt down, gestured over a patch of scrub.

"Flat," he grunted. He glanced up, pointed over the plains. "Flat all over."

I blinked. "Well, consider any doubts I had about your expertise banished. I can see it's flat, you imbecile."

"*Too* flat," he said. "Should be full of bushes 'n' saplings here. Scrub got trampled down."

"Why?" Dalaris asked.

Harges grunted. He stalked off and returned with a heavy rock. With another grunt, he heaved it forward. It struck the earth and then, suddenly, disappeared.

"Pits," he said. "Dug up all over here 'n' covered."

"Just in case someone were being pursued by horses," I said, realization dawning on me. "Centaurs would be nimble enough to dart around them."

"Horses, not so much." He shook his head at Dalaris. "Can't go no further, m'lady. Can't get no carriage 'round no pits."

"Just as well," I said, checking my dagger. "If there are traps here, the centaurs can't be too far away. I'll head out by myself."

"But . . ." Dalaris began. "That could be dangerous."

"Yes," I replied. "I would expect so."

"I should come with you."

"Excellent idea." I nodded at her. "My original idea was to sneak in, uncover evidence as to what they've been doing, and sneak out. But with your help, I think we can go in and deliver a stirring, strongly worded lecture on the impropriety of their raids. With any luck, they'll be shamed into confessing and vow to bring their raids up to standard."

Dalaris stared at me. I stared back.

"I'm being sarcas—"

"I know what you're being," Dalaris snapped. She sighed and rubbed her temples. "It's just . . . he was *my* husband. I feel so . . . so *useless,* standing here and letting you put yourself in danger."

I shrugged. "I assumed you paid me for that reason."

"Well, yes, but that doesn't mean I have to *like* it."

Maybe it was something in her voice—that soft, frustrated tone. Or maybe the way she seemed to shrink into herself, crossing her arms tightly. Or it could have been the way she pointedly looked away from me.

At that moment, I didn't care exactly *what* it was she was doing that made me smile so. There was just something so novel about someone who gave a damn for someone else.

Norgorber help me, I was starting to like this puppy of a woman.

But on the list of places I would not want to bring a puppy, a camp full of bloodthirsty centaurs ranked pretty high.

"Four hours," I said, holding up four fingers. "If I'm not back by then, you have my full permission to come after me, leave me, hate me, whatever. Agreed?"

Dalaris nodded, grudgingly. I glanced to Harges, who shook his head violently.

He took a step forward, thrust his hand out, made a beckoning gesture.

I glared at him for a moment before slapping the dented flask into his palm. He grunted.

"Just for that," I said, turning on my heel, "make it five hours."

"It isn't a matter of payment, stabled, it's a matter of *practicality.* We lost three warriors to the damn guards so we could carry your crap back here."

A voice. Thick, burly, bestial; like someone had been swallowing gravel.

"If you're saying you'd rather not be paid, then we'll be happy to shovel the gold we've been feeding you somewhere else, barbarian. Until then, you get paid to carry out orders, not second-guess them."

A voice. Deep, bellowing, rolling; distant thunder over a low hill.

"Gold won't do crap for us if we keep losing warriors doing these petty raids."

"Pettiness, you half-wit coward, is what the plan calls for. Have faith in Halamox's ideas."

"Kjoda *pisses* on Halamox's ideas, and if you want to bend down a little lower, he'll gladly piss on you, too."

"Keep talking and we'll see how well you piss after I put my hoof straight up your ass."

Isn't Taldane just the most beautiful language?

They'd been at this for the better part of half an hour now: grunting, snarling, throwing complaints, insults, and the occasional punch. And still, neither of them seemed to be at all interested in stopping.

I had to admit, the centaur reputation for tenacity was well earned, if this was any indication. And it was interesting to see how well that trait crossed cultural boundaries.

As I understood it, the majority of centaurs out there in the big wide world were clannish and wild, barely a step removed from the orcs, goblins, and other tribal humanoids that plagued humanity. Hunters, gatherers, raiders—most of them didn't aspire to be much more than that.

But occasionally, a few did. Now and again, a centaur put his mind to social mobility. He cut his hair, trimmed his beard, stopped pissing wherever he stood, and joined civil society. Valued as a strong warrior, he occasionally got as far as a four-legged humanoid could expect to get in many human-dominated societies—that is, occasionally he got invited into the house and not the stable.

I had always wondered what happened when the two breeds met.

And now, I was finding out.

One of the savages, a big, shaggy son of a mare wearing nothing but war paint and a truly impressive number of tattoos, squared off at the center of the camp. Behind him stood a number of other similarly half-nude clansmen and women, stamping irately. I assumed he was the leader—at least, he was the only one who talked about himself in the third person, so I guessed he must be pretty important.

He was the one voicing grievances, pounding a thick fist to his chest, snarling out his painted mouth, scowling out of beady eyes beneath a shaggy mane of hair. And every threat he made was backed up by snarls from the six savages behind him.

Not that this seemed to impress the other, cleaner centaurs any.

There were three of them: two males, one female, each about seven feet tall, burly humanoid torsos rising out of burly horse bodies. Their arms were crossed defiantly across their chests. Unlike their other kin, their hair was clean, and they wore polished armor and barding. One might have thought them completely civilized, were it not for the fact that they, too, pawed the ground aggressively with their hooves in anticipation of a fight.

"We've got gold enough to pay you for one more raid," the female centaur said to the savage. "You want it or not?"

"Kjoda doesn't mind taking your gold," the big one, Kjoda, said. "But it's not worth crap if we keep losing warriors because of your stupid ideas. You tell Halamox that, *stabled.*"

I saw the female's face contort in fury at that. My knowledge of centaurs was limited, but I knew enough to know the more civilized, city-dwelling ones—like her—found the term "stabled" to be something of a slur.

Which was doubtless why Kjoda had called her it. And which was doubtless why he was fondling the hilt of the greataxe strapped to his back like it was his lover.

Whatever the savage wanted to happen, it didn't. The centaur woman tilted her nose up and turned away, taking her cleaner cousins with her. The shaggier ones did likewise, skulking back to their side of the camp.

Neither of them noticed me, of course.

Funny thing about humans and humanoids alike is that they don't really look up unless they feel they're in trouble—usually to spew off a quick prayer to one god or another. Even if they had, they probably wouldn't have seen me, lying on my belly and peering out over the edge of the cabin's roof. But then, I hadn't moved since I got there.

Navigating my way through the traps and forest had proved not too difficult. Slipping past the sentries and into the shallow valley the camp was situated in was slightly tougher, but still, nothing I couldn't handle. The challenge came only now, when I realized just how big the camp was.

This had once been a hunting camp, if the various cabins were any indication. Whatever humans had been here had long since left, and the centaurs had moved in—the stabled ones, anyway. Their shaggier, barbaric kin still preferred sleeping out of doors.

The savages preferred to dwell on the far side of the camp, keeping to their bonfires, spending their time sharpening weapons and whispering to whatever noisome creatures they had in those big wooden cages they held at the edge of the camp.

Even if I hadn't just heard that little exchange, I could have told hostilities between the two groups were running high. Ordinarily, that'd be a good thing; if they weren't watching each other's backs, it meant they wouldn't be watching me slipping behind both of theirs.

Now, if only there weren't so gods-damned *many* of them.

At a quick count, I had guessed there to be maybe two hundred centaurs present. But after I found myself lingering up there awhile, I had been able to count closer to two hundred and seventy—eighty or so had been the clean kind. Combine that with however many were doubtless out raiding right now, then combine *that* with the six big wooden cages and whatever creatures they held, and . . .

I'm sure you can figure out why I was reluctant to move.

Night wore on. And as it did, more centaurs retired to sleep standing up, letting their bonfires dim. But there were still too damn many up, alert, and active for my tastes.

Not that there was ever an *acceptable* number of bloodthirsty centaurs.

But regardless of how many were present, I still had a job to do. The centaurs were strategizing and plotting, just as suspected. If I were a gambling woman—or a better one, anyway—I'd have laid odds that I'd find whoever was behind it here.

My eyes drifted to the edge of the camp. Situated farthest away from the uncivilized contingent, the largest cabin stood imposing and dark. Unlike the other cabins here, whose doors had been shattered to make way for centaur girth, this one still had a door on it. This one had something to hide.

Good enough place to start, I thought. But getting there would be an issue.

Would be, that is, if I were bad at my job.

I slipped to the edge of the cabin's roof, slid down the walls, and took off. The night was dark enough already that the tree branches that leaned down to smother the scant moonlight were just another little present for me. By the light of that half-masked moon, and the distant glow of the centaurs' fires, I picked my way around the edges of the camp.

I darted quietly from cover to cover: through underbrush, behind cabin walls, toward a nearby barrel. And it was behind this last that I froze. Because it was behind it that I heard footsteps approaching.

Moving now would be too risky. I slowed my breathing, stilled my body, closed my eyes.

"What'd those ugly things bring us, anyway?"

"Weapons, finally. Just like Halamox said they would."

Centaurs. Clean ones. Two of them. They came up to the barrel, fumbled around in the dark. I heard liquid sloshing into cups. Even through the short breaths I took, I damn near passed out from the reek of alcohol that flooded into my nose.

So I was hiding behind a cask. Full of whiskey, by the smell of it, and strong, at that. Made sense; it must take a lot to get a centaur drunk.

"'Bout time, you ask me," one of the centaurs said. "I tire of letting those barbarians do the fighting. I want a fight."

"Halamox says it's coming," the other said between gulps of the brew.

"Yeah, Halamox says a lot of stuff."

They wandered off, muttering to each other. I didn't wait for them to come back. It had been just luck that had made them more concerned with liquor than security. I might not get that again.

I swept out, picking my way deeper into the camp. A wide gap of space between the two sides allowed me to slip toward the uncivilized end. I moved quickly from the shadow of one tent to another, giving their dying fires a wide berth.

I couldn't help but feel a little insulted. The tribal centaurs were so embroiled in their own complaints that I felt like I could have started playing a trumpet and not been noticed.

"See Kjoda tonight?" Around a nearby campfire, a pair of them muttered to each other between strokes of whetstones on their blades. "Looks pissed. Not gonna take crap from the stabled much longer."

"Good," the other grunted. "I say we should've killed them before they got so many. More of these things keep showing up each day. Not gonna be able to take 'em for much longer."

"Weakling," the first snarled. "I could kill three in my sleep, at least."

"I could kill *four*. Kjoda just needs to give the word."

"If he don't? Then we get rowdy."

"Yeah," the other chuckled. "*Rowdy*."

Charming.

The discourse of centaur politics seemed enough to keep them distracted as I crept through their camp until I could get to the wooden cages at its edge.

I could hear the heavy sounds of animal breathing around me. Apparently, whatever was in these cages was not interested enough in centaur affairs to wake up. Still, that didn't mean I could be less careful. I'd had my share of dealing with guard animals before. I moved slowly, trying not to disturb anything that might make a new scent.

A low growling reached me from nearby. I glanced over, saw a pair of yellow eyes peering out from a large cage. Behind the lone watcher, five more wolves slumbered blissfully—presumably the ones the centaurs had used to find their weapons.

Fortunately, trained wolves weren't as suspicious as their feral kin. The one looking at me quickly lost interest and returned to sleeping with its pack.

Unfortunately, they could still be a pain in my ass if I had to get out of here quickly. I slipped toward the door of the cage and grinned at the sight of a metal lock.

Now, picking a lock is no mean feat: it takes years of practice to do it right. But jamming up a lock? That's easy.

I slid Whisper out of his sheath and into the lock, gave it a few twists until I heard something grind. Anyone wanted these wolves out now, they'd have to work for it.

I slipped away from the door before anyone could notice me and almost backed up into the largest of the wooden cages.

This one, massive as it was, was dead silent. I peered between its bars, looking into the darkness.

Luck had given me the night. Skill had got me this far. But it was pure instinct that made me jerk my head back just in time to avoid it being taken off by a massive, ursine claw.

Big as my skull, the hairy brown paw groped around the bars for a moment. When it found nothing, a pair of wide, yellow eyes peered out, crowned by a feathery scowl. The creature within made a short, rasping trill of frustration.

Paws. Feathers.

Some kind of bear . . . owl . . . thing?

Fantastic.

You sometimes hear of these things: insane unions between two beasts that ought not, by natural means, be able to crossbreed without a lot of liquor and a *lot* of regrets. Some say they're a god's disfavor made manifest. Others say it's evolution in action. Personally, I suspected it had a more logical explanation, such as a union of wizards and the aforementioned copious amounts of liquor.

It was a rare occasion that I actually didn't disapprove of crazy magic, but this was one of them. In the cage, another great shape stirred as a second of the creatures rose from its slumber. I crept to the front of their cage, saw the door secured by a lock no more sophisticated than the chain it held.

Not that I was expecting much from centaurs.

I slipped a hand to my belt, pulled free the tiny leather roll of lockpicks I carried inside it. With a quick glance around to make sure no eyes were upon me, I plucked out two picks and went to work.

I wouldn't have told you I was great at picking locks. No more than I would have told you I was good at understanding men or women. Truth was, I just knew what they all had in common.

Find the right spot, give it a flick, and watch them open.

The padlock clicked open, fell to the ground. I scrambled around the cage, scaled up its bars to its top, and simply waited.

It didn't take long for the curious creatures to realize what had changed. They nudged the door, watched it creak open, and came creeping ponderously out.

In the shadows, I hadn't realized just how gods-damned *big* they were. But as they came lumbering out on four meaty limbs, avian faces taking everything in, I guessed they both weighed a ton, at least.

Curiosity turned to exhilaration in a few short seconds. The creatures came loping out into the camp, silently making for the nearest cluster of centaurs.

I closed my eyes. And began to count to ten.

"HOLY HELL, THEY'RE LOOSE!"

I had gotten to four when the screaming began.

"Whose job was it to look after 'em?"

"IT'S GOT ME! HELP! HELP!"

"You gods-damned savages, get those things under control!"

"Stuff it under your tail, stabled!"

"SOMEONE, PLEASE!"

There were a lot of voices, a lot of screams, a lot of curses, a lot of terrified wailing. And none of them were louder or prouder than the blood-hungry screeches of the bird-bears.

Had I the time, I would have gladly stayed to hear how it all ended.

But time is money.

I leapt off the cage, broke into a run for the big cabin. The centaurs were all rushing for the center of the camp, content to ignore me in favor of the monsters currently making a scene. None of them so much as looked my way as I slipped around the side of the cabin. Peering into a window, I saw the dim glow of a lantern and nothing else. I took a breath, then hauled myself up and over the sill.

The room was quiet inside—quiet as it could be, considering the chaos outside. Bare but for the large tables set at either wall, a few barrels of whiskey stacked in the corner, and paper.

Loads and loads of paper.

By the light of the lantern hanging overhead, I could see them: maps pinned to the walls charting out caravan routes and guard patrols; various notes upon the tables, scribbled in a language I couldn't understand; books on military treatises and Taldan history.

If I was going to find anything, it would be here.

From outside came a scream, followed by an agonized screech from one of the bear-things. I cringed.

An amateur thief might have heard that sound, realized they likely only had a few precious minutes left before the camp got itself in order, and started getting sloppy. Overwhelmed by the fear that they would be discovered and subsequently mutilated, they would search too hastily, leaving things out of order, making evidence of their passage all too obvious. Then, realizing their looming fate, they would sit down and cry and wait for death.

Fortunately, I was a professional.

So while I was certainly *aware* of the possibility of being discovered and mutilated, I definitely did not cry.

I'd save that for when I had to beg for mercy.

I slipped over to the table, let my eyes wander over the papers instead of my fingers. Stories may tell of burglars who slip in and leave a bare treasure vault behind, but the reality is that the best burglars are the ones that no one even knows were there. As I liked to think of myself as at least fairly good, I wasn't about to touch anything until I was damn sure I could—

Aha.

I picked out a sentence I could read on one of the papers. Careful not to move the papers atop it, I gently pulled it out and looked it over. Written in common Taldane, dark ink, *fantastic* penmanship. But I was more concerned with what it said.

H—

I grow concerned by your brazenness. The assurances you offered that your alliance with the savage tribes would be to our mutual benefit has yet to manifest. Instead, I very nearly saw everything ruined by their raid. They didn't kill enough people for it to look convincing. The target was only narrowly eliminated. I remind you that subtlety is the price you pay for protection.

I have enclosed, with this week's missive, a dictionary, that you might learn the meaning of that word. In addition, the caravans have altered their routes. The maps I sent will tell you where to strike next. As usual, avoid the ones marked in red if you want your supplies to keep coming.

No signature, naturally.

Pity. But then, that would just have been too easy, wouldn't it?

Protection. Target. Eliminate.

These words, and the rather detailed map of caravan routes that only someone directing said routes would be able to pen, were merely suspicious. But it was the ink on the page that sealed it.

Granted, I've never been a noble myself, but I've known enough of them to know that it's fierce training they go through to prepare them for the rigors of being stupidly wealthy: there are manners to learn, languages to decipher, and penmanship so precise you could cut yourself on it.

I supposed whatever training the noble who wrote this letter underwent, it was too much to break even for the sake of sending a covert message.

A noble was behind it. All of it: the centaurs, the raids, Gerowan's death.

Dalaris would be very interested to hear this.

"Don't you walk away from me, stabled."

I really hoped I'd be able to share it with her.

Voices. Footsteps. Outside. Getting closer.

I darted to the corner of the room, leapt behind the casks of whiskey, pressed myself deep into the shadows, and held my breath.

Through the gap between the barrels, I saw the door open. A great shape bent low to enter. And when he righted himself, I could see the centaur in all his glory.

His big, giant, kill-me-with-one-hoof glory.

Funny, but from the waist up, he wasn't actually that bad to look at. His torso was broad and lean, his arms, corded with muscle, left bare by the breastplate and pauldron he wore. Beneath elegantly braided black hair and neatly trimmed beard, a rather regal face with a square jaw looked out.

Indeed, had he not been a freaky abomination of nature intent on slaughter, I might very well be tempted to introduce myself.

But as I mentioned, the horse-bit looked a little less inviting. Below, he was a massive destrier: black hair, thick legs, heavy hooves that could split my skull with a flick. A heavy sword belt with a heavier sword hung around his waist—human waist, not the horse waist.

"I'm hardly walking away from you, savage," the big centaur said as he walked toward a table. "That would imply I cared about you at all. I started walking back and you simply followed me."

"You know damn well what Kjoda meant." Kjoda, shorter and leaner, pushed his way in after the big one. "Two of my beasts are *dead* now, thanks to your kind."

"And five of my *compatriots* are dead thanks to your animals," the new centaur replied, sneering over his shoulder. "I'm being generous in calling it even, considering that your shoddy locks are to blame."

"Warriors say they locked them tight," Kjoda growled. "They aren't liars. No one lies to Kjoda. Without big muscle, we aren't gonna make it far when we start raiding big towns."

My eyebrow quirked at that. Centaurs were bad enough without ambitions.

"I lament your loss, truly," the civilized centaur replied. "We may discuss renegotiations in the morning, if you so choose."

"You said that last night. *And* the night before. And the night before *that*. And you never been here come the morning."

The centaur glanced briefly at his desk, then back to Kjoda.

"And what have we learned?" he asked.

My other eyebrow quirked at *that*. Handsome and witty was rare. But I suppose it was true what they said: the good ones are either married or horrific horse-beasts.

Kjoda turned and stalked away, muttering something about glue. He slammed the door shut with such force as to send the lantern swaying overhead. The big centaur stared at the door, arms folded, for a long time. Upon the floor, his monstrous shadow was painted even more twisted by the swaying lantern.

I mentally ran over the numbers in my head: about two hours since I had entered the camp had passed. That left about three left until I gave Dalaris permission to come after me—give or take one, depending on how antsy she got. I assumed the centaur came back to consult some charts, but he'd have to leave again, eventually, to get a drink or to take a piss or—

"Would you care to come out?" he asked.

Or he could just find me right away. That'd be fine, too.

"Mind you, I'm not adverse to searching for you," he said out loud. "But if I have to tear my command room apart, I'm going to be cross when I find you." He stamped a hoof upon the floor-boards, making the tables quake on their legs. "*Very* cross."

Damn it.

You got sloppy, Shy. Amateurish. You left the papers misplaced. Of *course* he noticed.

I held my breath, closed my eyes, ran over my options in my head. I could stay hidden, make him work for it. I could try to run for the window, maybe make it out . . . before he sicced his two-hundred-odd exceedingly mobile army of horse-people after me, each of which could run twice as fast as—

Yeah, no, maybe not that.

"Well?" he asked the room. "Keep me waiting much longer and I'll start to think you're a touch rude, thief."

"Now, sir." My words came as slowly as I did as I rose up behind the casks, my hands in the air. "I should accuse you of the same."

He whirled around, a scowl etched across his proud brow. I met him with what I hoped was an adequately-sheepish-yet-not-completely-spineless grin.

"After all, I have taken nothing from you yet," I said. "I am not *quite* a thief, and resent the implication."

No chance for retreat. I had to stall for time until I could think of something.

His face slowly softened as he took me in. I had to bite back my surprise as he swept low in a modest bow—not so much that I could have stabbed him, but far more gracious than one would typically expect in these circumstances.

"My apologies, lady," he said, straightening himself again. "Though I would hope that my state of mind would be understandable, given that you clearly intruded upon my camp without proper introduction." He tapped his chest. "Who does Halamox have the pleasure of meeting?"

"Anna, Sir Halamox. Anna Nimm." If I wasn't going to give a guardsman my real name, I sure as hell wasn't going to offer one to *this* guy. I managed a low bow of my own, careful to keep my hands visible.

"Anna Nimm." He spoke the false name slowly, as if he could taste it for a lie. "I won't humor you by saying you're welcome here. But I will forestall taking your life, for the moment."

"How generous of you," I replied. "I can see why your soldiers trust you." My lips curled in the slightest of smirks. "The clean ones, anyway."

Halamox eyed me coolly. "I take it, then, that you've overheard quite a bit. Speak plainly, human. What are you here for?"

"Merely lost, sir," I replied. "I stumbled into your camp and—"

"I'll not presume to insult your honor, madame, if you'll not presume to insult my intelligence." He stalked forward, making sure each hoof landed firmly to remind me just how big he was. "You were clever enough to recognize my command room. You are no hapless traveler."

I met his cool gaze with one of my own, slowly lowering my hands. Obviously, I hadn't expected him to buy that. But sometimes little lies are required to sell the big ones.

"I'm an adventurer," I replied. "Heard there was trouble in the woods after your raid on First Solace. Came to see if there was loot to be made."

The tension left Halamox in a great, snorting breath. While his eyes were still narrowed on me, he didn't seem *quite* as ready to kill me as he had been a moment ago.

"As you can see, we've not much here, madame," he said. "The Rockhoof Clan are a proud, simple folk. We take only what we need from the land."

"And what you want from the humans," I added, perhaps a bit hastier than was wise. "I'll thank you not to insult my intelligence, either, sir. I saw what your clan did in First Solace."

One of the barbaric centaurs would have gutted me for the insolence creeping into my voice. But Halamox, though he cringed, did not raise a hoof against me.

I knew his type. Observed the airs of city life from the outside, adopted their codes and mannerisms to fit in, found that it wasn't enough and tried all the harder. Whether human or centaur, people were all the same. He wouldn't kill me right now.

It just wouldn't be proper.

Like I said, I knew his type. And, as the lantern steadied overhead and bathed him in a consistent glow, I realized that I knew him.

"Unless I miss my mark, sir," I said, "I've seen you before."

"Have you, madame?"

"In the courtyards of the nobles of Yanmass, outside in their yards." But never in their homes, I refrained from adding. "You're from the city, are you not?"

"Your memory is apt or my reputation precedes me." Halamox inclined his head. "I and certain members of my company were popular choices for the instruction and training of the guards of the noble houses of Yanmass. Their coin afforded their guardsmen the fruits of my expertise."

"And doubtless, you learned a thing or two from them, yourself," I said. "Such as how to avoid their guard patrols."

"You are observant, Madame Nimm. I commend you."

"Not observant enough to understand, apparently. Why give up the noble life of a mercenary to become a common bandit?"

"Noble." He scoffed, an ugly sound tearing out of his throat. "Indeed, at times, I was left to wonder which aspect of my life was more noble: peddling my honor like a tramp or desperately attempting to ignore the whispers of 'monster' behind my back." He glowered at me, through me, hatred plain on his face. "No, madame. I was all too happy to give up that noble life for the fate of a centaur nation."

"A centaur . . . *nation*?"

I caught the incredulity in my voice just a moment too late and his glower intensified. But I could hardly help it; whoever heard of such a thing as a centaur nation?

"We are but tribes now," Halamox said. "Tribes pushed out of our own lands by human incursion. Tribes disunited and easy pickings for the savages of this world. Tribes forever wandering in search of a place to call our own." He gestured those big brawny arms out wide. "Taldor is a nation with too much land and too few citizens to use it. They will not miss what we carve out for own."

"Hence your need for weapons," I said. "Hence your raids."

"I have spent enough time among humans to know that all they respect is force. Like my savage kin, save the savages don't hide their lust for violence behind airs of superiority."

I furrowed my brow. "And what part of this demanded—"

"*No.*"

His voice was followed by the hiss of steel as his tremendous sword came flashing from his scabbard. He swung it about, as if to decapitate me in one fell blow. To my credit, I managed *not* to piss myself before the edge of that blade came to rest just an inch from my throat.

"I don't fancy myself a savage, madame," he said. "I am loathe to spill blood unnecessarily, but I have humored you enough. You are clearly no common adventurer out for coin. Your mind is too inquisitive and your tongue too refined. And unless I miss my guess, I have *you* to thank for the release of the beasts that killed my kin tonight."

I smiled at him, sheepish as I dared. "Would it soothe you to know, sir, that the locks *were* faulty?"

"It would," he replied. "But not nearly as much as it would soothe me to know my people had been avenged." He drew back his blade. "Pity. I was so hoping you'd give me a reason to spare you."

He swung.

"Would my employer do, sir?"

I know it's terribly gauche to be impressed with oneself, but you would be, too, if you could speak faster than a blade could swing.

And if it halted Halamox's sword, once more, from tearing my head off, so much the better.

"What?" He scowled down the length of his blade at me.

"My employer, sir," I replied, eyeing the blade without moving my head, lest it cut me. "As you say, I am no mere adventurer."

"I do not like liars, madame," he growled.

"There is not enough room between your blade and my neck *for* lies, sir," I said. "I was sent here at the behest of a noble whose trade you have disrupted."

Halamox glowered. "Which noble?"

Of course, there *was* room for lies here. Some of my best lying I've done with a blade at my throat, even. But occasionally, even someone as resourceful as me can't afford to speak anything but the truth.

"Sidara," I said. "House Sidara."

"They are of no concern to me. Nor are you."

"But we both will be, sir," I said, "if I don't return. The other nobles are already quite suspicious of your activities. If I don't return to my lady, she'll have no problem convincing them to rally a force to come rout you out." I glanced up at him. "You've been in their homes. You know how many guards they have."

Halamox furrowed his brow. Grit his jaw. He didn't *quite* buy my story, I could tell. But he hadn't hacked my head off, either, so I was happy.

And his hesitation told me more than he thought. Whatever noble was supporting him, he was not confident in their ability to protect him from the rest of them. Whatever hand was holding his leash, I guessed it was just one instead of many.

"Ah, curse my gentlemanly ways." Slowly, Halamox lowered his sword. "But I would hate for the nobles to think me a savage."

"Of course, sir," I said, allowing myself a breath of air. "And once I return to them, I will be happy to tell them whatever you—"

"When you return to them," he interrupted me, "it will be after I am paid."

I blinked, my facade slipping. Uh, what?

"I don't like liars, madame. But you seem like an honest sort. If you say you are a friend of nobles, I believe you."

His sword rose slowly, its tip pressing against my chin to raise my eyes into his smiling, haughty face.

"Just as I believe they will pay handsomely for your return."

7

Centaur Politics

Good rogues get away.
Bad rogues get killed.

But even the best rogues find themselves tied up every now and again.

The first time it happens, it's terrifying. The second time, it's embarrassing. But eventually, you learn how to deal with it.

It's just part of the job, really. And depending on who's holding the rope, it's not always that bad.

Not that having my hands jerked behind me, drawn around a stake, and tied together with some crude hemp was a high mark of my evening, but this wasn't the worst way it could have gone.

The worst way it could have gone was currently standing in front of me, grabbing my throat with one hand while the other pressed a jagged piece of metal masquerading as a knife against my cheek.

"Two-Toe and the Colonel." Kjoda's breath, hot and rank, washed over me as he snarled through a mouthful of yellow teeth.

"What?" I asked, and instantly regretted it.

"*Their names.*" The centaur's hand tightened around my throat, slammed my head against the stake. "I raised those beasts from cubs. Fed them meat, taught them to hunt, taught them to *kill.*" His knife's jagged teeth pressed divots in my skin. "And you killed them like you didn't even care."

"Well," I replied softly, "you trained them well. They killed quite a few of your own people, didn't they?"

He snarled, pounded a fist into the wood above my head. The shock of the impact ran through my entire body. Had he gone for my actual body, I'd be dead from that one blow.

I imagined most people would be screaming right now—after all, the idea of a sentimental centaur is shocking enough even without a blade ready to carve off one's face.

But if you could have seen me, at that moment, you would have seen nothing. You would have seen an expressionless face, a closed mouth, and a pair of unblinking eyes locked right on his.

Sometimes it's easy to forget what I do, the murderers and assassins and dealers I run with. Sometimes it's easy to forget how quickly blood gets spilled, how a little twitch with a little knife can end everything. But I never once forgot how to handle brutes like Kjoda.

Show no emotion. Say nothing. Don't let them look away from you.

Show them too much, they think of a reason to kill you. Turn away from them, they can't think of a reason to keep you alive. And if they're going to kill you, you make them look you dead in the eye when they do it.

Sem taught me that.

That lesson was about men rather than monsters, of course, but it's a gods-damned fine line between the two. And Kjoda had just enough of a glint in his eye to tell me the same rules applied to him.

And he turned that eye over my shoulder to the centaur standing behind me.

"Tighter," he growled. "I want to see her hands turning *blue* for what she did to me."

The centaur, one of the clean ones, snorted as she secured my wrists together. "The more damaged she is, the less we get for her return." She jerked the rope harshly. I winced as a shock of pain ran up my arms. "But if she causes trouble, Halamox says we only need her *mostly* alive."

"Gold." Kjoda spat on the ground. "You stabled would make me laugh if you weren't so damn sad. Ask them for gold, you only play by their rules." He looked back to me, brought his blade up under my chin. "Send them a corpse, you tell them they play by *yours.* And then *they're* the ones doing the asking."

I tilted my head up as the blade rose, felt a lump in my throat pass over its tip as I swallowed hard. Kjoda's eyes trembled, his jaw clenched and hand shaking. He looked over my face, searching for a reason.

He really loved those bird-bears.

This would almost be adorable if it weren't for the fact that my head was as high as it could go and his blade kept going.

A hand reached out, took him by the forearm, and forcibly lowered the blade. I held my sigh of relief as the centaur—the stabled one I saw before—walked up beside me and fixed Kjoda with a stern look.

"Gold brings food. Supplies. Corpses are something we have enough of and will have so many more of in the days to come."

There was something solemn in her voice, almost sad. She was right, of course; Halamox might want to carve out part of Taldor for his centaur nation, but carving was always messy, no matter how dead the goose was. A lot of people would die in the process, and she was doubtless certain that some of them would be her friends. I almost felt bad for her.

Of course, I'd feel worse if she weren't wearing my dagger around her waist like a trophy.

Kjoda sneered at her, then at me, then snorted and stalked off to rejoin a band of his fellows holding an impromptu funeral for the smoldering monster carcass at the center of the camp.

I glanced sidelong at the centaur, decided to try my luck. "Thank you," I said.

She returned a cold look. "I'd not see you gutted like a swine." She leaned down low, her nose inches from mine. "I'd prefer to see you trampled under a hundred hooves until we pulverized your corpse to fertilizer." She sneered as she stalked to a nearby barrel of whiskey and drew herself a hefty tankard. "You can thank Halamox that we've decided to do neither, though."

"I'd be happy to, if he'd come out."

There was a bit more venom in those words than I would have preferred. I counted it as a small blessing that the centaur only gave me a black laugh as she tossed back her whiskey and drew another cup.

"Halamox has greater things on his mind," she said. "Things I might not always agree with, but he takes the longer view. He dreams of a nation for us, of our own laws, our own rules, so that we don't have to bow and scrape for *your* coin." She raised her tankard high above her head. "I trust him. I salute him."

She tossed her head back, drained the tankard in one long drink. She let loose a belch and hurled it at my head. I narrowly ducked, letting it bounce off the stake and land at my feet.

"But I still would have killed you."

She snorted and stomped off to attend some other business.

I leaned back against the stake, tested my bonds, and found them appropriately tight. Quietly, I surveyed the camp.

The chaos the two beasts had caused was still being repaired. The civilized centaurs seemed concerned with the material loss as much as the death of their own. Tents had been ruined, food stores raided, and whiskey casks overturned, drenching various tents and cabins.

The barbarians' thoughts, however, were for their dead. Small clusters of them gathered around the blazing pyres that had been erected for the dead bird-bears.

Centaurs being a step above more monstrous humanoids, their ways were slightly more known to humans than your average orc or goblin, though still hopelessly alien. Respect was afforded those who proved an asset to the tribe. Hence why hulking, murderous beasts were given funerals and those who had died before they could do anything were given to the pile.

I found that interesting.

But not half as interesting as the mood pervading the camp.

The two centaur clans might have come physically closer in the wake of the chaos, venturing out of their respective areas of the camp to repair the damage, but this only seemed to increase their hostilities. The more civil ones contented themselves with casting accusing stares at each other. The rowdier ones made boisterous threats. The unstable ones continued to sharpen weapons while looking intently at their "allies."

Occasionally, one would venture close enough to hurl a curse at me. I said nothing. Looked straight ahead. Stood perfectly still.

It's a layman who believes stealth is all about sneaking in shadows and creeping up behind people. That's a big part of it, true. But so many rogues have met their ends by ignoring the first rule.

Sometimes, stealth is just about not drawing attention to yourself.

I reminded myself of this as I stood, stock-still, as a civil centaur came approaching from my left and a savage centaur from my right.

The former, a burly armored fellow carrying a lance over his shoulder, came wandering past toward the whiskey barrel nearby. The latter was dragging one of his dead comrades toward a nearby fire. They shot each other glowers as they passed one another, but said nothing.

And, more importantly, didn't spare so much as a glance for me.

I eyed the ground. The tankard the centaur had hurled at me lay by my feet. With as much movement as I dared, I reached out with one foot and hooked the toe of my boot into the tankard's handle.

I glanced at the barbarian's back as he walked away from me. I drew my breath and, with a prayer and a kick, sent the tankard flying.

Norgorber isn't the sort of god to do things out of the kindness of his heart. He's a selfish god for selfish people, a trickster and a thug with a mean streak long as most gods' patiences. Pray to him, you're bound to be disappointed.

But do something he finds funny enough, you just might be surprised what he gives you.

The tankard sailed through the air, caroming off the back of the savage's head. He whirled, a roar in his throat and a sword in his hand. Red-rimmed eyes swept from the tankard rolling on the ground to the centaur at the whiskey barrel drawing another cup, chuckling.

It was an awful lot to take in.

One could hardly blame him for not noticing the girl tied to a stake, standing perfectly still.

I certainly wasn't about to.

"*YOU!*" he snarled, stalking over his comrade's dead body. "You lookin' for a fight, stabled?"

The centaur peered lazily over the rim of his tankard as he slugged his whiskey. "I'm looking for quiet and a place that doesn't stink like shit. Since you can't give me one of those, maybe you can give me the other?"

"You're a clever grunt, aren't you?" The savage growled and raised his blade. "So clever you gotta hit me when my back's turned." He smiled. "Or is that cowardice? I always get them two mixed up."

The clean centaur snorted, tossing aside his tankard and stepping up to the savage. "When I want to hit you, you turd with legs, I'll do it to your face. Assuming I don't get it mixed up with your ass."

"Clever it is, then," the savage replied, thumping his chest. "Show me you aren't a coward!"

Completely still, I watched.

I watched as heads turned toward the commotion. I watched as the nomads drew their blades and came sauntering up behind their posturing comrade. I watched as the armored centaurs from the city filed in to back up their own boisterous friend. I watched insults turn to threats, threats turn to weapons, weapons turn to fury.

I watched this all, completely silent.

Really, at this point, they seemed to have everything well in hand.

"You human-loving, perfumed bastards better think hard about what you're doing," the barbarian growled as he stalked closer. "You've been making us do the heavy lifting, waiting for us to die. But it made us strong while you got soft."

"Lifting is all your breed is good for," the city centaur spat back, hooves pawing at the earth as he scowled at his rival. "You might want to recant while you still have your teeth."

A hush fell over the crowd, each side of the crowd trembling with restrained anger as it sized up the other. The civil ones saw a force that outnumbered them. The savages saw a small army that was, pound for pound, tougher than they were. Any fight here would end with a lot of bloodshed, they both knew, no matter how badly they wanted it.

For a brief moment, it looked like cooler heads would prevail.

Of course, then someone went and shot that to hell.

"HIT HIM, YOU COWARD!"

Had just another moment passed, they might have realized that the voice that cried out was no centaur. Had just another moment passed, they might have both looked to me and wondered why I was grinning so damn wide.

Maybe I just happened to say the right thing at the right time.

Because someone went and took my advice.

The savage threw the first punch, his sword hand lashing out to bring the crosspiece against the armored centaur's jaw. The clean one staggered with the blow, letting out a bellow as he reared up and brought hooves crashing down upon the barbarian's skull.

The savage collapsed.

A roar erupted.

And then, as intended, everything went right to hell.

The armored ones assembled themselves into a tight knot as they charged. The nomads howled, bringing their spears down as they rushed to meet their foes.

Fists flew.

Steel flashed.

Blood spattered.

And within the span of six seconds, the idea of rampaging bird-bears was nothing more than a pleasant memory of calmer times.

I didn't bother with stillness as I began to wriggle out of my ropes; it seemed everyone had bigger concerns than me at the moment. Tight they might have been, but the knots were about as clever as you'd think a centaur could muster.

That is, not at all.

"What's going on?"

The female centaur that had tied me came galloping up, running past me and skidding to a halt at the edge of the brawl. She stared out over the roaring, squealing carnage with mouth agape, wide eyes fixed upon the savagery unfolding before her.

And *not* the girl sneaking up behind her.

"What the hell happened here?" she whispered.

Poor girl. I don't think she ever learned.

Not as I reached for Whisper hanging from her belt. Not as I tore him free from his sheath. Not as I plunged his blade into her kidneys.

Five quick stabs—in and out, like a rusty machine—and she collapsed to all four of her knees. She let out a wail of pain that went unheard among the sounds of the brawl. Not that it mattered much—it only lasted another moment before I jammed Whisper into her neck.

Warm red life burst out, spattered on my leathers. She cast a shocked look at me through a face fast going white, still not quite certain what was happening even as her life leaked out onto the dirt. I almost felt bad for her.

Until I remembered she wanted to pulverize me into fertilizer.

I stepped back, let her limp body crash to the ground. I didn't take a lot of pride in that. It had been a messy job. But a job done messy was still a job done.

And I still had more of it to do.

I resisted the urge to run for the camp's exit. I could see a few centaurs hanging back from the brawl, cheering on their comrades. All it would take was a few of them to notice me gone and pursue me. Out on the plains, I'd be run down for sure.

I had to find something to keep them busy.

I rushed to a nearby bonfire, grabbed a nearby piece of wood and thrust it in. It started burning immediately; I had only moments before it was engulfed completely. Fortunately, I didn't need much more than that.

I darted to the barrel of whiskey, kicked its spigot off. With a grunt, I turned it on its side, the liquid sloshing around inside it. Another kick sent it rolling toward the brawl, leaving a trail of thick, reeking liquor as it did. It got lost in the melee almost immediately, smashed to pieces beneath a centaur's hooves and spraying liquor that went unnoticed amid all the blood.

And I took a moment to savor that moment.

Because in another, things were about to ugly.

I tossed the torch onto the ground. The trail of whiskey caught in an instant, raced across the earth and into the brawl. It went up immediately, catching leather, cloth, liquor-coated skin, whatever it could.

In a chorus of screams, the battle turned into a panic as the savage and civil alike went mad with fear. A brawl that beautiful gave the fire a feast, and it leapt from combatant to combatant, sending the fighters screaming for help even as their friends tried to get away from them.

I wished I had time to watch.

But I was already running.

I had grabbed up the torch, and as I rushed through the nomads' camp, I set it to every tent I could find. The dried hides went up like tinder, and in a few seconds the camp was bright as daylight with burning pyres.

As whatever fighters could be spared tried vainly to put out the flames, I was already back on the other side of camp. I tossed the torch into the nearest cabin, hoping its old, rotted wood would catch quickly. Centaurs went screaming, unsure which flaming ruin to help first: their friends or their supplies.

I hoped they had fun with that.

As for me, this seemed distraction enough. I tucked Whisper into my belt and went bolting for the exit. If any centaur noticed me fleeing, they didn't bother chasing me as they rushed for whatever water they could find. I kept to the shadows, out of their paths as they went galloping around the camp.

The mouth of the valley loomed large before me. It would be just a few more minutes out of the forest, across the plain, to Harges's carriage, and then we could get the hell out of here.

Admittedly, I thought as I came sprinting out of the valley mouth, I hadn't thought things would go this smoothly. Norgorber usually didn't like me this much.

At least, not as much as he liked a mean joke.

That's why I should have seen it coming, in the instant I heard hoofbeats behind me: the punch line galloping up.

I ducked the axe just as its head came cleaving through the air where mine had just been. I threw myself to the ground as a great, four-legged shape came leaping over me, hooves narrowly missing me as I rolled to the side and back onto my feet. I held up Whisper, still fresh with centaur blood.

This, of course, failed to impress Kjoda.

"My beasts dead, my kin dead, my camp ablaze . . ." Kjoda's teeth were yellow and stark through the red war paint on his face. "All from one two-legged whelp and Halamox's impotence."

"Sounds like you two have a lot to talk about," I said. Not that this was a particularly wise thing *to* say, but it wasn't like this could get worse.

"*WARRIORS!*" he howled, rearing up on his hind legs. "To me! The stabled have failed us! It's time we showed the humans we are not to be trifled with!" He leveled his axe at me. "And we start by sending this one's head back to its masters!"

He swung. I darted, scrambling into the underbrush.

I could feel the earth shudder beneath me as I slipped into the forest. More were coming.

You might have expected me to start panicking. And, truth be told, that would probably have been a sensible reaction. But just because there were now a bunch of centaurs hunting for me in the forest didn't mean things had gotten worse.

It just meant things were about to get dirty.

8

Steel Whispers

Spread out! Search the underbrush! She can't have gotten far!"

S   I wouldn't blame you for worrying for me.

"All the stabled couldn't handle one human? Hah! We'll show them."

After all, six centaurs against one tiny Katapeshi girl? Not great odds to begin with. If you were a gambler, I'd not begrudge a tiny bet against me.

"First her, then Halamox. Bring me her head. Bring me her broken body. Bring me her blood."

But I'll let you in on a secret: gambling's a fool's game. What kind of buffoon would risk his meager fortunes on something as fair and reasonable as dumb luck?

"If I find her first, I'm going to paint myself with her blood!"

No, no. Amateurs gamble. Professionals?

We rig the game.

"Come out, human! Make this easy on yourself!"

I'm not quite sure what Kjoda was expecting me to do here. Give up, I suppose.

That wasn't an option, of course. Neither was slipping away and running. Eventually, they'd chase me out of the forest, back to Dalaris. And her crappy carriage couldn't outrun these beasts. I had to keep them here. I had to *finish* them here.

Fortunately, as I peered at him from the underbrush, I couldn't help but feel Kjoda was going to make that easier than I expected.

He stood at the center of a small clearing, directing his clan with bellowing commands and powerful sweeps of his axe. And his clan, in turn, went tromping through the forest, spearing at the underbrush and stomping on the ground.

Not to sound too generalizing, but there's a certain mindset you come to expect from people in less civilized lands. From the lowliest orc to the mightiest lord in the Lands of the Linnorm Kings, hard lands breed hard people used to hard ways.

People like Kjoda, they rule by strength. They howl and stomp their feet and, so long as they keep bringing in corpses, they continue to lead. And all their people, they follow that example, becoming as brash and noisy as their leader. I don't blame them. They do what they must to survive.

But noisy people are all alike: whether they bellow or roar or just talk too much, they tell you everything about themselves within minutes of meeting them. They tell you their fears, their problems, their insecurities . . .

Or, in this case, they just tell you where they are.

I heard the brush rustling behind me. I heard hooves stomping the earth. I glanced over my shoulder and saw the centaur approaching. A youth, it looked like: lean and hard-bodied, but not brimming with the scarred muscle of his kinsmen. He was tromping through the underbrush, sweeping his spear back and forth in an attempt to flush me out.

And he was nowhere near my actual location.

Did they assume I was some kind of pheasant? That I'd just out and run and let them chase me down?

Ah, well. His bad luck.

I maneuvered around him as he came tromping through. Over the noise he was making, he never even heard me sneaking up behind him. I flipped Whisper over in my hand, angled the blade downward, and waited.

The youth glanced around for a moment and scratched his head. I assumed he was just now beginning to wonder if his strategy was all that effective.

Too late.

I leapt out of the bush without a sound. I jammed my dagger into the flank of his horse body and, with a jerk, yanked downward. He cut open like old leather, something thick and viscous spilling out of the wound. His hooves lashed out, his spear swung around, but these were only the spasms of someone in agony.

His scream was long, loud, and full of terror.

I jerked my blade out, went darting back into the brush, and scrambled away.

Hoofbeats thundered across the forest as his comrades came to see what was the matter. The youth collapsed in a pool of his own blood, hooves flailing as his body tried to figure out why it was no longer working. The rest of him, however, knew well.

"Help me!" he shrieked. "Please! Help!"

I winced. His voice was shrill, squeaking. He screamed like he didn't know what was wrong with him, even as he went leaking out on the forest floor. He couldn't be more than a teenager, out to prove himself to his brothers and sisters.

Poor kid.

But the world's full of poor kids.

"Holy . . ." one of them whispered. "Look what she did to him."

"She couldn't," another grunted. "She was so small . . ."

"What happened over there?" Kjoda bellowed.

"She got Munda!" another one shouted back.

"Avenge him! Find her!"

With apprehensive looks, they returned to the hunt. I couldn't help but smile. They moved a little slower now, a little quieter, and even beneath their war paint, I could see the fear written on their faces. Hard lands breed hard people, but hard people break like anyone else.

You just have to hit them in the right spot.

I glanced down at Whisper, painted with blood. Thick-bladed, he was always good for sending a particular kind of message. And the one I wanted to send was ugly and scarlet.

I peered out from the underbrush again, chose my next mark. A tall, burly-looking female. She carried a thick bow in her hands, arrow nocked, searching for a target.

Funny thing about hard people: they're suspicious, but never about the right things. They don't trust civilization because they think it makes people soft. But they never realize that soft people just learn how to work to make things easier.

Case in point. I could tell by the tension of her legs that she was ready for me if I were to come up behind her and try to stab her. If I were a hard woman, like her, I might try to do that and take my chances.

But I'm a civilized girl.

And I like to do things cleanly.

I slipped through the brush, pausing whenever another one of them tromped by, resuming when they cleared me. Inch by inch, I made my way toward the woman as she poked through the underbrush. I waited for her to pause, her legs tense and muscles bunched, and then . . .

I don't know if you've ever been to a farm, but they tend to take good care of their horses there. With good reason: for all their burliness, horses are pretty fragile creatures, particularly around the legs. They do everything standing up, so a horse with a broken leg, sadly, doesn't do well . . .

And a horse with a dagger jammed in her thigh? Well, she doesn't do much better.

I slipped out, reached around and cut at the interior of her leg. I felt something big burst in my hand. Her leg snapped out in response and immediately went limp as the blood drained from her. She screamed, falling to the ground as I sprinted away and ducked back into the brush.

"She got me!" she screamed.

Her companions came galloping over. Fear colored their faces more plainly than their war paint. Their eyes were wide as they looked down at their companion. They saw exactly what I intended them to see: someone no longer capable of hunting, of running, of even standing up. She was going to bleed out slowly and they could do nothing but watch the color drain from her face.

She shrieked again, holding her hand out.

"She's like a ghost," one of them muttered. "Maybe Halamox was right."

"Halamox was *not* right." Kjoda came stalking up. "We prove it tonight." He looked down at the female, frowned. "Sister . . . we'll get you to the healer, once we're done. But we can't let the human escape."

Deep down, she might have known that. But that was deep down, buried beneath all the fear and screaming they tried to ignore as they turned away and resumed the hunt.

But they were leery now, holding their weapons close, looking at every shadow. Fear can be handy in a hunt, but panic isn't. Panic makes you jumpy, makes you inattentive, makes you miss things . . .

Such as the woman scaling a nearby tree and sliding into its branches.

I found the thickest one, crept out as far out as I dared. Below, I saw them shaking, nervous, wary. Remember what I said about hard people? These ones were ready to break.

I just had to make the next hit suitably dramatic.

And fortunately, opportunity came pacing underneath. A big one, brimming with muscle and a bright mane of red hair, held a massive blade as he came stalking beneath my perch. His face was thick and broad, unused to holding the kind of nervousness currently on it.

And certainly, it was unused to surprise.

So when I dropped down from the tree and landed on his back, he didn't quite know how to react. All he made was a confused grunt as I reached up and grabbed him by the hair. All he made was a growl as I jerked his head back.

And by the time he thought to scream, my blade was already in his neck.

I heard the others shout their surprise as they saw him, blood fanning out of his throat in a bright red gout. I heard the others tear off running in various directions as their friend went to the ground, twitching and bleeding out. I heard Kjoda roaring curses at them as I sprinted toward the forest's edge.

That would keep them busy for a little bit, I thought. Long enough to get back to Dalaris's carriage and get the hell out of here. By the time they caught up to us, we'd be too close to Yanmass for them to engage.

I burst from the forest's edge. My breath was heavy, my heart thundering in my ears.

I don't think I even heard the sound of Kjoda's charge until he got me.

Something struck me in the back, knocked me to the ground. I felt the breath explode out of my lungs, felt the ground rise up and hit me like a fist. My head spun as I staggered to my knees. My breath came in short, ragged gasps.

I felt a shadow fall across me, fell to the side just in time to avoid a pair of hooves that came crashing down. I only barely managed to roll away from the axe blade that followed. By the time I found my legs, they were shaking under me. And when I looked up, Kjoda's eyes were like fires in the night.

"Two-legged scum," he snarled. "The stabled are fools to try to work with your breed."

"Well, listen," I said, "I just killed, like, a whole mess of them back at your camp. I thought you'd be happy."

He roared, reared back.

I made a lunge at him with Whisper. He batted it aside easily with his axe and nearly took my head off with the next swing. I leapt backward, again and again as he plowed ahead, swinging wildly.

He overextended. I leapt. Whisper found the flesh of his flank, tore at him. But I was too close. I heard his fist crack against my nose before I felt it. I flew backward with the force of the blow, staggered. I looked up at him. The wound in his side wept, but he didn't even slow down. I hadn't so much as tickled him.

That might explain why he was chuckling as he advanced toward me.

I wiped the blood from my nose, felt more flowing. I glanced around. Nowhere to run that he couldn't run me down. Nowhere to hide that he couldn't find me. Nothing between him and me except a big-ass axe and a lot of room to swing it.

Remember when I said I wasn't good in a fight?

All the fear that I had been keeping down since I got here started to creep back in. The axe in his hand suddenly seemed huge and menacing. His hide looked so thick as to be armor. And his smile grew so broad and sharp it could be its own weapon as he advanced toward me, slowly, taking his sweet time.

Like he knew I couldn't do a damn thing to stop him.

My heart beat faster. My hand trembled around Whisper's hilt. I stumbled as I backed away a step. The little part in my skull that was screaming for me to calm down was drowned by the big part in my skull that was just plain screaming.

Damn it. Damn it, damn it, *damn it.*

Sem always told me it would end like this.

Stupid asshole.

Kjoda drew closer. I couldn't see anything else but that big, savage smile growing wider with every gods-damned step. Not his axe, not his war paint, not the bright white light that suddenly engulfed him.

Hell, I damn near missed it when he burst into flames.

It happened so fast I didn't notice until he was already screaming. White-hot fire seemed to spontaneously erupt from him, engulfing him in a bright, wailing inferno. It wasn't the ugly red flame eating the camp behind us. This fire seemed . . . cleaner: white, pure, and so gods-damned bright I had to shield my eyes.

I felt a hand grab my wrist. I whirled around, Whisper held up. It was only because I saw myself, reflected in the lenses of Dalaris's spectacles, that I stopped.

"It's okay," she said, surprisingly calm considering the centaur burning to death behind us. "Breathe deep. Stay quiet."

She said something else. Something in a language I couldn't understand. It wasn't until I looked down and saw my fingers disappearing that I realized she was casting a spell.

Invisibility.

I didn't know she could do that.

I glanced over my shoulder as Kjoda fell to the ground in a smoldering heap.

I didn't know she could *that,* either.

And here I thought I'd be the only one with news. Turned out, I was going to have a lot to ask her as she wove another invisibility spell around herself, took me by the hand, and led me at a run away from the forest.

9

Drinking Solution

No lie, I once saw a dwarf down six healing potions at once.

It was a few days after I had left Katapesh, in the tavern of some border village. I was lifting a few coins to pay a caravan master to take me to Osirion when the doors burst open. Your typical motley assortment of adventurers came charging in: elegant elf, wizened wizard, obligatory halfling, that sort of thing. And on their shoulders was this dwarf, so covered in wounds I thought they'd painted him red as a joke.

They were coming back from a Forbidden Crypt of Evil Bad Crap or something like that, torn up and looking for a cleric. This village was too small for that sort of thing, so they shelled out money for everyone to give them every potion they had. Then they pried the dwarf's lips open, jammed a funnel in his mouth and crammed every last drop into his gob.

I *thought* I remembered him surviving, but I couldn't be sure. The party's thief started talking to me and we had drinks and then I had to leg it out of there before he realized I had swiped his purse.

Point being: people in this line of work have always had a fondness for healing potions.

Personally, I thought they tasted like licking the underside of a boot. When it came to restoratives, my tastes had always ranged toward the traditional.

"So, what'll it be?" I asked as I emerged from the kitchen, holding up a hefty bottle in either hand. "Are you more a wine girl or a whiskey girl?"

From her place on the sofa, Dalaris looked up at me. She looked as though she had aged six years in as many minutes, judging from the weariness on her face. Yet even that weariness wasn't enough to block out her incredulous offense.

"You just discovered a noble was in a plot to kill my husband," she said. "You were captured by centaurs and nearly killed by them. You have revealed a plot that goes deeper than anything I ever suspected, and all you can think about is *drinks*?"

"Well," I replied, "given all that's happened, I think I deserve one. Forgive me for thinking you might like to join me."

Dalaris sighed, shook her head. "Fine. Wine. Whatever."

"Sure thing. One glass of . . ." I raised the wine bottle, squinted at the label, and gasped. "*Rahadoumi Red?*"

Without a second thought, I tossed the bottle over my shoulder. It shattered against the wall and dribbled down the paneling. Dalaris's face turned the same shade of red.

"What was *that* for?" she demanded.

"It was from Rahadoum. I did you a favor."

"That bottle was vintage."

"A vintage bottle for *Rahadoum*," I repeated. "Drinking is a religious experience, woman. Never trust a godless man to know what good wine tastes like."

She muttered some further complaints—mostly about the mess I had left behind—but I ignored them. It's not like I could have made the place look much shabbier.

Sidara Manor was, as far as Yanmass's homes went, criminally modest. That is, it was merely as big as two houses, instead of the usual four or six. It had a well-stocked pantry if a rather shamefully skimpy wine cellar a few bedrooms, some lovely artistic décor and a living room that was merely spacious instead of cavernous. A staircase at the end of the living room rose to the second level, where bedchambers with simple quilts and shabby pillows lay.

It was nice. Almost cozy, compared to the echoing chambers of Herevard's manor. But it was all a little diminished by the layer of dust everywhere.

House Sidara's declining fortunes were no more evident than in the wear of Dalaris's living room. The portraits of ancestors were dusty and hung crooked on the wall. The rug was threadbare in places and torn in others. The brass sculptures were tarnished with age. All of this surrounded an aged, scuffed table flanked by a pair of sofas, Dalaris occupying one. As soon I sat down in the other, a fine cloud of dust rose up.

"Been a while since you had guests?" I asked, coughing.

"Been a while since I could afford servants," she replied, waving away the dust as it wafted over the table toward her. "Harges stays on mostly out of loyalty."

"He liked your mother, eh?"

"Sort of. He likes his horses more, and we can still find room in the budget to feed and stable them." She coughed. "He was a bit cross at how hard he had to run them to get back here, by the way."

"I'm sorry," I replied. "Next time I have to escape a pack of bloodthirsty centaurs, I'll try to do it in a manner that allows for more leisure."

Dalaris frowned at that. "So it's true, then. A noble is arming the centaurs."

"That's what the note said."

"And you're sure it's from a noble?"

"Darling, I think I know a rich man's penmanship when I see it."

"How do you know it's a man? It could be a woman! It could be a frame job or a—"

"A what?"

"A frame job," she said, making a vague gesture. "You know, where you frame someone?"

"Oh. You mean a left-handed backpat."

"A *what*?"

"Look, why are you trying to explain this away?" I wrenched the cork out of the remaining bottle. "You're the one that suspected a foul hand."

"I suspected a . . . a plot." Dalaris rubbed at her temples. "An assassination contract, an opportunistic merchant, a . . . a . . . *something*." She shook her head. "But now you're telling me it's a noble. And you suspect it was Gerowan's brother?"

"What's so hard to believe about that?" I tilted the bottle back, all but kissed it. The whiskey kicked like a mule and tasted like one, to boot. Pretty great stuff, all told. "Stuff like that happens all the time."

"I know, it's just . . ." She shook her head again. "I knew Alarin before I knew Gerowan. He was always so bright and exuberant, where Gerowan was shy and bookish. I ate dinner with him, went hunting with him, talked literature with him. He smiled at me. He held my hand and laughed and told me I had better give him some nephews and nieces he could spoil." She shivered, clawed unconsciously at her hand, trying to scrape away some filth that wasn't there. "Could he really lie to me? Right to my face like that?"

"If he was any good at it, he could."

She winced at my words. I sighed.

"Look, it makes sense, doesn't it? Alarin was shipping weapons to the centaurs. Gerowan caught wise. Alarin decided he had to kill him to cover his tracks."

"But why would he give weapons to the centaurs in the first place?"

"Quick coin, maybe. Halamox's money is good as anyone's."

"But . . . but . . ."

Dalaris's lips fumbled, searching for a refutation, struggling to find those perfect words that would prove it couldn't be what I said it was. But when she opened her mouth, all that came out was a soft, choked whimper.

She leaned back in the sofa, hugged herself. The facade of a noble seemed to melt off her with each heavy breath until all that remained was a girl. A scared little girl who wanted the world to just stop for a few moments and let her catch her breath.

I felt something cold in my chest, a pain I felt whenever I saw this.

Do this job long enough, there's stuff you get used to. Knives in the back, dead bodies in alleys, money slick with blood; see enough of it, it stops meaning so much.

But gods help me, I never did get used to the sight of that little girl.

She's in all of us, you know. Someone small, timid and trembling. We build up around her with our walls and our weapons and our scars and our proud talk until we can't see her anymore. But when we realize how big the world is and how very alone we are in it, all of that goes away. Walls come down, weapons rust, scars fade, proud talk falters.

And all that's left is that little girl.

Like the one that looked at me in the mirror the day I left Katapesh.

Like the one sitting on the sofa across from me.

"You feel betrayed," I said.

"I feel dirty," she replied. "I feel like . . . like I've just been sitting in filth and never noticed. Like someone was feeding me lies and I was all too happy to eat them." She looked up at me from behind those big spectacles of hers. "Do . . . do you know what that feels like?"

I looked down at the bottle, swirled it in my hand.

"Yeah," I said.

"How did—"

"Fortunately," I interrupted, "there's a very special magical spell that makes it all go away."

"What's that?"

I leaned over the table, offered her the bottle. She looked at me first like I was rude to do it, then at the bottle like it would be rude not to. She reached out, snatched it timidly, then looked at me.

"Didn't you bring glasses?"

"The magic doesn't work that way."

She eyed me suspiciously for a moment before looking back at the bottle. Then, like she was slaying a gods-damned dragon, she tossed it back and downed three big gulps with the kind of bravado that people who've never drank anything stiffer than lemon juice do.

Bless her heart, I thought, she is going to vomit *so* much.

She pulled the bottle free with a hacking cough. Tears fell down her cheeks. She shook her head, wiped her mouth with her sleeve.

"*No*," she all but roared. "No, I can't just *accept* it."

"Accept what?" I asked, taking back the bottle.

"Even if you're right, we can't just confront Alarin. We need proof. Hard evidence. Something that will link him to the centaurs and to Gerowan's murder." She drew in a long breath, face scrunching up. "And we'll find it in his manor."

I nodded. "Makes sense to me. Anyone with money keeps records of where it all goes, even if they keep it out of sight." I took another slug of the whiskey. "Tell me where his manor is, I'll break in and—"

"No." She turned a glare on me. "Absolutely not."

"Pardon?"

I couldn't quite tell if she was serious or if the whiskey had just hit her harder than I thought, but the look she gave me as she leaned over the table suggested she was either going to hit me or kiss me.

Or maybe both.

Still, I hoped she'd ask first.

"I sent you into danger once already," she said. "And you nearly died because of it."

I blinked. "Well, yeah. That's what you're paying me to do."

"I'm paying you to solve a murder, not get killed."

"It's sweet of you to care, but really, I do this sort of thing a lot. It's no big worry."

"I can't do that." She leaned back. "I can't be that calm about death, about people getting hurt. I'm surrounded by people who would eagerly kill a man if it meant a few more coins. I . . . I can't *be* like them."

"I should hope not, because this attitude certainly isn't helping." I cast a smirk over the bottle. "Besides, if I get in trouble, surely you can just speak a spell or whatever you did back at the camp."

"Don't joke about that."

"I'm not, honestly. In fact, I've been wondering how you did it." I took a sip and set the bottle down. "Did you have a scroll or a rod or some magical piece of crap?"

"No!" She sounded almost offended, looked almost embarrassed. "If you must know . . ." She glanced around the living room as though she expected someone else to be there. "That was me."

"You? *Your* magic?"

"You sound surprised."

"I am. If you can do magic, seems like all this sneaking around is infinitely more complicated than just showing up, shooting a fireball out of your ass, and calling it a day."

"That's not how it works! And even if it did, I don't know how to do that. I only know . . . certain spells."

"Certain spells that took care of Kjoda just fine."

"That was less a spell and more a . . . a talent. A trick Heaven gave me, my grandmother said." She glanced at her fingertips. Faint pinpricks of light hummed in response. "I've never fully understood it, myself. I never had to learn it. I've always been able to just . . . do it." She wiggled her fingers and the light disappeared. "The spells I learned are illusions, mostly. Spells that redirect divinations, alter images or turn me invisible."

"Like what you did at the camp." I hummed. "Spells to hide." I leaned back, draped my arms across the back of the sofa. "So, what are you hiding, darling?"

I knew the look she gave me: that quivering, lower-lip-biting, afraid-to-talk-but-more-afraid-to-keep-it-in look that everyone with a very big secret they've held for a very long time has. And I didn't have to wait long before she showed me.

She reached up, gingerly removed the spectacles from her closed eyes. And when she opened them again, it all made sense.

Why she wore those spectacles all the time. Why it felt so strange when she looked at me. Why she was sitting here, giving exactly half a damn more about my life than anyone else in the room did.

"Wow."

Gold. Polished, bright as the sun, pools of gold stared at me. And yet, gold seemed such a filthy thing—something people killed for and bled for. The color in Dalaris's eyes was something that burned altogether too brightly for feelings like that. The color in Dalaris's eyes was something warm that I wanted to wrap myself up in and fall asleep forever.

Either that or the whiskey kicked harder than I thought.

"We're not sure when it happened," Dalaris said softly, looking away. "My mother says somewhere around the time Yanmass was first established. But we know it was on my mother's side. We think a grandmother, at least four generations ago. One night, she was walking by a river, when . . ."

Dalaris collapsed with a sigh, held her arms out wide. I could tell by the wild flail of her arms that the whiskey was starting to hit her like the rear end of an ogre.

"The sky just opened up. A great white light lit up the night and down came a winged man. He introduced himself, told her she was beautiful, that he was fascinated with her, and . . ."

I leaned forward. "And what?"

Dalaris looked back flatly. "And Grandmother was apparently so taken with him that she hiked her skirts up then and there and it happened in the mud of the riverbank."

"Oh." I blinked. "I guess that would . . ." I looked down, coughed, absently ran my finger around the rim of the whiskey bottle. "It's just, tales like that usually have a little more romance and a little less . . ."

"Well, family legend was unclear. We weren't entirely certain that she wasn't batty until her daughter came about. Born like me." She gestured to her eyes. "But even more glorious. Hair like spun gold, skin like silver. She was beautiful. Then we went back to normal children until I came along."

"Impressive." I folded my arms, glanced her over. "So what's the technical term for you, anyway? Heaven-touched? Angelblood? Wingspawn?"

"The technical term for me is Lady Dalaris Sidara," she replied, annoyed. "When my powers manifested, I sought training for illusion spells specifically so I could avoid discussions like this." She reached out and seized the bottle. "People took advantage of my ancestor when her . . . heritage was made manifest. They thought she was easily manipulated."

I probably would have, too. People of especially strong moral fiber are easy to persuade, specifically because they believe they can't be persuaded. And I've never heard of a story that began with angelic copulation and didn't end with strong moral fiber.

And if the decaying fortunes of the Sidara household were any indication, everyone else had heard the same story, too.

"What about you, then?" Dalaris took a slug of whiskey, made an exaggerated gasp of satisfaction. "Surely your history is at least as interesting."

"What makes you think that?" I watched her set down the bottle with more than a little concern; both for the slur creeping into her voice and the diminishing liquor.

"Oh, come on," Dalaris insisted. "A beautiful lady thief? Far away in a distant land? There's got to be an interesting story there."

I stared at her thoughtfully for a moment. "There is."

"And?"

"And if you're drunk enough to call me beautiful, you're far too drunk to appreciate it." I slowly slid the bottle away from her, casting a wink. "Not that it goes unappreciated, mind you."

"I am *not* drunk." She leapt to her feet, swayed unsteadily for a moment. And then a moment longer. "Not *that* drunk, anyway. Madame." She folded her arms, attempted to look as intimidating as a drunk girl can. "I believe you *owe* me."

"Oh?" I grinned. "You're in complete control of your faculties, then?"

"I am!"

"Meaning you meant every word you said?"

"I did!"

"Fine." I stood up slowly, placed my hands on my hips, and looked her over. "Then kiss me."

The slack-jawed, unblinking look on Dalaris's face would have fit her better had I slapped her with a dead chicken.

"W-what?" she asked.

"If you really think I'm beautiful," I said, "then give me a kiss and prove it."

"It . . . it was aesthetic appreciation!" Color rose to her cheeks so quickly I thought she might explode into flames. "I merely . . . *appreciate* your looks." She held up her hands, flailing them wildly. "Among other things! It's not mere looks!"

"Then this should be easy."

I pressed my foot against the side of the table, slid it out from between us, and stepped forward, so close I could smell the liquor on her breath. She squirmed beneath my grin like a . . . a . . . a thing that squirms. I didn't know. I had had a few, myself.

"Well?" I asked. "Unless . . . you didn't mean what you said?"

"Of course I did," she replied hastily. "I'm a Sidara. We are bound to our word."

I held my hands out wide. "At your leisure, my lady."

Her arms stiffened at her sides. Her hands clenched into fists. She looked me dead in the eye, those golden irises gleaming a moment before they closed. Her lips trembled, then puckered, her entire face quivering as she leaned toward me.

For a moment, it looked like she was actually going to do it.

Or vomit.

Really, I wasn't sure which one it wound up being. She released a breath she had been holding in one gasp. Her eyes snapped wide open and she immediately pulled back.

"I . . . ah . . . that is . . ." She turned away, hurriedly heading for the staircase that led upstairs. "It'd be improper!" she cried out. "We have duties to attend to! Please, Shy, take your rest. I will figure out a way for us to infiltrate Alarin's manor! Leave it to me!"

"As you say, my lady."

I couldn't see my grin right then, but I imagined it was particularly insufferable.

"And . . ." Dalaris hesitated at the top of the stairs and looked over her shoulder. "I appreciate all that you've done for me, Shy."

With that, she scurried down the hall. I heard a door slam as she disappeared into her room, with her doubtless comfy bed and doubtless comfy quilts.

At that thought, all the aches my body had been delaying suddenly came rushing back to me. The idea of a bed—not specifically hers—suddenly sounded incredibly tempting.

I took a step forward, swayed, then collapsed back.

Then again, sofas were also tempting. Particularly when they came with bottles of whiskey nearby.

I plucked up my sleeping companion for the night, took another swig from its glass lips, and chuckled at the memory of Dalaris's bright red face.

Not that I felt particularly good about teasing her like that, mind you. If anything, I should have been the one offended. After all, her desire to kiss me was much less powerful than my desire to not discuss my past.

Of course, I knew she'd get embarrassed and run. She was unused to affections of my particular persuasion. She was a timid girl. A charming girl.

A good girl.

No need to go reminding her what a mistake she'd made by consorting with filth like me.

10

Silk-Collar Jobs

S ee, what you fail to appreciate is the simplicity of it all."

At my words, Dalaris looked away from the cabin window and turned her attentions toward me as I sat on the carriage's seat.

"It's common, I'll give you that," I said, holding my hands up. "But it's common for a reason. It's *effective*." I pantomimed with my hands. "I creep across a lawn at night, open a window, go creeping around while everyone's asleep." I slammed my fist into my open palm. "And anyone who *isn't* asleep, I *put* to sleep. It'd take no more than an hour, tops, and I'd have all the evidence we need."

She nodded along to all of this as I folded my arms and smiled at her.

"You want my opinion," I said, "it's the best possible plan."

The noblewoman assumed a thoughtful look, pursing her lips as she stared at the space above my head, as if weighing my argument.

"And if you want *my* opinion," she said, "you don't like *my* plan because it requires you to wear a dress."

At that, my smile didn't so much leave my face as run screaming and hurl itself off while on fire. What lingered behind was a frown I could feel like a scar. And I was quick to turn it down on the garb that covered me.

It didn't fit right—made for someone much bustier and with bigger hips than a skinny Katapeshi girl. It had way too many skirts—and they all stuck out in ugly frills around my legs. Its gloves were too small, its shoes were too high in the heel, its laces were cinched up so tight that I could feel my ribs crush.

And it was mauve. The color of evil.

Frankly, wearing this, I didn't see how I would be able to stab a man to death at *all.*

"I don't like your plan because it's a complicated, stupid mess," I growled. "I *like* dresses."

"Please," Dalaris scoffed. "During our brief and eventful time together, I've seen you wear nothing but leathers. I've had to squint to avoid mistaking you for someone with a beard."

I snapped open a feathery hand fan—the only thing that came with this dress that I kind of liked—and tilted my nose up.

"If you're trying to imply my slim physique makes me look mannish, I will remind you that my body is not yours to cast judgment on." I batted my eyelashes over the top of the fan at her. "Also, you've seen me naked. Pervert."

In truth, I didn't mind her comment too much—I've been called worse by better. But I found it hard not to savor moments, such as these, where she turned beet red and desperately sought to look anywhere but at my face.

I thought I might be developing a fetish.

"Well," she said, huffily, "I'm the one paying, so I say how this is done. And unless you can think of a better plan—"

"I just *said*—"

"*A better plan that does not involve you killing people,*" she finished, glaring at me, "then we go with this one." She flipped open her own fan, waved it like she could fan away her embarrassment. "You're the one that said you were a good liar. Consider this an opportunity to prove your superiority."

Outside, Harges called his horses to a halt. The carriage slowed to a stop a moment later, leaving me a moment to stew in my resentment.

In truth, she was right. I *was* a good liar, and her plan *wasn't* the worst in the world. Hell, it might even have been better than mine. It was easier to collect information when no one suspected you of actually trying to do that, after all.

But if it was a choice between painting a rich man's ass with honeyed words or clubbing him over the head and taking his stuff?

Well, call me a woman of simple pleasures.

The door creaked open. Harges stood dutifully to the side, looking positively miserable in the powdered wig and livery he had been dressed up in. I cringed in sympathy as I stepped out and onto the cobblestones.

"Announcing the arrival of Lady Sidara of House Sidara and guest," a nearby man, wearing *his* fancy outfit much more comfortably, called out.

Across a vast lawn, various servants and a few nobles looked up and spared half a moment to sneer in disgust before concealing their contempt behind a round of light applause.

I glanced behind me and saw the reason for their contempt. The circular driveway was host to a variety of fine horses of black and white, all of them pulling a variety of fine carriages of gold trim and pleasant wheels. Compared to them, Dalaris's worn carriage and powerful-looking draft horses looked as out of place as oak trees in a garden.

Not that the horses seemed to mind, if the way one of them raised her tail and dropped a load of dung on the pavement was any indication.

"Lord Amalien is expecting you, my lady," the well-dressed man said, approaching Dalaris as she stepped out of the carriage. He bowed low, gesturing across the lawn to the vast manor looming like a particularly foppish behemoth against the night sky.

House Amalien was remarkable in Yanmass if only because it seemed more a home and less a fortress. Its high, peaked roof was bereft of the hidden ballistae and watchtowers that other manors had. Its walls sprawled out to either side, baring windows without bars and doors without gates. The shrubberies in its lawn were shaped like animals. The servants were dressed like servants, not guards. The main doors were the size of a castle's and cast wide open, light and music and laughter spilling out from inside.

At a glance, it appeared Lord Alarin Amalien had absolutely zero cares for anyone who might enter his home.

Which made it seem like we really wasted an opportunity by choosing this plan, but whatever.

"Shall we, dear?"

I almost didn't recognize her voice by the prim way she offered it, but once I turned, I saw Dalaris standing beside me. The coquettish smile across her face all but transformed her from the nervous girl I had known before to a proper noblewoman. She stood taller, more confident, head held high and looking ever-so-slightly down on me. She extended her arm to me in a fashionable manner.

And I took it, as a proper lady should.

"By all means, darling," I said, forcing my voice a little higher.

Chin high, back straight, eyes forward, left arm upon hers, right cocked at just *such* an angle, and smile, Shy, always smile!

I had to remind myself once or twice as Dalaris escorted me across the lawn, but it came easily enough. This wasn't the first time I had posed as someone rich, brainless, or both, and since I was who I was, I was sure it wouldn't be the last. But nonetheless, as we passed the various painted, powdered, pampered nobles, I was reminded keenly why I had hated this plan so.

"Look at that, is that a Qadiran with her?"

"Maybe an Osirian. Or a Katapeshi? How exotic!"

"Indeed, exotic! Sidara's attracting a rather unusual fare."

"—such dark skin, how does she—"

"—hear they sell their own mothers for a—"

"—curious, maybe quaint, certainly exotic—"

One by one, the whispers of a few ignorant dopes might not be worth much. There are, after all, millions of stupid pieces of shit in the world. But that's precisely how stupidity flourishes; in bunches, in fast-growing weeds that choke delicately nurtured knowledge.

Thus, while I had certainly been called everything a gawping Taldan might call a Qadiran or a Katapeshi they *thought* was Qadiran—"thief," "barbarian," "warmonger"—it was only the words of the wealthy that ever irritated me.

After all, if I was a thief, I was still a person.

If I was merely "exotic," I might as well be a pet.

I was just about to stop and force Dalaris to reconsider my plan to stab everyone when I caught another, subtler set of whispers beneath the ones about my heritage.

"Look at her, why was she even invited?"

I glanced out the corner of my eye and saw them. A thin, bony woman wearing a tight-laced white dress and a hat with a stuffed pheasant adorning a positively epic poof of hair whispered to a portly man dressed in a tight suit whose moustache looked like a war crime.

"Pity, I suspect," another replied. "The late Amalien was her betrothed."

"Gods know what he saw in her. Did you see the carriage she showed up in? Ghastly."

"Have patience, Clarice. You know the poor thing's down on her luck."

"There's down on one's luck and then there's a curse from Heaven."

"I suspect when you're a Sidara, they're more or less the same thing."

They chuckled so softly I was certain only I could hear them. But when I glanced to Dalaris, I could see that I was mistaken.

The mask of nobility she wore was just that—a mask, and a fragile one. Her lips trembled and her jaw clenched, fighting to keep its smile up. And she tilted her head a little lower, that it might be harder to see the tears forming at the corners of her eyes.

How many of these parties had she been to, I wondered. How many times had she heard these whispers? How many times had she lain awake at night, wondering what they were saying about her?

I didn't know.

I only knew what to do.

I clutched her arm a little tighter. I reached out with my free hand and squeezed hers.

"Chin up," I whispered. "Courage. We have a job to do."

She nodded at me, forced her chin up. Her smile still trembled, though.

"Besides," I added quickly, "who are they to talk? That woman's wearing a dead bird on her head and likely paid out the ass for the privilege."

She laughed. Slightly louder than was ladylike.

And I smiled.

And walked with her, arm in arm, past the massive double doors opened wide, into the house of her husband's murderer.

11

A Rogue's Diplomacy

The exterior of House Amalien was magnificent. *Merely* magnificent. The interior was wealthy enough to tighten the trousers of every thief within sixty leagues.

Brilliant crimson carpet with gold trim layered over white tile so polished I could see up my own skirt. Marching pillars carved to resemble powerful, half-clad men held up the peaked ceiling. A vast, coiling staircase rose to galleries overhead, each one guarded by a marble-and-silver railing and housing countless portraits of countless ancestors. A small contingent of servants rushed about with a grace and discipline that would shame most armies.

And upon every tapestry, on the frame of every portrait, on the banister of every staircase and the breast of every servant's livery, the sigil of two crossed swords.

House Amalien's sigil.

Just like I had seen back in First Solace.

A peal of decidedly undignified laughter caught my ear. The party appeared to be in full swing, if the number of empty wine goblets in the hands of the seventy or so well-dressed nobles in attendance was any indication. And judging by the swiftness with which the servants rushed to refill them, things had doubtless been going swimmingly for a while. The fine fruits and cheeses went unappreciated, the dulcet tunes of the violin quartet in the corner unacknowledged. Tonight, the only culture heeded was the kind that came out of a bottle.

"I thought you said this was a wake," I muttered to Dalaris.

"We do things differently in Yanmass," she replied. "The nobles don't like to be reminded of their mortality. There will be a more somber funeral later, but for now . . ."

"Right," I grunted behind my fan.

I surveyed the crowd. Painted faces, men and women, conversing brightly behind fans, under hats and powdered wigs. Swigging wine, gorging on food, laughing and laughing like this was the best damn joke they'd heard in a while.

"So what's the plan?"

"There must be something here," Dalaris muttered in reply. "Someone with a loose tongue or a servant who knows too much."

I glanced around, immediately searching for the noble who wore a resentful scowl or the servant who looked a little too harried—someone who might talk.

My gaze settled upon a pair of them. A man and a woman with dark hair, currently waiting with silver platters full of wineglasses on a small circle of nobles. They looked like any other servants, clad in the colors and sigil of House Amalien, yet there was something a little too sharp about them, a little too hungry.

The male servant glanced my way and I tensed, only long enough to realize he was turning away so he wouldn't be seen yawning. He whispered something to the woman and she nodded, scurrying off to what I assumed was the kitchen.

"So you want to go searching for someone who'll talk?" I asked.

"We'll both keep an eye out," she said. "It shouldn't be too hard so long as we can avoid—"

"Dalaris! Darling!"

"—notice."

As the servants formed an army and the nobles the scavengers that follow in their wake, the man that came striding toward us was doubtless the general. Tall, well built, dressed in vest, breeches, and coat that fit his muscular frame perfectly, without a wig on his head or paint on his face, he came striding up. He wore no jewelry but for a ring around his finger, and no adornment but a glass in his hand.

Really, he didn't need any.

Alarin Amalien was the sort of man whose looks would only be tarnished by trinkets.

His green eyes glittered in the light of the candelabras. His sharp features were unmarred by the softness that other nobles wore comfortably. And beneath a perfectly trimmed beard, he flashed a broad, bright smile.

An honest smile.

Made me wonder how long he had to train to fake it.

"Alarin." Dalaris's smile turned genuinely warm as she extended a hand. "It's good to see you."

"And you as well." He took her hand in his, offered it a gentle kiss. "The rest of these copper-tongued flatterers, less so."

"You are generous to invite them."

"Gerowan would have wanted us to maintain cordiality to our guests." Alarin sighed, his smile turning weary. "And cordiality we shall maintain, regardless of who . . ."

His voice drifted off, along with his eyes, as his gaze slithered toward me. And in his eyes, I caught a glimpse of something I had seen many times before.

Not to sound *too* licentious, but this was hardly the first time a man had made that kind of eyes at me. Soldiers, senators, savages and scholars alike; all sorts of men had given me that look. At that moment, they didn't care about my name, my past, my motive. Their eyes were full of wonder and their heads were concocting a story as to how mysterious I might be.

Tricking a man isn't much harder than telling him that he's right.

So when I offered my hand, I did so with a soft smile and softer words in a thick Katapeshi accent.

"Lord Amalien," I said. "It is my inestimable pleasure to be among those honored by you."

His mouth fell open just a bit, hung there for half a moment, before he fumbled over his next words.

"Al. Alarin," he blurted out. "Please, call me Alarin."

Got him.

I contained my smile, even as he forced refined composure back onto his face. This sort of thing doesn't always work—and when it doesn't, it ends badly—but occasionally you meet a man like Alarin Amalien. A man who's seen more gold than grass and finds a shrubbery more interesting, a man whose attention is short and imagination is dim. Show a man like that something he's never seen before, and even a skinny Katapeshi girl in an ugly dress seems amazing to him.

"Alarin," Dalaris said, gesturing to me, "may I introduce Madame . . ."

She paused.

For a moment, I swore she was going to mess this up by giving him my real name.

"Shadeaux," she said. "Madame Shadeaux."

Then again, maybe it would have been better if she had.

"Madame Shadeaux," Alarin said, overemphasizing it with a terribly honest enthusiasm. He took my hand and gave it an equally excited kiss. "That's foreign, yes? Osirian?"

Well, at least he didn't say Qadiran.

"Katapeshi, my lord," I replied. "But you have a good ear. I take it you are well traveled?"

"Gods, but I wish." He made a long roll of his eyes. "I had aspirations to before father died. And before the unfortunate business with Gerowan, I was intending to leave much of this in his hands, leaving me free to see the wonders of the Inner Sea."

I nodded politely, taking note of how he referred to the murder of his brother as merely "unfortunate."

"Alas," he said. "This will compel my presence in Yanmass and surroundings for the rest of my years, until my heir is of age."

"If you ever get one," Dalaris replied. "And a wife, before that."

Alarin glanced toward me. "I have time."

I giggled, as he would expect me to. I squeezed his hand, as he would expect me to. I resisted the urge to roll my eyes, as Dalaris would expect me to.

"Come, Madame Shadeaux." Alarin drew me closer. "You simply must accept me as your escort for this evening."

"Oh!" Dalaris piped up. "But she—"

"Lady Sidara overwhelms me with her concern," I interrupted, forcing an already forced accent a little thicker. I looked at her pointedly. "But I assume that a man as learned as Lord Amalien will be nothing but a gentleman."

"She's right to be concerned," Alarin muttered, glancing around. "The fops here have been jumping at the mere whisper of the word 'Qadiran' for a generation now. A woman of such . . ."

Don't say "exotic."

". . . beauty as yours," Alarin said, "would likely blow their tiny gilded minds. You must grant me the honor of being there to see it."

My eyebrows rose in genuine appreciation. So Alarin wasn't all bad.

Dalaris tensed for a moment before glancing at me. "If it is her wish . . ."

"Oh, but it is," I said. "If my gracious host desires to . . . how did you say? Make minds blown? I can hardly disoblige." I smiled, took Alarin's arm. "Shall we, dear?"

"Originally, our house was founded on a desire for knowledge."

Alarin had his good points.

"It was my great-grandfather that had a desire to be a cartographer. He once set out from home with the desire to chart the entire world, to learn the language of every human he could."

Handsome. Pleasant smile. Large hands, but he didn't grab or pull or squeeze.

"Of course, he had scarcely gone two days out before he stumbled upon the richest vein of iron this nation had ever seen. And when he could be wealthy in knowledge or just plain wealthy . . ."

Well read, well versed, and curious, which are traits you scarcely see these days.

"He sold much of his ore to the Eighth Army of Exploration, and the emperor was all too happy to pay for the privilege to use it."

He was rich, too, which isn't always important, but never hurts.

"Our family migrated to Yanmass just two generations ago."

All told, Alarin Amalien was the sort of man I thought I could like very pleasantly.

"And we've since risen to great effect."

That is, you know, if he could ever shut his gods-damned face for a bit.

Not that I'd tell him that. I smiled gently, nodding along, speaking only to add a suitably mysterious quip that he probably thought sounded Katapeshi. I needed to keep him talking.

Not that there was any danger of that stopping. I could have stabbed him six times in the neck and he *might* have stopped to staunch the blood before going on about his family history.

Hell, he might not have even noticed the blade. He certainly didn't notice my attention drifting.

"Wine, madame?"

Thank Norgorber *someone* did, though.

One of the servants, the dark-haired, hungry-looking man I had noticed before, came up to me with a tray brimming with goblets. I would have taken the whole damn thing, had it not been unladylike to do so. Instead, I settled myself with just one—the one that looked the fullest—and smiled my gratitude at him.

He merely stared at me for a moment before turning and departing.

Ordinarily, I'd call that rude.

But comparatively, he was downright polite.

I glanced around the hall, noting with displeasure the suspicious glares cast my way and the way painted lips mouthed the word "Qadiran." Though any contempt they had for the race they imagined me was overshadowed by the respect—or the scraping simpering that passed for respect—for Alarin.

"*Lord Amalien!*" they called out. "*Favor us with your company!*"

"*Lord Amalien! Have you given much thought to my proposal?*"

"*Lord Amalien! Raise a glass to your gracious host, you dogs!*"

Alarin offered them nods, smiles, the occasional wave if he was indeed feeling gracious, but continued escorting me across the floor of his ballroom. I cast a glance at him from behind my fan.

"My lord is quite in demand at his party," I observed. "Would it not be polite to stop and grace them with your presence?"

"As though these jackals would recognize 'grace' if they saw it." The veneer of noble politeness slid from his face, leaving a contemptuous frown behind. "I know what each of them wants and I know how each of them wants to take it."

"My lord?" I put the expected timidity into my voice.

"My brother isn't even in the ground yet and already these swine would fit their fat asses in the spot he left behind." His words boiled with such anger I half-expected him to spit on his own floor. "Each of them would seek to take his shares of the wealth and responsibility and call themselves generous for doing it."

I observed him silently, hiding my scrutiny demurely behind my fan.

Contempt roiled across his features. His jaw clenched, his eyes narrowed, his nostrils flared. Odd that a man who should call the death of his brother merely "unfortunate" should react with such distaste to *others* acting boorishly about it.

Then again, his ire with them seemed keenest when he mentioned them clamoring after Gerowan's shares of the family fortunes. There were few things greedy people resented more than other greedy people. It could easily be that he resented the very idea of sharing wealth that he had already killed for.

"But I forget myself." Congeniality returned to him with a weary smile. "I forget that you're not native to Yanmass, my dear. This must all appear frightfully barbaric to you, treating a funeral like a courtship."

"We are no strangers to coin in Katapesh, my lord," I said as he guided me past a few pillars, into the shadow beneath one of the overhanging galleries. "It is, after all, a nation of bazaars and caravans. Deals are made at any occasion: funerals, birthdays . . ."

"Weddings?"

He placed a hand gingerly upon my shoulder, eased me in front of him. I suddenly felt the cool of marble upon my back as I pressed up against a pillar.

Goodness, but he did move quick, didn't he?

His smile remained gentle and easy, but his eyes were fixed on mine with a hunger deeper than any guest had shown their wine. I turned a smile away—exactly as he would expect me to—and looked at him shyly out of the corners of my eyes.

I had him now.

"Weddings are a place for such proposals," I said, "though it might be considered quite . . . forward to do so."

"You'll forgive me for not knowing the custom." His voice was a raspy purr. "Even here in more civil countries, I'm considered a bit forward."

He raised his arm, leaned forward and pressed his hand on the pillar beside my head. He loomed over me, looking down upon me. I'd seen this before—powerful people like to show it by getting in your space, show you what big people they are and how small you are.

They rarely realize that the closer they get, the less time they have to react when you pull the knife, but I digress.

"You would fit right in in the desert." I ran through the routine in my head—smile small, eyes direct, look interested and pretend this isn't creepy. I reached out, wrapped a hand around his wrist as he leaned closer. "Brashness is valued in men . . . and women."

"I should very much like to see it one day . . ." I felt his breath on my face as he leaned closer, smelled the wine on his lips.

"The desert?" I asked, letting my smile grow a little wider. "Or the brashness?"

"Yes."

He leaned down toward my face. My fan was up—not too quickly, not too slowly.

"Pardon my tongue, my lord," I said, "but were you not lamenting a lack of proper accord at your brother's wake? I would hate to offend your custom."

I held my breath and waited. Waited for him to snarl and curse his brother's name, waited for him to chuckle and make a sly remark, waited for him to give me anything, any word, any gesture that would tell me he did it.

I waited a very long time.

And when he reacted, it wasn't what I was looking for.

All the bravado leaked from his face as wine from a cask full of holes. The hunger left his eyes. What remained was something shallow and empty.

"Yes, I . . ." He turned away from me. "I suppose you're right, madame. Forgive my impetuousness. Gerowan wouldn't . . ."

Had he not turned away, he would have seen the puzzlement on my face.

I've known my share of murderers—exposed them, confronted them, shared wine with them. And I've known just as many faces that they wear. They moan, they sob, they weep. Sometimes they explode, they snarl, they threaten. They show any emotion they can think of, anything that they think would prove their innocence.

You rarely see them look quite so . . . empty.

That look, that drained, vacant stare, I had seen before, mind you. But on widows watching their husbands of twenty years being put in the ground, on eldest children who had to become parents for their siblings after their own died. Such a look appeared strange on Alarin.

"Lord Amalien."

A voice, hard and sharp as a blade, cut through the air. Alarin instantly wiped the grief from his face and turned to the shadow that had suddenly appeared behind him.

She was a woman, though to look at her, she might as well have been a spear. Tall and thin, she was wrapped in a tightly laced black dress with red trim, covering every inch of skin but a face that was full of sharp angles. Her lips were pursed in a tight frown beneath a hawkish nose, an elegant bun of red hair streaked with gray crowning a pair of glowering blue eyes.

"Your absence is noted." She spoke in soft, harsh words.

"Lady Stelvan." Alarin regained his composure in the time it took him to force a smile back onto his face. "I had wondered when you might show up. Fashionably late?"

"I arrived precisely when I intended to. Any sooner would involve me in senseless small talk that I have neither time for nor interest in." Her eyes drifted past his shoulder and all but skewered me to the pillar with her glower. "You are entertaining, I see."

"Ah, of course." Alarin glanced over his shoulder, took my hand and gingerly led me to his side. "May I introduce you, Madame Shadeaux, to Lady Vishera Stelvan, matriarch of one of Yanmass's older families."

"Older?" I asked.

"Very old," the woman replied, acid dripping from her voice. "Old enough to recall the last war with Qadira with *immense* clarity."

"Ah," I replied. "Well, we are not without our issues with Qadira in Katapesh, either."

Her glare intensified, as though she didn't believe I wasn't Qadiran or didn't see enough of a distinction between a Qadiran and a Katapeshi. When she glanced away from me, I had to restrain my sigh of relief.

"Permit me to keep this mercifully short, Alarin," she said. "I am here for the sole purpose of discussing the contract we left in the lurch three weeks ago."

"Indeed." Alarin's sigh was deep. "I take it you've still got your heart set on inheriting his contracts."

"I think with my brain, not my heart, Lord Amalien," Vishera replied sharply. "I understand I am in the minority of Yanmass in doing so, but I did not acquire my status through acting on weak feelings. Your brother controlled considerable amounts of ore that I should like to see dedicated to noble purposes."

"Purposes such as your weapons manufacturing," Alarin said.

My eyebrow perked at that, though I was careful not to betray *too* much interest, lest Vishera speak less freely around me.

As it was, when she glared my way, I rolled my eyes and turned away, taking a heavy drink from my wine. Satisfied at this Katapeshi girl's lack of interest in anything business, she turned back to Alarin.

"I have a legion of smiths and engineers waiting," Vishera said. "They merely need the metal to begin their process. Thousands of lives in hundreds of townships could be saved with the weapons I can create."

"As it happens, Lady Stelvan," Alarin replied, "I concur with your noble end. Improving the lives of the good people of Taldor is an utmost priority for me."

Vishera nodded stiffly.

"Which is why I've arranged a trade with Andoran. Gerowan's ore will be traded for more than fifteen hundred bottles of their finest wine."

"*Wine?*" Vishera hissed, her face twisting in anger.

"Wine. Exactly the kind that Madame Shadeaux is drinking." Alarin turned a smile my way. "What do you think, madame? Will they fetch a fair price?"

"As fair as any lady of the court," I replied, raising my glass to him. "My lord has exquisite taste."

I didn't lie about that, at least. It was *damn* fine wine.

"You're a fool if you think wine is what you should be investing in, Alarin," Vishera growled. "When Taldor's government collapses and we're stuck between Qadira and Cheliax like a sow on a spit, drowning in rabble from Andoran and Galt, you'll wish you had spent more on weapons."

"Madame Stelvan, you know I never begrudge anyone speaking business at a party," Alarin replied. "But I feel I should point out that it's dreadfully crass to advertise your weapons trade so brazenly. Especially when we've not seen a Qadiran across the border in years."

"Present company excluded." The noblewoman aimed her words in my direction.

I smiled back. "I applaud my lady's caution," I said. "And gently chastise her attentiveness. I have pointed out that I'm from Katapesh."

Vishera sneered at that, as though the thought of a difference between the two nations was simply laughable. I didn't begrudge her that any more than I begrudged it to anyone else who thought all southerners looked alike.

By which I mean I made a mental note to spit in her wine when she wasn't looking.

"I was taking the long view," Stelvan said. "If you desire proof of the need of self-defense, look no further than our own borders. Or is the murder of your brother at the hands of centaur thugs simply beneath your notice, sir?"

I held my breath, watching Alarin intently. I waited for him to show me something—a tremor of rage across that pretty face, an errant flinch—anything that would betray the slightest hint of guilt.

That bastard might as well have been carved from porcelain for all his face changed. He didn't so much as stop smiling.

"Your condolences are appreciated, dear lady," he said. "But I insist that your relentless doomsaying is unfounded."

"But it's true!"

I glanced over, saw that our discussion had drawn the attention of a few other nobles. One of them—a skinny fellow in a coat too big and a wig too small—approached us.

"Taldor's emperors been impotent since my grandfather's time," he said. "When the time comes, the grand prince will not look out for us, but for himself. And where will we be if we can't defend ourselves?"

"Funny thing about weapons," I interjected, though the glares cast my way suggested that this was highly unwanted, "once you've got them in hand, you start looking for a reason to use them."

Alarin chuckled at that. The skinny noble cleared his throat and looked away. But my eyes were on the lady herself. She fixed me with a gaze that suggested, had she a weapon in hand at that moment, she would not have had to look very far at all for a reason to use it.

"At any rate," Alarin said, "there are other contracts we may free up, prices adjusted accordingly. We can discuss them over dinner in a week." He smiled at Vishera broadly. "My cousin will be there. Perhaps you might bring your son?"

If Alarin's face was made of porcelain, then Vishera's was made of flint: a cold, harsh stone that quickly sharpened itself into a point so fine I thought it might impale Alarin then and there. Her eyes narrowed to slits and she spoke her next words through clenched teeth.

"Visheron is indisposed."

"Week after next, then," Alarin offered.

"He remains indisposed for the foreseeable future."

"Still? How do you ever hope to get him married off, Vishera?"

"Perhaps my lady simply desires to enhance the mystery for any potential suitor?" I offered, smiling. "After all, what woman would not find herself enamored with a wealthy aristocrat who does not show his—"

Admittedly, I *had* intended to goad her just a little. Her crack about my heritage still rankled me.

However touchy I was about being confused with a Qadiran, though, it wasn't nearly as touchy as she was about her son.

Or so I assumed, anyway, when she swung her open palm around and delivered a hard slap across my face.

The crowd around us fell silent. So silent I could hear my wineglass as it spilled across my chest and shattered on the floor. So silent I could hear myself in my own thoughts.

Easy, Shy. Don't stab her. Madame Shadeaux would not stab her.

"Well," Alarin observed dryly, turning back to Stelvan. "I feel as though perhaps you should leave, Lady Stelvan."

The noblewoman's face trembled with barely contained ire as she swung her glower from me to him to the surrounding nobles, all staring with keen interest. She said nothing as she turned and stalked toward the double doors, the various nobles and servants sweeping out of her way as she did so.

"Forgive me, darling," Alarin said, turning to me and taking my hand. "I should have warned you that Lady Stelvan is rather sensitive with regard to three subjects: her son, Qadirans, and being spoken to."

"So noted," I muttered, wiping at the wine staining my dress. "I don't suppose she cares much about the fact that I'm *not* Qadiran?"

"Not likely," Alarin said. "Her father was a rather unfortunate casualty in Qadira's last incursion across Taldor's borders. She's never really seen the virtue in differentiating between people from the deserts."

He glanced up and waved down a servant, who rushed over swiftly.

"Would you kindly escort Madame Shadeaux upstairs?" he asked. "Take her to a washroom and assist her in cleaning up? And make a note to have a bottle of wine sent in apology to Lady Stelvan."

"*Apology?*" The incredulousness in the glare I cast him was not exactly conducive to the act of a simpering noblewoman, but damned if he didn't deserve it.

"Forgive me again, madame," Alarin offered sheepishly. "There are certain protocols one follows in Yanmass's upper circles, particularly when it comes to people who account for a quarter of my business."

I stared at him thoughtfully. I drank in that smile of his, those perfectly even teeth and that single dimple on his right cheek. I watched the sincerity and apology reflected in every tooth.

Slowly, I matched it. Slowly, I nodded.

"Of course, my lord."

I kept his smile in mind as the servant beckoned me to follow. I recalled every crease it left on his face as the servant led me to the staircase at the end of the great hall. I remembered every twitch, every crook, every angle to that perfect, porcelain smile of his.

So that I might imagine how satisfying it would be to knock it clean off his face.

12

Perfumed Shadows

"Katapesh, was it? Can't say I've ever been far from Yanmass, let alone outside of Taldor's borders." The servant, a tall gangly fellow just out of his teenage years by the look, led the way across the upper gallery, beneath the stares of the ancestral portraits.

"Of course, there hasn't been much call to. I had dreams of visiting other nations, of course. I got a cousin in Galt . . . or I *had* a cousin in Galt. Got his head cut off in one of their revolutions. Put an end to my desire to see the world."

Balancing a tray of wineglasses, most of them empty or half empty, he turned sharply down a corner and traipsed down a long, carpeted hallway flanked by ornately carved doors.

"But I suppose there's no need. Master Amalien treats me well, pays me well. I've got food, a nice place to stay, good friends. Pity about the other Master Amalien—his brother cared for him deeply—but we've still got one."

He stopped at one of the doors and set the tray of wineglasses down on a nearby table.

"I'll need to visit the kitchen with those," he muttered.

He fumbled with a key ring, choosing a large silver key and fiddling with the doorknob.

"This is the master's personal washroom. Feel free to use anything you need to make yourself presentable, madame." He pushed the door open and smiled. "Anything else I can do for you?"

I resisted the urge to ask him to turn around so I could smash the wine tray against the back of his head for suggesting I wasn't "presentable."

Instead, I simply smiled.

"You've been quite helpful," I said. "Would you mind terribly informing Lord Amalien that I'll be a while? I've simply," I paused to sound suitably breathless, "*never* seen such magnificent quarters."

He puffed up, as though this were all *his* wealth I was admiring. "Lord Amalien will be thrilled to hear it. He does appreciate people who appreciate his tastes."

"Indeed." I quirked a brow, stepped a little closer. I let a finger curl around the inside of his vest, drew it down toward his belt. "Lord Amalien should be commended on his eye."

I saw the emotions play out on his face in rapid succession: the wide eyes of realization, the pursed lips of lust, the jaw-clenching terror of realizing what could happen if Alarin heard of him flirting with the woman he had eyes on. He tore away from me— and lucky he did, as a few more moments and the poor boy might have exploded—muttered a hasty farewell, and took off.

Missing a set of keys.

Don't get me wrong, bashing him over the head with the tray and then locking him in the washroom while I worked crossed my mind. But this way, even if he noticed his missing keys, he'd never find the courage to come questioning me for them. I had no idea how he'd explain this to his superiors. I didn't envy him.

But then, I didn't think of him for another second, either.

I set off down the hall—swiftly, lest I get caught—and began to try the doors. One after the other: a bedroom here, a library there, another bedroom here, a wine room there, a room that I could only assume was designed specifically for housing statues of naked ladies there . . .

By the tenth room I tried, with the knowledge that there were Norgorber knows how many other halls in this house, the daunting nature of the task had begun to wear on me. And by the eleventh, I had begun to wonder if I wasn't perhaps completely mistaken in my assumptions that Alarin had killed Gerowan.

Actual interaction with the man had left me with next to no clue as to his guilt. The man had barely shown me so much as a single emotion through that perfect porcelain of his face, and what little he *had* shown me was contradictory.

On the one hand, he had expressed open contempt for the nobles who had come to feast on his brother's assets.

On the other hand, he had referred to it as little more than an unfortunate incident and hardly seemed in poor spirits that evening.

On the *other* other hand, I just couldn't get that empty expression he had let slip out of my head.

Had he done it, then? What motive could he have had?

Money? He had sold Gerowan's shares in the family ore business off for *wine*. And while it had been some damn fine wine, I doubted it made him more gold than selling the ore for weapons to Vishera Stelvan—she did, after all, look like a very wealthy woman.

Perhaps he had been driven by a baser desire, then? Perhaps he had wanted Dalaris for himself, unable to give her away to Gerowan. But that hardly seemed any more likely. He had said little more than a few sentences to her.

Besides, I thought with just a *touch* of smugness, he seemed to go for the dark and mysterious type.

So, he hadn't done it for gold or for sex—what other motives even *were* there?

Revenge? Maybe Gerowan had once told him his pantaloons made him look graciously endowed in the posterior? Some folk would kill for an ass like that man had.

I was one door away from giving up and going back down to admire it when I tried the last door on the right. I inserted the key, gave it a twist, and . . . nothing.

I tried another key. And another. And another, until I had gone through the entire ring and not found a single one that would work.

This was not a door meant for servants.

Which meant it was not a room meant to be seen by just anyone.

Which meant it was not a door I could afford *not* to break into.

I once knew a Katapeshi man, an elderly fellow who had spent a lifetime accumulating vast amounts of gold. The only thing he had more of than wealth was paranoia. His vaults were guarded by sleepless hellhounds, countless spells, and a golem big as a tree and twice as heavy.

And if I had robbed *his* ass blind, I couldn't imagine a single door could stop me much.

I reached beneath my skirts, found the leather pouch I had strapped to my leg, and fished out my lockpicks. With a quick glance down the hall to see if anyone was coming, I set to work.

Alarin being a wealthy man, the lock on the door was of rather solid quality. Which meant it took me six shakes of a rat's ass to break, rather than two. I turned the knob, pushed the door open with a creak.

A cold, dark room greeted me. Unlike the bright warmth designed to flaunt the styles and wealth of the other rooms, this perfectly square, cramped office was home to no ornamentation and barely any furniture.

A bookshelf loomed large against the wall, but the tomes lining its shelves were stark and had titles like *Mercantile Law* and *Taldan Trade Agreements: A History,* and likely didn't have any fight scenes or sex scenes in them. Naturally and quite understandably, I didn't look at them for very long.

More noticeable was the massive slab of a desk seated against the window. Among the sheaves of papers and ledgers dotting its surface, I spotted an abacus, a scale, and various maps indicating caravan routes.

I wagered this was where Alarin did much of his business, then. Which meant this was where I wanted to be.

I darted to the desk, began skimming the papers. I'd done this sort of thing before—scroll jobs, we called them back in Katapesh—and my eyes were already searching for what I knew had to be here: a stray receipt for a business that could serve as a front for something shadier, a letter penned in code that no one would recognize unless they knew what to look for . . .

But with every page flipped, my search yielded nothing. Nothing that wasn't completely expected for an office, that is: receipts, ledgers, shipping notices. And none of them looked even a little suspect. The caravan maps looked all in order, the receipts were exactly for what you'd expect Alarin to work in, and even his penmanship was perfectly . . .

Wait.

I caught a glimpse of something wedged between the letters, stuffed there without a second thought. I tugged it free, flipped it over. It was crumpled up, like it had been tucked away hastily, but even that hadn't destroyed the broken wax seal at its edges.

I edged closer to the window, drew back the curtain to let a bit of moonlight in. Elegant lettering greeted me.

Lord Amalien,

You will excuse the lack of formalities preceding this letter. I had hoped to break your seal and discover a business proposal to more formerly align your mining companies with my smithies. Imagine, if you will, the infinite span of my displeasure to discover yet another overture to merge family instead of business.

This may seem curt, Lord Amalien, but my patience and concern dwindle in equal measure with regard to this subject. I have no interest in a marriage between my son and your cousin, Analine. I have no interest in reading lists of her apparent virtues of homemaking and entertaining. I have no interest in formalizing our relationship through marriage.

I understand that this practice is becoming more accepted among families that mistake exotic for sensible, but Visheron is possessed of immense potential. Potential, if I may be blunt, that could only serve to be diminished by a union of inferior stock.

Kindly do not send additional inquiries unless they are about business.

Yours,
Lady Vishera Stelvan

I experienced, in that moment, two revelations.

The first, that Lady Stelvan was just a bit of a bitch, was hardly a discovery.

The second, however, all but made my heart leap out of my chest.

They matched.

The letters. The penmanship. The styles.

They matched.

I remembered back in Halamox's camp, the letter I had found in his cabin. Plain as a gods-damned wart on a goddess's nose, I remembered that perfect, unerring—a *precise* match for the letter I held in my hand.

Stelvan.

Lady Vishera Stelvan.

She was the one supporting the centaur attacks. She was the one smuggling weapons to them. She was the one feeding them information.

She was the one who had Gerowan killed.

Her sigil had been on the crates that had been lost. Her caravan routes had been the ones protected while she directed the centaurs to attack others. Her clues had given the centaurs the insight they needed to attack First Solace.

It all added up.

Except for the most important part.

Why?

To get at Gerowan's shares? Awful big risk to take just for a little more money. But then, I'd met men and women both who killed more for less.

My head hurt as the story I had built inside it came crashing down. Alarin, I thought I knew. Alarin made sense. Vishera, I didn't know at all.

But I knew who would.

I glanced up. The moon was waning. I'd be missed by now, I was sure. My lips twitched as I started rehearsing my most brainless smile, going over in my head what I was going to say.

"Oh dear, I'm terribly sorry," I said, "this house is simply so large and complicated. Not at all like what we have in Katapesh. I left the washroom and I suppose I lost my way."

That sounded pretty good.

"I agree with that, wholeheartedly."

That did not.

A voice came from behind me. A hand followed.

A black glove clamped over my mouth before I could even think to scream. A blade flashed in the dark, pressed against my throat before I could even think to fight back. And by the time I could even think to pray to whoever up there might be listening, I could hear a thick, rasping voice in my ear.

"You are *far* from home, Shaia."

13

Scars Left by Thin Knives

Ask a warrior, a ranger, a priest: they all have just one word for "trouble."

Pack of goblins? Trouble. Hobgoblin army? Trouble. Rampaging dragon strafing the countryside, devouring virgins or whatever? Yeah, that's trouble, too. And they solve all their trouble the same way: by stabbing, shooting, or burning it.

In my line of work, a greater sense of delicacy is required. And if you do this sort of thing long enough, you start developing different definitions of trouble.

There's the fleeting, annoying, gnat-behind-your-ears trouble that you can solve with a quick knife in the dark. There's the kind of trouble that makes sweat pool on your brow and makes your hands go real steady and your fingers like whispers.

And then there's the kind of trouble that tastes metallic in your mouth. The kind you swallow and let cut up your throat and make your chest clench before it settles in your belly like a cold knife in your guts.

I'll give you three guesses as to what kind of trouble I was in. First two don't count.

I remembered everything in fragments, shattered pieces of a window with a brick thrown through it. I remembered a knife at my throat. I remembered a heavy force cracking against the back of my head. I remembered hitting the floor, the world swimming around me before it dove into a dark place and took me with it.

And once I woke up, I remembered nothing but pain.

My heart pounded. My skull throbbed. My breath ran dry down a throat scratched raw. Everywhere I looked, I saw only blackness. The stink of my wine-soaked breath mingled with the reek of my sweat and conspired to choke me.

And around all of this—in every pain and ache, scraped raw over my skin and sunk deep in my bones—was that feeling: that cold-knife trouble lodged in my stomach.

I shook my head. Shook all my other thoughts clear out my ears so that I had nothing left but emptiness and quiet.

"Time and breath. So long as you've got those, you've got the means to survive."

Sem told me that, once.

I listened back then. I survived back then.

And so, like I did back then, I slowed down. I closed my eyes. I breathed.

Heart pounding, skin sweating, cold fear: I couldn't use these. They told me nothing I didn't already know.

The stuffy breath, the pain in my body, the sweat peeling down my skin: I could use these.

I breathed. The reek of wine on my breath hit my nostrils. A drop of sweat slipped into my mouth. In another moment, I could smell the burlap of the sack tied around my head.

I breathed. Feeling came back to my body, blood crept back into my limbs. I could feel the wood of the chair beneath me. I could feel the bite of rope binding my wrists together behind me.

I breathed. I heard no sounds of the night or of the wind. I heard no whisper of people or shuffle of feet. I wasn't in Alarin's manor anymore, then, but I was still somewhere close, somewhere confined.

I breathed. I felt a cold breeze, followed by a cold word, followed by a cold blade—

Ah, hell.

"Are we awake, Miss Ratani?" A voice, harsh and sharp as a spade that digs a grave. "Have we slept well?"

The tip of a blade prodded beneath my chin, tilted my head up. Through a clenched jaw, I replied.

"We have not," I said. "We would suggest that proper rest is rather impractical when one has one's head smashed from behind." I sniffed. "But then, we also assume the question was rhetorical."

"Still so smug." The voice became a hiss. The blade traced its way down to the hollow of my throat. "Even now, tied up and with a blade at your throat, you can't help but mouth off, can you, Shaia?"

"It's not you, darling," I replied with far more confidence than a woman in my position should. "I hate to give you the wrong impression of me, but this isn't even the first time this week I've been tied up and had a blade at my throat. The novelty's a touch diminished."

"Are those really the last words you want to leave before I send you to Hell, Shaia?" The knife prodded a little deeper. I felt a drop of blood blossom on my neck.

"No," I gasped. "But you're not going to kill me."

"Oh?" The voice took on a softness as the blade trailed across my throat. "And why is that?"

"Because there's only one person who calls me Shaia."

The blade came to a halt right at the base of my throat. I swallowed a cold, hard lump and felt the point brush against my neck. I whispered and felt every word reverberate in its steel.

"And she once told me that she'd never hurt me."

Do it long enough, lies start coming easy. You slip on names, histories, emotions as easily as you put on a cloak. It stops being a sin and starts being just one more part of a job.

It's honesty that gets hard. Every truth you speak tastes bitter in your mouth. And speaking plainly is so hard it makes having your throat cut open seem not so bad in comparison.

Or maybe that's just me.

Because those were words I had hoped I'd never say again.

Words died. Breath went still. Everything fell so silent I could hear the knife have a conversation with my throat. The beating of my heart, the blood rushing into my jugular made a plaintive plea. I heard the knife mull it over as its edge slowly slid along my neck, steel lips dancing across my skin in coy kisses. And all throughout the silence, that cold-knife fear in my belly wrenched itself a little deeper.

A snort of contempt. A muttered curse. The knife left my throat with a whisper. I took a moment to let out a breath as that fear slid itself out of my guts.

A breath, it turned out, was all I had. For an instant later, the sack was torn from my head and my eyes were sent fluttering against the sudden light that assaulted me.

Not that it took long for them to adjust. What little light there was was dim and flickering, cast by a few old candles set in rusted wall sconces in a tiny, drab room. And yet, for as little light as there was, it was still enough to afford me a good view of my captor as I looked up into two cold, pupil-less eyes.

And that cold-knife fear jammed itself right back into me and gave itself a good, hard twist.

I took her in. That bone white hair, cut so severely around her long, pointed ears. That slim, athletic build wrapped so tightly in black assassin's leathers. Those eyes—that cold blue stare that had seen a thousand men beg for mercy and hadn't so much as blinked when they watched her cut their throats.

And I smiled sweetly. And I said . . .

"Hey, Char-Char."

Let it never be said Chariel Longstride, assassin of the Brotherhood of Silence, suffered an abundant sense of humor.

Also, let it never be said she didn't have a mean backhand. Because I barely had time to register the sneer across her face before her left hand shot out and slapped me square across the face.

"Son of a *bitch*," I snarled. "Slapped twice in one night? Do I have a sign on my back or something?"

"What you've got, Shaia, is a scent." The knife came back under my chin, tilted my face up to look at her. "And it's of a *rat*."

"I resent that," I replied, eyes pointedly on the knife. "A rat is someone who turns over her companions to the authorities. I never uttered a word to a guard that wasn't more spit than language."

"Hardly seems the time to be pedantic, doesn't it?" Chariel asked.

"If I'm going to die here, I want the record set straight. I never ratted you out, Char."

"No." Her hand shot down, seized me by the hair. My cry was drowned out by her growl as she wrenched my head back and loomed over me, blue eyes bearing down upon me like two blocks of ice. "You just *left*."

I opened my mouth to say the first thing that came to mind. After thinking better of it, I closed my eyes.

"I had my reasons."

"Yeah. I bet you did."

She released my hair. My head slumped forward as she stalked away from me. The candles flickered as she walked by, as though they wished they could just snuff themselves out at her passing. And in their quivering light, I could get a better look at my surroundings.

The paint on the walls was peeling. The carpets were torn and ragged. Portraits of people I didn't recognize bearing names I didn't know hung crooked on the wall. Everywhere, furniture covered in white sheets loomed like a child's idea of specters. The room and everything in it did not so much have a layer of dust as it had a suit of armor made entirely of grime.

Still, it was big. Big enough to house a lot of furniture and a couple of boarded-up windows. I wagered we were in one of the abandoned manors at the edges of Yanmass, from back before the city got big and being any kind of wealthy short of "insanely" became unacceptable.

That made sense. I knew the Brotherhood liked to keep property in every city in Taldor. Just a couple of nice, out-of-the-way spots that would be ideal for, say, killing, dismembering, and then disposing of someone who had once stolen a large amount of money from them.

Just as an example.

"See, here's what really irritates me . . ."

I glanced over to Chariel. By the light of a nearby candle, she inspected her blade, studied the tiny drop of my blood adorning its tip.

"I like to think I'm merciful," she said. "There are quite a few things I can forgive. Betrayal, murder, theft . . . I don't always hold a grudge against these."

I would imagine she didn't. Some of our best friends were ardent practitioners of those arts.

"But when someone wrongs me . . ." She turned her scowl on me. "When someone wrongs the *Brotherhood* . . . and they simply saunter under my nose like I won't find them? That insults me. *That* irritates me."

"I went into hiding for *months*," I protested. "Whatever anyone says about your nose, Char, it's not nearly so big that it could cover the whole city. Frankly, I'm not even sure how you got into the city, let alone how you found me."

"Yanmass is built and governed by paranoid nobles who see doom at every corner." She smirked at me. "Are you that surprised to learn there are more than a few secret ways in and out of the city? As for how we found you . . ."

I didn't have to ask. An instant later, the answer came stalking in from the shadows.

"We covered our tracks," a man said. "No one will be following us."

"One guard got nosy," a woman added. "Nothing a few gold and a few words didn't fix."

Ah, hell.

I should have realized it. I should have recognized them. My eye picked them out of the crowd for a reason.

Sem would have told me to trust my instincts.

The man and woman spared a haughty smirk for me as they entered the glow of the candlelight. Their hair was as dark as I remembered from the party, but they had changed their servants' uniforms for black garb. Hell, now that I saw them in more appropriate clothing, I could almost recognize these two. I thought we might have shared whiskey together, once.

Idiot, Shy. Of course the Brotherhood had agents in Yanmass's manors. Why the hell wouldn't they? How the hell could you have been so stupid as to think they wouldn't recognize you?

"So, what are we thinking?" the woman asked. "A quick chop job? Ship her carcass out piecemeal for the boys back in Oppara to see?"

"Too messy," the man said. "You'd want to keep her whole, right? So the bosses know we really got her? We could ship her out in a barrel of wine." He looked to Chariel. "What do you think, Longstride? Just tell us what you want us to—"

"Leave."

The woman's face screwed up in ire. "We just got here."

"She's dangerous, Chariel," the man added. "All the bosses said so. We're supposed to keep eyes on her."

"And considering your past with her," the woman muttered, "maybe we should . . ."

She never finished that sentence.

Chariel didn't threaten her. Didn't throw knives, didn't cut throats, didn't spill blood. That would have been tactless, coarse. You didn't get to be as respected as Chariel by being coarse. No, you got to be where she is, at the very top of a long, black list held by the Brotherhood's highest heads, by being good.

Good enough to send a man and woman cold and breathless with just a look.

Kind of like the look she shot them.

"Yeah, all right," the man said, turning to leave. "Call us if you need help, Chariel."

"Better give us credit for the kill," the woman muttered as she followed, earning a jab in the ribs from her companion.

The two of them stalked off, disappearing into the shadows as Chariel watched them go. When she was certain she was alone, she turned back to me, strode over to the chair I was bound to. Slowly, she looked me over, her gaze cold and sharp as any knife, so that I didn't dare move.

I merely stared back, silent, following her gaze as she looked down at my wine-stained dress. She reached down, idly played with one of its billowing straps across my shoulder.

"Mauve?" she asked.

"Yeah," I replied.

Slowly, she stalked around behind me, her hand sliding away from the strap and onto my shoulder. I felt her fingers squeeze gently as she leaned down behind me and drew her knife back. There was a quick, sudden jerk.

"You look better in black," she said as the ropes fell from my wrists.

"Wasn't my idea." I rose up, knuckled out a kink in my back as I turned to face her. "It was the only dress available for the disguise."

She looked at me. The smile that crept across her face was small, so small you could barely even call it a ghost of a grin. But it was gentle, it was warm, and I had spent more than one night thinking of it.

"Always up to dirty business, Shaia? Even when you got out?"

"Do you remember what I told you back when we first met?" I asked. "You can take me out of Katapesh . . ."

"But I can't take Katapesh out of you. I remember."

I grinned. "I missed you, Char-Char."

And she stopped smiling.

Anyone who plays this game—from the rat kid who lies to guards to the shadow lord who shakes hands with the men he intends to kill—has more than one face. Chariel was no different, even if she didn't have as many as I did.

Most people—the men whose throats she cut in the night and the men who paid her to do it—never saw more than the one face: the cold mask she wore, dark as deep winter and unflinching even when blood was spattered against it. A lucky few had seen her smiles, those small little curls of lip that danced across her face and were gone in a flash, like pixies.

But there was a face she saved just for me. A mask of black silk, soft and sad, when her eyes became melting snowflakes and a frown deeper than night painted her face.

A face she had shown me only three times.

Once, when she woke up beside me.

Again, when she knew I was leaving.

And now.

I wished I could tell you it didn't tear me up worse each time to look at it.

"I told you I hate that name," she said, turning away from me.

"That's never stopped me from calling you it before." I shot her a grin in the hope she might shoot me one back.

But the gods didn't love me quite that much.

"Things were different before," she said. "Before, we were on the same side." She gave me a look, cold and deep. "Before, I didn't have an order and a fat sack of gold telling me to kill you."

I held her gaze, unsmiling, unblinking. I cleared my throat and glanced away. "Yeah, well . . . you haven't killed me yet."

"I should have," Chariel said. "Calistria knows I should have. It'd make things a hell of a lot easier."

"Char, we've been in this work too long to believe that killing makes things easier."

"Well, things sure as shit aren't easier with you still alive." She whirled on me with a snarl. Her eyes hardened to shards of ice, pinned me against the wall as she stalked toward me. "You betrayed us, Shaia. You betrayed the Brotherhood, you betrayed the job, you betrayed *me*. And I could have lived with that if you had done the smart thing and fled Taldor and gone where we couldn't find you, but you stayed here."

Her lips pursed. She narrowed her eyes.

"And we found you."

I swallowed something cold and hard. It settled in my belly like a lead weight.

"And?" I asked. "What happens now?"

"You insulted me once, Shaia. Don't insult me again by acting like you don't know."

Yeah, I did know.

From the minute I decided to leave Oppara to the minute I showed up on Herevard Helsen's doorstep with a big, fat letter of blackmail, I knew what was going to happen to me, eventually.

Same thing that happens to everyone who burns the Brotherhood of Silence.

Except for me, it'd be worse.

See, the Brotherhood doesn't do small-time. They've got dreams. Big, bloody, dirty dreams. And I was at the centerpiece of one of them when they brought me onto the streets of Oppara and shoved me in front of the carriage of one Senator Ignatio Calavus.

Taldor had been dying for centuries. Everyone knew it. And no one knew it better than the bickering men and women in Oppara's senate. Most of them could be trusted to do the smart thing: play nice with the Brotherhood, kick them a few favors and get out with as much gold as they can carry when the hammer falls. But men like Ignatio come from old blood with old visions of when Taldor was great, and believe in things like honor and virtue and romance.

Honor that compelled him to step out of his carriage and see this poor, down-on-her-luck Katapeshi girl that had stumbled in his way. Virtue that compelled him to take her in, this wretched soul without anyone to care for her. Romance that compelled him to fall in love with her, never suspecting she was there to put a knife in his back so someone more amenable could step up and take his place.

A normal assassination would bring up concerns of political motives. But if we could make him seem a faithless lover and me a vengeful woman spurned, the whole thing would be written off as a big tragedy. I'd be smuggled out before I could go to trial and his successor would play the way the Brotherhood wanted.

It wasn't a bad idea, really. Chariel's idea. We put a lot of work into it, her and me and about a dozen other Brotherhood higher-ups.

Not really sure why I chose to run away before we could do it, if I'm honest.

Maybe I didn't feel like sharing the gold we would get from it and decided to leave when I could get a bigger payday from looting Ignatio's vaults. Or maybe I knew that those privy to the Brotherhood's bigger assassination schemes were usually the next to get their throats cut.

Or maybe, when Ignatio looked me in the eyes and told me he loved me, I believed that he did.

I've made a thousand mistakes in my life, starting with my birth. Leaving the Brotherhood was just one of my latest. But when I fled for Yanmass, hoping to stay low until I could get to Galt, I never thought it'd end like this.

With Chariel's knife drawn on me even as she looked like she was about to cry.

"Char-Char," I said, breathing hard as she edged closer, "put the knife down."

"Don't call me that, Shaia. Don't say a damn thing."

"Chariel, *listen* to me—"

"It's kinder this way, you know." Her voice was a soft whisper. "I send you back to Oppara, they torture you, cut your eyes out and feed them to you. With me, it's just one stroke, in and out. You won't feel a thing."

"You don't have to do this," I lied, poorly.

"They saw you, Shaia. Two of the Brotherhood *saw* you. And they saw you with me *last*. They'll know. They'll think I betrayed them, like you betrayed them."

She swept forward suddenly. Her arm was over my throat. Her knife was pointed against my neck. Her jaw was clenched and she drew in sharp, ragged breaths in a desperate bid to chase away the tears forming at the corners of her eyes.

"Like you betrayed *us*."

"They wanted me to kill him, Chariel," I said, gasping as I struggled to pull her arm away. "They wanted me to marry him and then *kill* him. I had to leave. What else could I have done?"

"You could have told me."

"What could *you* have done."

"*I would have come with you.*"

Both of us went wide-eyed, silent and breathless at that. She hadn't expected to say it. I hadn't expected to hear it. And I sure as hell hadn't expected to feel so damned guilty for not even having considered it.

You know you've made some bad decisions in life when you feel morally inferior to an assassin.

And I assure you, if I hadn't felt a knife digging into my neck, I would have reflected more on them.

But this wasn't a time for thought. This was a time for instincts. And all of mine told me to scream.

So I did.

"There's another way," I gasped out.

And Chariel paused. Those big, pointed ears of hers started quivering, listening.

"The Brotherhood doesn't forgive," I said, "but it does do business. It trades, Chariel. And I've got a trade I can make it."

"You robbed them of a senate seat," she said. "An Opparan senate seat."

"One seat in Oppara," I said, "compared to the whole of Yanmass I could give them."

She narrowed her eyes, but made no other move.

"I'm onto something, Char. Something big. And it involves some of the biggest houses in Yanmass. Dirty business they'd keenly like to keep anyone from knowing."

"And would pay to keep it that way." Chariel hummed thoughtfully. "There's old money out here in Yanmass."

"Old money, old power." I eyed her knife. "The Brotherhood can't turn that down."

"They can turn it down from someone who's burned them before," Chariel muttered.

"But not from one of their top assassins," I shot back. "You run this to them, tell them you vouch for me, they'll listen."

"And if this is a lie, they'll cut my ears off along with yours."

"It's not a lie."

"It's *always* a lie, Shaia."

She had me there.

"Maybe," I said. "But I've never lied when you could get hurt, too."

And she just stared at me for a moment.

Like I said, everyone in this line of work has more than one face. Me? I had a dark, nasty closet full of them. But there was one of them that I kept buried deep, one I rarely took out, one that I had only shown three times before.

Once, when I met Sem.

Again, when I met Chariel.

And right now.

And she looked at me. And what she saw in my eyes, looking dead into hers, was enough to get her to drop her knife.

"If you stay in town," she said, "and where we can see you . . . I can get you a few days."

"A few days?" I sounded slightly more incredulous than a woman in my position ought to.

"Maybe a week," she replied. "And if you can't get us something by then . . ."

"Yeah, yeah," I muttered. "I know."

She eased her arm off my throat, drew away from me. That cold face, the face she showed so many others, returned as she looked me over.

"Stay here," she said. "Give me a minute to talk to the Brothers out front."

She began to stalk away and paused, casting a single glance over her shoulder.

"I'm going to tell you this exactly once, Shaia," she said. "Do *not* try to screw me."

And I simply smiled sweetly at her as she disappeared into the darkness.

Ah, Char-Char.

I never once had to try.

14

Empty Bottles

All right, so, the good news is that I don't think that Alarin's behind Gerowan's murder. I recommend you hold onto that bit, because that's about all the good news you're going to get. What is this? Whiskey? I thought I finished this bottle.

"Anyway—woo, that stuff packs a kick, doesn't it?—I found a note in Alarin's study from one Lady Vishera Stelvan. Apparently, he's been pushing rather hard for a marriage between her son and a cousin of his. That in itself isn't too interesting, unless Alarin thought Gerowan was a problem for some reason, which isn't too likely.

"Sorry, did you want any? No? Well, don't say I didn't offer. Anyway, the note I found there completely matched the penmanship of the note I found in Halamox's stable—I mean, his camp. Hah. Sorry. Long night. Anyway, I was going to come back down and tell you about it when someone smashed me in the back of the head with a dagger hilt.

"I'm fine, for the record. Nothing another few sips of this can't cure. Now, I don't want to bore you with the details, but it turns out I have maybe . . . four days to solve this thing before someone cuts me into little pieces and feeds me to sharks—or rats. Sometimes it's rats. Naturally, if I die before solving it, you can keep the latter portion of my payment, no worries.

"So, long story short, I'm thinking I'll break into Stelvan's manor tomorrow night and see if I can't find anything explaining if she's behind Gerowan's murder and, from then, we can use it to accuse her in a court of law. Then you pay me, I ride off into the sunset and—and this is crucial—we don't spend a lot of time asking questions."

I took a deep breath. I smiled across the table. I swirled the whiskey in my cup and took another sip.

"So," I said, "how was the rest of the party? Did you have a good time?"

To her credit, Dalaris, as she stared at me and blinked once, looked like she had taken the news rather well.

"*WHAT?*"

For about a second.

"Okay," I said, holding up my hands, "I know that *technically,* just screaming 'what' is more of an exclamation, but I still count it as a question and I was *quite* clear in—"

"No! *NO!*" Each of Dalaris's words was punctuated with a flail of her fists that I might have found petulant, were they not also accompanied by bright bursts of light from her eyes. "You can't just come in and tell me this! You can't drop this . . . this *madness* on me!

"Which part? There was a lot of mad stuff I just told you."

"All of it! *Any of it!*" Dalaris shrieked. "I was *mostly* willing to explore the possibility of Alarin because I was largely convinced he wasn't at fault!"

"And he's not. What's the problem?"

"The problem is that not only are you telling me that you suspect House Stelvan, a house so far beyond mine that it could have me expelled from Yanmass with a harsh word, to be involved in Gerowan's murder, but there are also assassins after *you* for looking into it and that I shouldn't so much as care?"

"Oh, *now* I see where you're upset." I laughed, took a sip of my whiskey. "No, see, the assassins are totally incidental to the fact that House Stelvan had your husband killed. Really, they're my problem, no need to worry about them at all."

"No need to worry about them," she repeated flatly.

"Right."

"No need to worry about the assassins."

"That's what I said."

"No need to worry about the hired killers connected to a larger network of hired killers, each of them hungry for your blood and perfectly willing to kill you and anyone who knows you should you take one wrong step."

"Okay, see, if I repeated everything like *that*, I could make you sound awfully foolish, too." I shook my head. "But trust me when I say your safety hinges on you not worrying about it. The less you know about my business, the better."

"Trust you? Trust *you*?" She shot to her feet, sending a cloud of dust rising from the sofa. "Trust the woman who disappears and almost gets herself killed on a nightly basis? Trust the woman who finds conspiracies behind every curtain and has a new suspect every night? Trust the woman—"

"Trust the woman who you paid to get the job done." I had cut off peoples' hands with more kindness than I cut off her sentence, but these hysterics had begun to grow tiring. I looked at her coldly over the rim of my glass. "You hired me to find Gerowan's killer. That is precisely what I'm doing, *Lady* Sidara."

Sem once told me I had a habit for needling people. Said it was what made me so good with a knife. I just had some instinct for figuring out exactly where I could hit people to make them hurt.

I never really believed it. I had always thought I was just lucky.

And, indeed, maybe it was just my bad luck that made me say exactly the right words to exactly the wrong person. But in the very brief moment that occurred after Dalaris's mouth fell open with disbelief and before her eyes suddenly went aglow with bright, angry light, I had a moment to think that maybe Sem had a point.

She screamed a word. I felt a wave of force roil over me, knocking the table and the couch over and sending me rolling backward. I was stunned—so stunned I didn't even *think* to shed a tear for my poor, innocent spilled whiskey. When I staggered to my feet, my thoughts weren't for fleeing or fighting. Rather, my eyes were locked onto the creature before me.

Her eyes burned. Brighter than any crude pyre or earthly flame, her anger was that of twin suns, searing and painful to look at. It painted her skin in a bronze glow, making her look more molten metal than flesh and bone. Her body held itself tense, her jaw clenched, her hair whipping about her with some unseen force. The timid little noble I had met was gone, and I was left with some terrible creature from beyond.

So I guess maybe I *did* needle people a little too much.

"Dalaris, I—"

"*Dalaris?*" she spoke, her voice given terrible resonance. "You want to call me by that name now? No desire to call me '*lady*'?"

"I only meant that—"

"You only meant to mock me," she spat. "You only meant to goad me, to make me feel like I don't belong here, like all the others."

"The other nobles?"

"No, you're *worse* than them." Dalaris stalked toward me, tall and menacing and narrowing her burning gaze upon me. "They scheme, lie, steal, cheat, but because they're fools with more money than sense. But you." She thrust a finger at me and I held my breath, wondering if a spell would follow it. "*You* should know better."

I felt something a bit like anger prick at the back of my neck. "I should, should I?"

"Someone like you," she growled, "you've seen what becomes of the victims of crimes. You've seen the children who starve when their food is stolen and the widowers who weep when their wives are never coming home. You lurk in shadows, with your blades and secrets, and you watch the people you hurt and you don't even *care*."

If it was her angelic bloodline that enabled her to channel sorcerous powers, I wondered if the ability to also channel insufferable sanctimony was a necessity to doing so or merely a perk.

Regardless of the fact that she probably could have made me burst into flames with a flick of her finger, I stood my ground. I balled up my hands into fists, stalked forward to meet her. And though my glare wasn't, you know, *fiery*, I liked to think it conveyed my displeasure.

"And you think you know me?" I asked. "Tell me how you came about this delightful insight into my character, hm? Been reading my thoughts? Or was that whole spew about shadows and secrets just something you read in a steamy novel?"

"Do you deny it?" she asked. "Do you deny doing any of those—"

"Of course not, you idiot. I wasn't born rich. Or with powers. Or because my great-aunt whatever had an ass so sweet the heavens themselves parted. I was born to slaves in a shitty little corner of a shitty little city of a shitty little country and I had to *fight* to get out of it."

"Fight," she said, sneering. "Like you're so noble."

"Not noble. Never. You can't eat honor, and virtue won't keep you warm at night, sister. I had to earn those things, carve them out of the city's hide with the tip of my knife. But you're wrong when you said I didn't care." I leaned forward, forced every word through clenched teeth. "I *loved* every minute of it."

She recoiled, as though struck. "I should never have hired you. I should never have—"

"Then what would you do?" I pressed my luck, reached out and shoved her a little with one finger. "Go run to the guards? Find a noble knight? You'd get a lot of platitudes and good intentions and never hear so much as a gods-damned *word* of what happened to Gerowan. People like you want to believe that justice is all shiny paladins and sweeping proclamations, but it's as ugly and dirty as anything else that comes out of civilization, sweetheart, and *I'm* the girl who doesn't mind getting down into the dirt."

She opened her mouth to retort, but I had heard enough. I held up a hand, spoke forcefully.

"I'm in too deep to get out now," I said. "You don't want to pay me, fine. But if you ever hope of finding justice for your lost love, I—"

"*I NEVER LOVED HIM.*"

It might seem a bit odd that *that* statement should be what rendered me speechless, as opposed to all the, you know, fire and magic and stuff. But I couldn't help it.

"What?" I asked.

The fires dissipated from her eyes, fading into nothingness. What was left behind were her wide, bright eyes, brimming with tears. The molten glow of her skin, the regality of her poise, all vanished.

What was left behind was a girl. Even smaller and more scared than the one I had met way back in Herevard's manor.

I could hardly blame her for running.

Hell, I didn't even blame her for shoving me aside as she tore up the stairs and disappeared down the hall.

I don't live with regrets. Any rogue worth the coin in her pockets doesn't. The sole regret you're permitted is the one you feel just after the floor drops out from under you and the noose tightens around your neck. And so I certainly didn't regret telling her what I did. She should know—she should *have* known—the dirty business she asked me to do.

And yet, sometimes . . .

Do this job long enough, you stop noticing things. You don't see a nice tree brimming with apples, you just see cover you can duck behind. You don't see sunshine, you look for the shadows it casts where a knife might be lurking. You forget the nice things in life.

And you forget not everyone sees the same things you do.

I looked up the stairs and sighed. I knew I should go talk to her.

I mean, she spilled all the whiskey, so it wasn't like there was anything else to do.

I trudged up the stairs, turned down the hall. The living room of House Sidara at least kept up a vain attempt at remaining dignified, but the upper reaches of the manor had given up all pretense. The walls were cracked and bare of portraits. The floors splintered at the edges where the carpet had frayed. It all seemed less like a home and more like a rich man's tomb.

The door to Dalaris's room was at the end of the hall. I knocked once, heard no reply. Slowly, I eased it open and slipped in.

I almost felt uncomfortable being in her room. Not for any sense of decency, mind you—"decency" is just one of those fancy words they made up to keep anything productive from getting done, like "virtue" or "law"—but because it was so . . . so . . . *not* where I should be.

It was not decadent. Not grand, like I imagined a rich woman's room would be. It was big and had a big bed to match, but it was a comfortable-looking affair with a heavy quilt, two large pillows, and a well-worn stuffed rabbit given an honored position in the middle. The wardrobe was modest, the sofa was threadbare, and the portraits weren't the grand, ancestral homages of downstairs. Rather, they were small, intimate things: painted memories meant for just one person.

I had never known a home bigger than a shack. A place like this felt weird, alien to me. Too warm, too close, too . . . *bright*. I wanted nothing quite so much as to leave.

Well, almost nothing.

I slunk to the bed, where Dalaris sat, staring through teary eyes at the wall. She said nothing as I sat down beside her and stared with her. I was fine with that. A lot is said when no one's talking.

But when she finally broke the silence, it was with a whisper.

"When my mother died, my first thought was to run away," she said. "I wanted to get away from Yanmass, from Taldor, from anything political or made of gold. Maybe I'd join a wizard's college or become an adventurer."

Now would have been a good moment to have whiskey to sip, if *someone* hadn't ruined that.

"There wasn't anything for me here," she continued. "Anything that wasn't dead, anyway." She sighed, and her eyes drifted to a portrait hanging over her bed of a well-dressed woman with a gentle smile. "But it feels like people only get louder when they die. At least in Yanmass." She looked down at her hands. "So I chose to stay. I had a duty to House Sidara. I had to continue things."

"And you picked Gerowan," I said.

"He was polite, gentle, kindly . . ." Dalaris closed her eyes as she recounted. "He was . . . *fond* of me. We were good friends. But there was always something between us, the knowledge that neither of us would be doing this if it weren't necessary. And if it was a choice between Gerowan and one of those swine at Alarin's party . . ."

I nodded appreciatively. "Smart."

"So, when he died . . . when he was murdered . . . I was horrified and sad and . . . and . . ." She swallowed hard. "I felt something almost like . . . *relief.* Gods, how horrible is that?"

"Eh." I shrugged. "Not like you *wished* it upon him."

"He was my betrothed."

"'Betrothed.' He was more a word to you than a person. And it's not like you're not trying to do right by him now."

"It was a mistake," she said. "I shouldn't have gotten you involved. I should have handled it myself."

"If you could handle it yourself, you wouldn't have found me. But you did find me. And now we're both in a hole so deep that the only way out is to just keep digging."

"How does that make sense?" She looked at me, puzzled. "Do we . . . dig *up*?"

"All right, that? That thing you just said? Stuff like that is why you couldn't handle it yourself." I smiled at her. What I *thought* was an encouraging smile. "Were it me, I wouldn't have done it. But you're not me, are you? Even if your grandma hadn't porked an angel—"

"Shy, please."

"—you'd still be who you are. And I know that, because you are who you are, you'd hate yourself far more if we didn't find who was behind Gerowan's murder."

She looked down at the floor again. "You really think it was Lady Stelvan?"

"For the moment. I think she's our best bet."

Dalaris shook her head. "But if you get hurt—"

"Don't be stupid." I reached down and squeezed her hand. "Only amateurs get hurt."

She looked down at her hand, then up at me. And I knew the look in her eyes. I had seen it a thousand times in the eyes of those hopeful suitors, in those believers in redemption, in Chariel right before I disappeared . . .

She was looking at me like she looked at a flower growing out of a pile of manure. She was looking for light in a dark place, the possibility that there was more to me than just snide words and latent alcoholism. The possibility that someone, somewhere down the line, would be very happy with me.

Yeah, I had seen that look before.

Many times.

Right before their eyes went glassy.

But there was no need to ruin the mood right now, was there?

15

Knocking at the Back Door

Once they hear the word "thief," everyone thinks of the same thing. You probably thought it, too, when you heard it.

A moonlit—or moonless, if you're feeling dramatic—night, right? The clouds shift overhead, revealing a single figure, clad so head to toe in black leather that they might as well be a shadow—sexless, ageless, almost formless. There's a single glint of silver as a grappling hook is drawn and thrown. And with all the speed and grace of a spider, they skitter up the wall to a rich man's home—or I hear fortresses of evil tyrants are popular with the bards these days—and slide in like a ghost.

That about right?

I've heard them all. In Katapesh, it's a slinky, black-clad stranger who breaks into a greedy merchant's house. In Andoran, it's a proud abolitionist spy infiltrating a prison to break free some slaves. But it's more or less the same thing: black clothes, dark night, sneaky-sneaky, breaky-breaky, stealy-stealy.

Usually, I prefer the more subtle route: disguises, subterfuge, a heaping helping of lies. But sometimes, that's just not feasible.

And, I thought to myself as I pulled up the grappling hook behind me, the classics are classics for a reason.

I leaned out from the windowsill, cast a glance down. It was a twenty-foot drop to Vishera's courtyard. If the fall didn't kill me, then the numerous guards in black-and-red livery would. To be honest, I was a little surprised I'd made it as far as I had. House

Stelvan's gardens were markedly slim on the statues, fountains, and artistic shrubberies that peppered the other nobles' houses. Likely, that was to make it more difficult for would-be thieves—or, more likely, the Qadiran spies that Vishera apparently feared lurking in the night.

Which was ridiculous, of course. Qadirans were all about their sun goddess, Sarenrae. Norgorber would never send a cloudy, moonless night—the kind that would let someone slip across a heavily guarded courtyard, for example—to a Qadiran.

Fortunately, Norgorber has an understanding with Katapesh.

I slipped back into the window, eased it shut behind me and slid out of the frame. The light inside the manor was dim—only a few candelabras lit—but I couldn't take the chance that someone would look up and see my shadow.

This high up, a fall into House Stelvan's living room would kill me as surely as a fall in the courtyard. I'd just leave a much more elegant corpse.

The main hall to Stelvan's manor was positively enormous. Dalaris's could hold two couches and a table comfortably. But within this massive hall, it was like its own world. At the great doors were two flanking, severe-looking statues of ancient ancestors. Farther down was a dining table replete with twenty chairs on each side. Scattered about were sofas and tables and cushions and relaxing chairs as big as thrones. All of this sat under the watchful eyes of the omnipresent ancestral portraits of Yanmass—and Vishera's ancestors looked particularly uptight.

Even so, I'd have called the whole thing, with its many crimsons and blacks and violets, beautiful.

I *would* have . . . if not for the guards.

They stood so still, I would have called them more pieces of furniture if it weren't for the occasional shifting of stances they took. One by one, they stood at the various large windows and stared out, deliberately searching the night for anything the guards outside might have missed. They were clad in the same livery as the ones in the courtyard, and I could see swords at their hips and the glint of mail beneath their shirts.

Their eyes were locked on the windows—or, occasionally, on each other as they casually traded conversations. I smiled at my fortune. These were no eager young recruits who searched everywhere. Nor were they hardened veterans who could sense trouble in the air. No, I had been lucky enough to find the guards who were too old to care out of enthusiasm and too young to care out of loyalty.

I pulled a black hood up over my face and leaned forward. The rafters crisscrossing the house looked solid enough: old, but well made. Nonetheless, I crept out onto them slowly and with great, deliberate care. Like a cat, hands in front and feet back, I tested each beam before sliding onto it. I wasn't worried about them giving way under me—I didn't weigh that much, no matter how much I had been drinking lately. But a groan from an ancient timber or a squeak from a rusty connector would give even a lazy guard a reason to look up.

"Anything out there tonight?"

Fortunately, they didn't seem too interested.

"Yeah, I saw an entire squadron of Qadirans marching through the street." A slightly bored-sounding voice wafted up from below. "And behind them, Sarenrae herself was driving a chariot pulled by six naked angels, all of them singing—"

"You can just say 'no, I didn't see anything.'" The first voice sighed. "You don't have to be an asshole about it."

I peered over the beam. This high up, the guards looked tiny. But Stelvan's main hall was so vast it might as well have been an amphitheater. In the silence of the night, the echoes of their voices carried all the way up.

"Every night is the same routine," the bored guard said. "Even a place this big doesn't require *this* many guards to be awake all night. We don't even know what we're supposed to be looking for."

"Whatever the mistress says you're looking for," the other guard replied. "You don't want her to catch you slacking off."

"She'd have to leave her study for that to happen. I hear she's taking her meals in there now."

"She controls the entire weapons trade of Yanmass. She has bigger concerns."

"Still, a little leadership would go a long way to improving morale around here. If not the mistress, then perhaps her son could—"

The conversation was abbreviated by the sudden sound of an open palm slapping a cheek. The echo carried through the hall, drawing a glance from the rest of the guards. Looking down, I saw the second guard seize the other by his collar and draw him close. Their voices dropped to a low mutter and I could just barely make out what they were saying as I leaned over the beam and strained my ears.

"Don't you *ever* speak of the master," the second guard hissed. "The mistress pays you to watch, not speculate. Got it?"

The first guard nodded dumbly, then scurried off to his post as the other guard released him. I rubbed my own cheek in sympathy, remembering the sting of Vishera's slap quite well.

In a way, it was kind of nice to know that it wasn't personal. Apparently, *anyone* who mentioned her son was worthy of slapping.

And it was even nicer to know that the mistress was currently indisposed.

I glanced toward the end of the great hall. A massive staircase, wide enough to accommodate five men side by side, rose up from the marble floor to climb to the upper levels of the manor. A large balcony stretched left and right, doubtless leading into the upper halls.

I couldn't help but be impressed; I knew a few fortress-commanders who would writhe in envy at the scope of Vishera's manor.

I, myself, had a passing appreciation for the fact that her rafters stretched all the way to the staircase. I decided I would leave her a thank-you note.

Carefully, I crept across the rafters toward the end of the hall. Once I reached it, I spared a quick glance for any guards that might have been watching. Their eyes fixed on the windows, I hugged the beam and swung myself to its underside. I lowered myself to the balcony and rushed for the left hall.

I pressed myself close to the wall, slipped behind a pillar. I peered down the hall. White marble columns marched its length, flanking a dark crimson carpet. Elegant doors lined the walls, each one marked with gold filigree that glowed in the dim light of lamps hanging from the domed ceiling.

It looked *almost* like precisely what you'd expect to find in a rich woman's house.

Of course, usually, you'd expect guards up here.

It made sense, right? The upper levels were where the jewels, artwork, and important stuff was kept, wasn't it? Someone as paranoid as Vishera would doubtless want her most priceless shit watched over closely.

And yet, the halls were completely bereft of life. No guards. No sentries. Not even a servant was present.

There could be a few reasons for that, of course. Possibly Vishera preferred to front-load her protection, assuming no one would get past her guards downstairs. Or maybe she simply didn't have enough money to staff the entire household.

Or perhaps a woman so paranoid as to suspect an imminent incursion of Qadirans hundreds of miles away would be paranoid enough to not even trust her own guards with her most priceless secrets.

I scratched my chin. That would seem to make sense, but no rich person ever left their treasure *totally* unguarded.

Which meant . . .

I glanced to the floor, narrowed my eyes, and searched until . . .

"Hello, beautiful."

There. Six paces ahead. Stretched between the two nearest pillars. It was a thin little thing, barely thicker than a strand of spider's silk and painted a shade of crimson that made it indistinguishable from the carpet. Any other idiot would have stumbled into it, for sure. And frankly, I probably would have, too, had I not taken the time to search.

But this wasn't the first tripwire I'd ever seen.

I looked up to the walls, saw the arrow-slots neatly hidden just after the pillars. It was a good setup: some bumbling oaf comes in, trips the wire without even noticing, takes another two steps and finds himself skewered by six arrows before he knows what hit him.

Classic.

And expensive.

Here's a piece of advice: the amount of money spent on a trap to keep someone from advancing is always guarding an object worth at least three times that amount.

Call it Shy's Law.

And as this particular arrow-trap was worth at least six thousand, there must be some nice stuff down this hall.

I crept out, stepped gingerly over the tripwire, and kept my eyes open for traps. Good thing I was, as my trip down the hall yielded a pressure plate hidden under the carpet, a pendulum-blade hidden in the wall, and a bust of an old bald guy.

Granted, I didn't know if that bust was one of those weird trapped busts where the guy shoots lightning out of his eyes if you walk in front of him or if Vishera just had an ugly relative she wanted to remember, but I ducked under it, all the same.

And as I went, I checked each door, pressing my ear to the wood and listening. The guards said that Vishera was in her study all the time. If I had to wager, I'd say that anyone paranoid who had anything worth hiding would keep it near them.

Or maybe I was looking forward to the opportunity to break in, sneak up on her, and choke her. Either way, once I heard a noise, that'd be my best bet.

And yet, all the doors I tried were dead silent. One after another, I didn't hear a gods-damned sound. I was starting to suspect I'd have to crack them open and search them all, but then I reached the fourth door.

Ear to the wood. Breath held. Eyes closed. Concentrate.

Footsteps.

There we go.

I reached for the handle, paused. The door was held with a rather hefty-looking lock. It was gussied up with gold and silver, but it was still the kind of lock you'd use to guard either a lot of money or a guy you really, *really* wanted to kill later.

Still, nothing I couldn't work with.

I pulled my picks out of my pocket, knelt down, and went to work. It took a bit of tweaking, poking and wiggling, but eventually I found a smile creeping on my face as I heard the sound that every rogue loves hearing.

Click.

Click is good.

Ka-chunk.

Ka-chunk, though? Ka-chunk is not good.

I heard wood sliding behind me. I heard a spring go off. I heard wind whistling.

And if I had been just a hair slower, I'd have been hearing three thick darts punching into my kidneys rather than the wood of the door. And even though I had fallen to the floor in time to avoid the trap, I couldn't help but curse.

Vishera had to have heard that. She had to have known what that sound was, too. No more time to play it slow, then; I had to get in there and silence her before she could raise an alarm. I pulled Whisper out of his sheath, threw the door open, and swept into the room, searching for an old lady with a throat that needed cutting.

What I found, though, was a naked lady.

A *huge* naked lady.

She loomed before me, ten feet tall and reclined on a sofa adorned with a leopard's pelt. Skin so pale it was almost translucent, the barest scrap of silk valiantly trying and failing to offer modesty to the curves of her body. Beneath a mane of raven hair and above the vaguest of come-hither smiles, a pair of brilliant blue eyes sparkled.

She was beautiful, to be sure.

Even if she was a painting.

And even if her breasts were so gigantic that they'd probably make the Inner Sea shift six miles east whenever she bent over.

The portrait hung on the far wall, dominating the spacious room. And as huge as it was, it'd be much easier to ignore if every other wall wasn't caked in other canvases of various sizes, each of them sporting an echoing theme of "insanely endowed woman lying on dead animal." It's not like there was any furniture to speak of except a table, a wine bottle, and an easel with a woman awaiting the painting of the second massive breast to compliment the first.

I wasn't quite sure *where* Vishera would be hiding incriminating evidence in this, er, "gallery." But hey, good to know she had hobbies.

"Beautiful, aren't they?"

I whirled at the voice, knife up and ready to stab. But the face that looked at me didn't look particularly worried. Hell, he didn't even seem to notice I *had* a knife as he came walking out of a nearby curtained doorway.

He was a sort of classically—or generically—handsome fellow. His tall and lean body was in a tunic way too loose and breeches way too tight, leaving way, *way* too little to the imagination. A velvet cap hung lazily over a mop of unruly black hair. His features were narrow and sharp, reminiscent of an axe head. But it was his eyes, dark and smoldering, that drew my attention.

Though apparently, the same could not be said of my eyes. The man seemed to look right past me as he walked up to the easel and gestured toward his incomplete newest portrait.

"This one, though," he said, his voice a dark, sultry sort of sound, "this one will be my masterpiece. It's almost intimidating. I am entering brave new territory. Note the leaves encroaching at the borders, stopping just shy of the beauty, as if to suggest that even nature could not improve upon her. And here, see? The babbling brook shyly creeps by, to suggest deference to her."

I looked over the portrait, noticed the leaves and brook, and nodded.

"Right." I scratched my chin. "So, uh, what do the colossal tits suggest?"

"Please." He held a hand to his chest, turned away dramatically, apparently offended. "The beauty of the form is, perhaps, exaggerated, if only to accentuate the life-giving power apparent in all women."

"Yeah. Okay." I nodded, squinted at him. "So, have you *seen* many women, or—"

"Droll." He sneered down a rather long nose at me. "I trust you didn't decide to grace me with your presence solely so you could misunderstand my work." He glanced toward the door. "Of course, given the amount of trouble you had to go through to get here, I can't actually imagine why you *would* have come."

"Yeah, I meant to talk about that." I swept over to the door, glanced out to make sure no one was coming before easing it shut. "Are *all* the rooms here hidden behind poisoned dart traps, or what?"

"Poisoned darts?" The man lofted a sculpted eyebrow. "Upon last inspection, it was still the pendulum of death. I suppose that explains the banging I heard two months ago." He walked to the wine bottle, poured himself a glass. "Mother's been doing some renovation, I suppose."

"'Mother?'"

I turned to him, eyes wide, just as he turned to face me. And suddenly, I saw it: the narrow features, the harsh angles of his face, the way I kind of wanted to strangle him a little.

"Holy hell, you're Vishera's son."

"Mm." He took a long bow. "Lord Visheron Stelvan, at your service. Or at least, as much service as I can accomplish within the confines of my quarters." He paused. "Since you didn't know who I am, I take it you're *not* here to see me."

"Not really, no."

"Pity. I *thought* it wasn't my birthday. Mother usually sends me a new model once a year or so." He ran his eyes up and down me and made a face that made the urge to strangle him grow stronger. "I don't think she'd send me someone quite so boyish, though."

"Well, sorry, friend." I bit back my resentment and shrugged instead. "I was actually looking for, er . . ."

"Mother, I take it." He swirled his wine and snorted. "Or something Mother took. Or someone Mother killed."

"Actually, yeah. Does she do this sort of thing a lot?"

"One does not reach the lofty heights that Mother has without being a heady cocktail of ambition and ruthlessness, my dear. After all, how else would one explain locking one's offspring up for his life?"

I blinked. "She just keeps you in here, then? Like a prisoner?"

"More or less. Don't let me mislead you: the prison is lavish, to be certain, but Mother, shall we say, frowns upon the idea of me being seen outside the house."

"Yeah, I gathered. What with the poison dart trap and all. How long have you been here?"

"Hm." Visheron tapped his pointed chin, looked up at the ceiling. "Thirteen years? Perhaps eleven?"

Well, that might account for him not having a very clear idea of what women looked like, I guessed. That aside, I couldn't help but feel a little bad for him; cells are cells, and I'd seen enough to know how awful they are.

"Damn," I muttered. "What the hell could a son possibly do to make his own mother lock him up like a criminal?"

Visheron laughed. "Oh, had I been a criminal, Mother would doubtless have been pleased. She'd have a use for me, then, at least. Sadly, at around twelve, it became clear that my talents and interests lay in art and not in her many lessons on geography, economics, and military tactics." He took a long sip from his glass. "She had such hopes for me, of course. Alas, when I started to manifest and still took no interest, she had me sealed away."

I pursed my lips. "Manifest" was one of those words that never preceded anything good, like "begat" and "foretold." And yet, I had to ask.

"Manifest . . . how?"

Visheron grinned broadly, and there was something rather unpleasant in his smile. He gestured across his face.

"I take it you see Mother in me, but tell me what else you see."

"I see a decently handsome man with a curious taste in aesthetics."

"*Decently?*" Anger flashed across his features, but soon simmered down to mere ire. "Very well, perhaps you require a more forward demonstration."

He doffed his cap, smoothed back the hair from his scalp. And had I a curse sufficiently blasphemous at hand, I probably would have been spewing it right then. It wouldn't have been dignified, of course, but hell.

How exactly was one *supposed* to react to the sight of two black horns jutting from a man's scalp?

"Norgorber's nuts," I whispered. "You're a fiend."

"Half of one, at least," Visheron said. "I like to think the better half."

"What the hell is Vishera *doing* in this house?"

"You weren't aware?" He blinked at me, ran a finger across a horn. "I was certain you were some manner of do-gooder here to put an end to her particular brand of wickedness."

"Not as such, no. I'm here to find out if she had something to do with a murder."

"Ah. The Amalien fellow, yes?"

"You know?"

"I hear things."

"Then she did it."

"It wouldn't surprise me if she did." Visheron quaffed the rest of his wine. Shrugged. "But it wouldn't surprise me if she didn't. Mother is both vengeful and aloof. She likes to keep eyes on her fellow nobles, but doesn't often sully her hands with murder. Apropos of nothing, have you any interest in stripping naked so that I might draw you?"

My face screwed up. "What? No!"

"I see. Well then, I'm afraid I'm no longer interested in this conversation." He yawned, began to stalk toward the curtained doorway. "Do lock the door on your way out. Mother will know you've been here by the sprung trap, but I'd hate for her to think I had anything to do with it."

"What? Where am I going to find what I need, then?"

"Try the library. East wing. Third door on the left, I believe." He began to slip inside the doorway. "Mother does love her books."

I sighed. That was something, at least. I turned to leave, but spared one more moment.

"One thing."

Visheron paused, looked over his shoulder.

"If you thought I was someone here to stop your mother," I said, "why were you so forthcoming with information about her?"

He licked his lips. "It'll be funny. Mother never did have a sense of humor." He winked. The light of the lantern glimmered off his horns. "I think I got mine from Father."

16

Bloodlines

Tribal Politics of the Hold of Belkzen . . .
The Armies of Exploration: A History . . .
Qadira: More Than a Menace?

I scratched my head as my eyes went down the various rows of books in Vishera's library. They all went on like this: massive tomes, none less than a hand thick, each one detailing government, military tactics, or various studies of Qadiran politics. Which, I supposed, was exactly the sort of thing you'd expect to find in her library.

For some reason, I expected there would be at least *one* romance novel.

But the library, such as it was, was only fifty by fifty feet. It consisted of nothing more than a large chair and three walls, each one bearing shelves laden top to bottom with books, and I had gone over each of them over the past hour or so I had been here.

I didn't find one romance novel.

I didn't find one book with naughty pictures, either.

And I sure as hell didn't find a single shred of evidence I could bring back to Dalaris.

Meaning this entire trip was starting to look like one huge waste of time.

And time was something I was going to be running out of very soon. It couldn't be much longer until the sun rose. Norgorber didn't love me enough to pull shadows out of the sun's ass just for my benefit. And if I wasted much more time here, I'd be facing a new guard shift, fresh and attentive and with plenty of daylight to spot me by.

Of course, maybe that was Visheron's whole intention in sending me here. He might not have had any love for his mother, but my breasts weren't *nearly* large enough for him to like me any better. And he *was* half-devil . . . or half-demon? Something nasty made a nasty with his mother and turned out something nasty, at any rate. And while I hate to subscribe to stereotypes, fiends don't live in Hell for no good reason.

That must be it, I thought as I looked around the bookshelves again. Visheron was just screwing with me. I had to have been an idiot to have believed a man with horns bursting out of his head. Unless Vishera was fond of hiding pieces of incriminating evidence inside books, and I wasn't about to go through each of them looking for—

I paused.

I blinked.

Son of a bitch, how did I not notice that?

There. Western wall. Between the third and fourth bookshelves. A crack that was just a touch wider than the cracks between the other shelves. I knelt down, felt a cold breeze whisper from it.

I hopped to my feet, ran my hands across the spines of the book. I pressed my fingers against each of them, testing them, probing them. *On Kyonin's Stratagems* jiggled; no good. *Cheliax: Traitor Nation* shifted easily; not that one. *Twelve Steps to a Closer Relationship with Abadar* . . . did not move.

There we are.

I took it in both hands, pulled it out. There was a heavy-sounding *click.*

And no *ka-chunk* followed.

The book came out halfway, then slid back in, pulled by a mechanical lever. The bookshelf slid back into the wall, then slid out of the way, revealing a dark room behind. I was tempted to laugh. Or to groan. In the end, I settled for cursing myself. "Stupid girl."

Of course. A false bookshelf. I should have seen that coming. But who could blame me for not?

I thought these things were only in stories.

I slipped in, felt my foot catch on something. The bookshelf slid itself shut behind me, triggered by whatever plate I had found. Pitch blackness closed in around me, smothering my senses.

I had to feel my way forward in the dark, though I could tell by the claustrophobic confines that this was a space built between the walls of the library and the next room.

For what purpose, I was soon to find out. As I continued creeping forward, I felt the floor turn to stairs beneath my feet, leading downward in a narrow switchback. I continued down, stepping as lightly and carefully as I could afford, lest I trigger something else.

My caution felt vaguely useless, of course. After all, it didn't make a whole hell of a lot of sense to be careful when I was walking blind down a hidden passage in the house of a crazy woman who might have killed a man and apparently had a fetish for under-worldly pleasures.

My pace slowed until I came to a halt.

Suddenly, I found it rather hard to move, realizing I was up to my neck in shit.

This wasn't what I signed on for. I had thought this was going to be simple: break into a rich person's house, find something, get out under the cover of darkness. Just like I had done a hundred times back in Katapesh with Sem.

But Sem wasn't here. This wasn't Katapesh. And Vishera wasn't just a rich woman.

Her son was half fiend. Part of me shuddered to think that Visheron might have been the product of a demon forcing itself onto her. But there was another part of me, a part lodged somewhere in the pit of my stomach, that shuddered at another possibility.

What if a half-fiend was exactly what she had been looking for? What if Visheron was the price she had paid for something darker? People made unholy pacts with the beasts below all the time; hell, Cheliaxians had it as part of their national character. Whatever reward Vishera had earned from it, I was walking right into it.

I had to get out of here. Escape while there was still time. Run back to Dalaris, tell her it was a wash. No evidence, no nothing. Give her the money back, run elsewhere, get out of here. Escape Chariel. Escape the Brotherhood. Escape everything. Run away, run away, run—

"*Hello?*"

I froze.

"*Is someone there?*"

That wasn't the sort of voice you wanted to hear down in a dark, dank secret passage. That wasn't the sort of voice you wanted to hear *anywhere*. It slid itself into my skull and slithered down into my chest on a hundred centipede feet and coiled around my ribcage.

"*I can hear you breathing.*"

And, as far as signs that I should turn and run go, they didn't get much clearer than that.

And every instinct in me was screaming for me to listen to that. It was just one voice telling me to stay.

Family will cut you for a coin. Strangers will stab you for a laugh. But among thieves, Shy, there's trust. Because you and me? We've got no one else.

I closed my eyes. I sighed.

Sem probably wasn't talking about Dalaris way back then. But it wasn't any less true. She may not have skulked in the dark or carried a knife, but she didn't have anyone else, same as me. And if I left now, she'd be left to deal with this on her own.

I didn't expect that thought to bother me as much as it did.

And I certainly didn't expect it to make me resume my descent.

But today was just full of surprises.

I continued down. A faint blue light crept in, slowly ruining the pitch blackness. It grew as I went deeper down the stairs. The air grew colder. But it remained silent. So silent I could almost pretend that I hadn't heard the voice at all, that it was just a trick of a stressed mind fraught with frightened thought.

In the darkness, a line of blue light framed a black rectangle; a doorway in the darkness. Whatever Vishera was hiding down here, I had found it. And because she had gone to all the trouble of burying it under her house, I was certain she didn't intend for just anyone to open it.

I ran my hands along the frame, found the hidden latch just next to the handle, clearly intended to be sprung when someone hastily tried to jerk the door open. Too dark to see what it was supposed to trigger, but I didn't have to. I closed my eyes, drew in a deep breath.

And with it, the scent of oil.

It rose in faint coils of stink from beneath my feet. I glanced down, stepped to the side and, carefully, gave the handle a quick jerk before leaping away.

Ka-chunk.

Two gouts of flame erupted in the dark, lighting up the darkness as they came spewing upward in a wall of flame that would have incinerated me had I stayed just close enough. But their fury was brief, and soon they dimmed to small candle flames beneath a grate on the floor, providing a rather pleasant glow.

I had just made another move for the door when I heard it.

Ka-chunk-chunk.

Two chunks? Who could afford *two* chunks?

I leapt back as I heard a panel in the wall open, just in time to see a small torrent of chittering, screeching creatures come flying out. Their carapaces glittered against the dark in the dimming light of the fire, and I saw them strike the wall and then go skittering away, just barely making out pincers and curling tails.

I couldn't help but whistle in admiration.

I had never even *heard* of a trap that shot scorpions.

Whatever the hell Vishera was hiding, it must be *incredible*.

And after the few minutes it took me to take care of the lock, I was more than ready to find out. I pushed the door open, a weighty iron thing, and it slid with the faintest of groans, opening up into a thirty-by-thirty room bathed in the soft blue light from a globe hanging near the ceiling overhead.

Magic, obviously. And ordinarily, I might be impressed by that. If it were even remotely the most magical thing here.

You hear tales of wizard treasures and immediately think of the same thing: some ancient, arcane study overflowing with books and magical tomes, a cauldron bubbling with various alchemical apparatus, reagents scattered everywhere, maybe a skull with a candle on it—wizards always keep skulls, for whatever reason. Freaks.

Compared to that, I think Vishera's hoard would be downright disappointing.

Not for lack of volume, mind you. Everything you'd expect to find was there: staves with weird symbols on them, wands in all manner of suggestive and sinister shapes, rolls upon rolls of scrolls, a table fit with alchemical tools and several potions.

But it lacked the rather haphazard charm you'd expect of a doddering old wizard's study. Everything here was neat and organized. The staves and wands were arranged on racks like spears, the scrolls sat in their own little shelf-niche, the alchemical vials and tubes were all clean and sterile. Orbs, amulets, rings, whatever—they all had their little places. At the center of it all stood a column of smooth, stainless bronze, my distorted reflection staring back at me from it.

In a way, this all unnerved me.

I don't trust magic, but I always understood why a wizard—or sorcerer or whatever they like being called—would hoard. The appeal of owning a lot of shiny things, whether or not they shot fire out of them, was something I easily related to.

But there was something too calculated about this setup. I remembered working with a nasty son of a bitch in Katapesh who specialized in ransoms—namely, the part where he'd hack off a limb to send to the loved ones to encourage them to pay. I remembered his many saws and scalpels and cleavers and how he had obsessively cleaned and neatly arranged them.

Vishera's "workshop," for lack of a better word, reminded me too much of it. Clean hands, dirty deeds.

In all the cleanliness, though, I couldn't help but see the sole point of disorderliness. There, upon a desk next to the alchemical apparatus, I saw sheaves upon sheaves of papers left hastily out in the open. Something she hadn't tidied away yet. Something she had been reading recently.

I flipped through them, studying them. My suspicions were immediately confirmed: her penmanship matched the letters at the centaur camp precisely. She had been behind the attacks, probably behind Gerowan's murder, as well. But for what cause?

I read on to find out.

Experiment 12, Day 33

Results dissatisfactory. Herbs do not have the desired effect of inducing conception. Suspect either faulty recipe— reminder to self: do not bargain with Yhevesh the Black again—or improper application of herbs.

Unfortunate results for subject. She has, regrettably, died during the attempt. Reminder to self: Advise accountant to set aside room in the budget to pay the aggrieved family member. If he refuses, have him removed.

Experiment 14, Day 2

Results EXTREMELY dissatisfactory. Total failure. Potion caused immediate termination of child and near-instantaneous death of mother. Located in First Solace. Good stock. Extremely regrettable. No family.

Mood darkening. The Thing continues to mock me, continues to say that he could easily help me. Reminder to self: practice meditation. Repeat: Do not listen to The Thing. The Thing always lies. It is the nature of The Thing. The Thing does not know. The Thing could not know.

Update on Project Stable

Received report that the centaurs have struck again. Two caravans lost. Total losses: 16 crates of ore (Amalien), 20 crates of silk (Helsen), 12 crates of sundries (Marvalen), 10 crates of weaponry (self). Reminder to self: invest in Helsen silk. Centaurs continuing to take largest toll on his trade.

Irritated. Centaurs continue to strike at caravans, refusing to go for settlements. Seem to be stockpiling instead of pushing their offensive. Other houses continue to refuse to acknowledge they are a threat. Direct centaur leader to press attack or withhold further support.

UPDATE: IMPORTANT

Ancestry of Subject S. just received.

Suspicions confirmed. Compatible genealogy.

Apprehend immediately once Amalien support has been terminated.

Norgorber's nuts.

Sometimes, the gods curse you. Sometimes, they help you. And sometimes they hand you a suckling pig on a golden platter.

Gods damn it. Stelvan suddenly made a lot of eerie sense to me. She was directing the centaurs to both undermine her competitors and convince the people that they were a threat. And the smart gold said that, when she was ready, she'd be the one to see the centaur "threat" quashed so that Yanmass would heed her for whatever she wanted to say next.

And if she was behind the centaur attack, then it stood to reason she knew about Gerowan's murder. Hell, she was probably behind it, if this "terminate Amalien support" business was any indication.

The rest of the letter I didn't understand. Ancestry? Genealogy? Subject S?

A problem for another time. Everything I had here, I could use as leverage to find out the rest. Once I got this in Dalaris's hands, she could get it where it needed to go. I rolled the whole mess up and stuffed it into my belt and was already on my way out the door when I heard it.

"Leaving so soon?"

The voice. I had almost forgotten it. I had *almost* been able to pretend it was just a waking nightmare. But it spoke closely to me now, purred in my ear and reached into my chest.

"Rather rude, isn't it? You didn't even say hello."

You don't stay in this line of work for long by making stupid decisions. And listening to a voice that came out of nowhere and wedged itself into your ears like a knife definitely counted as one.

And yet . . .

I had seen a lot of Vishera's arsenal and more of Vishera's machinations already. But I was about to piss off a woman with a lot of ways to make my life terrible. I couldn't leave without knowing every trick she had, even if one of them was a creepy, disembodied voice. *Especially* if that creepy, disembodied voice was something she intended to spring on me later.

Right.

I turned and walked back into the room, pretending that I was making sense.

"*Ah, very good. Here, dear girl. Toward the back. Behind the bookcase.*"

At the very back of the room, a bookcase full of tomes stood. It didn't take me long to find the hidden switch that made it slide away. It took me even less time to realize what a mistake I had made.

Because the first thing I saw when the bookcase slid away was the eyes: big, black, smoldering things set into a face that I would consider impossibly handsome.

If not for the ebon horns bursting out of his skull.

Batlike wings twitched behind him. Cloven hooves clopped upon the floor as he stepped forward. In the blue light, I could see the perfection of his muscular, naked body. And yet that perfection seemed all the more perverse as his lips spread wide and revealed a smile full of sharpened teeth.

"Ah," the fiend said in a deep, resonant voice, "how nice of you to visit."

17

The Father of Fiends

I breathed.

In and out. Shallow and quick. I breathed.

Because it was damn near the only thing I could remember how to do.

I stood transfixed by him: his beauty, his malice, his everything. The slope of the hollow of his neck, the curve of the fangs in his mouth, the veins of his wings and the burning smolder of his gaze. Everything about him was so horribly perfect, I could only stare. I should have run, should have screamed, should have taken out my blade and started stabbing and hoped for the best. But all I could remember how to do was breathe.

Several minutes passed and I was still breathing.

So I figured that was a pretty good sign.

And that's when I noticed the shackles.

Encircling his slender wrists were clasped iron rings, runes emblazoned across the metal in bright red script. Chains slithered down to the floor, holding him in place within a delicately arranged circle of salt, one magically burning candle arranged at each of the four cardinal directions.

I didn't know much about summoning fiends, but I knew that this particular one wasn't going to be much of a threat.

The fear and awe that had held me suddenly ebbed away. It somehow felt difficult to be afraid of a creature so thoroughly imprisoned.

"You're staring, mortal," he said, his voice resonating in my ears.

"Well, yeah." I coughed, discreetly turning my eyes upward and away from his waist. "You *are* kind of naked."

"Indeed." His grin was broad and sultry. His chains rattled as he gestured at his own form. "And am I not magnificent, mortal? Do you not quiver at the very sight of me?"

"You're quite . . ." My eyes darted downward for a tasteless second before I looked back up. "Uh, yeah. Yeah, very magnificent."

"Do not feel ashamed, mortal." His eyes flared to life, embers suddenly stoked. "Gaze all you like. Look upon me and feel your shame, your will, all your useless emotions slipping away. Look upon me . . ." He hissed, a long pointed tongue sliding out between his teeth. "And *obey*."

I stared back at him for a moment, then shook my head.

"I'd rather not," I said.

The fires in his eyes died out. His very pretty face turned into a very pretty pout.

"Why not?" he asked.

"Don't really feel like it, is all."

"You don't . . ." He shook his head and snarled. "I am *perfection*, a work of art honed to a razor's edge in the forges of the Abyss. Why do I fail to stir lustful obedience in you?"

"I don't know." I shrugged helplessly. "You're not my type, I guess."

He narrowed his eyes upon me. "Woman, I am an incubus, the very incarnation of carnal desire, formed specifically to prey upon mortal lust. I am, factually, *everybody's* type."

"Listen, nobody likes a braggart. Let alone a braggart devil—"

"Demon."

"Demon. Sorry."

He deflated with the force of his sigh, shoulders slumping and wings drooping. His hair fell over his eyes as he shook his head.

"These damnable enchanted shackles drain my powers," he muttered, "make it impossible for me to dominate. Were I not thusly captive, I would make you my unwitting slave before I fed upon your soul."

"I bet you'd be great at it, too, champ." I patted the papers in my belt. "I take it you're The Thing mentioned in these documents?"

"Fennoc." He made a half-hearted bow. "Fennoc the Devourer."

"Of course," I sighed. Fiends always had names like 'the Devourer' or 'the Conqueror' or 'the Thrice-Damned.' No one never met a Fennoc the Forthcoming or Fennoc the Pleasant Conversationalist, did they?

I was about to mention this to him when it suddenly hit me. I took in his horns, his eyes, his jawline, and realized I had seen them before.

"Son of a bitch," I muttered. "You're Visheron's father?"

"Who?"

"Visheron? The fellow who lives upstairs? The guy with the horns and the breast fetish?"

"Ah. The spawn."

Between a mother that locked him up and a father who referred to him as "spawn," I was beginning to see why Visheron had turned out the way he had.

"He's your son," I said.

"'Son' is a term that carries affections I do not have. I did not raise him. I have never spoken to him. I only know he exists because the woman told me. I was simply coerced into creating him. Nothing more."

"Coerced?" I squinted at him.

"Yes. Coerced. Is that surprising?"

"Kind of. I mean, given that you're from Hell—"

"The Abyss."

"Right, the Abyss. Given that, I thought your type were usually the ones to do the coercing."

"Normally, yes. Mortal minds are weak and their bodies are weaker. The time it takes to break both and feast on the soul is little more than the blink of an eye to me. Hence, when we are called from beyond, we answer quite willingly, with intent of seducing and—"

"Yeah, no need for details." I held up my hands. "I can guess what you do."

"Such was what lured me to this world. The idea of a mortal in possession of such wealth and power as the woman was pleasing to my masters. I had every intention of using her as my doorway to further souls."

I glanced at his shackles. "I take it that didn't happen?"

His face drew tight. The heat in his eyes turned to something cold and bitter. "She was ready for me. With circles. With shackles. With trinkets to guard her mind. She laid me low and . . . *used* me."

My eyes widened. I wasn't sure if I was more surprised that a mortal could *do* that or that a fiend would sound so offended at them doing so.

"Her sole interest in me was in creating the spawn," Fennoc hissed. "Once she had grown swollen with him, she locked me away and did not speak to me except to compel answers regarding his powers." His lips curled into a slow smile. "Though I have gathered he is quite the disappointment."

"Well, he's not a great artist," I said.

"The woman was expecting power. She desired a sorcerer, a warrior, something with the strength of the Abyss in its veins. Not an artist."

"And what did she want that for?"

"Is it not obvious, mortal? Even a fool could see that she is ruled by her fears. She is consumed with nightmares of the collapse of her nation, her fortunes, her lineage. She sees enemies everywhere: Qadirans to the south, Galtans to the north, Cheliax and Andoran to the west."

"Cheliax." A nation ruled by fiends in all but name. I had heard the stories. "That's what she wants. She wants to use fiends to make Taldor strong, like they are."

"Would that were true. She sadly lacks faith in our motives." Fennoc chuckled. "She envisions Taldor mighty again, with her brood at its head. But above all else, she requires control. Control she cannot assume over my kind."

"So she wants your power, but not your unpredictability. Seems logical."

"Indeed? I suppose any sufficiently advanced madness must seem indistinguishable from logic. Alas, the poor woman is convinced that if she cannot summon a suitable leader for Taldor, she can breed it."

Breed it.

Words flashed in my mind. Elegantly carved letters on the parchments in my belt.

Experiment. Subject. Child and mother. Died. Regrettable. Total failure. Inducing. Conception.

I wished I had words foul enough to say what was going through my head at that moment. As it was, I could only stand there with my mouth open. The words that came, eventually, were slow and weighed with horror.

"Her son is the failure," I whispered. "But she didn't kill him. She wants to breed him." I looked at Fennoc. "But with what?"

He smiled broadly. "My powers are dampened, but even now, I can hear your thoughts, mortal. You are so deliciously close to figuring it out. I can hardly contain myself."

I growled, started to curse. And then two more words flashed in my skull.

Subject S.

S.

Sidara.

Amalien support. Genealogy. Ancestry. Celestials. Angels. Pinnacles of control.

Dalaris.

"Son of a bitch," I said. And when simply saying felt insufficient, I screamed. "*SON OF A BITCH!*"

"Aha. You've found it, have you? Isn't it so delightfully depraved?"

"She's going to use Dalaris. *Gods!* That's why she had Gerowan murdered. She didn't want the Amalien fortunes, she wanted to make sure no one would miss Dalaris when she was gone. And she used the centaurs to cover it up! That . . . that . . . evil . . . wretched . . ."

"I assure you, mortal, that all the curses you are thinking remain insufficient for your outrage." Fennoc drew himself up, gestured to his chains. "And I daresay that the only thing that would satisfy you is setting me free."

I snapped from my reverie of fury to look at him curiously. "What?"

"Think of it," he whispered. "All the wickedness she has done pales in comparison to what she will yet do. You need only set me free to make sure that does not come to pass. Unlock my shackles. Disrupt the circle. In the span of two breaths, I can be at her throat and drag her back to the Abyss with me."

His voice slithered into my ears, settled in my belly on cold, scaly coils. Every word came with the flicker of forked tongue and the glimmer of dark eyes.

"Your friend will be safe," he said. "And you could be the one to save her. You could be the one to go to her, to hold her in your arms, to tell her that all will be well."

Images filled my head, blossomed like flowers. I could see Dalaris now, that weak and helpless girl, so desperate that she reached out to a scoundrel like me for help. I could smell her tears, hear her wails, feel my lips whisper the words that would tell her it would all be fine.

"You will be her hero," Fennoc purred. "You will have done something great and beautiful with your life. All the sorrow and suffering you have taken to get here will all be worth it, if you can but save someone else. No one need ever die because of you again. Not like Sem."

Sem.

Sem didn't raise a fool.

I whirled on Fennoc, my blade held up like I earnestly believed it could do a damn thing to him.

"Stay *out* of my head," I snarled. "And don't even think I'm dumb enough to let you out. I know enough about demons to know they don't keep their promises."

"Oh?" Fennoc looked bemused in that bullshit can't-blame-me-for-trying way.

"You're creatures of wicked whimsies, unable to control your basest desires, unable to resist inflicting pain."

"That's not quite true," he countered. "We can be patient. For example, we can keep someone talking long enough for the mechanical guardian of this chamber to activate its protocol and sneak up behind them."

I squinted. "Huh?"

My ears pricked.

Metal on stone. Metal on metal. Blade drawing. Wind splitting.

Mind hesitating. Body acting.

I leapt forward.

Too quick to be dead, too slow to be bloodless. Something sharp bit into my back, split the leather and carved a red line in my flesh. I tumbled forward, narrowly stopped myself from disrupting the circle around Fennoc. I whirled, Whisper in my hand as I looked upon my attacker.

If you ever happen to find yourself in a madwoman's forbidden sanctum brimming with magical paraphernalia, here's a tip: never assume the nondescript column is *just* a column.

It had been, of course, when I arrived here. I still recognized my reflection in the polish of its stainless bronze, save that I looked a degree more terrified now. But what stood before me now, I had no words for.

Its body was rail thin, perched upon two spindly legs ending in sharp claws. Long, thin arms jointed in three places extended outward. The remainder of it looked like the column, but only for a second longer. In another moment, it seemed to . . . unfold itself. What remained of the column extended outward, becoming another pair of long arms. And topping it was a bronze mask carved in an expressionless face of a genderless creature, its hollow eyes fixed on me.

"*Subject detected,*" it said in a hollow, tinny voice. "*Do not attempt to resist. It will all be over soon.*"

It turned all four of its arms toward me and I saw the wicked instruments they ended in: a syringe; a writhing probe; a small, whirring saw; and a long scalpel wet with my blood.

"The hell is that thing?" I screamed.

"A golem. Custom-made." Fennoc hummed. "It activates around this time. She likes its timeliness."

I glared over my shoulder. "Why didn't you say something earlier?"

Fennoc shrugged. "It's funnier this way."

I had a wittier retort to that than the scream that escaped my mouth, but it's hard to think when you're dodging. The golem lashed out suddenly, metal joints squeaking, saw blade whirring. I darted beneath the blow, scrambled away as its syringe-arm thrust at me and bit into the stone floor.

"*Do not scream. Do not cry.*" Its voice echoed off of the hollows of its mask as it turned its empty eyes upon me. "*This is all for the best, you will see.*"

I had to get out of Fennoc's cell. Had to get more room to maneuver. Of course, the only place with more room was filled with horrible magic items that could possibly explode if disturbed by a violent melee, but—

The scalpel-arm lanced out as I scrambled to my feet, bit into my bicep and drew a scream.

Focus, Shy. Focus.

I whirled, Whisper in hand, to face the machine. The clock-work creature turned—or at least, half of it turned. Its torso rotated with a grating clicking sound to face me and, with its legs still facing the opposite way, it began to approach me by walking backward.

Not that this thing was all that pretty to look at to begin with, but it was just *freaky* now.

It was still a machine, I reminded myself as it advanced methodically toward me. It was put together, it could be taken apart. It was a matter of finding the right spot to hit.

I narrowed my eyes as it moved closer and drew my blade back. Its spindly arms shuddered with each step it took, its joints continuing to squeak and click as its empty gaze settled upon me. I tensed, held my breath. It raised its saw-arm, ready to strike.

It lunged. I leapt back, snapping my arm forward in one fluid movement. Whisper flew from my hand, tumbled through the air, and bit. There was a sound of metal clanging. The golem jerked back as Whisper lodged right in the left eye of its metal face.

For a moment, it stood there, frozen with a foot of steel stuck in its face.

And then in another moment, it clicked, whirred, and kept right on coming.

Really, I wasn't sure what I expected to happen.

Screw it. Plan B, then.

I glanced to my right. Alchemical apparatus: tubes, potions, vials. I grabbed the greenest one—green is always useful, right?—and hurled it at the clockwork monster. It shattered against its carapace, spilling green slime all over the metal. I grinned broadly, waiting for the inevitable hissing clouds as the acid ate away at the armor.

But none came. The slime just dribbled down the creature's chest and pooled on the floor.

What kind of lunatic bottles regular, nonacidic slime?

No time to wonder. I continued grabbing bottles, hurling bottles, shattering bottles. Black oil, yellow ooze, red ichor; it looked like someone had vomited a rainbow on the clockwork, but it was still coming.

"I know you are afraid, but it is all for the better. You will make Taldor strong. Do not cry."

It lunged at me, swinging its saw-arm in a broad arc. I only narrowly stepped out of the way, darting toward the nearby rack of staves. Its blade stopped a mere inch away from the rack, the clockwork suddenly freezing.

Interesting. The damn thing must have orders not to disturb anything in the sanctum.

In which case, this next bit was probably going to piss it off.

If it were capable of being pissed off, anyway.

I whirled to the rack of staves, looked for the most twisted, ugliest one—those are the most powerful ones, right? Wizards love twisted stuff—and held it out before me like a lance aimed at the clockwork.

"Now!" I screamed.

The staff, to my inexplicable surprise, did absolutely nothing.

"Go!" I shook it at the golem.

It simply lay there in my hands, not doing anything more impressive than your average stick.

"Come on, asshole! Do something!"

Apparently, whatever the magic words were to this thing, those weren't it.

The golem sprang forward, syringe-arm thrusting out to impale me. I leapt aside, tumbled low as its arm swept over my head, narrowly missing me. Whatever magic bullshit was working this thing, it wasn't stupid. It was learning my moves, even as my moves were slowing down, thanks to the blood weeping out my back and the soreness racking my body.

I crawled backward, holding the staff out defensively before me.

"It doesn't work like that, woman," Fennoc called out from inside his cell. "The staff's spell requires contact. A touch."

He'd been around here long enough. He would know, wouldn't he?

I crawled to my feet as the golem turned on me. Muscles were aching. The wound in my back was still bleeding. I was losing breath quickly. This thing was a machine, reliable and sturdy—the longer the fight went on, the better odds it had.

Had to even them.

Had to make it count.

I took the staff in both hands, gripped it like a club. The spell needed contact? I was going to give it all the contact it could handle.

I rushed toward the golem. It whirred, as if in surprise, and swung at me. I darted to the left, grunted, and swung at its helm with all my might. It connected solidly. I heard a snapping sound.

And in the brief instant between the staff snapping in two and the bright burst of light that followed, I suddenly realized that most people don't take advice from demons for a reason.

Light filled the room. A wave of concussive force erupted, knocking me off of my feet and sending me flying backward, where I struck the wall and dribbled down to the floor like a wine stain. There, breathless and dazed, I lingered.

Moments passed as I tried to find my breath. More moments passed as I tried to find my feet. I don't know how long passed before I was finally able to stand up mostly straight and look through swimming vision.

But in all that time, I didn't get stabbed. That had to be a good sign, right?

I looked for any sign of my opponent and found several. In pieces. All over the room.

Its syringe-arm was at the threshold of Fennoc's cell. Its arms and torso were scattered across the floor. Its legs wobbled unsteadily before me before collapsing. Its empty head lay at my feet, clicking and whirring, along with the assortment of magical detritus inside that had been scattered across the room like entrails.

Had all those potions I had hurled at the thing somehow weakened it? Or had it just gotten the worst of the blast, and I'd been lucky?

I didn't care. At that moment, the fact that I was alive—aching, bruised, bleeding and about to collapse, but still—was more than enough to make me happy.

Until I heard another ticking sound. Until I heard another set of metal boots setting down upon the stone floor. Until I wondered if there were more than one of those things here.

I almost didn't want to look up. And when I did, the noise I made was half groan, half scream. Another column nearby, tucked away in a corner I hadn't noticed, was unfolding itself. Its saw-arm came to life with a screeching song. Its hollow voice spoke.

"*Do not be afraid. This will be painless.*"

"No," I whispered. And I meant it.

I couldn't take another. The last one had almost killed me. I searched for anything that wasn't either broken, shattered, or likely to kill me. And found nothing but Whisper on the floor nearby. I grabbed him up, but he felt weighty in my hands, as though he already knew he was useless.

"She keeps a command scroll," Fennoc said from his cell. "In case they go rogue. There, on her shelves. Second from the top, at the very end."

I was at the shelf and rifling through it, my fingers brushing against the scroll, when I realized that he was probably lying again.

This was likely the most fun he'd had in ages, watching me stumble about blindly, using magic that would kill me. That scroll would likely set me on fire or turn me into a newt or . . . or . . . some other magic crap.

I chose the one next to it—no telling if this would be any better, but I'd at least not give Fennoc the satisfaction of deceiving me.

The floor trembled with the metallic groaning of armor as the golem advanced, saw-arm raised high and screeching.

I tore the scroll open, glanced over it—the magic words were meaningless to me, but at least they were written in Taldane. Lucky break. No telling what it would do, but I had to try. I started reciting the words phonetically, straining to be heard over the squeal of metal as the golem advanced toward me. From the cell behind me, I could hear Fennoc.

"What? What are you doing? That's the wrong one, you—"

I didn't hear him. I ignored his voice, forced mine louder as I continued to read. The golem rushed toward me, blade outstretched, so close I could see the reflection of my lips in its bronze just as I finished the last word.

Bright light.

Breath left me.

Feet left the ground.

I felt airy, insubstantial, like I was being lifted up and away.

Wrong scroll, then.

Ah, well. Today was just full of lessons, wasn't it?

That was my last thought as the light grew brighter, blinding, engulfing me until everything around me simply disappeared. And a moment later, so did I.

18

Safehouse

I've mentioned I hate magic before, right?

I'm starting to think you might not realize just how much I hate it. I could write essays on how much I hate magic. I could paint portraits depicting, artistically, my loathing for magic. Men would fall to their knees and forsake gods upon seeing these portraits. Women would weep.

I came out of the spell—teleportation or some crap like that—and emerged into a dark room. My internal organs seemed to arrive just a hair after the rest of me did. That would explain, anyway, why I collapsed on the ground and expelled everything I had eaten onto the tiles.

Tiles. Cold. Clean-smelling. I knew that, if nothing else. Wherever I was, it was completely pitch black. And though I had probably tipped off whatever else might be here with me by the spatter of my lunch on the floor, I didn't dare call out.

On your feet. Find a wall. Get your back covered.

Old instincts die hard, and the instincts you get in a Katapeshi back alley don't come much older. I leapt to my feet and scrambled backward, one hand out to feel for what I might be coming up against, the other hand on my knife. I found cold brick before anything else and quickly pressed myself up against the wall.

A natural human reaction, to panic in the dark, which is why so many things that want to eat us like to lurk in lightless depths. Fear is good, keeps you alive. Panic just makes you tastier. Do this work long enough, you start to know that fighting blind is like any other trick: do it enough times, you get a routine.

Step one: get your back to a wall. Check.

Step two: listen. I slowed my breathing, listened past the thumping of my heart, extended my ears. Thirty seconds is the minimum; anything that doesn't need to breathe for that long is in there with you, you've got bigger problems.

Step three: find out what you're working with. I reached overhead, extended my arm all the way before I felt the ceiling. Six and a quarter feet tall, more or less. I pressed my arm against the wall, edged to the right and felt a corner after about two paces. Small rooms, small comforts. Anything in here with me, I'd have heard it by now. But who was to say this wasn't a cell or a trap or some other magic bullshit?

Step four: pray. But that's usually assuming steps one through three didn't go well. Since I didn't think Norgorber would be listening, even if he was the kind of god to grant wishes, I didn't bother.

I continued edging along the wall, my hand outstretched, until I felt it brush against something round and cold. My fingers lingered a hair too long and the room was immediately filled with a bright, blinding light.

Since I didn't get incinerated, disintegrated, or turned into a swan or some other magical crap, I didn't mind shielding my eyes while they readjusted to the light cast by a globe, like what I had seen beneath Vishera's house. When they did, I saw I wasn't in a cell.

And I wasn't alone.

On the floor in front of me was the top half of the golem, its various limbs twitching with a slow, mechanical mindlessness. The rest of it—its legs and torso—were somewhere else. It must have reacted to the magic, got part of itself torn through while the rest was left behind in Vishera's laboratory.

And *that's* why I hated magic. It only ever works out by chance. You stick someone with a knife, it does what you think it'd do. You use magic garbage on someone, who knows what'll happen?

Still, at least it worked out in my favor this time. I took a breath and began to look around the cell. No, not a cell . . .

Really, I don't know what you'd call it. Four walls, a ceiling, a door. Same size as a cell, but none of the fun stuff: no shackles, no benches, no pile of filth in the corner or bed of straw. Aside from my puddle of vomit, the room was scrubbed clean from top to bottom, barely any dust on the floors, the walls . . .

Or the crates stacked against them.

Not many, only four, and not very big. It took only a little knife-work to pry open one of them. Inside, I found jars of preserved food, dried peaches, strips of salted meat that I didn't think anyone would mind me helping myself to. The crate beneath that held canteens of water and a few bottles of wine, as well. Beneath that: durable, simple traveling clothes. And under that, short blades and other concealable weapons.

Someone, apparently, was ready for a long trip.

The last organ to resettle itself inside me was my brain. The realization hit me hard. This must be an escape route. Whatever her paranoid fantasies of Qadirans invading or Cheliax breaking into her house, Vishera wanted to make sure she had a way out. That scroll I used must teleport to a fixed location, a place she could make her escape from.

But where? Another house across the street? Another city in Taldor? Or an entirely different nation? Was I in a safehouse she had constructed elsewhere, dozens of her thugs waiting behind the door to gut me once I came out? Was I even on the same *plane?*

As much as these thoughts terrified me, they weren't what made a cold pang of dread settle in my stomach.

How far away, I wondered, was Dalaris?

It wouldn't be long before Vishera realized she'd been infiltrated. It'd take her even less time to extract whatever information she needed out of Fennoc. And once she learned her secret was blown, she'd move her timetable up and make her move on Dalaris.

Which meant I didn't have much time to reach her.

Which meant I'd better stop fretting and see where the hell this gods-damned door behind me led.

A turned wheel. A groan of metal. The door swung open into darkness that was free of goons, elementals, demons, or whatever the hell might have been waiting to kill me.

Small comforts.

I found the wall in the dark, felt my way out. I could feel the ground slope up beneath me. Cold brick turned to damp, sodden earth. As the path shifted ever upward, something ahead of me shimmered, as though the darkness were water that someone had thrown a stone out of.

Two more steps and I emerged out of darkness and into night. Which, while still darkness, was a darkness I remembered. A vast, grassy plain stretched out before me. Behind me stood the hole I had just emerged out of. After a breath, it shimmered again and the image of more grass grew over it.

More gods-damned magic.

The urge to vomit at this realization was suppressed by the urge to get back to Yanmass and get Dalaris out of danger before Vishera could act.

Fortunately, I could see Yanmass from where I was. Unfortunately, it was nothing more than a collection of pinpricks of light in the distance. Easily a day's trip on foot. And that was a day I didn't have.

But before I could feel the stress of that realization hit me, a brighter light caught my eye. I glanced down the hill I was standing on, across the plains to the collection of lights on the road nearby.

And my heart quickened at the thought that I might have just had one of my first lucky breaks.

I recognized these lights. First Solace, the caravan-rest, stood not a mile away from here. Which meant I could get a horse there and be back in Yanmass in a few hours.

I squinted as the lights within the little village grew brighter. Funny, I didn't remember there being quite so many lights there last time.

Nor did I remember it being quite so on fire.

And I definitely didn't remember it being surrounded by a horde of centaurs, running rings around and firing flaming arrows into it.

Some folk might have screamed at this realization. If I hadn't thought it would mean vomiting again, I might have as well. But as it was, I merely sighed and started down the hill.

After all, I had the feeling that I would need to save my screams for later. There was bound to be a lot of call for it tonight.

19

The Sound of Thunder

So I bet you, like most sane folk, would wonder at the logic of trying to sneak into a besieged camp when you need to be elsewhere.

After all, given that I only barely made it through the rings of centaur warriors running around First Solace, the chances of me making it out on a horse were slim to none.

You'd probably point out, like most sane folk would, that I'd need one hell of a miracle to pull that off. And you'd also probably point out that Norgorber isn't exactly the sort of god that gives out miracles.

To which I would probably call you a bit of an asshole, and then point out that even a slim chance of a miracle was better than the day's journey back to Yanmass that would surely see Dalaris dead.

I *would* do that, anyway, if I weren't running screaming across a field.

Arrows were flying over my head: fiery volleys shot from the marauding centaurs behind me, returned shots fired from defenders behind the low walls ahead of me. I didn't bother trying to dodge them—after all, it's not like either of them were actually aiming for me. But that stopped being a comfort around the third time one just barely grazed my ear. Now, I ran with my legs blood-less beneath me, everything in me in my lungs, trying to force breath through me as I rushed for the relative safety of First Solace.

"Incoming!" I could hear one of the defenders cry out as I neared the wall. "Bring it down!"

"No, you idiot!" someone else barked back. "Shoot the things with *four* legs!"

Among this chatter, I didn't hear anything like "hold your fire" or even "aim away from the girl on the field." But then, I suppose I wouldn't have, either. At the very least, they didn't shoot me or stop me from reaching the wall and vaulting over it. Not that a Katapeshi girl in black leather out of nowhere wasn't suspicious, but I imagined they had more important things on their minds.

Such as everything being on fire.

My legs gave out, sent me collapsing against the wall. As my lungs strained for breath and my body worked blood back into the rest of itself, I got a good look at just what kind of a world of shit we were in.

The warehouses were currently up in flames. Caravan guards were rushing to them with buckets of water from the nearby well, coaxed by the shrieking terror of whatever merchants happened to be stranded here. The soldiers on the walls were a hodgepodge of other merchant guards, armed with bows, crossbows, and whatever else that shot as they clumsily returned fire over the walls.

But I could tell from their errant firing that they weren't doing much more than shooting anything that moved. Just as I could tell that they wouldn't be doing much good against an enemy as mobile as the centaurs. I didn't even *need* to see the collection of dead and wounded guards lying at the center of the caravan village.

Of course, since I *did* see them, I had a keen appreciation for just how badly this was going.

I reached out to whoever was on my left—a young guard with a dented helmet and a crossbow he was currently cranking back—and slapped his leg.

"Hey. *Hey!*" I barked, drawing his attention. "Who's in charge here?"

"The merchants, idiot," the guard said. "They better pay extra for this crap."

"No, who's in charge of the defense?"

"How should I know? I didn't sign on for a defense."

I slapped my own face. "Norgorber's nuts. Just tell me who started shooting back first."

The guard grunted, pointed down the line. I caught glimpse of a plumed helmet, and beneath it, a grizzled-looking face. He barked an occasional order to the two or three guards around him, which went ignored by the others.

A veteran, then.

Good enough.

I crept low around the wall, reached him in short order. "How long ago did they strike?" I asked.

He didn't bother to look back at me. He barely even bothered to growl. "Half an hour. Came out of the gods-damned night. Tore apart a wagon I just sent out and circled the town."

"Any idea how many?"

"Too many." Finally, he bothered to look around. "Who the hell are you?"

"Yes, asshole. *That's* the important question right now." I spat on the ground. "Which way did they come from?"

"East," he said. "Now either pick up a bow or start praying. Once we run out of arrows, we're gonna need gods."

Not the most helpful individual.

But I didn't need him to be. I edged my way to the eastern wall, peered out over its ledge. I saw it immediately: a denser cluster of centaurs here, running in a smaller circle. They were protecting something. And as I peered past them, to a nearby hill bathed by moonlight, I could guess what.

I reached down to check that my knife was still with me. Then I took a deep breath and started heading toward First Solace's gate.

You might, like most sane folk, wonder what I was planning on doing. And like most sane folk, if I told you, you probably would have called me insane. And I would have told you that I didn't have the time to debate sanity when Dalaris's life was at stake. I would have told you that I wasn't insane.

I would have, anyway, if I didn't kind of agree with you already.

You ask a warrior, they'll tell you that every one of their weapons tells a different story. You ask a wizard, they'll say that every spell is its own song with its own sorrow.

But if you ask someone in my line of work if sneaking ever gets complicated, they'll tell you what I'd tell you.

Same shit, different shadow.

Head down. Knife close. Short, quick, decisive movements. I slipped across the battlefield just as I slipped through Vishera's house, just as I slipped through the alleys of Katapesh.

I kept low to the ground, picked my way between fallen trees, high scrub grass, bramble patches—any terrain that looked too rough for centaurs to bother trampling. I had just crept behind a fallen log when I heard the sound of thunder and felt the earth shaking under me.

I froze, forced my breath shallow. There was an animal urge in me to run, but I forced it down; I was in defensible terrain, I told myself. I was safe.

And I was really close to believing it until I felt the log shudder and four hooves went flying over me.

I was too breathless to scream out. Fortunate for me. The centaur that leapt over the log had enough air to clear my head and land in front of me. He didn't bother looking back, merely let out a whooping cry as he drew his bow and shot another flaming arrow toward First Solace.

He was followed by a dozen more of his shirtless, hairy kin—
who, thankfully, opted to go around my log rather than over it.
They ran in a long circle, one of three, firing haphazardly into the
caravan-rest.

From here, I could see their run curving inward. With each
circle they ran around the camp, they drew a little closer to First
Solace. I could see the other centaur groups doing likewise, inching
closer and closer to the caravan-rest. I supposed once they got
within range, they'd make use of those big spears strapped to their
backs.

Clever tactic, I had to admit. Whittle down the human
defenders bit by bit before closing in for the kill, all the while being
harder to hit than if they simply charged straight at the camp.

I wondered when Halamox came up with this strategy.

I'd have to remember to ask him, if he didn't cut my head off.

Once the centaurs had cleared me by another mile, I got up
and started moving again. From log to scrub grass to stone, I
picked my way across the field toward the nearby hill. The moon
shone brightly, revealing a hulking, four-legged figure atop its
crest, watching the carnage below.

Like a proper general. Hoofed bastard probably thought he
was one, too.

I circled around to the far side of the hill, came up quietly
behind him. It had been a few days, but Halamox looked no less
intimidating. His hair was groomed and pulled back, his armor
polished and his greatsword gleaming brightly in the moonlight.

Halamox had wasted no time in indulging his fantasies of
being the leader of a great liberating army. He had a nearby table
full of maps, charts, strategies—all the hallmarks of a war-weary
general, right down to the tastefully placed mug of ale.

Admittedly, I might have thought this was kind of cute if he
weren't, you know, killing a lot of people.

I hid beneath the ridge of the hill, peering over as I saw him conversing with another centaur—this one armored and groomed, like him. They exchanged a few words before the other one saluted and galloped off, likely to deliver whatever orders Halamox had just given him.

I worked quickly, slipping up onto the hill and creeping toward his table. I seized his mug and gave it just a bit of a spill, enough to put a few drops on the table. By the time he turned around, I was already slipping back beneath the hill and circling around. I kept an eye on him as he drank deeply from his mug and smiled broadly. Then I came up behind him, cleared my throat noisily.

"Nice night for a raid, isn't it?"

I tensed, ready to leap away should he whirl on me with that big sword of his. But to my surprise, he merely glanced up at me with weary resignation, as though I were more annoyance than anything else.

Considering what I had done to his camp, I felt a little insulted.

"Madame Nimm," he muttered. "Still alive, I see."

"You must have known I would be when you found Kjoda's corpse cooling in the forest." I shot him a rather daring wink. "You're welcome for that, by the way."

He sneered, letting his hand slide to the hilt of his sword. "Kjoda was a kinsman to me."

"Save the drama for your victory speech," I said, waving him off. "You and I both know that Kjoda was a rival preventing you from assuming control of the tribal centaurs." I glanced over my shoulder at the raid as the lines drew nearer to First Solace. "Looks like you're enjoying the fruits of my labors."

"Kjoda was a powerful warrior and you cut him down like a dog." There was a distinct lack of accusation in Halamox's voice— if I wasn't quite so tired, I'd have said it sounded like a compliment. "Still, I cannot deny your contribution."

He trotted past me, to the edge of the hill, and gestured out over the carnage below.

"It's only fair that you see the future you helped carve." He raised his arms high, as though the flames below were a work of art he was proud of. "This is our first step. The tribes need evidence of my leadership, of the victories I can give them. This is the second caravan-rest we've hit. A few more and Yanmass will be starving and weak. With the centaurs I attract from these victories, we will be in a position to burn the city to the ground."

"Uh-huh." I folded my arms, shot him a glance. "And you think Taldor won't respond in force?"

He smiled at me. "They would have to catch us first. We will burn, take what we need, and move on. Over and over, striking where they are weak—and there are many weaknesses in Taldor. Sooner or later, Oppara's senate will give us what we want. We shall have land of our own to settle, thanks to you." He sniffed. "Perhaps I'll name a village after you." Then he waved a hand and went back to his table. "Or perhaps I'll just do you the favor of not skewering you where you stand. I can't say my warriors will be as forgiving." He plucked up his mug and took a deep drink. "So I suggest you be on your way."

"Well, hell, since you're in such a generous mood, maybe you want to do me another favor?" I gestured over to First Solace. "Call off the raid."

He chuckled. "I like you, two-legs. You're funny."

"I'm not joking," I said. "I need a horse to get to Yanmass and I can't get there unless you pull back." I held up my hands. "And I'm not going to say I don't have an offer, either. Do right by me, I'll do right by you."

"I stand at the precipice of destiny," Halamox said. "A hundred warriors will soon be thousands, and I will stand at their fore as their king." He smirked as he brought his mug to his lips. "What could you possibly offer me?"

I smiled back as he took a long, deep drink, and spoke softly. "The antidote."

His eyes went wide—good sign. He looked at his mug, then back to his table, and saw it: the spill, the splash of ale on the table. I knew the look in his eyes. Every man who fancied himself powerful had the same look: darting and fervent, piecing together paranoia as they realized how many enemies they had.

That's when I knew he believed me.

And why wouldn't he? The creeping sneak thief that had set fire to his camp? That had cut down his rival in cold blood? Why wouldn't she be able to poison him?

It didn't matter that I hadn't, of course—I certainly wasn't going to tell him. I just needed him scared and uncertain.

"You vile little—" Whatever he was going to call me was buried under the sound of his sword being torn free from its sheath as he stepped toward me. "Give it to me. Give it to me or I will *cut you*—"

"Go nuts." I held my arms open wide, gestured to my middle. "Run me through. Cut my head off. Whatever. Enjoy the next two days before the norgroot coursing through your veins finally kills you." I winked at him. "The nobles of Yanmass requested norgroot specifically. They wanted you to suffer."

Halamox's mouth hung open for a moment before he roared and swung his sword at me. A frantic, clumsy blow—I sidestepped it easily.

"*Lying!*" he roared, whirling on me. I slid beneath the arc of his blade as he cleaved empty air. "You're *lying!*"

"Yeah, sure. I'm lying."

I danced out of reach of his blade. I fought to keep a grin off my face as I saw the weariness in his. He was weighing everything now—was that ache in his arm just a cramp or part of the poison? Was the headache he had just from staying up too late?

The ugliest part of what people like me do isn't the knives in the back or the poisons in drinks. It's the picking locks, the springing traps, the pulling levers that make the gears grind. Because it's not long before you start seeing the whole world like that. Governments, businesses, people: they're all just machines. Twist them the right way, they'll do what you want.

Just like Halamox was doing when he turned that big, panicked face to me.

"Pretend I'm lying," I said. "Comfort yourself with that knowledge. Cling to it as you die over the next two days." I let my grin seep through, ugly and dark. "Tell it to yourself when your ghost watches your tribes crumble and the remnants of your great centaur 'nation' get mopped up by a handful of adventurers looking to get paid from the rich turds in Yanmass. I'll be there, laughing from Hell."

His sword fell, along with his face. They both suddenly seemed too heavy for him. His steel bit into the earth, hung limp from two big, weak hands. And his mouth hung open, eyes big and pale enough to see a future where all his work was for nothing.

Like I said, twist them the right way . . .

"Alternately," I said, "we could make a trade."

. . . and they'll do what you want.

He regained at least a little of the composure he had, forcing his mouth closed and raising his head high. He thrust his sword into the earth, folded his arms over his massive chest, and glowered at me.

"I don't care if you burn down First Solace or all of Yanmass," I said. "You just chose a night to do it that was personally inconvenient to me. Call off your horses. Let me hitch a ride to Yanmass. If I reach it before midnight, I'll have the antidote sent to this hill."

"Midnight?" He gawped. "That's only two hours from now."

I shrugged. "Guess you better act fast, then."

He stalked toward me. I stood my ground. He glared down at me. I looked back up, impassive. However civilized he claimed to be, he was still part animal. And he was trying to use that animal part of him to trigger an animal panic in me.

And to be fair, it almost worked. I could see all the ways I could die: those massive hands that could strangle me effortlessly, those giant hooves that could stomp me into the earth, that huge sword that could hack me in two. My body screamed at me to run, to cower, to betray my lie and give it all up.

But there were lots of things scarier than animals. I was about to see a few of them that night, I was certain.

And so I stood my ground, met his eyes, and sniffed.

"A horse will never get you there fast enough," he muttered. "I'll take you. And you'll give me the antidote personally."

I shrugged. As compromises went, I'd heard of worse. I was certain I could think of some bullcrap to give him before we got to Yanmass.

He stalked to the edge of the hill, trotted down it to go reach his warriors. I glanced over at First Solace and frowned. There were more bodies, more fires, more carnage in the caravan-rest than when I had come out here. Part of me wondered if, had I acted a little faster, been a little cleverer, some good people might still be alive now.

But sorrow's a heady liquor. Drink too deep of all the good you could have done, you wind up dead.

At the moment, I had only enough worry in me for one woman. And as I looked to Yanmass in the distance, I could only hope that Halamox was as fast as he said he was.

20

Skulkers

When I was young—too young to be where I was—I once saw a dead body lying in the alley next to the alley I called home. Old woman, no visible wounds, might have been mugged, might have just been unlucky.

I was fresh, then. Never held a blade, never had a dose of pesh, never had a sip of wine. Death was still something scary, something bad that happened to good people. I remember I got scared, started to cry, started to panic.

And Sem had taken me by the shoulders and said: *"Cry over every corpse, you'll run out of tears. Don't worry about why she's dead, worry about whether or not what killed her is still here."*

Sem wasn't a sage. But there was wisdom in those words.

In this business, foresight's good, but hindsight will get you killed. The people you've burned, the lies you've spun; look over your shoulder too much, you'll never see what's ahead of you.

That thought always brought me comfort.

Not a lot, but enough.

Enough comfort to leave First Solace and its many dead behind. Enough comfort to leave the centaurs running back to the woods, confused and angry. Enough comfort to have plucked a bottle of whiskey from First Solace on our way back and given it to Halamox upon our arrival, claiming it to be a cure.

Sure, there would be more dead. Sure, the centaurs would come back. Sure, Halamox might eventually figure out he'd been deceived. But those were things I'd put behind me.

Ahead of me were the streets of Yanmass, dark and slick and disappearing beneath my feet as I rushed down them. Ahead of me, the lights of House Sidara burned in the windows, tiny and soft fireflies in the distant darkness.

There was something about those lights, so unlike the cold and distant brightness of the bigger manors' lampposts and massive windows. House Sidara's distant lamps looked gentler, softer, like the glow from hearths in the windows of cozy homes I used to peer into on the colder nights in Katapesh.

Some nights, huddled under an awning in a dark alley, I'd dream about running into one of those homes. And for a minute there, in the darkness of Yanmass, I could almost pretend that was just what I was doing: running headlong toward a home that would welcome me.

But as dangerous as hindsight is, dreams are worse. Dreams are an excuse not to look at reality. And as nice as it would have been to pretend that I'd go running into that warm home and its soft light and be welcomed, my reality was something darker, colder, and armed with big sharp blades.

I saw them as I neared the yard: men and women in dark clothing, their swords painted black as they prowled the unkempt lawn of House Sidara. I slowed my stride, forced my breathing slower, ducked low as I crept up to its fences and hid behind a shrubbery. But even as my breathing slowed, my thoughts raced.

Too late. Too gods-damned late.

Stelvan's thugs. They had to be. She had found out. She had discovered my presence. She knew everything. She was already out for Dalaris. She probably already had Dalaris.

I was too late. I wasn't fast enough. I wasn't smart enough. All those people dead in First Solace, all for nothing, all because I—

Easy.

I could almost hear Sem's voice in my head.

Breathe.

The old words that had seen me through those cold nights in Katapesh.

Look.

Hindsight was useless. Whatever I had failed to do, pointless to dwell on. What lay ahead of me, that was what I had to focus on.

I peered around the shrubbery, forced my mind quiet and my breath slow.

I counted three of them: two men, one woman, all wrapped in black cloth and holding short blades in their hands. They crept low to the ground, eyes open as they scanned the walls of House Sidara, stopping to scrutinize bushes and dry patches of lawn.

They were still searching, then. If they had found Dalaris, they'd already be gone.

Still time, I told myself, letting out a long breath. *There's still time.*

How much time, I didn't know. But it couldn't be much.

Which meant this was going to be ugly.

My knife slid into my palm. I hopped the fence, crouched low behind a shrubbery and watched the three of them creeping across the lawn.

Their blades looked sharp enough for dirty work, but their movements—the overexaggerated hunch, the tiptoeing creep, the slow pace—were the marks of amateurs. These were people who had an idea of what they thought stealthy business *looked* like, but had never seen a true professional work.

Some lessons you learn the hard way.

I watched them until one of them slipped farther away from the others, rounding a corner. I cast a quick glance to make sure the other two weren't looking before I slipped away from the bush. I darted quickly to the next hedge, then one more before he was in my sights.

A short burst of quick movement. A hand clapped over his mouth. A swift jab in the side of his neck. His body fell, he twitched briefly, his eyes glassed over. And the last thing he saw was his blood leaking out onto the lawn.

That's how a professional does it.

Not quite as glamorous as black-painted blades and creeping around at night, but it gets the job done.

I turned back, slipping back to the shrubberies. I caught a glimpse of one of them searching a nearby wall, maybe for a secret passage he thought was there. The last one, the woman, was nearby inspecting another bush. They must have been at this for a while if they were searching the gods-damned foliage.

Almost seemed a shame to kill people whose last task on this dark earth was to look real hard at a plant.

But I'd live with it.

Another short sprint and I was behind him. I wrapped my arm around his throat, pulled him close. He had just enough time to let out a gasp before I jammed my blade into his side, singing out an ugly poem in three short, bloody stanzas.

I released him, slipped back into the bushes. He let out a long, agonized groan as he fell to the ground, clutching the wound in his side.

He'd bleed out in another few minutes. Sloppy work. Hell of a way to go. Not something I was fond of doing in the first place, but like I said, I had to get ugly.

His groan drew his companion. She came running to see what was wrong and, bless her heart, she immediately let out a cry for her fallen friend and ran to his side. With his last moments of life, he reached up a shaking finger and pointed over her shoulder. She whirled around, eyes wide in shock.

I like to think she didn't even see me when I thrust my knife up into her chin. I like to think that everything just went dark and she fell down, lifeless, atop her friend, who soon followed her into limp, bloodless slumber.

But I couldn't afford to wonder if she had.

I slipped up to the wall, peered up and into one of the windows. Against the soft firelight, I could see shadows moving. More Stelvan guards, searching Dalaris's home. But they weren't moving fast, which meant they had no idea that three of their friends were currently watering the lawn.

Good news.

At a rough count, I could see maybe ten of them in there.

Less good.

I couldn't take them all head-on and there wasn't enough cover or time to cut them out the careful way—besides, Dalaris would never forgive me for getting so much blood on her carpets.

No. My best bet was to get in, find Dalaris, and get out. But if a dozen thugs hadn't found her so far, my luck didn't look a lot better.

She must have been using her magic to hide. Vishera probably had some item that could detect magic, but I'd be willing to bet that most of these other nobles also had similar junk—she couldn't deploy big magic of her own without all of them noticing and seeing what was up.

Nothing for it, then. I'd have to get in, do my own search, and hope Dalaris revealed herself to me.

This was all assuming she hadn't already left. But something about her told me she hadn't. She was smart, yes, but also sentimental and timid; I'd known enough of those types to know they clung close to home in case of danger.

Unless I was wrong. In which case, I'd be found, captured, and tortured for information before being executed and dumped in a ditch somewhere.

So, you know, educated guesses and all.

I kept low and close to the wall, made my way around the house to the servants' entrance around back. I froze at the corner, knife in hand, at the sight of a body squatting by the wall in ambush. But after I waited a few breaths, I could see it wasn't taking any of its own. A body, but not breathing; and not squatting, but slumped, with an empty crossbow in his hands and a lot of red streaking his beard.

Ah, Harges, you poor bastard. I hoped he'd at least wounded one of them with that thing before they got him.

I'd have given him more of an elegy than a cringe and a hop over his corpse, but I knew he'd want me to think of Dalaris before his body. So I slipped past him, through the shabby stables out back and toward the servants' entrance. The door was shut. I reached out and jiggled the handle, feeling no resistance of a lock. I pressed my ear against it, could hear a muted grumble from beyond the wood.

Guard at the door. Naturally. And from the feel of it, he was leaning against it.

I readied my knife in my right hand, took the door handle in my left and jerked it open. There was the barest of cries as the guard came crashing down and landed before me. I suppose he would have made a louder noise had I not jammed my blade up under his throat.

I hauled the body out of the way, pressed the door shut as quickly as I dared, and waited for the sound of an alarm. Nothing. No one had noticed him disappearing.

If I were an idiot, I'd say Norgorber was looking out for me. But since I wasn't, I'd just say he was enjoying the corpses I was leaving in my wake.

I pulled the door open, slipped into the kitchens. Small by noble standards, they were nonetheless rife with tables, cabinets, and the shadows they cast. I darted between them, made my way to the door leading out to the living room, and peered out.

The place was a mess: furniture overturned, portraits torn down, bookshelves toppled. The guards were tearing it apart in their search for Dalaris. Even if she were invisible, this was too crowded for Dalaris to hide. She would have gone upstairs, I wagered.

And if she hadn't—capture, torture, death, ditch, and so forth, you get me.

I slipped into the room. Fortunately, the chaos left in the guards' wake left a lot of places to hide that they weren't keen on searching again. I made my way swiftly and quietly to the stairs and darted up them, all the while praying that I wouldn't be spotted.

No alarm was raised. Good.

No knife was in my back, either. Better.

Either Norgorber was watching over me or someone else was, for I slipped down the hall and into Dalaris's bedroom without so much as a sound. As I expected, I found it tossed—bed overturned, dresser drawers pulled out, wardrobe emptied. But to my relief, I found no signs of a struggle—no bloodstains anywhere, no signs of magic being expelled.

Dalaris wouldn't have gone without a fight. They hadn't gotten her.

But still, there was no sign of her, either. Had I been wrong? Had she fled already? Gone and disappeared into Yanmass somewhere? My body ached at the idea of combing an entire city for her, and my heart followed at the thought of Vishera's men prowling the alleys for her, knives bared and glistening in the dark.

My eyes drifted to the wall.

For as much carnage as I'd seen in my life, it never bothered me half as much as the scenes that followed: those times when I arrived too late and could only guess at what had happened. A warehouse in Katapesh with corpses stacked like crates, a home in Oppara drenched in blood, a young girl's cold corpse in a cold alley in a cold city, looking almost peaceful as she lay on the stones staring up into the night sky with empty eyes . . .

Compared to that, I'd forgive you for thinking that a rich girl's trashed room wouldn't be that noteworthy. But it's funny the things you notice in those moments of aftermath; it's never the blood or the bodies, but the little things that give you just the barest idea of who these people were before they died. Sometimes it's a corpse reaching blindly out for aid that never came, a message written in blood, a single locket clasped in a dead girl's hands . . .

Or, in this case, a portrait crooked on the wall.

Dalaris's mother, still serene despite the scene before her, hung at an angle. Someone had started to pull her off the wall, realized how dumb it was to be looking for a fully grown woman behind a portrait, and let it fall back haphazardly. Perhaps that might sound like an odd thing to notice here.

Just like it might seem odd that I took the time to carefully right the portrait. I'd explain why, but I don't know if I could. It wasn't going to fix anything, wasn't going to make the shit I was in any less deep. But, like I said, it's funny the things you notice in the aftermath.

Just like it's funny the things that make you feel like it can get better, somehow.

I stepped back from the wall and instantly froze as a hand fell on my shoulder.

I resisted the urge to thrust my knife backward. I was still breathing, so whoever had gotten the jump on me didn't want me dead. But it wasn't until I heard that voice that I relaxed a little.

"Shy," Dalaris whispered.

I turned. The magic around her faded, shed like a cloak. The air shimmered as she came tumbling out of the invisibility spell and collapsed into my arms. Her body shook with contained sobs as she buried her face in my shoulder.

"Hey, kid," I whispered as I pulled her closer.

That probably wasn't the right thing to say. But hell if I knew what I was doing—I didn't usually let people get so close to me without one of us being drunk and nude.

"I heard them in the night," she whispered, voice trembling. "One of them knocked over a vase and I got up and looked downstairs and they were coming in through the window. So I ran and used a spell and . . . and . . ."

"Yeah, I know." I stroked her hair, pulled her closer. No idea what good it would do—but I remembered all three times someone had held me like this, and those were the closest I'd ever come to feeling good about myself. "It's all right. Everything's going to be fine."

For all the lies I'd told in my life, I'd never felt guilty until that one.

"It's Stelvan's people down there," I whispered. "She's up to some foul shit in her house, Dalaris. We've got to get out of here."

I laid my hands on her shoulders, gently eased her away from me. She looked back at me with those huge, intense eyes. The tears at their corners made them seem like they were living, twitching things ready to leap right out of her skull. But those tears didn't go farther than the corners of her eyes. She was going to be all right.

Relatively, anyway.

"No one saw you?" I asked. "Before you used your spell?"

Dalaris shook her head. "No one. They don't know I have magic, so—"

"So they didn't come ready for it," I muttered.

I crept to the door, put my ear to it. No sound of footsteps upstairs; Vishera's thugs must still be rooting around below, searching for a secret passage or something. No better chance than now.

"Okay," I said. "We're going to head to the end of the hall. I'll climb out the window, head down to the grounds below. You're going to have to jump down to me." I glanced over my shoulder at her. "Can you do that?"

Dalaris stiffened, nodded. I couldn't help but smile. There are two types of people in this world: tough people beneath a layer of tears and teary people beneath a layer of toughness. Dalaris, thankfully, was the former.

"We'll get away from here, head for Alarin's manor. We'll be safe there and I can explain everything Stelvan is up to." I put a hand on the door handle, took a breath. "Ready?"

"Ready," Dalaris whispered, coming up behind me.

"Stay low, move quick, stop when I stop." I pulled the door open. "And if I tell you to run, you run for the window and never look—"

That last part was supposed to be "look back." But it was hard to concentrate just then.

What with the magic wand pointing in my face and all.

I had just enough time to look past the bony arm clutching it and into the cold blues of Vishera's eyes. Her thin lips spoke a word I couldn't understand. A dark light burst from the tip of the wand; a hungry light, one that drank the stars and moonlight seeping through the window and doused the room in blackness.

I staggered backward, shielding my eyes. I blinked them clear and, for a moment, looked at my hands. Skin still on, bones not turning to snakes or whatever. Maybe it took me longer than it should have to realize that nothing was happening.

I looked up, saw Vishera quirk a brow at me, a lot less worried than she should be that her spell had failed. I took my blade in hand, rushed toward her.

And that's when it hit me.

I opened my mouth to scream; nothing came out.

I raised my knife to stab; it was too heavy for me.

I turned to run to Dalaris; my legs turned to jelly beneath me.

My stomach sank inside me. My throat tightened up. Fever boiled behind my eyes. I felt things inside me go dark, cold. I felt the magic eat, grow fat on my pain, settle in the pit of my stomach, glutted and content and grinning.

I hate magic.

"*SHY!*"

Barely any light, just enough to see Dalaris falling over me. She grabbed me by the shoulders, tried to pull me to my feet. Her eyes were looking over me and, bless her, for a moment they looked big and bright enough that they might just see what the hell Vishera had done to me.

And then they were filled with something else. A brightness that ceased to be welcoming and became searing.

That same brightness blossomed on her hand as she thrust it out toward the darkness beyond. A bright ray of flame burst from her fingers, lashing out into the gloom. I could hear a scream from beyond, smell leather catching ablaze.

Good girl. She got one of them.

Not the right one, though. Another word, harsh and arcane. Another light, purple and crackling. Violet arcs of electricity coursed across Dalaris's skin and she went rigid as a board. Paralyzed, she toppled over, face frozen in terror, eyes wide and unblinking. I tried to reach out for her, but my limbs wouldn't work. They lay limp on the floor, bloodless hunks of meat that couldn't so much as twitch their fingers.

Which was rather unfortunate, because in another moment, Vishera's scrawny, withered neck was well within reach and fit for strangling.

She knelt beside me, looked me over with a cold, appraising stare, like I was some piece of tarnished jewelry she was considering throwing away. Apparently reaching a decision, she sneered at me.

"We've had quite an adventure today, haven't we?" she asked, voice harsh and ragged.

"How . . ." I gasped.

"It wasn't easy, if it makes you feel any better," Vishera said. "I knew the lady of the house was using magic to hide from me."

"So you used something . . . some kind of ring . . . some bullshit."

"That would have been easy, but no. I don't like tempting the other houses into thinking they need to keep up with my little collection of trinkets." She glanced to the wand in her hand, slid it back to join the other wand in her belt. "I'm risking quite a bit by bringing these little dears out to begin with, I wager."

So I was right. It was hard to feel good about it, though.

"But once one of my men saw you returning to the city, I knew it was only a matter of time before you came here," she continued. "And thus, only a matter of time before she revealed herself to you. It was a waiting game, and an insufferably long one. I discovered your handiwork in my laboratory just moments before I received word that my centaurs were attacking First Solace." She sighed, reached out and patted my cheek. "I suppose you've figured it all out, then?"

"You killed Gerowan," I gasped. It hurt to talk, but I needed to say it. I wasn't sure how long I had left. If the truth was all that was to survive, so be it. "Used the centaurs to do it . . . promised them weapons . . ."

"Indeed," Vishera said. "A nationalist is, at best, an incredibly useful idiot. A nationalist without a nation, even more so. I was hoping to use the centaurs to persuade the other nobles of our lack of preparedness, allowing them to be more pliable when I had a champion to lead us in our defense against Qadira. Sadly, Visheron proved too . . . placid. Flush with his father's charisma, yet lacking any of his desires. Too flaccid, too whimsical to be of much use. I require someone with more . . ." Her eyes drifted toward Dalaris. "Purpose."

My gag reflex was, unmercifully, not paralyzed. I felt bile rise in my throat. I struggled to raise my hand, achieved nothing more than a limp flop of fingers.

"Leave her alone," I gasped.

"Would that make you happy?" She chuckled. "I don't intend to harm her. I require her in proper condition to bear an heir."

"Bitch." I tried to spit. "You crazy, evil—"

"No." Her reply was as cold as a stale wind over a grave. "I accede to none of your base accusations, desert filth. I am doing what needs to be done to protect this land and its people. Qadirans press in from the south, Galtans from the north, and Cheliax is all around us. Taldor is weak, rife with fat, slovenly nobles and weak, impotent princes. It requires someone bolder to protect it from the evils of this world.

"The blood of fiends is not enough. They're merely slavers in waiting. Celestials, too, lack the ambition and daring needed to keep us safe. But the blood of both, in one vessel . . . just think about it. The power of Hell, the presence of Heaven . . . I can create the hero that Taldor needs to be strong again."

"You're right. That's not crazy." I glanced up at the smug smile painted across her face. "They don't have a word for what kind of lunatic you are."

It might seem foolish to use my last breaths for a quip, but it wasn't like I could stab her. At the very least, my relentless wit might bug her a little when she was trying to sleep.

So, you know, bright sides.

"Of low birth, low vision, low intelligence," Vishera said, shaking her head. "It's not in your scope to even question me, much less understand me." She wearily rose up, old body creaking. "But had I the inclination to explain your lack of vision, you don't have the time to listen." She tapped the wand against her hip, smiling cruelly. "The magic will do its work soon enough."

She glanced down at the knife lying in my limp hand.

Still, one wonders if it's just a touch too cliché to simply wait for you to die.

She had just begun to reach for the blade when the door burst open once more. One of her thugs, a tall man, came breathlessly into the room.

"Madame," he said, panting. "They've arrived sooner than we expected. A few of them outside the house, but there'll be more."

"Ah?" Vishera sighed and rose back up. "Well, then, I suppose that moves things up." She gestured to Dalaris. "Collect the specimen. Return to the manor." She sneered at my prone form. "Leave this one as a warning."

I could almost feel it.

I could feel my legs working, desperate to rise up. I could feel my fingers twitching, trying to grasp the knife's hilt. I could feel myself leaping out, grabbing the thug as he awkwardly plucked up Dalaris's frozen form, saving the day, saving everyone.

But it wasn't happening.

I lay there, no more breath for words, no more life in my limbs. That dark light inside me grew hungry again, began gnawing at my insides. A fever swept over me, made my vision go dim at the edges as the thug carried Dalaris out the door.

I knew, then, which god had been watching over me. And it was Norgorber all along. Letting me think I was going to make it out all right, then leaving me to die here on the floor . . . that was just the sort of thing that would make that old bastard smile right before he took my soul.

It was so cruel, I could have screamed.

But I didn't.

As my vision faded into darkness and the fever swept over me like a tide, I resolved to save my very last breath so I could spit in Norgorber's face.

21

Back-Alley Lullabies

I opened my eyes and knew something was wrong.

I mean, *really* wrong. I'd been in trouble before. I'd been chased by hounds through streets, held my breath as hobgoblins tried to sniff me out in tunnels, held my blood in with one hand and cut blood out of someone else with the other. I'd been in filth so deep that my feet couldn't even touch bottom.

But I never thought I'd screw up so bad that I'd be back in Katapesh.

And yet, here it was. Sprawling before me like a dead serpent, I could see the dusty streets of the bazaar. All around me were the merchant stalls, people holding objects so shiny as to render their faces dark by comparison, leaning out and shoving their wares at passersby. The people of the streets brushed past me, pushed me aside in a river of skin and sweat flowing all directions at once. The symphony of the streets—the merchants barking, the customers haggling, the prostitutes propositioning, and all the cursing when a deal went awry—filled my ears.

It even smelled like home: the stale desert air chasing away the reeking facade of perfumes and spices and bringing out the more authentic odors of alley garbage and someone filthy smoking pesh.

This wasn't right.

I had just been in a house. It was dark, incredibly dark. Yet I could feel the Katapeshi sun bearing down on me, the sweat dripping off my brow and into my eyes, and—

No! No, that wasn't it. I was in a house. I was with someone. A woman . . . right? I shook my head. Yes, there had been a woman. There *had* been. It wasn't a dream. She was real.

But, then, why couldn't I remember her name?

I had it. I could hear it, almost see it in my mind, along with her face and the rest of the house. But it was fading, shrinking with every breath, becoming fuzzy and dissipating into shadows in the back of my head.

My head.

It hurt. Like something inside my skull was trying to burrow its way out. I could feel my temples throbbing beneath my fingertips as I clutched them, shut my eyes tight. The skin burned, hotter than the sun, so hot that it felt like if I could just carve a hole in my skull, get a little air in there, I might . . .

"Shy."

My name. Spoken so fondly.

"Shaia."

In a voice that made everything seem better just to hear it.

"SHY!"

Someone seized my hands. Something heavy fell into them. I looked down at the bulging purse in my hands, heavy with coin. I looked back up into a broad, familiar grin and a pair of green eyes offering me a sly wink.

"You're up, champ," Sem said. "If I were you, I'd run fast."

And then Sem was gone, a skinny shape tearing off down the road and disappearing into curtains of pedestrians.

"Sem!" I cried after. "Wait!"

"There!" Another voice barked out, harsher and crueler. "There's the money! Come here, you filthy rat!"

I turned, looked up. Men were barreling down the street toward me, wearing official-looking clothes and shiny armor, scimitars drawn and eyes wild beneath dark brows. They looked huge, effortlessly shoving complaining pedestrians out of the way.

And I was so small.

I turned, took off running. The streets were searing in the heat—they burned my bare feet. But only a little; my feet, they were already hard, even after only a few weeks of doing this. This wasn't unusual, this running.

This was my life.

Mine and Sem's.

"Get back here!"

Their voices were bellowing roars behind me, but I just laughed. I used to cry when I first heard them, but this was becoming easy now. They were so big and clumsy, always fumbling through the crowds as I darted through them. They pushed and fought to take even a single step as I darted between the skinny legs of the men and tumbled under the skirts of the shrieking women.

Sem was already long gone, would be waiting for me back at our little hideout. All I had to do was get there.

Easy.

I felt so light. No tears in me. No screams. No memories. I flew through the crowds, around the adults' legs as they spat curses down upon my head. I tore down a nearby alleyway, the coins jingling a little song just for me. Pesh-smokers, distinguishable from the refuse only by their hazy eyes, looked up at me as I ran to the end of the alley where a low wall stood. I scrambled up the debris to the top of it, swung briefly as I got my balance, and looked out over the world.

My world.

Katapesh.

All its filthy alleys and rising smoke and rich, opulent spires in the distance. Up here, I could almost pretend I was the only one in the whole city, the girl who could outrun the guards and take its coin at will. I laughed long and loud.

"Shy?"

My name.

"*Shaia.*"

But not Sem's voice.

"*Shaia!*"

A woman's. Thick with suffering. The kind of intimate, short-supply sorrow that one only ever offers one other person in their life.

"*Shaia, what did they do to you? Wake up! Answer me!*"

I looked around. I was alone. I couldn't tell where the voice was coming from. But I heard it so clearly, like it was coming from inside my own head.

"*Still breathing . . . Hold on, Shaia. Please, just hold on.*"

And, without knowing it, my lips whispered a name I didn't know.

"Chariel?"

"There you are!"

Rough hands reached up, grabbed me by the scruff of my shirt and jerked me back harshly. The coins fell from my hands—Sem would be so disappointed—and I fell backward into a pile of refuse.

And then I kept falling. Into a darkness so dank and suffocating I couldn't breathe. I opened my mouth to draw in a breath, but only a scream came out as the darkness swallowed me up.

Silence.

And then . . . light.

Dim light. Tiny, fuzzy orbs dancing at the periphery of my vision. My body shuddered with the force of the breath I took, a sharp, painful rasp that felt like razors in my lungs. My head was swimming, my vision dark at the edges, but I could still see them.

Lights.

Lamps.

Street lamps.

They were whirring past me, sliding in and out of my vision as I slipped, weightless, down the street. I could feel something under me: holding me up, carrying me away.

"Shaia," a voice unused to the terror it held whispered. "Stay with me. Look up. Look at me. Look into my eyes."

Eyes. Staring down at me. No whites. Cold and blue as ice, Chariel's were. A killer's eyes. Weird that they made me smile, like they did now.

"That's it, Shy," she said. "Just keep looking at me. Hold onto me. I'm going to fix this."

So big. So blue. Her eyes just kept getting bigger and bluer until they burst right out of her head and exploded into a vast, yawning sky over me.

And I was gone again.

Hot stone on my back. Warm wind on my skin. I had once found the breeze refreshing, a reprieve from the sun. But now, it felt like something stifling, a cage of heat and sweat that closed in around me a little more every time the wind stirred.

I watched the sun crawl across the sky, turn it from blue to red to purple to black as it sank away. Down below in the bazaars, street lamps were lighting—coin never slept down here—making it hard to see the stars when there was so much light down below. Even the moon seemed smaller.

Somehow, every day I spent in Katapesh, everything seemed to shrink.

"Someday."

And yet, that voice never got small. Even when it was a whisper, it was still so loud and clear.

I sat up, grabbed my knees and leaned back. Sem looked black against the night sky, right at home in the darkness. Sem had always been good at that sort of thing. I only ever visited the shadows, but they always reached out to welcome Sem back.

To me, Katapesh was both a home and a prison. To Sem, the city always seemed like just one more stop before returning home to the shadows. And it never seemed more apparent than that night.

"I can't stand it anymore," Sem said, looking down on the streets below. "Pulling coins out of pockets, breaking windows, stabbing people in alleys . . . I was made for more than this." Sem looked at me, eyes bright and green like a cat's. "We were made for more than this."

"We were?" I crawled across the roof toward the edge. "Could have fooled me. I figure if I were made for big things, my mother wouldn't have chased me out of the house with a knife." I flashed a grin to my right. "Won't she be kicking herself to learn that I was made for bigger things?"

Sem returned the grin. "Yeah, well, there's no way she'd believe you. I'll have to go down there and tell her myself."

"Yeah." I chuckled. "'Well, Mother, you may think I'm trash, but this *other* piece of trash says I'm not. So there.'" I laughed a louder, hollow laugh, as though my mother could somehow hear it. I looked down at my hands, resting on my knees in threadbare trousers. "I want to get out, Sem."

"I know," Sem said. "I told you we would one day, right?"

"Yeah. One day."

I felt the hand before it even touched mine. Sem was like that, with a touch that things just responded to. Locks danced open, doors whispered shut, knives leapt like living things. And when I looked down and saw that dark hand on mine, the air no longer felt so oppressive.

Not even when I heard what Sem had to say.

"Two days from now."

"What?" I felt numb, like the idea was too impossible to even hear. But when I looked up, Sem's eyes were hard and real.

"Two days. I know how to get out."

I shook my head. I didn't want to hear this. I couldn't bear to realize this wasn't real, that Sem was just talking nonsense. "No. There's not enough money to get somewhere else, Sem. There's not—"

"We do a job," Sem said. "A quick one. And it gets us all the money we need to go anywhere, do anything we want."

The words, the idea, the very possibility made my heart flutter, feel like a moth banging against a window trying to get out. And I could tell that Sem felt the same way.

But Sem wasn't smiling.

"Shy. I've got to kill someone."

I screamed.

The sound tore itself out of my throat from some place inside me where the darkness gnawed. I heard it echo against stone, repeat a thousand times over. I felt stone on my back, cold and slick with my own sweat. Cold stone surrounded me, candle lights burning like dying fireflies at the edges of my vision. But for all the chill around me, I felt like I was boiling with fever.

My breath came in short, ragged gasps, each one growing fainter, each one struggling to claw its way out of my mouth. And as they grew quieter, I could hear the voices.

"I don't care about your gods-damned price, worm." Chariel. Colder still than this stone. "The people I work for are the people you can't afford to piss off."

"It's not a matter of price, but of *possibilities.*" Tessan. The priest from earlier, so long ago it felt like another life. I recognized his shrill whine, the terror in his voice. Chariel had that effect on people. "I don't know what magic I'm dealing with here. Or even if it *is* magic. You say you just found her like this? What makes you sure she didn't just have a bad night of drinking?"

I heard the whisper of steel coming out of leather. I heard the sound of a cloth collar being seized. I heard a little man become a little boy.

"I wouldn't come to you if I hadn't found her collapsed in a manor with three corpses on the lawn. And I wouldn't be ready to cut your eyes out over a night of bad drinking." Chariel hissed. "It's magic. *Fix it.*"

"I . . . I don't know how!" Tessan all but squealed. "I have no idea what's wrong with her! If I had the spellbook that caused it, perhaps, I—"

"You don't have that. I don't have time to find it. Your options are either to fix it, tell me how to fix it, or figure it out when your god tells you after I send you to him."

I heard the soft, tender shriek that only a woman like Chariel could induce in someone. I heard Tessan scramble across stone, strike something hard.

"W-wait, there is something . . . a scroll. It can cure almost anything. But . . ."

"But what? Use it."

"If it were that easy, I would have given it to you already. But each temple only receives one of these from the high church. If I use it, they have ways of knowing. And even your Brotherhood can't threaten the Church of Abadar."

Chariel fell silent for a moment. "How much?"

"I just said—"

"You said Abadar. God of merchants. He always has a price. I'll pay it."

Tessan almost laughed. "It's . . . the cost would be . . ."

I felt Chariel's eyes on me. I felt something cold well up beneath me. I heard her voice.

"I'll pay it."

I opened my mouth, tried to say something. To beg her to do it? To warn her not to? To ask her to just kill me and end this?

I didn't know.

The chill was creeping in on me, reaching out to the fever boiling inside of me. I could feel my throat closing even as I craned open my mouth. I had no words. I just needed to scream. And yet, nothing would come out.

"*Shy?*"

Nothing ever came out.

I blinked. And there I was again, back in Katapesh. In a rich man's home on a rich man's carpet with a rich man's son lying at my feet.

Bleeding out of a hole I had put in his neck.

"Shy?"

Sem's voice in my ear. Sem's hand on my shoulder. Sem's knife in my hands.

And the rich man's son's blood on the floor.

That boy—he couldn't have been older than sixteen, just a few years older than me—was staring up at me. His eyes were wide and attentive, like I had just told him a joke and he was waiting to hear the punch line. Hell, to look at him, I almost thought he hadn't even noticed that I had stabbed him. His lips were trembling. And I thought, for some reason, that he had the most important thing in the world to tell me, but he couldn't.

And then I wondered if that was what it'd be like when I died.

"Shy."

I looked up. Sem looked back at me, took the knife out of my hands, covered them and all their messy bloodstains with a cloth.

"It's not your fault."

I stared down at the rich man's son and his blood on the carpet and his blood on my hands and his eyes staring at me. I stared back and couldn't say a damn thing.

"He was going to get the guards," Sem said. "We had to. I should have done it myself. I should . . ." A pause. "It was what we came here to do, anyway. We had to send a message, right? That's what they're paying us for. Now we can get out of here, Shy. We can leave. Do you understand?"

I didn't.

But I knew I would.

Sem took my hand. We ran down the stairs. We ran out the door. We kept running for a long, long time.

I closed my eyes. I drifted into somewhere dark, somewhere cold, far from Katapesh and far from Sem.

And I understood.

After that night, killing became the way out for me. It started off defensive, with me lashing out with a blade whenever I felt threatened—and after that night, I always did. But then, as I kept doing it, I got better at it. And somewhere along the line, it became the easiest thing in the world.

I understood that now.

Just like I understood I was dying.

No Katapesh. No Sem. No Chariel. No Dalaris. They were all dreams, one way or another, fleeting things I could never keep ahold of.

All that awaited me now, as this darkness of mine poured out of my eyes and mouth and covered me like a shroud, was Norgorber. I'd open my eyes and find him there, leering at me, grinning like he was about to tell me whatever that dead rich man's son had been before I cut open his throat.

Ah, well.

I had a nice run of things.

It wasn't just the killing. There was other stuff there, too. Maybe Norgorber would look kindly on me for that.

Maybe.

I'd never know, though.

For in another instant, all that chill and cold dark vanished. The fever inside me became something altogether too hot and too bright to be contained. It burned through me like a wildfire, ate at the shadow as surely as the shadow ate me. I felt it sear through my flesh, burn through my veins, claw its way up my throat, and when it pulled itself out, it did so on a scream that lasted for what felt like hours.

But somehow, it burned itself out.

Bright light cleared away from my eyes. It hurt to blink, hurt to breathe, hurt to move. But it hurt in a way unlike whatever Vishera had done to me. It hurt in a way that told me I was alive.

I looked around me, saw the chamber of the temple I had seen Gerowan's corpse in not too long ago. I lay on an altar, beneath the frowning stare of Tessan. A scroll in his hands turned to ashes, fell from his fingers. He shook his head at me and turned away, as though he couldn't quite see the worth in what he had just done.

But someone else did.

I felt her arms wrap around me, pull me up, draw me close. I felt her bury her face in the hollow my neck. I felt the warmth of her breath and the tightness of her embrace and her slow, shuddering breath against my body.

Chariel didn't weep. Chariel never wept.

Chariel didn't say a damn thing.

That wasn't how she did things. She was a woman that wasted nothing. She was an assassin. And she moved through life with the exact knowledge that everything she did would one day hurt somebody.

And though I never said it, I wondered if she knew that saving my life would do that, too.

22

A Late Winter,
A False Spring

I saw magic for the very first time on a street in Katapesh.

It was a wizard—or a sorcerer? I can never tell the difference—a young man, tall and skinny with facial hair, just out of puberty. There was a crowd gathering around him, and Sem and I were at the front.

Somehow, I reluctantly let him talk me into giving him a coin. I'd tell you I was drunk, but I was just young, so same thing, really. Anyway, he took one of my coppers in his hands, whirled it around a little, made a puff of light and smoke and, when he handed it back to me, it was a shiny gold piece.

Don't get me wrong, I didn't throw it back in his face, but even then, I didn't trust it. I had fought off six other kids in the street for that copper and he turned it into gold? Just like that? I couldn't believe it.

Then, when I tried to buy something with it and the illusion spell wore off and it turned out it was just a crappy chunk of wood, I finally understood magic.

If you didn't pay attention, you'd think that magic-users did what people like me did: they went places they shouldn't, got past things designed to keep them out, and did in a few seconds what a warrior does in a lifetime of hacking and slashing.

And if you were stupid, you might even think that magic-users were better at what we did than we were.

But there's a crucial difference. Wizards study, sorcerers harness, but people in my line of work? We *learn*. We watch, we observe, we try and we fail and we get back up. Magic-users go through life confident in their powers, never learning the price of failure. So they never plan for failure. And they never see it coming.

Much like that street wizard never saw it coming when Sem and I jumped him outside of a tavern, kicked him in the teeth, and stole his money.

Point being: Magic is cheating. And not good cheating, either.

So when I walked out of the temple of Abadar, ostensibly free from whatever Vishera had done to me, I still didn't feel right. The fever that had plagued me was gone, whatever visions I had seen were gone, and though I was a little shaky on my knees, I still felt otherwise fine.

But I didn't feel *right*. I didn't like that someone could just do that to me, send me back to Katapesh like that, all with the wave of a stick and a fancy word. I didn't like that there were people like that in the world: rich people, magic-users, assholes who just took whatever they wanted without earning it.

And I didn't like that Dalaris was out there with one of those people right now.

"He said it was poison."

I glanced over my shoulder. Chariel leaned against the temple door, staring at me, arms folded over her chest, lips set in a frown, cold blue eyes unblinkingly fixed on me.

Which was about as close as she got to "concerned," so hey, that was nice.

"Magic poison. Not the honest kind. Some kind of thing that makes you weak." Chariel shrugged. "I wasn't listening for a lot of what he said. But he managed to cure it." She looked straight at me. "It wasn't easy. Or cheap."

"Yeah." I rubbed the back of my neck. "Sorry about that." I managed a weak smile at her. "Next time I get blasted by a power-mad devil-woman's evil spells, I'll try to do so in a more cost-efficient manner. Maybe a nice, easy-to-patch fireball to the—"

"Don't."

Everyone expects an assassin to be fast. And when motivated, Chariel's quick. But a *good* assassin is deliberate. And so every step she took toward me felt like a knife working its way under my skin.

"Don't act like you can solve this with jokes."

"I wasn't."

"Or with running. Or with disappearing. Or with drinking. Or with killing."

"I was just—"

"I know what you were doing." Her face twitched, a mask cracking at the edges. Her voice became a snarl and she narrowed her eyes. "Because you *always* do this. You *always* run: into a bottle, into someone else, or into thin air. But you always run when you're feeling scared."

"I'm not scared."

"I heard you." Chariel swept up to me, looked down at me with a scowl. "In the temple, I heard you crying out. I heard you sobbing. I heard you—" She stumbled over her words, looked away briefly. "I heard you say that name again."

I rubbed my temples, let out a long sigh and turned away from her.

"You're doing it again," she hissed.

"No, I'm not."

"You're running."

"I am *not*."

"Then what would you call it?"

"I don't know!" I whirled on her, gestured to the empty air between us. "This thing? This right here? This is the sort of thing I'd expect from, say, a farmer's daughter. Becoming entangled with a remorseless assassin should not come with *nearly* this much emotional bullshit."

"Don't flatter yourself," she hissed. "I'm not staring out a window, waiting for you to return. I'm not a simpering little broken heart. I'm simply *tired*. I'm *tired* of your cowardice, your ineffectiveness, your running—"

"*Would you stop saying that?*" I don't know how to roar dramatically. I just kind of squawked out something. "I'd be running if I were smart! And if I were smart, I'd be gone by now! I'd have left before you and your thugs caught up to me! I'd have left when that dumb girl asked me to solve her problems! I'd be *gone,* understand? I'd be *gone* instead of standing here . . . standing . . ."

With nothing.

That's how it always ended, somehow.

No matter how hard I worked, no matter how much blood I spilled, it never seemed to make a difference. Coins, power, people; it didn't matter. At the end of everything, I'd be standing there with empty hands. Alone.

But gods—for a little while there, when Dalaris looked at me like I could do something, like I was the one that could help her . . .

Things almost seemed all right.

I felt a hand on my shoulder. I closed my eyes.

"We could go," Chariel said. "Together, this time. Leave the Brotherhood, leave Taldor, leave everything. They can't follow us past Galt."

"I can't."

"The hell you can't. I've seen you—"

"Char . . ." I took her hand in mine, turned to face her. "I can't. I can't leave her."

Chariel didn't have the emotional capacity to look wounded; that sort of thing had been beaten out of her long ago. But the twitch across her face, the crease of anger in her brow—I knew that was as close as I was going to get to her looking hurt. It didn't feel great.

"You and her . . ." she said. "Do you . . ."

"Not like that." I shook my head. "She's just . . . she was counting on me."

"A lot of people were." Chariel glared at me. "*I* was."

"Yeah, but I always knew you were going to take care of yourself. The Brotherhood, they wouldn't miss me once I was out of Taldor. No one was going to mind that I disappeared. But Dalaris is different. She's got the blood of Heaven in her. She can probably trace her lineage back to a god, and even *they* aren't looking out for her right now."

"You expect me to believe you want to be a hero?"

"No," I said. "I don't expect much of anything except that . . ." I sighed. "Even if everything else goes to hell, at least someone should come out of this okay. And neither you nor I deserve for it to be us."

I didn't know if Chariel believed me. Hell, I didn't even know if *I* believed me.

I had a good thing in front of me. Vishera sent me to hell with just a flick of a little wooden stick. I knew the scope of her plans and I knew what she had under her house. And even if I somehow made it out of there, there was still the Brotherhood's presence here.

I was in over my head.

And if I was smart, I'd run for it. Chariel was right, the Brotherhood wouldn't pursue us beyond Taldor's borders. She would know how to evade them long enough for us to get to Galt and beyond.

I wasn't the sort to believe that the kind of heroics that happen in operas even existed, let alone that I could be part of them. I wasn't the sort to believe that I'd be the person that hope came to rest on.

I wasn't that kind of person. I was smart. And the smart thing would be to run.

And somehow, every time I tried to tell myself that, my mind just drifted back to Dalaris and those big eyes of hers and how I wondered if I once had eyes like that.

And I knew I couldn't go.

And even if I didn't believe it, even if I wasn't a hero, I was a damn good liar. And I looked at Chariel like I believed it. And, as her face softened as much as she was able, I knew she believed it, too.

"What are you going to do?" she asked, sighing.

"Kill the richest woman in Yanmass, I guess." I shrugged.

"Just like that, huh?"

"I've got a plan?"

"Do you?"

Of course I didn't. I had just barely come out of whatever pit Norgorber had dragged me into. But I had an idea, at least.

"I do," I said. "And I need your help."

She cringed. "The Brotherhood can't get involved in this. We've got too many pieces in play."

"Not the Brotherhood. You. I need you to deliver a message for me. Go outside the city walls, there's a centaur there who's . . ." I paused, scrutinized. "How many curse words do you know, anyway? You're going to need a lot for this to work."

23

Into the Maw

Gods are hard to come by in this line of work.

The decent, loving deities don't approve of thievery. The evil, vicious deities don't feel thievery is quite enough to warrant their blessings. And the less interested deities don't feel any particular need to look out for you.

Thus, those of us with a talent for getting places are left with Norgorber.

Not a good god. Not a kind god. He's a sneering, weasely, vicious little prick of a god. But if you know what he likes, you can sometimes beseech him. Selfishness, he approves of. Murder, he likes. But what he really loves is when someone sets themselves up for such a tremendous, spectacular failure that he can't help but lean out a little and push them into it.

Which is why tonight, I was beseeching him.

Because I was about to give him a show he wouldn't soon forget.

And it all began with me walking up to the gates of House Stelvan and looking up.

You'd think it'd look foreboding, what with being the domicile of a madwoman and all, but it looked a touch cozy that night. The stars were out, not a cloud in the sky, and the lights above twinkled as softly as the warm light beaming out of the manor's many windows.

A good night to get killed.

I jiggled the gate's handle, found it locked. In short order, I had my tools out and the door picked. It swung open with a noisy creak—Stelvan could spring for a torture dungeon but not oil for hinges, I guess—but that was fine. I wanted them to hear me coming.

I took my time strolling down the walkway through Stelvan's gardens. The last time I had seen these shrubberies and statues, they were cover—places to hide and shadows to slip in. Here, in the light of the stars, I could see the delicate care put into their maintenance: the rounded cheeks on the sculpture of a young lady, the precise corners of a square-cut hedge, the bright smile of a stone child standing at the center of a fountain.

This, I supposed, is what Vishera thought she was protecting. To me, it was just a rich person's junk: wealth thrown about to show everyone else how wealthy she was. And maybe if I hadn't met her, I would think Vishera was just one more of them.

But I had looked into her eyes.

I had heard the fear in her voice.

And in it, I had heard the same hungry terror that had been in the voice of every orphan, every urchin, every rat in every back alley I had ever met in Katapesh. They had been poor kids with nothing but a hunk of bread to their name, but they lived in perpetual fear of even that much being taken from them. And when you're rich, you have a lot more that can be taken from you.

I just saw riches. But Vishera saw love, saw tenderness, saw all the care she had poured into making this manor her home. And in her mind, I suppose that's all it was: a home. Her home. One she would do anything to protect.

And when put that way, was I right to stop her?

I don't know. You want philosophical questions, go ask a priest.

I was here to stab a bitch.

I walked up to the massive doors, found them locked. Unfortunate. I was planning on kicking them in. It was going to be all dramatic and whatever. Ah, well.

I picked the lock, folded up my tools, and tucked them into the back of my belt. I slid my knife into my hand; not that it would do me much good, but it was something. I put my shoulder against one door and shoved.

It opened with a slow groan, revealing Vishera's massive grand hall.

And the three dozen or so guards within, blades drawn.

I took a deep breath, fought down that common-sense urge to run, and walked in, shutting the door behind me.

I glanced across the many men and women surrounding me. I saw their blades, leveled at me. I saw the reflection of my eyes, calm as they could be, in the gleam of their steel. What I *didn't* see was any of that steel embedded in my flesh and soaking in my blood.

So, hey, off to a good start.

"Expecting me?" I asked.

One of them, a fellow with slightly nicer trim to his garb, stepped forward. "We had warning this time." He cast me a sneer. "See how much nicer it is when you don't come crawling in like a rat?"

"I'll admit, I didn't expect it to go quite this well." I glanced pointedly around at the guards and their weapons. "So, are we going to have wine before you kill me or what?"

"The mistress requested we speak properly before engaging in combat." The head guard sniffed. "You could try running, if you'd like. But . . ." He allowed himself a little grin. "We took the liberty of moving a few of our people in behind you once you came in through the gate."

"Courteous." I eyed the dagger in my hand. "So, what's your mistress want to know?"

"She found her study compromised." He ran a finger along the lapel of his coat. "The man I inherited this uniform from was in charge of security on the night you broke in. We'd like to know what you took, so that his soul might be at peace."

"His soul, huh?"

"Well, the mistress is more concerned with what delicate equipment might have been compromised by your intrusion."

"That sounds about right." I folded my arms. "So, I tell you, then you kill me? Sounds like a short conversation."

"The mistress is willing to be lenient. Her progress cannot be further hindered, obviously, so any deal would involve your silence." He held up his hands, put on a grin that I *think* was meant to be reassuring. "There are magical means to this, completely painless. With just a few words, we can seal away your voice with minimal effort."

"Compelling," I said.

"Afterward, the mistress is willing to locate a suitable domicile for you. A monetary stipend will be set aside for you. Trivial to her. You could lead your life in comfort and silence."

"Uh huh. And why not just torture me for the information?"

His face turned to a sneer. "The mistress wishes me to inform you that she considers torture to be more the purview of *your* people."

I pursed my lips, nodded slowly. Not that I should specifically be offended by that kind of statement—what with all the *other* horrible stuff going on here—but it didn't make it any easier.

"That said," he continued, "should you prove uncooperative, we may hesitantly resort to such unpleasantness."

"Well, I wouldn't want things to be unpleasant. But . . ."

I paused as I heard a distant sound. Something heavy hitting stone. I smiled.

"But?" the guard pressed.

"But I've got no reason to trust you. And even if I did, I've become a little attached to my voice." I grinned, held my hands out wide. "True, I prefer to do things quietly. But on occasion, I do love a good . . ."

I licked my lips.

"*Spectacle.*"

A long moment passed. Nothing happened. The guards traded baffled looks. The one in the lead stared at me blankly. I held my hands out for just a moment longer before sighing and looking back at the door.

"Ah, damn." I rubbed the back of my neck, then turned back to the guards. "Sorry, I thought I had it all timed out."

"What?" the head guard asked.

"See, I was going to hold my hands out, say 'spectacle' like I did, and then—"

The doors flew off their hinges.

An arc of steel cut the air where I had just been standing. I tumbled away as the splintered doors sailed through the air and landed in the crowd of guards, knocking a few of them to the ground.

Hooves clopped on stones, massive sword screeching as he dragged it behind him, eyes burning like fires as he surveyed the crowd before him.

Halamox made a hell of an entrance, I had to hand it to him.

It would have been more impressive if he had come in when I had said "spectacle," sure, but, anyway . . .

I leapt to my feet, my back to the guards. I held up my dagger and pointed it at Halamox and screamed.

"There he is, boys! I told you he'd come! Gut the horse before he reaches the mistress!"

The guards, bless them, looked confused. Halamox, however, looked anything but.

"*Betrayer!*" he howled as he leapt forward and into the crowd.

After the first skull split beneath a hoof, the guards caught on pretty quick.

His sword swung wildly, cleaving bodies even as the guards surged forward, thrusting their blades into his mass. He didn't seem to mind—hell, he didn't seem to notice. Halamox just kept swinging, just kept stomping, just kept roaring.

And he was joined. From behind, two more centaurs—the refined kind with armor—came bursting through the door, spears in hands.

"Crush the human filth!" Halamox roared. "They've betrayed us!"

And soon, they added themselves to the chaos.

Whatever scenarios the guards might have rehearsed for, I was pretty sure this wasn't one of them. Training failed, giving way to instinct. Fear and fury painted their faces as they realized this was no longer three dozen guards tormenting a Katapeshi girl. This would be a fight for their lives. They rushed forward, screaming and stabbing.

Halamox and his centaurs welcomed them. Their own war cries drowned out the shrieks of the guards, their own weapons dwarfed the guards' puny swords. The wounds they took, they returned with savage blows. And by the time one of them finally went down under a flurry of steel, she did so with half a dozen corpses at her feet.

And me?

I was crawling for the stairs.

I'd like to tell you this was all according to plan. I'd like to tell you I truly was that brilliant. But if you knew me well enough, you wouldn't believe it.

Still, give me some credit. I had a *little* idea of what I was doing.

I knew Halamox would still be close to the city walls. He had tired himself out taking me back to Yanmass and I wagered he'd still be pissed about my duping him and forcing him to call off his raid. Of course, he wouldn't be able to get in on his own.

Hence, having Chariel deliver a profanity- and threat-laden message on behalf of Vishera to them and then escaping to lead them on a merry chase that "accidentally" led to a secret entrance into the city was the next logical step. I trusted Halamox's time in the city would let him find Vishera's manor.

You'd probably expect something to go wrong with this plan. I wouldn't blame you; there's a lot that *could* have gone wrong. I could have taken too long to get to the manor, the guards might have killed me right away, Halamox might not have taken the bait . . .

But fortunately for me, I have an excellent sense of timing, the guards were under orders from Vishera not to kill me immediately, and, for that last part, it turns out I was just a big enough pain in his horse ass to warrant this kind of slaughter.

I scrambled to my feet as I reached the stairs and glanced over. The remaining dozen guards or so had adopted more careful stances as they tried to close in around Halamox and his companion, but the two centaurs weren't making it easy. They continued to bellow and swing their weapons in wide arcs, and the guards continued to jab and dart at them.

And no one seemed to notice me much.

"You boys have fun with this," I muttered and sprinted up the stairs.

I had to make it to Vishera's laboratory, through the secret room in her study. Dalaris would doubtless be there, if it wasn't too late.

If it *was* too late, Vishera would be there. And then I'd stab her.

Either way, I was planning on getting something done tonight.

It was when my foot hit the top of the stairs that I heard the crackle of electricity. I had just enough time to glance down the hall and see the spark of cobalt before it came screaming out at me. My body was paying closer attention than I was, though; I instinctively leapt forward, feeling the tingle of the lightning bolt between my shoulder blades as it arced past my back and struck the wall. I fell to the ground, smoking splinters falling in a shower around me.

I was back on my feet in a moment, my knife in my hand and my eyes locked down the hall.

By the crackling blue light at the tip of a crooked wand, I could see the rage painted across Vishera's face as she snarled at me.

"So, suffice it to say," I said, clearing my throat, "I'm going to have to decline your offer of mercy."

Credit to the old girl, she didn't waste time with dramatic, villainous speeches. She simply leveled the wand at me again and hissed.

I darted toward her, zigzagging as I did so. She spat a curse at me, trying to fix her wand's tip on me. She couldn't have been a good aim in her best days, let alone with age catching up to her. When she finally shrieked the command word, the wand erupted with another bolt of electricity that arced well over my head.

I flipped the blade in my hand, slipped low as I closed the final few feet between us. I narrowed my eyes on her belly, felt the muscles in my arm bunch up in anticipation. Two quick stabs, I told myself. Right into her kidneys. Then run away and let her bleed out. Quick, messy, ugly. But it'd get the job done.

One held breath. Three more strides. I was right on top of her. I tilted my blade up, swept up close to her, and . . .

Bounced right off what felt like a solid brick wall between us.

I fell to the ground, looked up at the air itself rippling around her. Why I didn't think she might have some kind of magic piece of crap that would protect her from me, I'm not sure.

Maybe I was just feeling lucky.

"Scum," she snarled, turning the wand on me. "You have no appreciation for what I'm doing."

"Accurate."

I was back on my feet, darting around her as she tried to aim the wand at me. She might be protected by magic, but there was no amulet that could cure being an old, slow, creaky woman. I slipped around her, kept at her back. I couldn't touch her, but I could keep behind her and that toy of hers.

"Thousands within Taldor's borders," Vishera snapped as she tried to whirl on me. "And they all rely on *me*! On what *I* can do! Their prince can't protect them, their senate doesn't care about them! I'm the only one who gives a damn!"

"Yeah," I said, "you care enough to kidnap, murder, and rape for it. You're just misunderstood, you poor angel."

My eyes slipped around her person, looking for whatever trinket might be keeping her shield up. I saw something peeking out of her pocket, a column topped with something silver. It looked like it might fall out if I could just get her to . . .

"You're like them," she snarled. "Just like the Qadirans. The only reason you'd stand in my way is if you were in league with them."

"Funnily enough, I'd be content to let you do whatever crazy crap you're doing here." I switched directions, darted back around her. "But you happened to involve a friend of mine."

She whirled to try to keep up with me. The trinket fell out of her pocket, jostled by the sudden movement, and rolled across the floor.

I leapt for it, seizing it and rolling into a tumble. I ended up on my back, staring down the length of Vishera's wand as it crackled with electricity.

With nothing else to defend myself with, I hurled the trinket at her. It tumbled through the air, bounced off the shield—still tragically up—and struck the wall.

It shattered into tiny fragments. Not a column, then. A vial. And as it smashed against the wall, the first thing I noticed was a viscous substance on the wood.

The second thing? Vishera's scream.

"*NO!*" She reached for the vial, as though she could still grab it. "*Visheron!*"

"Visheron?"

For a moment, I wondered if she had used some kind of magic garbage to put his soul in that vial or something equally crazy. But, in a painfully swift moment, I looked at the glistening substance on the walls.

And I remembered what value she saw in Visheron.

And I fought the urge to vomit.

"Norgorber's nuts, lady." I sprang to my feet. "You are *sick*."

Her sole reply was a scream as she raised her wand. And I was already running.

Wires tripped beneath me. Pressure plates shifted. I heard a small symphony of clicking sounds in the walls around me. I tumbled low as twin gouts of flame burst from either wall above me. I leapt forward as a hidden blade shot out of the floor beneath me. I skidded to a halt as a chorus of darts shot out of the wall to my left and embedded themselves in the wood to my right.

Vishera shouted a command word. I heard the lightning bolt crackle behind me. I turned and ducked into the nearest open door, narrowly avoiding the arc of electricity that streaked past.

I slammed the door behind me, took a deep breath, and surveyed my surroundings.

Ordinarily, I wouldn't feel *quite* so relieved at being surrounded by so many large-breasted naked women. But Visheron's room, and its many lewd portraits, was at least a reprieve from his mother's attempts to kill me.

The artist himself lay not too far away from the door, sprawled out upon a sofa and completely naked. I held my finger up to my lips for an embarrassingly long time before realizing I didn't need to. Visheron wasn't moving.

I crept to his side, held my hand up close to his mouth. I felt breath, but faint. This was no natural sleep. His mother must have drugged him before she . . . she . . .

There was really no way to describe it without spilling my guts on the floor, so I was content to let it be.

I heard footsteps coming up the hall. I glanced around, saw a nearby sculpture of a ridiculously well-endowed naked woman. Hopefully, she wouldn't mind if I put her tremendous bosom to more practical use. I slipped behind the sculpture just a moment before the door went flying open.

Vishera came stalking in, the tip of her wand alight with electricity. The first thing she did was storm over to her comatose son. I would have called it motherly if I wasn't sure she was just checking to make sure her source of demonic seed hadn't been knifed.

By the light of the candles burning in the room, I could see Vishera's face. The rage on her visage exaggerated the harsh lines of her wrinkles, making them look more like scars. Her gray hair, usually neat and orderly, was tousled and hung about her face in sweaty strands. And her eyes . . .

Well, after seeing her eyes, the lightning bolts didn't seem quite the most menacing thing in the room anymore.

I held still, took slow, shallow breaths as I watched her from the shadows. She skulked around, searching the room for me. Slowly, she inched toward the sculpture. I resisted the urge to flee, closed my eyes. She cast only a sneering gaze at the buxom stone woman so graciously serving as my cover and then stalked away.

Rude.

But I wasn't about to protest. Vishera stormed off into the rear of the room, toward her son's sleeping chambers. I took the chance, slipping out silently and creeping out the door.

I wouldn't have long before she realized I wasn't in there. Seconds, maybe. I had to make the best of this situation. Which, in this case, meant figuring out how to kill her. Gods knew I wasn't going to get out of here with Dalaris so long as that woman was looking for me.

And to that end, I'd forgive you for thinking that it was stupid to head back to the study. I'd certainly understand if you called me a fool for pulling on the secret book and revealing the hidden door.

And I'd probably agree with you that going down into a cramped room with the very real possibility of being trapped there with a psychotic woman full of things that could make me explode was a dumb idea.

But I'd like to see you come up with a better one.

I slipped down the spiraling staircase, into the darkness. Down here, at least, I had the shadows. At the very least, I had something here I could use against Vishera.

And as I went deeper, I realized that the shadows might be about all I had.

24

And Down the Gullet

L ike any other job.

No matter what I had to rob, who I had to kill, where I had to sneak, one job was the same as any other. So long as I got out alive, I could call it a win. So long as I got what I needed, I could call it a total victory.

This? This was like anything else.

That's what I told myself as I came creeping down into the room, through the pitch-black darkness. This was just another job. No matter how weird it might have gotten, I could get through this. I could do this.

I came pretty close to believing it, too, until the voices started.

"Hm?"

Deep. Resonant. Sultry.

"Ah, look who came back."

Fennoc.

"This is to be expected, of course. They rarely stay away for long."

I ignored him. Or tried to. It's easy to ignore a literal incarnation of demonic sex speaking in your head, but only in theory.

Down the stairs, through the hall, stepping lightly for any traps that might have been reset. Through the door, into the dim blue light of Vishera's laboratory. Just like before.

The first thing I saw was Vishera's golem. I started, holding my knife up defensively. In another moment, I relaxed as I saw it lying in a tangled heap in the corner. All the various ichors from the various jars I had thrown at it still seeped from it; I must have done more damage to it than I thought.

The next thing I saw was Dalaris.

A table stood in the center of the room, beneath the dimly glowing orb of light in the ceiling. Upon its face, she lay, stripped down to her undergarments and strapped to it, unmoving. I immediately rushed to her side, felt for a pulse.

It was there. Faint, but there. Her eyes were rolled back into her head. Her mouth hung open, exuding a soft breath. She was still alive. Drugged, like Visheron.

"I can smell your concern for her from here, mortal." Fennoc's voice hissed from nearby. "It reeks. Kindly take it outside, won't you?"

I glanced to the nearby door of his cell. It stood with all its complicated locks still undone—Vishera hadn't time to redo them, I suppose. But even from beyond it, I could feel his gaze upon me, sense the wicked curl of his smile.

"Shut up," I muttered.

"Stressed, are we? Whatever for?" He chuckled blackly. "Ah. What's this? A quickened pulse. A heart beating just a tad too fast . . ."

"I said *shut up*."

"And such rudeness. Feeling rather trapped, are we? There's no way out of here, you know. Of course you know. You used the only way out on your last little jaunt to visit me. Poor dear."

I consigned myself to ignoring him, began sawing at the straps holding Dalaris down. I could still do this. I could pick her up, carry her out, get out during whatever confusion remained . . .

"Oh. What's that? A whiff of hope? Or is that desperation? Or denial? I can't tell the difference, if I'm honest."

"You're never honest," I snarled, finally breaking free the first strap.

"I can be, when it's beneficial to me. Or when it's amusing. Such as when I say you really should saw faster . . . or perhaps, just look up."

A cold knife of fear in my belly. I didn't want to listen to him. But upon hearing the crackle of electricity, the fervent breath of a furious old woman, I slowly glanced up.

Vishera stood in the doorway, wand leveled at me, cobalt electricity forming at the tip. Too close for me to dodge. Too far for me to get to. Nowhere to run, nowhere to hide. She began to speak the command word. I did the only thing I had left to me.

I cheated.

I leapt behind the table, ducked down behind it. The command word caught in Vishera's mouth. I saw her eyes go wide. She jerked the wand back, terrified that she had almost accidentally electrocuted Dalaris.

"Careful there," I said. "One false move and your future hellbaby grandchild forever remains a twinkle in your eye, old woman."

"Coward," she hissed. "You'd forsake her to save your own skin? Come out and face your punishment."

"Lady, we can debate the semantics behind that accusation if you want, but I'm pretty sure you're not in a position to call *anyone* names." I slowly rose up behind the table. I pressed my knife to Dalaris's throat. "And I *know* you're not in a position to make demands."

"Oh." Fennoc chuckled. "That's unexpected."

"Shut up," Vishera spat in the direction of Fennoc's cell. She glared at me, spoke through clenched teeth. "Do not dare harm her."

"It'd be a kinder fate than what you've got in store for her," I replied.

"You mistake me for a monster," Vishera said.

"I'm pretty sure it'd be a mistake to settle on a word as polite as 'monster.'"

"The girl will be taken care of," she continued, slowly lowering her wand. "I intend for her to have the best care while she carries my heir. She will want for nothing, have everything she desires—"

"Unless she should desire a life outside of carrying hellspawn, right?"

"Technically," Fennoc interjected, "the spawn would be of Heaven and the Abyss."

"Shut up," I snapped.

"Once the heir is born, she may retire elsewhere." Vishera rolled her shoulders. "A nice island to the south, perhaps? Maybe a home on the frontier. Or perhaps she would desire to see her house restored to its former glory, right here in Yanmass. Her family's honor would be restored. And safe."

"She'd never be safe in the same city as you."

"On the contrary," Vishera replied. "When my heir achieves his full power, when he is ready to take control of Taldor, there will be no place safer than within his family. His will be a glorious reign, a secure reign, and no one will know his power more keenly than those closest to him."

"And if it's a girl?"

Vishera shrugged. "I see no reason why a woman could not lead Taldor as well as any man."

"Bravo, madame." Fennoc chuckled again. "Your egalitarianism truly inspires."

"Shut *up*!" Vishera and I snapped in unison.

"But . . ." The old woman sighed, offering me a smile. "This is all wasted breath, isn't it?"

She took a step forward. I tensed, drew the knife a little closer to Dalaris's throat. But she didn't so much as flinch.

"You had the chance to run," she said. "You knew I would not have pursued you. Yet you came back. You enlisted the aid of my centaur pawns, slew my guards, came all the way down here . . ." She gestured to Dalaris. "For her."

Her smile grew so long and cruel as to make Fennoc's look mild by comparison.

"And you think to convince me that you'll kill her? Right here? Right now?" She shook her head. "We both know there is only one way out of this, my dear."

I looked down at Dalaris. Slowly, I felt a frown weigh upon my face. My knife dropped away from her throat. I sighed.

She was right. There was only one way out of this. And I did know it.

But damned if I was ready to admit it.

A quick snap of my wrist. A cry of alarm. My knife went flying from my fingers.

It tumbled through the air, struck the globe of light above Dalaris. The crystal shattered into a dozen fragments and the magical substance within hissed out of existence, bathing the world in darkness.

Vishera let out a series of curses as she whirled about with her wand. But the sparks forming at the tip of it were nowhere near bright enough to allow her more than a tiny bit of light. She held it out before her, searching for me.

But I was already gone.

Low to the ground, breath soft, feet swift, I swept to a nearby wall and put my back to it. I felt papers rustle behind me; a bookshelf. I held my breath as I watched the tiny light of her wand dart fervently in the darkness.

There'd be no hope of finding my knife in the gloom. Nor would it matter; whatever shield she had was still up. Even if she was a little more screwed than before, I was still just as screwed as I had ever been.

Do this line of work long enough, you see a lot of people meet their end in a lot of different ways. And somehow, it's always the opposite of what you think it'll be. I've seen brave warriors beg and cry for their mothers before they've died. I've seen brilliant wizards struck dumb and speechless by their impending demise. I always wondered how I'd go.

I supposed that all depended on how I lived. And here, at the end of it all, I knew that I had been an immense pain in the ass to an awful lot of people.

No need to give that up now.

"So, I bet you're used to being called insane by now," I said from the dark. "But has anyone pointed out how stupid you are?"

Vishera whirled in my direction, thrust her wand out. But her clenched jaw spoke no words. She scanned the darkness, searching for me.

"You've got more money than anyone else in Yanmass," I continued. "And you spent it on *this*?"

"It's the only way," she snarled.

"What, really? You didn't think to hire an army of mercenaries or something? Or maybe buy a nice catapult? You're sure maybe you didn't really just want a little bundle of hellfire to bounce on your knee?"

"*Silence!*"

Her roar was followed by another command word. A bolt of lightning shot out, struck the bookshelf and set it ablaze. But I was already gone, crawling across the floor until I arrived at the wall behind her.

"No, I get it. You want a way to secure your legacy."

She whirled once again, trying to get a fix on my voice. I crept slowly against the wall, low to the ground.

"Your father was killed by Qadirans, right? You want to avenge him by reshaping Taldor in an image of your family. You don't want vengeance against Qadira, you want vengeance against the people who failed him."

"They were weak." She thrust her wand out. "Cowards. We'll all be better off—"

"Yeah, I've heard that part. But this isn't for them, is it? No one comes up with a plan *this* insane just for the sake of someone else. Let alone a woman as rich and spoiled and selfish as—"

Another word. Another burst of lightning. I could feel it snake past me this time. It struck an alchemical apparatus behind me, shattering the many vials and beakers and spilling viscous liquids onto the floor.

And I was moving again. She was angry now, hurling more lightning in the dark in an attempt to strike me. Good. I could work with that.

Whether I could survive it was another matter.

I kept crawling around until I felt it: cold iron at my back. I slid my way to my feet.

"It's never about them. It's always been about you and your fears. Because you know what all this is for, right?"

"Shut up!" She whirled.

"You just don't want to go out like your father."

"Be *quiet!*" She leveled her wand in my direction.

"Some nameless fool who died for nothing."

She spoke a word.

And I fell to the ground.

I kicked backward. The door to Fennoc's cell went swinging open. The lightning bolt from Vishera's wand went arcing over my head, bolted into the cell. And there, it struck something solid.

There was a brief grunt.

And then a brief silence.

And then? Very long, very low laughter.

I could feel him. Fennoc's malice radiated out of him like a fire. It was the same disquiet, the same eerie sensation that I had felt before, amplified to a proportion that bore me to the ground. His hatred, his fury, it felt too big, unleashed . . .

Unshackled.

The sound of metal clinking upon stone. The sound of hooves striding forward. The sound of leathery wings stretching.

I could only bear to hear him. I looked up only once to see him striding past me, black even against this darkness, and then looked down to the floor again, lest he notice me.

But I didn't need to.

His eyes were for her alone.

I glanced up and saw the terror painted on Vishera's face as she thrust the wand out impotently before her.

"No!" she gasped. "The spell! The shackles, they . . ."

"Such a delicate business, binding a demon," Fennoc said. "The most powerful wizards study the process for years, dedicating their lives to figuring out its intricacies. And even they make mistakes. And you, dear?"

He strode toward her.

"You are but a hobbyist."

She screamed, command word after command word, hurling bolt after bolt of lightning into him. He cackled, luxuriated in the electricity, even cried out in what sounded like ecstasy; but he did not stop. He continued walking leisurely toward her until she finally turned to run.

And then, he reached out for her. His hand passed through the shimmering air of her shield effortlessly and seized her by the throat. She let out an ungodly moan as he raised her into the air. Through the darkness, his smile was bright and his eyes blazed with fire.

"Now then, darling," Fennoc said. "After being your guest for so long, I have been looking forward to returning the favor. Let me show you . . ."

Fires burst into being around his body, spread out until they surrounded him and Vishera both.

". . . where *I* call home."

Her shriek was lost in the roar of fire as the flames engulfed both of them. They burned bright enough to fill the entire room in one blinding inferno. And then, just as swiftly, the conflagration faded.

And the two of them with it.

And I was left alone with the darkness.

25

Stains on the Carpet

Once you get past all the traps, monsters, and frequent eviscerations, adventurers have it pretty easy, don't they?

No, I mean it. Everything in a dungeon is a pretty straightforward affair. You get some idiots to go down into a hole with you, you kill everything you come across, you trip a few traps, maybe say a fond farewell to a companion who got unlucky and took an arrow to the face, then grab a lot of treasure and head back to whatever piss-soaked inn you crawled out of to spend it all on booze and floozies.

Simple, right?

That's what I should have done. Hired on with some meathead warrior and some bearded wizard and gone down to plunder vaults of orcs or whatever. And if I had less of an aversion to getting stabbed by orcs, I probably would have done it.

But you do this line of work long enough, you come to realize that the only person who ever goes into it is the sort of person that can't do things straightforward. This line of work is meant for those of us who can't look someone in the eye unless we're telling them a lie, those of us who don't feel comfortable unless someone else is worse off than us, those of us who can't ever quite seem to figure out when we've got a good thing going and should just stop.

Like now.

I looked down at my empty wineglass, tilted it back to drain the last few precious drops that remained, and then held it expectantly above my head. A little fellow—skinny, bright-eyed, and full of energy—came scampering up to me, flashing his servant's uniform like it was a gods-damned war banner.

"Mistress?" he asked.

"More," I replied.

"Of course." He had the bottle ready; which figured, since this was my fifth glass. "If this vintage is not to your liking, I can find you another. Lady Sidara instructed us to offer you whatever you wish."

"Yeah. Isn't she a peach."

I leaned on the railing, stared down upon the main hall of House Amalien and the crowd gathered therein. Fat men, pale women, all of them dressed in fineries, all of them swilling wine and eating parts of animals that you weren't supposed to. All of them had come for the big news.

And the big news was currently standing in the middle of the room.

I had to say, for a guy who hadn't spoken to anyone that wasn't a painting for most of his life, Visheron was quite the extrovert. His goatee neatly trimmed, his clothes fine and flouncy, his hat expertly angled to hide the horns on his head, the young artist commanded the attention of at least two dozen aristocrats, all of them cackling at some joke he had told.

More than a few of the women there cast him rather sultry gazes. But, as their chests didn't look like they would bring them crashing to the earth, I didn't see Visheron paying much attention to them.

Most of his attentions, it seemed, were for the tall, regal-looking man that came into his circle with a pair of wineglasses. Alarin cracked a joke of his own, no doubt just as stupid, that sent the circle laughing again, almost as hysterically. Which figured, since Alarin was almost as rich as Visheron was now. And soon, they would be ridiculously rich.

I suppose you might be wondering how *that* all happened.

Shortly after Vishera's untimely departure, I freed Dalaris and dragged her, half-paralyzed from the drugs, out of the hole and into the house. There was no sign of Halamox or his centaurs, unless you counted the dozens of corpses they left behind.

They *were,* however, several dozen armed guards from House Amalien, with Alarin at their head, looking quite curious as to why I, bloodied and singed, was dragging his dead brother's former fiancée down the stairs and into the great hall in her underthings.

Frankly, I was more surprised that it took them so long to respond. If they hadn't sensed the insane amounts of magic coming out of the house, then surely they'd noticed the centaurs tearing things up. Personally, I had suspicions that Alarin was content to let a little carnage be wrought upon his only rival in the city before intervening.

But I hadn't been about to voice those suspicions when his guards all trained their crossbows on me.

Fortunately, though, I hadn't had to. In another few moments, all our eyes had turned to the stairwell as Visheron, clad in a flimsy robe and nightcap, had descended.

I still don't know if it was sorcery or his own natural charisma that did it, but Visheron revealed that his mother had disappeared earlier—likely due to fear from being targeted by the centaurs—and had summoned him from Oppara to continue her business.

Dalaris and myself he explained as having been abducted by the centaur invaders and rescued by his house guards at great sacrifice.

I could tell, even then, that Alarin hadn't believed it. Not all of it, anyway. But Alarin was rich and, like any rich man, understood that the truth should never get in the way of money.

"Mistress?"

I glanced to my side, took the wineglass from the servant and set about draining it. He, helpfully, slipped back against the wall and waited for me to finish it again.

That's how, two days later, I wound up here, in a fancy dress, drinking fancy wine at a party celebrating the official pact of House Stelvan, House Amalien, and House Sidara.

Trade agreements would be announced soon, guards at caravan-rests would be replenished to fend off centaurs, and everyone would be rich and happy.

In the hall below, a smile crossed Visheron's face, a little too wide and a little too sinister to resemble anything but his father's. For my part, I didn't like the idea of him having all of his mother's wealth. True, he wasn't his mother. But he was the son of a vicious, horrifying psychopath and a demon, so the thought of him having access to all her money, magic, and forbidden knowledge didn't make me feel optimistic for anybody he entered a pact with.

But, then again, Alarin was a merchant, so they couldn't be *that* dissimilar in views.

My concern was for their third partner.

I found her, standing well away from Visheron and Alarin's circle of sycophants. Her back was to a pillar. Her eyes were on the wineglass she hadn't so much as taken a sip from. She did nothing more than occasionally smile and nod to the few people who remembered there were three houses in the pact.

Understandably, she hadn't been well in the past two days since being freed from Vishera's laboratory. She was twitchy when she was awake, restless when she tried to sleep, withdrawn and quiet. I expected she would be for some time. You don't walk away from a situation like that without some scars. And if you're lucky, all you get is visible ones.

I couldn't begin to fathom what she was thinking, behind those massive spectacles. For the same reason, I couldn't begin to fathom why she had agreed to this "pact" in the first place. Her fortunes were meager compared to Alarin and Visheron's. Whatever they saw in her, they doubtless wanted to exploit. Surely, she could see that.

But perhaps she didn't want to see it. Perhaps she didn't want to think about it. Perhaps she just wanted this all to be over as soon as it could. I could understand that. She wanted to put all of this behind her: Gerowan, Vishera, the centaurs . . .

And me.

That thought came dangerously close to knocking me sober. I looked down at the remains of my wineglass, drained it and held it out.

"The vintage is to your liking, mistress?" the servant asked, rushing forward.

"Very," I said. I handed him the glass. When he moved to refill it, I simply took the bottle. "So much so that I'm going to take the rest of it. That's fine, right?"

"Er . . . I could . . . get you a bigger glass, if you liked?"

"I wouldn't want you to trouble yourself." I shot him a smile and a wink. "A glass wouldn't last me the walk back, now would it?"

"I'm afraid I don't—"

"Good thing no one asked you to." I turned and began to stalk toward the stairs, taking another swig from the bottle.

"But what do I tell Lady Sidara?" he called after me.

I paused, stood there for what felt like a very long time.

"Tell her . . ." After a moment, I sighed. "Don't tell her a damn thing." I walked away and held the bottle of wine high above my head. "Just give her one of these."

In all my favorite stories, the hero always disappears without a trace. Whether they're a lover, a mysterious warrior, or a daring rogue, it always ends the same: the people they just saved look for them to thank and find not a single shred of evidence that they were ever there.

So maybe I was being slightly less than classic when I left a trail of wine-stained clothes and an empty bottle on the floor as I wandered naked through Dalaris's house, but whatever. She was going to get servants, soon, and I wanted to make sure they earned their keep.

I felt slightly cheated by the wine. I was too drunk to be quick and careful about this, but not nearly drunk enough to be clever. So I simply stumbled up the stairs to the small room where I had been staying.

I found my leathers in the wardrobe—Dalaris had put them there, thinking perhaps that I'd stay awhile longer—and slipped into them. I strapped my belt around my waist, my knife hanging off of it at my hip. What little else I had, I gathered up and tossed into a satchel that clinked with the sound of coins.

My reward.

In all this, I had almost forgotten Dalaris owed me money. And now, I had almost forgotten that she had paid it. How much had it been? Five hundred platinum? I couldn't remember. Nor could I even think what to do with it.

It was this city.

That's what I told myself. I'd been here too long, gotten too distracted. Once I was gone, I could find my head and a way to spend all this. Maybe I could go to Oppara and get really drunk . . . or go to Galt and get really, *really* drunk. Or maybe I could . . .

"You left without saying goodbye."

I froze. I could feel Dalaris's eyes upon me, looking right through me, so keenly that I was afraid to turn around and see them myself.

"So, that's it?" she asked, her voice soft. "You're just . . . going? Without a word?"

"Well, obviously not *now*," I said. "You just ruined that."

"Don't joke," she replied. "And don't pretend that you can just walk away from this."

"I'm not pretending."

"I just thought . . ."

"I know what you thought." I sighed. "You thought that I'd be here for you, right? Your trusted advisor in the shadows? Your streetwise friend, here to steer you clear of these shady merchants and their deals? Well, I can't. I've got better things to do than sit here and watch over a rich girl."

I had been hoping I wouldn't have to make a clichéd tough-girl speech, to be honest. Because I had also been hoping that this wasn't going to turn out this way. Of course, I should have seen it was going to be one typical, gritty farewell, and—

"No, you idiot."

I paused.

That, I had not seen coming.

I turned and faced her. She held her spectacles in her hands. Her eyes, big and brimming with light, stared at me. No longer so wide and scared as they had been, they focused like arrowheads upon me, pinning me to the spot.

"I can handle myself here," Dalaris said, walking forward. "I know what Alarin is like . . . and I know what Visheron *is.* They're little more than bright, shiny egos that need occasional polishing. I'll be just fine here."

"Then why—"

"Because you won't be fine." She gestured to the door. "Out there. Outside of Yanmass's walls. Whatever's looking for you will keep looking for you. Here, between the three of our houses, you can be safe."

"Safe, huh?" I dared a grin. "You want to keep me like a pet?"

"That's not what I—" She looked away for a moment. "It's just that . . . I owe you."

"You *owed* me. And you paid me. We're even."

"Maybe I just . . . don't want you to leave, then. I don't have anyone who's looked out for me like you have. I don't have anyone who's just been there for me. You protected me." She looked back at me and it hurt, just a little. "Let me protect you."

And something inside me ached.

All this time, Norgorber had spared me death, evisceration, electrocution, and worse, and I knew he had done it just so he could have a great laugh when everything came crashing down around me.

And this was it.

Right now, I was just drunk enough, just desperate enough, just terrified enough to know what I had to say next. And when I said it, it felt like pulling a knife out of my throat.

"But you can't protect you from me," I said.

"What?"

"I . . ." I shook my head, thought maybe I could just pretend I hadn't said that. But now the knife was out and the words just kind of bled out of me. "I've been doing this for too long, Dalaris. I've been in too many shadows, cut too many throats. I don't know how to stop. I don't see people anymore, I just see . . . *tools*. I see ways out, I see ways to get ahead, I see ways to get away, but I don't see people I can just sit and be with."

"But you could! If you tried, I know you—"

"You don't know me." I smiled at her. The kind of smile that hurts to wear. "I don't know me. But I know you. I know you came from bad luck, even if you were born from Heaven. Someday, someone was going to try to use you. Hell, you'll have people trying to use you for the rest of your life. I believe you when you say you can handle Alarin and the others, but if you were to tell me you could handle me?"

"I could try," she said, with all the conviction of a guilty schoolchild.

"Could you? Could you look me dead in the eyes when I came home with my hands soaked with blood and believe me when I told you it was an accident?"

She looked at me for a long moment. When she looked away, I no longer felt pinned. But I didn't feel free, either. I felt like something very precious was leaking out of me.

"That's what I thought."

I plucked up the satchel, slung it over my shoulder, and began to walk for the door. But as I passed her, I stopped. I put a hand on her shoulder, drew her close to me.

"Neither of us really had a choice, you know," I said. "But you've got a better chance than I have. I'm glad to have given you that."

She whispered something in my ear that might have been goodbye. Or it might have been a plea to stay. I'm not really sure. I wasn't really listening.

I was already on my way out, trying to stifle my laugh. Gods. *I'm glad to have given you that.* Had I really said that? Could I have been any more saccharine? Ah, well. At least it made her feel better. After all, that's why I said it, right?

Yeah.

All of that. It was all for her.

That's what I told myself.

And when I left the house and shut the door behind me, I could almost believe it.

My trip out of Yanmass was without fanfare, as it should have been. I was afforded a few queer looks from gentle ladies peering out their carriage windows as they rolled by. A house guard grunted something in my general direction while he and a few of his friends loitered outside a gate, clearly on break. But once it became clear I was moving toward the large gates leading out of the city, everyone seemed fairly content to let me be.

I wondered how much they knew of what had happened in Stelvan's manor. There were a few rumors, of course: that Vishera's former centaur lackeys had attacked out of revenge, that Vishera had been murdered and this person claiming to be her "son" was an impostor, that the people cleaning up the manor reported sounds of dark whispers and the sensation of being stared at.

No one could confirm anything, of course. All anyone seemed to agree on was that Dalaris emerging from Stelvan's manor in her undergarments was a clear sign that she had been carrying on a lengthy affair with me, Vishera, Visheron, the house guard captain, or all four, and that anything else was just a story made up to excuse her lewd behavior.

Dalaris didn't refute this; it was preferable to having them know what really happened. I didn't refute it, either; it was a much more interesting story.

If all that people remembered of my stay in Yanmass was that I was an exotic mistress to one or more rich women, that was fine by me, even if I hated the idea of being called "exotic." Norgorber knows there are worse things to leave behind.

For example, a reputation for bilking an angry nobleman out of his time and money with some trumped-up blackmail. I hadn't found the time to send Herevard an apology letter. Ah, well. I'm sure he knew.

Still, I wondered if it was too late to stop in and tell him. I wondered if it was too late to con him into thinking I had some other dirt on him. I glanced around Yanmass's many avenues lined with statues and manicured lawns, passed its many squares with blossoming gardens and babbling fountains, walked beneath its many eaves of beautiful trees and under the many gazes of finely wrought statues.

I had a really good thing here for a while, didn't I?

Made me wonder why I gave it all up to help Dalaris. Sure, she was cute in that damsel sort of way, but not so cute that it was worth losing all this. And yet, now that all of that business was behind me, I wondered if it was too late to go back to her, to tell her I changed my mind, to stay here and be pampered and never have to run away from anything ever again.

And before I knew it, I was at the gates of Yanmass.

And I wasn't alone.

Against the finery of the city, Chariel stood in the center of the gateway like a stark shadow. Her black leathers made her look like a soot stain from a fire burnt far too long on the white pavement. And her eyes, so blue and so deep, sapped all the warmth out of the afternoon sun.

She approached me. I froze. It's never a good sign when an assassin comes at you in full daylight with plenty of forewarning.

"You look well," she said, stopping just a foot away from me. "I trust you've recovered from your ordeal."

"I have. Thanks."

She nodded, eyed the satchel draped over my shoulder. "And earned yourself a reward, too, I see."

"It's not much, but yeah." I rubbed the back of my neck. "Listen, I know you did right by me with that magical poison business. If you want repayment . . ."

"Shaia," she said. "I charge the Brotherhood one hundred gold pieces just to get out of bed. I can handle it."

"Ah. Of course." I cleared my throat. "Well, thanks, then."

She said nothing. She simply stared at me, like her eyes were knives digging into my flesh.

Silence is an assassin's greatest weapon, they say. But when they said it, I'm pretty sure they didn't mean that the silence would get so awkward you'd want to kill yourself.

"Were you hoping to leave without seeing me?" she asked, suddenly.

I looked back at her. "If I was, I probably wouldn't have used the main gate."

"But you didn't seek me out before leaving, either."

"Maybe I knew you'd come and find me, first."

"Maybe," she repeated, flatly.

Another long moment passed. We avoided each other's gaze, lest the words brewing behind our lips come spilling out. We weren't used to honesty, people like us. It was painful to hear, even more painful to speak.

And yet, somehow, no matter how hard we tried . . .

"Was it all for nothing, then?" she asked.

"I told you, I'd pay you back if you wanted—"

"I'm not talking about the poison, idiot," she snapped. "Not *just* the poison, anyway. I'm talking about all of it: the favors I pulled, keeping the Brotherhood off your back, doing your little dirty work to get your centaurs into the city. All that and you're just going to leave?"

"What, you expect me to pay those back?"

"Yes!" She shook her head. "No. I'm not sure. I just thought that . . ." For a moment, something that looked like pain flashed across her features. But in the next, her face twisted up into a snarl. "I don't *do* this, you know. I don't pull favors, I don't make compromises, I don't have conversations like *these*. I'm not meant for it. But somehow, for you—always for you—I end up changing everything and feeling like an idiot for it."

I opened my mouth to say something.

Like "You're not an idiot," maybe. Or "It's all right to feel feelings beyond a vague sense of murderous rage." Or maybe even "This is incredibly awkward, let's just find a dark alley and see what happens."

But I couldn't. I couldn't say any of it.

Because I knew where it would lead. Everything I could say, anything I would say, it would all just end with me and her back to our old ways. And I'd find a new reason to cheat her, to double-cross her, to steal from her, or to just run away from her.

And no matter how badly I wanted to tell her I wouldn't, I just couldn't see a future in which I didn't hurt her again.

Do this line of work long enough, hide in the shadows long enough, run away from trouble long enough, you forget how to do anything else. Hurting people just comes naturally, like you don't even have to try to make someone bleed.

She looked away from me for a moment. "I said . . ." She paused, choked for a second. "I said we could run, put the Brotherhood behind us, go far away from here together." She looked back at me. "I still will. If you ask me to."

Quiet is my business. I've spent days stalking a mark, not uttering a single word. But the longest silence of my life was when I stared into those big blue eyes, quivering with tears, and didn't so much as breathe.

Yeah, it hurt seeing that tear slide down her cheek. But there are worse pains in the world.

I got one of them just a moment later when she walked past me, back into Yanmass, and disappeared without so much as saying goodbye.

And just like that, I was running again.

More like walking, but you get what I mean. This is simply what I do. Drunkards swill, addicts puff, and I just keep walking away. Into peoples' problems, out of peoples' lives, and so on and so on until I die.

Sometimes they chase me, of course. My problems in Yanmass were bound to. Halamox was still out there, somewhere, undoubtedly still pissed at how many times I had manipulated him. The Brotherhood was still out there, probably no more happy that their chief assassin had failed to kill me. Both of them would be looking for me, and there was an awful lot of land between Yanmass and wherever I was going.

I'd forgive you for thinking I was crazy if you could see me walking out of Yanmass smiling at that thought.

Don't get me wrong, I was walking away alone and without much to my name, as usual. And I had left behind my share of wounds that would probably take a long time to heal. Dalaris would have her work cut out for her fending off the rich vipers of the city. Chariel would learn to hate me again. A demon somewhere in the Abyss knew my name, and that wasn't good at all.

But these were problems I'd always have. There would be time enough to worry about them much later, when I was in a warm bed and full of wine and regrets.

For now, I had enemies. For now, I had an open road. For now, I had a knife at my hip and a satchel full of coin. For all my problems, I had enemies I could sneak up on, throats I could cut, shadows I could hide in.

For everything else . . .

Well, that's what they make liquor for, isn't it?

About the Author

Sam Sykes is the author of the fantasy novels *The City Stained Red*, *The Mortal Tally*, and *An Affinity for Steel*. For more information, visit **samsykes.com** or find him on Twitter at **@SamSykesSwears**.

Glossary

All Pathfinder Tales novels are set in the rich and vibrant world of the Pathfinder campaign setting. Below are explanations of several key terms used in this book. For more information on the world of Golarion and the strange monsters, people, and deities that make it their home, see *The Inner Sea World Guide*, or dive into the game and begin playing your own adventures with the *Pathfinder Roleplaying Game Core Rulebook* or the *Pathfinder Roleplaying Game Beginner Box*, all available at **paizo.com**.

Abadar: God of cities, wealth, merchants, and law.

Abyss: Plane of evil and chaos ruled by demons, where many evil souls go after they die.

Andoran: Democratic and freedom-loving nation. Formerly controlled by the Chelish Empire, and before that by the Taldan Empire.

Andoren: Of or pertaining to Andoran; someone from Andoran.

Angels: Race of good-natured creatures native to good-aligned planes like Heaven.

Brotherhood of Silence: Powerful guild of thieves and assassins based in Taldor.

Bugbears: Large, humanoid monsters related to goblins. Extremely violent and ill tempered.

Calistria: Goddess of trickery, lust, and revenge.

Celestials: A collective term referring to any native of a good-aligned plane, such as Heaven.

Centaurs: Intelligent creatures with the upper bodies of humans and the lower bodies of horses. Often found in nomadic tribes on the edges of more established nations, though some integrate fully into humanoid society.

Cheliax: A powerful devil-worshiping nation formerly ruled by Taldor.

Clerics: Religious spellcasters whose magical powers are granted by their gods.

Demons: Evil denizens of the Abyss, who seek only to maim, ruin, and feed on mortal souls.

Devils: Fiendish occupants of Hell who seek to corrupt mortals in order to claim their souls.

Divination: School of magic allowing spellcasters to predict the future, learn secrets long forgotten, find hidden things, and foil deceptive magic.

Dwarves: Short, stocky humanoids who excel at physical labor, mining, and craftsmanship. Originally from the Darklands, the dwarves ascended to the surface millennia ago during the Quest for Sky.

Elementals: Beings of pure elemental energy, such as air, earth, fire, or water.

Elves: Long-lived, beautiful humanoids who abandoned Golarion millennia ago and have only recently returned. Identifiable by their pointed ears, lithe bodies, and large eyes that appear to be one color.

Fiends: Creatures native to the evil planes of the multiverse, such as demons, devils, and daemons.

First Solace: Caravan-rest located near Yanmass.

Galt: Nation locked in perpetual and bloody democratic revolution. Fond of beheadings.

Goblins: Race of small and maniacal humanoids who live to burn, pillage, and sift through the refuse of more civilized races.

Golarion: The planet on which the Pathfinder campaign setting focuses.

Golems: Magical constructs, usually humanoid in shape, built to mindlessly serve a master.

Halflings: Race of humanoids known for their tiny stature, deft hands, and mischievous personalities.

Heaven: Plane of good and law ruled by angels, where many good souls go after they die.

Hell: Plane of evil and tyrannical order ruled by devils, where many evil souls go after they die.

Hellspawn: Someone with fiendish blood, such as from ancestral interbreeding with devils or demons, often identified by horns, hooves, or other devilish features. Rarely popular in civilized society.

Hobgoblins: Larger, more intelligent kin of regular goblins. Highly organized and militant.

Incubus: Demons formed from the souls of evil mortals who derive sexual gratification through pain and violence. Incubuses appear as muscular and attractive humanoid males with batlike wings.

Inner Sea: The vast inland sea whose northern continent, Avistan, and southern continent, Garund, as well as the seas and nearby lands, are the primary focus of the Pathfinder campaign setting.

Katapesh: Mighty trade-oriented nation south of the Inner Sea. Also the name of its capital city. Ruled by mysterious masked beings known as Pactmasters. For more information, see *Pathfinder Campaign Setting: Dark Markets, A Guide to Katapesh.*

Katapeshi: Of or related to the nation of Katapesh.

Kyonin: Forest kingdom seen as the elven homeland and largely forbidden to non-elven travelers.

Lands of the Linnorm Kings: Cold northern nation ruled by an alliance of the eponymous Linnorm Kings.

Lender: Term of respect for a priest of Abadar.

Maheto: Taldan city in the northern foothills of the World's Edge Mountains, home to masterful dwarven artisans whose weapons and other products are in high demand throughout the empire.

Molthune: Expansionist nation in central Avistan, ruled by a military government and perpetually at war with its northern neighbor, Nirmathas.

Norgorber: God of assassins, secrets, and murder.

Ogres: Hulking, brutal, and half-witted humanoid monsters with violent tendencies.

Oppara: Coastal capital of Taldor.

Orcs: Race of humanoids with green or gray skin, protruding tusks, and warlike tendencies. Almost universally hated by more civilized races.

Osirian: Of or relating to the nation of Osirion, or a resident of Osirion.

Osirion: Ancient nation south of the Inner Sea renowned for its deserts, pharaohs, and pyramids.

Paladins: Holy warriors in the service of a good and lawful god. Ruled by a strict code of conduct and granted special magical powers by their deity.

Pesh: Narcotic drug made from a type of cactus.

Plane: One of the realms of existence, such as the mortal world, Heaven, Hell, the Abyss, and many others.

Platinum: Widely used form of metal currency worth ten times as much as gold.

Qadira: Desert nation just south of Taldor, with whom it has a long history of war and resentment.

Qadiran: Of or related to Qadira; someone from Qadira.

Rahadoum: Atheist nation where religion is outlawed.

Rangers: Hunters and warriors specialized in surviving in a particular terrain; often employed as scouts, guides, and skirmishers.

Sarenrae: Goddess of the sun, honesty, and redemption. Often seen as a fiery crusader and redeemer.

Scrolls: Magical documents in which spells are recorded so they can be released when read, even if the reader doesn't know how to cast that spell. Destroyed as part of the casting process.

Sorcerers: Those who cast spells through natural ability rather than faith or study.

Stabled: Derogatory term for centaurs who have embraced humanoid society, used primarily by nomadic centaur tribes.

Taldan: Of or pertaining to Taldor; a citizen of Taldor.

Taldane: The common trade language of the Inner Sea region.

Taldor: A formerly glorious nation that has lost many of its holdings in recent years to neglect and decadence. Ruled by immature aristocrats and overly complicated bureaucracy, and perpetually on the brink of war with Qadira.

Wizards: Those who cast spells through careful study and rigorous scientific methods rather than faith or innate talent, recording the necessary incantations in a spellbook.

Yanmass: Wealthy frontier city in northern Taldor supported primarily by caravan trade between the Inner Sea region and lands farther east.

Turn the page for a sneak peek at

Reaper's Eye

by Richard A. Knaak

Available December 2016

1

The Rescue

Daryus Gaunt eyed the two armored figures over the froth-covered rim of his mug, taking in every detail of the pair. Despite his apparent disinterest, he remained on edge until the two crusaders took their leave of the tavern.

They had not recognized him—but then, he hardly looked like the earnest warrior he had been when he had worn their same uniform. Scars etched his oddly narrow features, many covered unsuccessfully by the thin, black beard edged with gray. Some of the jagged marks had been earned when he had been a crusader, but the rest—along with the beard—had been earned acting as a sword for hire for whoever was willing to pay.

Daryus could have saved himself so much trouble by simply not making Nerosyan his base. Doing so was like poking the proverbial bees' nest. The Order of the Flaming Lance had a significant presence here. If even one crusader recognized him, he risked losing his head.

After all, the order had very little sympathy for *traitors*.

He set down the empty mug, then rose. Next to him, the two surly thugs muttering to one another about some future robbery immediately eased out of his way. Contrary to his name and his grandfather's supposed elven lineage, Daryus Gaunt was a mountain of a man, just a few inches shy of seven feet. It made his hiding in a stronghold of the order an even more questionable choice to that handful aware of his situation.

Five ales had done nothing to temper Daryus's mood, but he always stopped after five no matter what a part of him desired. The five drinks represented part of his failing, part of his betrayal. Daryus might have so far escaped punishment, but he couldn't escape his own guilt.

The Crimson Hammer Tavern might not have been one of the best-known establishments in Tumbletown—much less the city of Nerosyan itself—but it was a place where those in desperate need of a practiced sword could find such. "Desperate" was the key. Prospective employers had to be willing to wend their way deep northwest into one of the worst parts of the city.

Tonight, Daryus noted two potential contracts. One was a squat, robed figure who tried to keep his face covered with a scarf. The former crusader guessed him to be a merchant attempting to smuggle something either into Nerosyan or out of it. At present, the rotund man conversed with a pale, eye-patched swordsman who Daryus knew would do his best to part the fool from his money without fulfilling the contract.

The other possible client was a thin young man with long blond hair and furtive eyes who gave Daryus a studious glance before heading toward a grizzled ex-pirate from the River Kingdoms by the name of Divalo. Daryus gave the young man some credit. He had picked one of the more trustworthy swords in the tavern. Despite his background, Divalo would live up to his contract and even make certain that any other swords the young man needed would do the same on pain of death.

Seeing no reason to remain, Daryus made for the door. It had been a fortnight since he had returned to the Diamond of the North, as Nerosyan was also known. The name had little to do with any glamorous aspect of the city and more with the base design of the massive fortress initially built here. There was no better forti-fied city than Nerosyan—a good thing, since it was close enough to the Worldwound to attract the attention of demons.

Thinking of the Worldwound, Daryus hesitated just shy of the door. It was not out of any thought of adding a sixth ale to his count, but rather the hope that the rumors he had heard might still prove true. The word was out that some Pathfinders were planning an expedition into the demon-blighted land. What insane reason they had for doing so, the former crusader did not care. All he knew was that Pathfinders paid well. They would need a strong arm out in the Worldwound if they hoped to even survive their first night.

Gripping the swinging door carefully, Daryus slowly opened the way. A slight creak accompanied the door's movement. The tavern's owner liked to keep all the doors creaky, the better to know when someone exited or entered. Daryus appreciated that aspect, too, save now when he wanted to make certain that no one outside might hear him.

But the two crusaders were nowhere to be seen, even to his skilled eye. If they had recognized him and arranged a trap, they had done a fine job. Daryus doubted it, though.

Some might have wondered at his choices, a renegade at the heart of the crusader city. Even the explanation he gave himself— that they would never expect to find him so close by—was one that Daryus knew he wouldn't have accepted from anyone else.

Shrugging off both the obvious contradictions in his decisions and the reasons behind them, Daryus headed deeper into Tumbletown. For all their power, the crusaders did little to clean out the area. It wasn't due solely to the tremendous effort needed, though. The area around the Crimson Tavern and its like allowed the crusaders to have a particular place to find those tools they would not admit they needed at times. Daryus had seen the supposed clients who he knew were actually servants of the various crusader orders. Even the most pious of the orders' higher-ups occasionally needed those they considered scum.

Only a few dim oil lamps and torches lit the way through the grimy streets and the filthy buildings lining each side. There had been attempts in the past to better illuminate the area in a pretense of making everyone safer, but those had lasted only long enough for someone to steal the lamps. The lesson remained. Only those who could defend themselves could walk these streets at night.

A light some distance to the southwest and high above momentarily caught his attention. While not as large as the city's four main defense towers, Starrise Spire—or, more specifically, the magical beacon floating above it—was a useful landmark when trying to wend through the darkened streets toward where he lived. The only other landmark of any use to Daryus besides the city's towers was the great Cruciform Cathedral, situated dead center in the city. More a fortress than an ordinary cathedral, that massive redoubt housed Queen Galfrey and the rest of Mendev's leadership, those soldiers and bureaucrats charged with organizing all the disparate crusader orders into a solid defense against the Worldwound's demons.

As he moved on, Daryus set one gloved hand on the hilt of the longsword dangling at his side. All it would take was one swift motion to ready the blade for battle. He had been forced to draw it three times since arriving in Nerosyan, but not of late. Most of the regulars knew Daryus Gaunt by reputation now and avoided trouble with him.

Help . . .

He came to an abrupt halt. Cocking his head, he listened.

Silence reigned.

With a grunt, Daryus moved on. Five ales might not be enough to affect his faculties, but exhaustion could. He hadn't slept in three days. As a young warrior, three days awake would have meant little to him, but of late it seemed to Daryus that his strength flagged quicker and quicker. Still, there were few he knew of in Tumbletown with more skill than him, so he wasn't overly worried.

Help!

Again, Daryus hesitated. He listened, only hearing a slight wind struggling through the tightly packed buildings and narrow streets.

Help!

He frowned. It was almost as if he heard the voice in his *head*.

"Help me! Please!"

That cry he heard out loud. Moving with a speed and grace his form belied, Daryus drew his sword. He took one step toward where he believed the faint cry had come.

The clink of metal against metal made every muscle in his body tense. Daryus considered the possibility of a clever crusader trap, but quickly disposed of the notion. The cry seemed too true, too honest.

"Help!"

Daryus got a fix on the direction. With swift but stealthy steps, he headed toward the pleading voice. Whether it was male or female, he couldn't say, but it didn't matter. Every instinct in Daryus pushed him to helping the unseen caller. A renegade he might be, but he couldn't fight his basic nature.

As he entered a side alley, something just ahead of him moved in the shadows. With his left hand, Daryus brought the sword around, but only found empty air.

A second clink warned him just before the point of a narrow sword would have pierced him through the throat. Instead, Daryus managed to bring up his own weapon in time to deflect the attack. The oncoming tip scraped his cheek, adding to collection of scars.

Daryus's fist followed his sword, striking his adversary hard in the chest. The shadowy figure grunted as the force of the blow sent him back a step.

Despite eyes already attuned to the darkness, Daryus had trouble making out the other swordsman's features. No matter how hard he tried, the face remained indiscernible.

The sword did not. Out of the corner of his eye, Daryus spotted the weapon coming at him again. As he shifted his own blade to meet it, he noted another attack coming from the opposite side.

There was no time to reach the small dagger he wore in his belt. Daryus thrust his other arm up, willing to take a shallow slice on his cloth-covered arm rather than have his head skewered.

Deflecting the first sword, Daryus spun to meet the wielder of the second. He had the satisfaction of feeling his blade cut into the other attacker's arm.

Despite the wound, the second figure made no sound. Daryus knew that he faced not only seasoned fighters, but determined ones.

The cry for aid had ceased, making the mercenary wonder if he had arrived too late. However, he knew that the point no longer mattered; he was now committed to the struggle, whatever and whomever it concerned.

The first attacker tried to take him again. Daryus's left-handed counterassault kept the shadowy fighter off guard, while at the same time, he kicked at the legs of the second figure. He drove his latter attacker down on one knee, buying time to better deal with the first.

"Beware above!" the same voice that had cried for help called.

Rather than thrust at his foe, Daryus had to instead leap back. Even then, he barely missed being crushed under the weight of yet a third figure.

Sword already in play, Daryus lunged at the newcomer. He caught the crouching fighter on the side, but the other managed to roll away before the sword could do more than scrape what Daryus guessed to be a light breastplate.

Daryus sensed the movements of the second assailant. Determined to do something to keep the odds from turning further against him, he threw himself against the kneeling figure.

As they collided, Daryus twisted his sword around and shoved as hard as he could.

Although the blade sank deep into the other's throat, his foe's only response before dying was a grunt. Daryus began to wonder whether they could even speak at all.

He hardly had the sword free from the collapsing body before the third of his attackers returned. Despite a hint of illumination from the street beyond, the face continued to be as featureless as those of the original pair. Daryus knew magic when he saw it, and hoped that the obscuring shadows were the extent of their abilities. The trio did not strike him as spellcasters, but rather paid assassins given a trick or two. Still, even one more trick might prove too much for Daryus.

Both attackers converged on Daryus. He fended off their initial attacks, at the same time managing to analyze which of the pair was the more dangerous. As for his foes, they seemed satisfied to harass him, almost as if waiting for something *else* to happen . . .

A clatter arose from his right. Daryus, already suspecting just what the pair had been waiting for, was startled that the *fourth* figure seeking his death could be so clumsy. The murky form stumbled into Daryus's waiting hand.

With all the force he could muster, Daryus threw his latest adversary toward the others. One fighter managed to evade the living missile, but the second wasn't so lucky. The two fell in a heap.

"Beware! One more! One more!" came the voice, this time from what seemed somewhere on the ground to the right.

Daryus couldn't see anyone there, but he responded to the warning. Drawing his dagger, he brandished the smaller blade at the most likely direction from which any additional enemy would attack.

It was all he could do to keep his grip as the sword point thrusting out of the darkness clashed against his dagger. Daryus spun around, forcing the barely visible sword's wielder back while still keeping the foremost of his other adversaries at bay.

Lunging toward his latest foe, he slipped past the sword enough to reach the hand gripping it. He drove the dagger as hard as he could into the wrist.

This time, Daryus was rewarded by a pained cry. The sword slipped free. Daryus grabbed the wounded limb, then pulled his opponent toward him.

So near, he finally caught a glimpse of a face, a peculiarly nondescript face that even Daryus's expert eye could not identify by region. A faint beard covered most of the lower half, but that was perhaps the only detail of any note.

A rough hand shoved Daryus back. The face disappeared into the same sort of odd darker-than-dark inkiness obscuring the faces of the rest.

Daryus used the force of the push to enable him to roll to the side. As he turned on his back, he brought up his sword.

The point caught the attacker coming up behind him under his armored chest. Before the wounded fighter could stagger back, Daryus shoved the sword deeper.

As he did that, a strange change came over his dying enemy. Not only did the inkiness fade, but the attacker's entire body shimmered. A bland face identical to the other fighter briefly materialized, then itself faded into something else.

And suddenly a *pitborn* stood before Daryus.

As a crusader, Daryus had come face to face with the demon-tainted creatures before. Generally human in face and form, they bore the curse of some past coupling between a human and one of the foul denizens of the Abyss. Daryus's former order had seen pitborns as little more than demons themselves, though while many were indeed evil, Daryus knew that others could be as pure of heart as the oath-sworn warriors with whom he had served.

The last, it appeared, did not apply to the fanged, thick-browed figure collapsing by Daryus. His dying gaze held only rage, a look that faded a moment later as death took him.

Daryus scrambled back as both the attacker he had knocked over and wounded and the remaining pair regained their footing. He had been fortunate up until now, but even with two dead and possibly two wounded, the odds were still against him, especially if *all* of the three were pitborn. The demon-touched often wielded some level of sorcerous power, which explained their ability to mask themselves in the midst of a crusader stronghold.

Instead of attacking, though, to Daryus's surprise, the two in front of him retreated. Weapons ready, they vanished into the shadows behind them.

Daryus turned to the last, only to find the disguised attacker sprawled in a heap. Suspecting a trap, Daryus approached cautiously. As vicious as the dagger wound had been to the assassin's wrist, it should not have killed him so quickly, if at all.

In death, the pitborn's true countenance lay revealed. Small, sharp horns curled up from his forehead. His gaping mouth revealed sharp teeth. However, it was the pitborn's throat that demanded Daryus's attention.

Something had ripped it out with animalistic tenacity, something evidently capable of moving swiftly and silently.

Not one to question his fortune, Daryus looked around for the caller. He was not surprised to find himself alone. Whoever had been the intended target of these assassins had wisely fled. Unfortunately, that left Daryus alone to deal with the bodies. Bodies were not uncommon in Tumbletown, but three dead pitborn would certainly stir the attention of the city's crusaders. There would be a search of the area, with questions about who in the area would have the skill to kill not one but three.

It would not be long before someone led them to Daryus.

Daryus knew a spot where he could put the bodies, a place where no one would find them for years, if ever, based on the two skeletons he had discovered there the first time he had stumbled into it. He wiped his sword and dagger off on the body with the ruined throat, then sheathed the weapons and hefted the dead pitborn over his shoulder. He could have carried two at once, but that would have made it harder to draw a weapon should someone come upon him. Besides, a single body he could prop against a wall and pretend in the dark was a drunken comrade.

The hiding place in question was a narrow passage between two old, stone buildings to the west of his dwelling. Sometime far in the past, the entrance to the passage had been bricked up to make the two structures seem one. The only way to still reach it was from the roofs above, which was how Daryus had stumbled on it in the first place. He had not expected to have to slide into it, nor had he expected the skeletons with the telltale chips in their ribs indicating death by sword. Now, though, what had been an unfortunate chance discovery was proving to be of use.

For most people, the time needed to dispose of one body, let alone three, would have been measured in hours. Daryus managed to remove the first two in such quick order that he surprised himself. Only then did he realize just how well he had eased into his current life. His earlier existence suddenly seemed farther away than ever.

Gritting his teeth, Daryus returned for the last. Not once had he seen anyone on the street, but he doubted his luck would hold much longer. With growing impatience, Daryus returned to the scene of the struggle . . . and found no trace of the last corpse.

What he did find was a small and curious-looking animal sitting near where last he had seen the body. The long, sinewy mammal licked one of its forepaws, upon which Daryus noted small bits of dark moisture.

The brown-furred creature raised its head to look at him. Daryus had not seen many weasels in this region, but knew what they looked like. This one was average in size and slightly wide in the mouth. There was nothing out of the ordinary about it save that its left eye seemed injured and twisted shut.

Without warning, it scampered over to Daryus and started up his leg. Thrusting the dagger in his belt, the former crusader seized the vermin by the scruff of the neck and brought it to eye level.

The weasel wrinkled its nose, but otherwise didn't react. It seemed perfectly at ease dangling several feet above the ground as it stared with the one eye at Daryus.

A quick survey of the area revealed no sign of either the intended victim or the last body. Daryus knew he had risked himself far too long for what he now felt was no good reason. Indeed, he began to wonder if perhaps he had been set up by someone intending either robbery or vengeance. Perhaps *he* had been the target all along.

Remaining wary, Daryus abandoned the area, taking what precautions he could to keep from being followed by anyone. If in fact he had been set up by a rival, or had simply become the object of some thieving gang's attention, he didn't want company joining him at home.

Not certain what else to do with the weasel, Daryus set it down and started off. He didn't get far before realizing that the creature was following close.

Daryus waved it off, but the weasel continued to follow. Its lack of concern for the dead or missing assassins suggested it hadn't been a pet of theirs. Yet if it had belonged to whoever had cried out—assuming there had actually been someone in the first place—Daryus wondered why the animal's owner had left it behind.

Daryus's abode was little more than a shack attached to the back of a warehouse. In the early days of the city, the shack had probably acted as the warehouse guard's quarters. The warehouse had changed hands and functions over the generations, becoming now the front for a merchant of disreputable means. Daryus paid the man's scarecrow of a daughter a month's lodging at a time. He knew that they also saw him as an unpaid guard for their goods, for if something happened to the warehouse, then Daryus would lose his dwelling and the money he had paid out that month.

Other than a creaking oak bed with a blanket to act as mattress, the lone room had only two other pieces of furniture. The well-stained table and accompanying bench were where Daryus spent his time when not sleeping. A half-empty bottle of foul-tasting red wine that reminded Daryus of the swill he had once drank in faraway Sauerton sat atop the table, looking inviting despite his familiarity with its sharply acidic taste.

Just as he shut the door behind him, the weasel slipped through into the room.

"No you don't!" He made a swipe for the sinewy creature, but the weasel twisted out of range. It darted to the bench, leapt atop, then made its way to the table and the waiting wine bottle.

Daryus pursued, only to pull up short as the weasel suddenly turned its one-eyed gaze back at him. The stare was so intense that the renegade crusader almost expected the animal to talk.

Which it did.

"You save Toy's life!" it piped in the voice Daryus immediately recognized as the one calling for help. "You save Toy's life, but now we must beware! They will seek to obey their master's will! They will come again with more! We must leave this city!"

Daryus reached for his sword. "What are you?"

Toy impatiently shook its head, its single open eye never leaving Daryus. "No time to waste on foolish questions! Must act! Must act before he acts!"

"Who?"

The weasel hissed. It reared, revealing that it was definitely male. "An evil walking on two legs! An evil that will now come looking for both of us, Master . . . unless Toy and Master stop him first!"

And then, without warning, the weasel opened his *other* eye as well—an eye simultaneously of fire and ice, blood red and bone ivory.

A *demon's* eye.

Once a notorious pirate, Jendara has at last returned to the cold northern isles of her birth, ready to settle down and raise her young son. Yet when a mysterious tsunami wracks her island's shore, she and her fearless crew must sail out to explore the strange island that's risen from the sea floor. No sooner have they delved into the lost island's alien structures than they find themselves competing with a monstrous cult eager to complete a dark ritual in those dripping halls. For something beyond all mortal comprehension has been dreaming on the sea floor. And it's begun to wake up ...

From Hugo Award winner Wendy N. Wagner comes a sword-swinging adventure in the tradition of H. P. Lovecraft, set in the award-winning world of the Pathfinder Roleplaying Game.

***Starspawn* print edition: $14.99**
ISBN: 978-0-7653-8433-1

***Starspawn* ebook edition:**
ISBN: 978-0-7653-8432-4

PATHFINDER TALES

STARSPAWN

A NOVEL BY **Wendy N. Wagner**

When caught stealing in the crusader nation of Lastwall, veteran con man Rodrick and his talking sword Hrym expect to weasel or fight their way out of punishment. Instead, they find themselves ensnared by powerful magic, and given a choice: serve the cause of justice as part of a covert team of similarly bound villains—or die horribly. Together with their criminal cohorts, Rodrick and Hrym settle in to their new job of defending the innocent, only to discover that being a secret government operative is even more dangerous than a life of crime.

From Hugo Award winner Tim Pratt comes a tale of reluctant heroes and plausible deniability, set in the award-winning world of the Pathfinder Roleplaying Game.

Liar's Bargain print edition: $14.99
ISBN: 978-0-7653-8431-7

Liar's Bargain ebook edition:
ISBN: 978-0-7653-8430-0

PATHFINDER TALES

LIAR'S BARGAIN

A NOVEL BY Tim Pratt

The Hellknights are a brutal organization of warriors and spellcasters dedicated to maintaining law and order at any cost. For devil-blooded Jheraal, a veteran Hellknight investigator, even the harshest methods are justified if it means building a better world for her daughter. Yet things get personal when a serial killer starts targeting hellspawn like Jheraal and her child, somehow magically removing their hearts and trapping the victims in a state halfway between life and death. With other Hellknights implicated in the crime, Jheraal has no choice but to join forces with a noble paladin and a dangerously cunning diabolist to defeat an ancient enemy for whom even death is no deterrent.

From celebrated dark fantasy author Liane Merciel comes an adventure of love, murder, and grudges from beyond the grave, set in the award-winning world of the Pathfinder Roleplaying Game.

***Hellknight* print edition: $14.99**
ISBN: 978-0-7653-7548-3

***Hellknight* ebook edition:**
ISBN: 978-1-4668-4735-4

PATHFINDER TALES

HELLKNIGHT

A NOVEL BY
Liane Merciel

Captain Torius Vin has given up the pirate life in order to bring freedom to others. Along with his loyal crew and Celeste, the ship's snake-bodied navigator and Torius's one true love, the captain of the *Stargazer* uses a lifetime of piratical tricks to capture slave galleys and set the prisoners free. But when the crew's old friend and secret agent Vreva Jhafe uncovers rumors of a terrifying new magical weapon in devil-ruled Cheliax—one capable of wiping the abolitionist nation of Andoran off the map—will even their combined forces be enough to stop a navy backed by Hell itself?

From award-winning novelist Chris A. Jackson comes a tale of magic, mayhem, and nautical adventure, set in the vibrant world of the Pathfinder Roleplaying Game.

Pirate's Prophecy **print edition: $14.99**
ISBN: 978-0-7653-7547-6

Pirate's Prophecy **ebook edition:**
ISBN: 978-1-4668-4734-7

PATHFINDER TALES

Pirate's Prophecy

A NOVEL BY
Chris A. Jackson

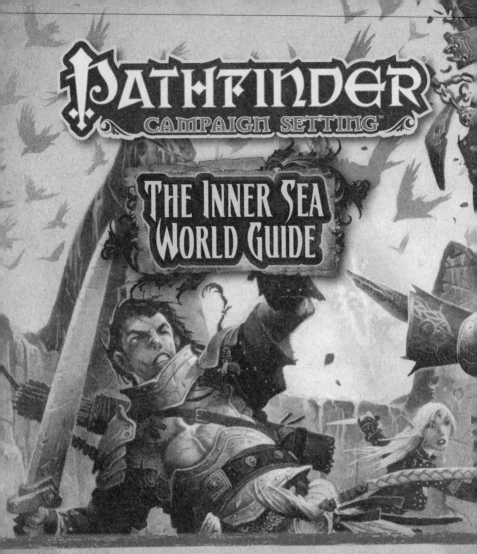

PATHFINDER®
CAMPAIGN SETTING™

THE INNER SEA WORLD GUIDE

You've delved into the Pathfinder campaign setting with Pathfinder Tales novels—now take your adventures even further! *The Inner Sea World Guide* is a full-color, 320-page hardcover guide featuring everything you need to know about the exciting world of Pathfinder: overviews of every major nation, religion, race, and adventure location around the Inner Sea, plus a giant poster map! Read it as a travelogue, or use it to flesh out your roleplaying game—it's your world now!

EXPLORE YOUR WORLD!

paizo.com

paizo®